# *Earth Song*

Medieval Song Quartet #2

Catherine Coulter

Thorndike Press • Thorndike, Maine

Published in 2000 by arrangement with Signet, a division of Penguin Putnam Inc.

Thorndike Press Large Print Basic Series.

The tree indicium is a trademark of Thorndike Press.

The text of this Large Print edition is unabridged.
Other aspects of the book may vary from the original edition.

Set in 16 pt. Plantin.

Printed in the United States on permanent paper.

**Library of Congress Cataloging-in-Publication Data**

Coulter, Catherine.
Earth song / Catherine Coulter.
p. (large print) cm. — (Medieval song quartet ; 2)
ISBN 0-7862-2356-1 (lg. print : hc : alk. paper)
1. Cornwall (England) — Fiction. 2. Great Britain — History — 13th century — Fiction. 3. Large type books. I. Title.
PS3553.O843 E27 2000
813′.54—dc21 99-056259

NEWARK PUBLIC LIBRARY-NEWARK, OHIO 43055
3 2487 00585 5128

STACKS

# *Earth Song*

***Also by Catherine Coulter in Large Print:***

The Countess
The Deception
The Edge
Midsummer Magic
Calypso Magic
Moonspun Magic
Chandra
Fire Song
The Offer
The Cove
The Heir
Lord Harry
The Rebel Bride
The Wild Baron

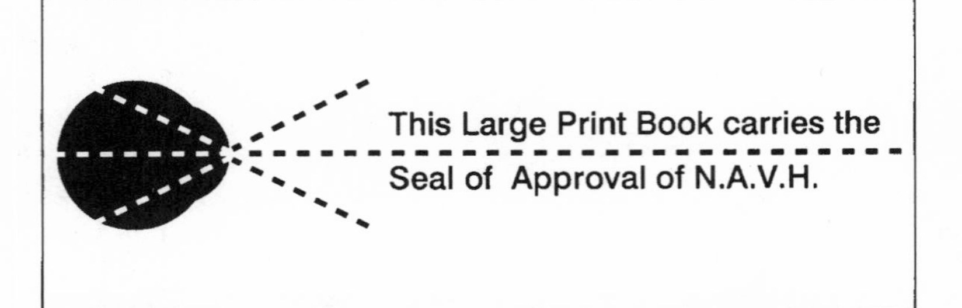

To Carol Steffens Woodrum
Bright and beautiful
and loved very very much by
her auntie Catherine.

# 1

*Beauchamp Castle*
*Cornwall, England*
*April 1275*

"You must wed me, you must!"

Philippa looked at Ivo de Vescy's intense young face with its errant reddish whiskers that would never form the neat forked mustache he hoped for. "No, Ivo," she said again, her palms pressed against his chest. "You are here for Bernice, not for me. Please, I don't want you for a husband. Go now, before someone comes upon us."

"There's someone else! You love another!"

"Nay, I do not. There is no other for me right now, but it cannot be you, Ivo, please believe me."

Philippa really did expect him to leave. She had told him the truth: she didn't love him and didn't wish to marry him. Instead of leaving her chamber, instead of releasing her, he simply stood there staring at her, his arms loose now around her back.

"Please leave my chamber, Ivo," she said again. "You shouldn't have come. I shouldn't have let you in."

But Ivo de Vescy wasn't about to leave. "You will wed with me," he said, and attacked.

Philippa thought, even as he lifted her off her feet and tossed her onto her back on her narrow bed, that a man bent on winning a lady was not best served using rape as an argument. She jerked her face back as he wetly kissed her cheek, her jaw, her nose. "Please, this is absurd! Stop, now."

But Ivo de Vescy, newly knighted, newly pronounced a man by his stringent sire, saw his goal and dismissed the obstacles to his goal as more pleasurable then risky. Philippa would want him soon, he told himself, when he pressed his manhood hard against her, very soon now she would be begging him to take her. He finally found her mouth, open because she was primed to yell at him, and thrust his tongue inside.

It was like putting flame to dry sticks. He was breathing heavily, wanting her desperately, pinning her now-struggling body under his full weight. He got his hand under her long woolen gown, shoved aside her thin linen shift, and the feel of her smooth flesh relieved him of his few remaining wits.

Philippa twisted her head until his tongue was out of her mouth — not a pleasant experience, and one she didn't care to repeat. She wasn't worried until Ivo managed to slither his hand over her knee. His fingers on her bare thigh turned him into a heaving, gasping creature whose body had become rigid and heavy on top of her.

"Stop it, Ivo!" She wriggled beneath him, realized quickly that this would gain her naught — indeed, would gain her even more of a ravening monster — and held perfectly still. "Listen to me, Ivo de Vescy," she whispered into his ear. "Get off me this minute or I will see to the destruction of your precious manhood. I mean it, Ivo. You will be a eunuch and I will tell my father and he will tell yours why it happened. You cannot ravish a lady, you fool. Besides, I have as much strength as you, and —"

Ivo groaned in his dazed ardor; he unwisely thrust his tongue into her mouth again. Philippa bit him hard. He yowled and raised his head to stare down at the girl he wanted so desperately. She didn't yet look as if she wanted him, as if she was ready to beg him for his ardor, but it didn't matter. He decided he would try a bit of reason even as he thrust his member against her in a parody of the sex act.

"No, Philippa, don't try to hurt me. Listen, 'tis you I want, not Bernice. 'Tis you and only you who will bear my sons, and I will take you now so that you will want to be my wife. Aye, 'twill happen. Don't move, sweeting."

His eyes were glazed anew, but Philippa tried again, speaking slowly, very distinctly. "I won't marry you, Ivo. I don't want you. Listen to me, you must stop this, you —"

He moaned and jerked his belly repeatedly against hers. They were of a height, and every male part of him fitted against her perfectly, at least in his mind. Philippa decided it was time to do something. She was loath to harm him; he was, after all, Bernice's suitor and perhaps future husband. Her sister wouldn't want him to be a eunuch. But he was in her chamber, pinning her to her narrow bed, breathing into her face, and planning to force her.

When his fingers eased higher on her thigh, she yelled into his ear, and he winced, his eyes nearly crossing, and moaned again — whether from passion or from the pain of her shrill cry, Philippa didn't know.

"Stop it!" she yelled once again, and pounded his back with her fists. Ivo touched her female flesh, warm and incredibly soft, and thought that finally she wanted him, would soon be begging him. Her legs were so long he'd begun to wonder if he would ever reach his goal. Ah, but he'd arrived, finally. He pressed his fingers inward and nearly spilled his seed at the excitement of touching her. He was panting now, beyond himself. He would take her and then he would marry her, and he would have her every night, he would . . .

"You bloody little whoreson! Devil's toes and St. Andrew's shins, get off my daughter, you stupid whelp!"

Lord Henry de Beauchamp was shorter than his daughter, blessed with a full head of hair that he was at this moment vigorously tugging. His belly well-fed, but when aroused to fury, he was still formidable. He was nearly apoplectic at this point. He clutched Ivo's surcoat at his neck, ripping the precious silk, and dragged him off Philippa. But Ivo didn't let go. He held tightly to Philippa's waist, his other hand, the one that had touched her intimately, dragging slowly back down her thigh. She pushed and shoved at him and her father tugged and cursed. Ivo howled as he fell on the floor beside her bed, rolled onto his back, and stared blankly up at Lord Henry's convulsed face.

"My lord, I love Philippa, and you must

—" He shut his mouth, belated wisdom quieting his tongue.

Lord Henry turned to his daughter. "Did the little worm harm you, Philippa?"

"Nay, Papa. He was lively, but I would have stopped him soon. He lost his head."

"Better his head than your maidenhead, my girl. How comes he to be in your chamber?"

Philippa stared down at her erstwhile attacker. "He claimed to want only to speak to me. I didn't think it would become so serious. Ivo forgot himself."

Ivo de Vescy had more than forgotten himself, Lord Henry thought, but he merely stared down at the young man, still sprawled on his back, his eyes now closed, his Adam's apple bobbing wildly. Lord Henry had nearly succumbed to a seizure when he'd seen Ivo de Vescy atop his daughter. The shock of it still made the blood pound in his head. He shook himself, becoming calmer. "You stay here, Philippa. Straighten yourself, and, I might add, you will keep silent about this debacle. I will speak to our enthusiastic puppy here. Mayhap I'll show him how we geld frisky stallions at Beauchamp."

Lord Henry grabbed Ivo's arm and jerked him to his feet. "You will come with me, you randy young goat. I have much to say to you."

Ivo deserved any curse her father chose to heap on his head, Philippa thought, straightening her clothing, and her father had an impressive repertoire of the most revolting curses known in Cornwall. She thought of Ivo's hand creeping up her leg and frowned. She should have sent her fist into his moaning mouth, should have kicked him in his spirited manhood, should have . . . Philippa paused, wondering exactly what her father would say to Ivo. Would he tell him to forget about Bernice? Would he order Ivo out of Beauchamp Castle? This was the *third* man who'd acted foolishly . . . well, not so foolishly as Ivo, and it wasn't amusing, not anymore. Bernice didn't think so, and neither did their mother, Lady Maude. Lord Henry wouldn't order Ivo away from Beauchamp; he couldn't. Bernice wanted Ivo Vescy very much. Lady Maude wanted him for Bernice. Philippa wanted him for Bernice as well.

Philippa felt a thick curl of hair fall over her forehead and slapped it away, then sighed and tried to weave it back into its braid. Life wasn't always reasonable; one couldn't expect it to be. But there had been five suitors for Bernice's well-dowered hand.

Two of the men had swooned over Bernice, but she hadn't shared their enthusiasms. The other two had preferred Philippa, and Bernice, unaccountably to her sister, had decided it was Philippa's fault. And now Ivo de Vescy, the young man most profoundly desired by Bernice, the one with the sweetest smile, the cleverest way of arching only one eyebrow, and the most manly of bodies, had turned coat.

What was Lord Henry saying to him? Philippa couldn't allow Ivo to be turned out of Beauchamp. Neither Bernice nor Lady Maude would ever forgive her. They would both accuse her of trying to gain Ivo's affections for herself. Bernice would probably try to scratch her face and pull out her hair, which would make life excessively unpleasant.

Philippa didn't hesitate a moment. She hurried quietly down the deeply indented stone stairs from the Beauchamps' living quarters into the great hall with its monstrous fireplace and a beam-arched ceiling so high it couldn't be seen in the winter for all the smoke gushing upward. She didn't stop, but speeded up, slipping out of the great hall into the inner ward and running toward the eastern tower. She climbed the damp stone stairs, slowing down only when she reached the second floor and the door to her father's private chamber. His war room, it was called, but Philippa knew that her father frolicked away long winter nights in that room with willing local women. Without hesitation she eased the door open a crack, just enough for her to see her father standing near one of the narrow arrow slits that gave out over the moat to the Dunroyal Forest beyond. Ivo de Vescy, his shoulders attempting arrogance, stood straight as a rod in front of him. She heard her father say sharply, "Have you no sense, you half-witted puppy? You cannot have Philippa! Bernice is the daughter who is to be wed, not Philippa. I will not tell you this again."

Ivo, sullen yet striving with all his might to be manly, squared his shoulders until his back hurt and said, "My lord, I must beg you to reconsider. 'Tis Philippa I wish to have. I beg your pardon for trying to . . . convince her of my devotion in such . . ." He faltered, understandably, Philippa thought, easing her ear even closer.

"You were ravishing her, you cretin!"

"Mayhap, my lord, but I wouldn't have hurt her. Never would I harm a hair on her little head!"

"Hellfire, boy, her *little* head is the same height as yours!"

That was true, but Ivo didn't turn a hair at the idea of having a wife who could stare him right in the eye. "Lord Henry, you must give her to me, you must let me take her to wive. My father will cherish her, as will all my family. Please, my lord, I wouldn't have hurt her."

Lord Henry smiled at that. "True enough, young de Vescy. She wouldn't have allowed you to ravish her, you callow clattermouth. Little you know her. She would have destroyed you, for she is strong of limb, strong as my hulking squire, not a mincing little bauble like other ladies." There was sudden silence, and Lord Henry stared at the young man. There came a glimmer of softening in his rheumy eyes and a touch of understanding in his voice. "Ah, forget your desire, young Ivo, do you hear me?" But Ivo shook his head.

All softening and understanding fled Lord Henry's face. His fearsome dark brows drew together. He looked malevolent, and even Philippa, well used to her sire's rages, shrank back. Surely Ivo would back down very soon; no man faced her father in that mood. To her shock and Lord Henry's, Ivo made another push, his voice nearly cracking as he said, "I love her, my lord! Only Philippa!"

Lord Henry crossed his meaty arms over his chest. He studied Ivo silently, then seemed to come to a decision. Frowning, he said, "Philippa is already betrothed. She is to wed on her eighteenth birthday, which is only two months from now."

"Wed! Nay!"

"Aye. So be off with you, Ivo de Vescy. 'Tis either my lovely Bernice or —"

"But, my lord, who would claim her? Whom would you prefer over me?"

Philippa, whose curiosity was by far greater than her erstwhile ravisher's, pressed her face even closer, her eyes on her father's face.

"She is to wed William de Bridgport."

*De Bridgport!*

Philippa whipped about, her mouth agape, not believing what she'd heard. Then she caught the sound of her mother's soft footfall and quickly slithered behind a tapestry her grandmother had woven some thirty years before, where only her pointed slippers could be seen. She held her breath. Her mother passed into the chamber without knocking. Philippa heard some muttered words but could not make them out. She quickly resumed her post by the open door.

Philippa heard her mother laugh aloud, a

rusty sound, for Lady Maude had not been favored with a humorous nature. "Aye, Ivo de Vescy, 'tis William de Bridgport who will wed her, not you."

Ivo stared from one to the other, then took a step back. "William de Bridgport! Why, my lord, my lady, 'tis an old man he is, a fat old man with no teeth, and a paunch that . . ." Words failed Ivo, and he demonstrated, holding his hands out three feet in front of his stomach. "He's a terror, my lord, a man of my father's years, a —"

"Devil's teeth! Hold your tongue, you impudent little stick! You know less than aught about anything!"

Lady Maude took her turn, her voice virulent. "Aye, 'tis none of your affair! 'Tis Bernice we offer, and Bernice you accept, or get you gone from Beauchamp."

Philippa eased back, her face pale, images, not words, flooding her brain. De Bridgport! Ivo was right, except that de Bridgport was even worse than he had said. The man was also the father of three repellent offspring older than her — two daughters, shrill and demanding, and a son who had no chin and a leering eye. Philippa closed her eyes. This had to be some sort of jest. Her father wouldn't . . . There was no need to give her in marriage to de

Bridgport. It made no sense, unless her father was simply making it up, trying to get Ivo to leave off. Aye, that had to be it. Ivo had caught him off-guard and he'd spit out the first name that had come to mind in order to make Ivo switch his ardor to the other sister.

But then Lady Maude said, her voice high and officious, "Listen you, Ivo de Vescy. That giant of a girl has no dowry from Lord Henry, not a farthing, hear you? She goes to de Bridgport because he'll take her with naught but her shift. Be glad de Bridgport will have her, because her shift is nearly all Lord Henry will provide her. Ah, didn't you know all call her the Giant? 'Tis because she's such a lanky, graceless creature, unlike her sweet-natured sister."

Lord Henry stared in some consternation at his pallid-faced wife whose pale gray eyes hadn't shone with this much passion since their first wedded night, a very short wedded night, and slowly nodded, adding, "Now, young pup, 'tis either you return to York and your father or you'll take my pretty Bernice, as her mother says, and you'll sign the betrothal contract, eh?"

But Ivo wasn't quite through, and Philippa, for a moment at least, was proud of him, for he mouthed her own questions.

"But, my lord, why? You don't care for your daughter, my lady? I mean no disrespect, my lord, but . . ."

Lord Henry eyed the young man. He watched his wife eye de Vescy as well, no passion in either eye now, just cold fury. Even her thin cheeks sported two red anger spots. Ivo was being impertinent, but then again, Lord Henry had been a fool to mention de Bridgport, but his had been the only name to pop into his mind. And Maude had quickly affirmed the man, and so he'd been caught, unable to back down. De Bridgport! The man was a mangy article.

"Why, my lord?"

There was not only desperation but also honest puzzlement in the young man's voice, and Lord Henry sighed. But it was Maude who spoke, astonishing him with the venom of her voice. "Philippa has no hold on Lord Henry. Thus she will have no dowry. She is naught to us, a burden, a vexation. Make up your mind, Ivo, and quickly, for you sorely tax me with your impertinence."

"Will you now accept Bernice?" Lord Henry asked. "She, dulcet child, tells me she wants you and none other."

Ivo wanted to say that he'd take Philippa without a dowry, even without a shift, but sanity stilled his impetuosity. He wasn't stupid; he was aware of his duty as his father's eldest son. The de Vescy holdings near York were a drain at present, given the poor crops that had plagued the area for the past several years. He must wed an heiress; it was his duty. He had no choice, none at all. And, his thinking continued, Philippa wasn't small and soft and cuddly like her sister. She was too tall, too strong, too self-willed — by all the saints, she could read and cipher like a bloody priest or clerk — ah, but her rich dark blond hair was so full of colors, curling wildly around her face and making an unruly fall down her back, free and soft. And her eyes were a glorious clear blue, bright and vivid with laughter, and her breasts were so wondrously full and round and . . . Ivo cleared his throat. "I'll take Bernice, my lord," he said, and Lord Henry prayed that the young man wouldn't burst into tears.

Maude walked to him, and even smiled as she touched his tunic sleeve. " 'Tis right and proper," she said. "You will not regret your choice."

Philippa felt like Lot's wife. She couldn't seem to move, even when her father waved toward the door, telling Ivo to repose himself before seeking out Bernice. In an instant of time her life had changed. She didn't understand why both her parents had turned on her — if turn they had. She'd always assumed that her father loved her; he worked her like a horse, that was true, but she enjoyed her chores as Beauchamp's steward. She reveled in keeping the accounts, in dealing with the merchants of Beauchamp, with settling disputes amongst the peasants.

As for her mother, she'd learned to keep clear of Lady Maude some years before. She'd been told not to call her "Mother," but as a small child she'd accepted that and not worried unduly about it. Nor had she sought affection from that thin-lipped lady since she'd gained her tenth year and Lady Maude had slapped her so hard she'd heard ringing in her ears for three days. Her transgression, she remembered now, was to accuse Bernice of stealing her small pile of pennies. Her father had done nothing. He hadn't taken her side, but merely waved her away and muttered that he was too busy for such female foolishness. She'd forgotten until now that her father hadn't defended her — probably because it had hurt too much to remember.

And now they planned to marry her to William de Bridgport. They wouldn't even provide her with a dowry. Nor had anyone mentioned it to her. Philippa couldn't take it all in. From a beloved younger daughter — at least by her father — to a cast-off daughter who wasn't loved by anyone, who had no hold on her parents, who was of no account, who had only her shift and nothing more . . . What had she done? How had she offended them so deeply as to find herself thus discarded?

Even as Ivo turned, his young face set, she couldn't make herself move. Finally, when Ivo was close enough to see her, she did move, turned on the toes of her soft leather slippers, and raced away. The toes of the slippers were long and pointed, the latest fashion from Queen Eleanor's court, and they weren't meant for running. Philippa tripped twice before she reached the seclusion of her chamber. She slid the bolt across the thick oak door and leaned against it, breathing harshly.

It wasn't just that they didn't want her. Nor was it that they simply wanted her away from them and from Beauchamp. They wanted to punish her. They wanted to give her to that profane old man, de Bridgport. Why? There was no answer that came to mind. She could, she supposed, simply go ask her father why he and her mother were doing this. She could ask him how she had offended them so much that they wanted to repulse her and chastise her.

Philippa looked out the narrow window onto the inner ward of Beauchamp Castle. Comforting smells drifted upward with the stiff eastern breeze, smells of dogs and cattle and pigs and the lathered horses of Lord Henry's men-at-arms. The jakes were set in the outer wall in the western side of the castle, and the wind, fortunately, wafted away the smell of human excrement today.

This was her home; she'd never questioned that she belonged; such thoughts would never have occurred to her. She knew that Lady Maude cared not for her, not as she cared for Bernice, but Philippa had ignored the hurt she'd felt as a child, coming not to care over the years, and she'd tried instead to win her father, to make him proud of her, to make him love her. But now even her father had sided with Lady Maude. She was to be exiled to William de Bridgport's keep and company and bed. She felt a moment of deep resentment toward her sister. Bernice, who'd been the only one to garner the stingy affections Lady Maud had doled out as if a hug or a kiss were something to be hoarded.

Was it because Philippa was taller than her father, a veritable tower of a girl who had not the soft sweet look of Bernice? Lady Maude had told Ivo that she was called the Giant. Philippa hadn't known; she'd never heard that, even from Bernice in moments of anger.

Was it because she'd been born a girl and not a boy?

Philippa shook her head at that thought. If true, then Bernice wouldn't be exempt from displeasure, surely.

Philippa wasn't really a giant, just tall for a female, that was all. She turned from the window and looked blankly around her small chamber.

It was a comfortable room with strewn herbs and rushes covering the cold stone floor. She had to do something. She could not simply wait here for William de Bridgport to come and claim her.

It occurred to Philippa at that moment to wonder why Lord Henry had gone to such pains to educate her if his intention were simply to marry her off to William de Bridgport. It seemed a mighty waste unless de Bridgport wanted a steward and a wife and a brood mare all in one. Philippa had been Lord Henry's steward for the past two years, since old Master Davie had died of the flux, and she was becoming more skilled by the day. What use was it all now? she wondered as she unfastened her soft leather belt, stripped off her loose-fitting sleeveless overtunic of soft pale blue linen and then her long fitted woolen gown, nearly ripping the tight sleeves in her haste. She stood for a moment clothed only in her white linen shift that came to mid-thigh. Then she jerked the shift over her head. She realized in that instant that she'd seen something else in the inner ward of the castle. She'd seen several wagons loaded high with raw wool bound for the St. Ives April Fair. Two wagons belonged to the demesne farmers and one to Lord Henry.

She stood tall and naked and shivering, not with cold, but with the realization that she couldn't stay here and be forced to wed de Bridgport. She couldn't remain here at Beauchamp and pretend that nothing had happened. She couldn't remain here like a helpless foundling awaiting her fate. She could hear Bernice taunting her now: . . . *an evil old man for you, a handsome young man for me. I'm the favorite and now you'll pay, pay* . . .

She wasn't helpless. In another minute Philippa had pulled a very old shapeless gown over an equally old shift and topped the lot with an overtunic that had been washed so many times its color was now an indeterminate gray. She replaced her fashionable pointed slippers with sturdy boots that came to her calves. She quickly took strips of linen and cross-gartered the boots to keep them up. She braided her thick hair anew, wound it around her head, and shoved a woolen cap over it. The cap was too small, having last been worn when she was but nine years old, but it would do.

Now she simply had to wait until it grew dark. Her cousin Sir Walter de Grasse, Lady Maude's nephew, lived near St. Ives. He was the castellan of Crandall, a holding of the powerful Graelam de Moreton of Wolffeton. Philippa had met Walter only twice in her life, but she remembered him as being kind. It was to her cousin she'd go. Surely he would protect her, surely. And then . . . To her consternation, she saw the farmers and three of her father's men-at-arms fall in beside the three wagons. They were leaving now!

Philippa was confounded, but only for a minute. Beauchamp had been her home for nearly eighteen years. She knew every niche and cavity of it. She slipped quietly from her chamber, crept down the deep stairs into the great hall, saw that no one noticed her, and escaped through the great open oak doors into the inner ward. Quickly, she thought, she must move quickly. She ran to the hidden postern gate, cleared it enough to open it, and slipped through. She clamped her fingers over her nostrils, shuddered with loathing, and waded into the stinking moat. The moat suddenly deepened, and her feet sank into thick mud, bringing the slimy water to her eyebrows. She coughed and choked and gagged, then swam to the other side, crawled up the slippery bank, and raced toward the Dunroyal Forest beyond. The odor of the moat was now part of her.

Well, she wasn't on her way to London to meet the king. She was bent on escape. She wiped off her face as best she could and stared down the pitted narrow road. The wagons would come this way. They had to come this way.

And they did, some twenty minutes later. She pulled her cap down and hid, positioning herself. The wagons came slowly. The three men-at-arms accompanying the wagons to the fair were jesting about one of the local village women who could exercise a man better than a day of working in the fields.

Philippa didn't hear anything else. From the protection of her hiding place she flung several small rocks across the road. They ripped into the thick underbrush, thudding loudly, and the men-at-arms reacted immediately. They whipped their horses about, drawing the craning attention of the farmers who drove the wagons. As quickly as she could move, Philippa slipped to the second wagon and burrowed under the piles of dirty gray wool. She couldn't smell the foul odor of the raw wool because she'd become used to the smell of the moat that engulfed her. The wool was coarse and scratchy, and any exposed flesh was instantly miserable. She would ignore it; she had to. She relaxed a bit when she heard one of the men-at-arms yell, " 'Tis naught!"

"Aye, a rabbit or a grouse."

"I was hoping it was a hungry wench wanting to ride me and my horse."

"Ha! 'Tis only the meanest harlot who'd take you on!"

The men-at-arms continued their coarse jesting until they heard one of the peasants snicker behind his hand. One of them yelled, "Get thee forward, you lazy lout, else you'll feel the flat of my sword!"

# 2

*St. Erth Castle, Near St. Ives Bay*
*Cornwall, England*

The sheep were dead. Every last miserable one of them was dead. Every one of them had belonged to him, and now they were all dead, all forty-four of them, and all because the shepherd, Robin, had suffered with watery bowels from eating hawthorn berries until he'd fallen over in a dead faint and the sheep had wandered off, gotten caught in a ferocious storm, and bleated themselves over a sheer cliff into the Irish Sea.

Forty-four sheep! By Christ, it wasn't fair. What was he to do now? He had no coin — at least not enough to take to the St. Ives Fair and purchase more sheep, and sheep that hadn't already been spring-shorn. He couldn't get much wool off a spring-shorn sheep. He needed clothes, his son needed clothes, his men needed clothes, not to mention all the servants who toiled in his keep. He had a weaver, Prink, who was eating his head off, and content to sit on his fat backside with nary a thing to do. And Old Agnes, who told everyone what to do, including Prink, was also doing nothing but carping and complaining and driving him berserk.

Dienwald de Fortenberry cursed, sending his fist against his thigh, and felt the wool tunic he wore split from his elbow to his armpit. The harsh winter had done him in. At least his people were planting crops — wheat and barley — enough for St. Erth and all the villeins who spent their lives working for him and depending on him to keep them from starving. Many lords didn't care if their serfs starved in ditches, but Dienwald thought such an attitude foolhardy. Dead men couldn't plant crops or shoe horses or defend St. Erth.

On the other hand, dead men didn't need clothes.

Dienwald was deep in thought, tossing about for something to do, when Crooky, his fool, who'd been struck by a falling tree as a boy and grown up with a twisted back, shuffled into view and began to twitch violently. Dienwald wasn't in a mood to enjoy his contortions at the moment and waved him away. Then Crooky hopped on one foot, and Dienwald realized he was miming something. He watched the hops and the hand movements, then bellowed, "Get thee gone, meddlesome dunce! You disturb my brain."

Crooky curtsied in a grotesque parody of a lady and then threaded a needle, sat down on the floor, and mimed sewing. He began singing:

> My sweet Lord of St. Erth
> Ye need not ponder bare-arsed or
> Fret yer brain for revelations
> For you come three wagons and
>    full they be
> Ready, my sweet lord, for yer
>    preservations.

"That has no sensible rhyme, lackwit, and you waste my energies! Get out out of my sight!"

> My sweet lord of St. Erth
> Ye need not go a-begging
> In yer humble holey lin-en
> There come three wagons
>    full of wool and
> But a clutch of knaves to guard
>    them-in.

"Enough of your twaddle!" Dienwald jumped to his feet and advanced on Crooky, who lay on the rush-strewn floor smiling beautifully up at his master. "Get to your feet and tell me about this wool."

Crooky began another mime, still crouched on the floor. He was driving a wagon, looking over his shoulder; then fright screwed up his homely features. Dienwald kicked him in the ribs. "Cease this!" he bellowed. "You've less ability than the bloody sheep that slaughtered themselves."

Crooky, exquisitely sensitive to his master's moods, and more wily than he was brain-full, guessed from the pain in his ribs that his lord was serious. He quickly rolled to his knees and told Dienwald what he'd heard.

Dienwald stroked his hand over his jaw. He hesitated. He sat down in the lord's chair and stretched out his legs in front of him. There was a hole in his hose at the ankle. So there were three wagons of raw wool coming from Beauchamp. Long he'd wanted to tangle with that overfed Lord Henry. But the man was powerful and had many men in his service. From the corner of his eye Dienwald saw his son, Edmund, dash into the great hall. His short tunic was patched and worn and remarkably filthy. His hose were long disintegrated, and the boy's legs were bare. He looked like a serf.

Edmund, unconcerned with his frayed appearance, looked from his father to Crooky, who gave him a wink and a wave. " 'Tis true, Father? Wool for the taking?"

Dienwald looked again at the patches that were quick wearing through on his son's elbows. He shouted for his master-at-arms, Eldwin. The man appeared in an instant and Dienwald knew he'd heard all. "We'll take eight men — our most ferocious-looking fighters — and those wagons will soon be ours. Don't forget Gorkel the Hideous. One look at him and those wagon drivers will faint with terror. Tell that useless cur Prink and Old Agnes that we'll soon have enough work for every able-bodied servant in the keep."

"Can I come with you, Papa?"

Dienwald shook his head, buffeted the boy fondly on the shoulder, a loving gesture that nearly knocked him down into the stale rushes. "Nay, Edmund. You will guard the castle in my absence. You can bear Old Agnes' advice and endless counsel whilst I'm gone."

The stench was awful. By the evening of that first day, when the wagons and men camped near a stream close to St. Hilary,

Philippa was very nearly ready to announce her presence and beg mercy, a bath, and some of the roasting rabbit she smelled. But she didn't; she endured, she had to. They would reach St. Ives Fair late on the morrow. She could bear it. It wasn't just the raw, bur-filled wool, but the smell of moat dried against her skin and clothes and mingled with the odor of the raw wool. It didn't get better. Philippa had managed to burrow through the thick piles of wool to form a small breathing hole, but she dared not make the hole larger. One of the men might notice, and it would be all over. They would sympathize with her plight rightly enough, and let her bathe and doubtless feed her, but then they would return her to Beauchamp. Their loyalty and their very lives were bound up with Lord Henry.

She pictured her cousin Sir Walter de Grasse and tried to imagine his reaction when she suddenly appeared at Crandall looking and smelling like a nightmare hag from Burgotha's Swamp. She could imagine his thin long nose twitching, imagine his eyes closing tightly at the sight of her. But he couldn't turn her away. He wouldn't. She prayed that she would find a stream before arriving at Crandall.

To make matters worse, the day was hot

and the night remained uncomfortably warm. Under the scratchy thick wool, adding sweat to the stench, the hell described by Lord Henry's priest began to seem like naught more than a cool summer's afternoon.

Philippa itched but couldn't reach all the places that were making her more desperate by the minute. Had it been imperative that she jump into the moat? Wasn't there another way to get to the forest? She'd acted without thinking, not used her brain and planned. "You think with your feet, Philippa," Lord Henry was wont to tell her, watching her dash hither and yon in search of something. And she'd done it again. She'd certainly jumped into the moat with her feet.

How many more hours now before she could slip away? She had to wait until they reached the St. Ives Fair or her father's men would likely see her and it would have all been for naught. All the stench, all the itches, all the hunger, all for naught. She would wait it out; her sheer investment in misery wouldn't allow her to back down now. Her stomach grumbled loudly and she was so thirsty her tongue was swollen.

Her father's guards unknowingly shared their amorous secrets with her that evening.

"Aye," said Alfred, a man who weighed more than Lord Henry's prize bull, "they pretend it pains them to take ye — then, jist when ye spill yer seed and want to rest a bit, they whine about a little bauble. Bah!"

Philippa could just imagine Alfred lying on her, and the thought made her ribs hurt. Ivo had been heavy enough; Alfred was three times his size. There were offerings of consolation and advice, followed by tall tales of conquest — none of it in the service of her father against his enemies — and Philippa wanted to scream that a young lady was in the wool wagon and her ears were burning, but instead she fell asleep in her misery and slept the whole night through.

The next day continued as the first, except that she was so hungry and thirsty she forgot for whole minutes at a time the fiery itching of her flesh and her own stink. She'd sunk into a kind of apathy when she suddenly heard a shout from one of Lord Henry's guards. She stuck her nose up into the small air passage. Another shout; then: "Attack! Attack! Flank the last wagon! No, over there!"

Good God! Thieves!

The wagon that held Philippa lurched to a stop, leaned precariously to the left, then righted itself. She heard more shouting, the sound of horses' hooves pounding nearer, until they seemed right on top of her, and then the clash of steel against steel. There were several loud moans and the sound of running feet. She wanted to help but knew that the only thing she could possibly do was show herself and pray that the thieves died of fright. No, she had to hold still and pray that her father's men would vanquish the attackers. She heard a loud gurgling sound, quite close, and felt a bolt of terror.

There came another loud shout, then the loud twang of an arrow being released. She heard a loud thump — the sound of a man falling from his horse. And then she heard one voice, raised over all the others, and that voice was giving orders. It was a voice that was oddly calm, yet at the same time deep in its intensity, and she felt her blood run cold. It wasn't the voice of a common thief. No, the voice . . . Her thinking stopped. There was only silence now. The brief fighting was over. And she knew her father's men hadn't won. They would tell no tall tales about this day. She waited, frozen deep in her nest of wool.

The man's voice came again. "You, fellow, listen to me. Your guards are such cowards they've fled with but slight wounds to nag at them. I have no desire to slit any of your throats for you. What say you?"

Osbert wasn't amused; he was terrified, and his mouth was as dry as the dirty wool in the wagon, for he'd swallowed all his spit and could scarce form words. But self-interest moistened his tongue, and he managed to fawn, saying, "My lord, please allow this one wagon to pass. Thass ours, my lord, my brother's and mine, and thass all we own. We'll starve if ye take it. The other two wagons are the property of my lord Henry de Beauchamp. He's fat and needs not the profits. Have pity on us, my lord."

Philippa wanted to rise from her bed of wool and shriek at Osbert, the scurvy liar. Starve indeed. The fellow owned the most prosperous of Lord Henry's demesne farms. He was a freeman and his duty to Lord Henry lightened his purse not overly much. She waited for the man with the mean voice to cut out Osbert's tongue for his effrontery. To her chagrin and relief, the man said, " 'Tis fair. I will take the two wagons and you may keep yours. Say nothing, fellow," the man added, and Philippa knew he said those words only to hear himself give the order. Her father's farmers would race back to Beauchamp to tell of this thievery, and likely bray about their bravery against overwhelming forces — and take her with them, if, that is, she was in the right wagon.

Suddenly the wagon moved. She heard the man's voice say, "Easy on the reins, Peter. That mangy horse looks ready to crumple in his tracks. 'Twould appear that Lord Henry is stingy and mean."

Philippa wasn't in the right wagon. She was in one of the stolen wagons and she had no idea where she was going. For that matter, when the farmers returned to Beauchamp they wouldn't have any idea who'd attacked them.

Dienwald sat back on his destrier, Philbo, and looked upon the two wagons filled with fine raw wool, now his. He rubbed his hands together, then patted Philbo's neck. The guards had fled into Treywen Forest. They would be fools to ride back to Beauchamp. If they did, Lord Henry would have their ears cut off for cowardice. Other parts of their anatomy would doubtless follow the ears. The farmers would travel to St. Ives. He knew their sort. Greedy but not stupid, and liars of superb ability when their lives were at stake. He imagined them playing the terrified and guiltless victims very well. He imagined them carrying on about this monster at least seven feet tall whose face was nearly purple with scars, who'd threatened to eat them and spit them out in the dirt.

And they wouldn't be far off the mark. That was the beauty of Gorkel; he hadn't said a word to the terrified peasants; he didn't have to. Perhaps Lord Henry would even let them keep the proceeds from the sale of their wool — well, not all, but enough for their efforts. And St. Erth now had enough wool for Old Agnes to weave her gnarly fingers to the bone; and in addition, he had two new horses. Not that the nags were anything wonderful, but they were free, and that made them special. It wasn't a bad outcome. Dienwald was content with his day's work. He would remember to give Crooky an extra tunic for his information.

"Don't dawdle," he called out. "To St. Erth! I want to reach home before nightfall."

"Aye, my lord," Eldwin called out, and the wagon lurched and careened wildly as the poor nag broke into a shuffling canter. Philippa fell back, bringing piles of the filthy wool over her face. She couldn't breathe anything save her own stench until she managed to burrow another breathing hole. Where was St. Erth? She'd heard of the place but didn't know its location. Then her stomach soured and she thought only to keep herself from retching. The nausea overpowered her and she clawed through the layers of wool until her head was clear and the hot sun was searing her face from overhead.

Philippa kept drawing deep gulping breaths, and when her stomach eased, she grew brave enough to look around. The man driving the wagon had his back to her. She craned her neck and saw the other wagon ahead, and beyond the first wagon rode six men. All were facing away from her. Which one was the leader, the lord? They were all poorly garbed, which was odd, but their horses seemed well-fed and well-muscled. Philippa, her stomach snarling even more loudly, tried to ignore it and take stock of her surroundings. She had no idea where she was. Gnarled oak trees, older than the Celtic witches, grew in clumps on either side of the pitted dirt road. She fancied she would get an occasional sniff of the sea from the north. Mayhap they were traveling directly toward St. Ives. Mayhap all was not lost.

Philippa continued thinking optimistically for another hour. They passed through two small villages — clumped-together huts, really, nothing more. Then she saw a castle loom up before them. Set on a high rocky hill, stunted pine trees clustered about its base, was a large Norman-style castle. Its walls were crenellated and there were arrow loops, narrow windows in the four thin towers and walls at least eight feet thick. It was gray and cold, an excellent fortress that looked like it would stand for a thousand years. It stood guard like a grim sentinel over mile upon mile of countryside in all directions. As the wagons drew nearer, Philippa saw there was no moat, since the castle was elevated, but there was a series of obstacles — rusted pikes buried in the ground at irregular intervals, their sharp teeth at a level to rip open a horse's belly or a man's throat if he fell on them. Then came the holes covered with grass and reeds, holding, she imagined, vertical spears. The wagons negotiated the obstacles without hesitation or difficulty.

Philippa heard a loud creaking sound and saw twenty-foot gates made of thick oak slowly part to reveal a narrow inner passage some thirty feet long, with withdrawn iron teeth of a portcullis ready to be lowered onto an enemy. The wagons rolled into an inner ward filled with men, women, children, and animals. It was pandemonium, with everyone talking at once, children shrieking, pigs squealing, chickens squawking. There were more people and animals here than in the inner ward at Beauchamp, and Beauchamp was twice as big. Even the chickens sounded demented.

Philippa barely had time to duck under the wool again before the wagons were surrounded by dozens of people cheering and shouting congratulations. She heard the thick outer gates grind close again, and it seemed a great distance away.

Philippa felt her first complete shock of fear. Her optimism crumbled. She'd done it this time. She'd truly acted with her feet and not with her brain. She'd jumped into a slimy moat and then into a wagon of filthy raw wool. And now she was alone at a stranger's castle — a prisoner, or worse. She was so hungry she was ready to gnaw at her fingers.

The wagon lurched to a sudden jolting halt. Dozens of hands rocked the wagon. Philippa felt them grabbing at the wool, felt their hands sifting through the layers, nearer and nearer to where she was buried.

Then she heard the leader's voice, closer now, saying something about Gorkel the Hideous and his magnificent visage, and then her stomach announced its rebellion in no uncertain terms and she fought her way up through the wool until she flew out the top, gasping, gulping the clean air.

"God's glory," Dienwald said, and stared.

A little boy bellowed, "What is it, Papa? A witch? A druid ghost? Thass hideous!"

Gorkel shuddered at the apparition and yelled, " 'Tis more hideous than I! God gi' us his mercy! Deliver us from this snare of the devil's!"

Dienwald continued to stare at the daunting creature lurching about, its arms flapping, trying to keep its balance in the shifting wool. The creature was tall, that much was obvious, its head covered with wool, thick and wild and sticking straight out. Then the great wigged hag gained its footing and turned toward him downwind, and he gagged. The noxious odor surpassed that of his many villeins who didn't bathe from their birth until their death.

The creature suddenly began to shake itself, jerking away clumps of wool with its grubby fingers, until its face was cleared and he saw it was a female sort of creature staring back at him with frightened eyes as blue as the April sky that was just beginning to mellow into late afternoon.

His people were as silent as mourners at a pope's tomb — an achievement even St. Erth's priest, Cramdle, had never accomplished in his holiest of moments — all of them staring gape-mouthed and bug-eyed. Then slowly they began to speak in frightened whispers. "Aye, Master Edmund has the right of it: thass a witch from the swamp."

" 'Tis most likely a crone tossed out for thievery!"

"Nay, 'tis as Gorkel says: thass not human, thass an evil monster, a punishment from the devil."

Edmund yelled, " 'Tis a witch, Papa, and she's here to curse us!"

"Be quiet," Dienwald told his son and his people. He dug his heels gently into Philbo's sleek sides. He got within five feet of the ghastly female and could not bear to bring himself closer. He fought the urge to hold his nose.

"I'm no witch!" the female shouted in a clear loud voice.

"Then who are you?" Dienwald asked.

Philippa turned to stare at the man. She wasn't blind. She saw the distaste on his face, and in truth, she couldn't blame him. She touched her fingers to her hair and found that her cap was long gone and the thick curls had worked free of the braid and were covered with slime from the Beauchamp moat and crowned with clumps of the squalid wool. She could just imagine what she looked like. She felt totally miserable. People were making the sign of the cross as they stared at her, horror and revulsion on their faces, calling upon a dizzying array of saints to protect them.

And she was Philippa de Beauchamp, such a wondrous and beauteous girl that Ivo de Vescy had tried to force her so she would wed him. It was too much. By all the saints, even William de Bridgport wouldn't want her now. She imagined herself standing before him covered with slime and wool, her smell overwhelming. Surely he would shriek like the little boy had. She pictured de Bridgport turning and running, his fat stomach bouncing up and down. She couldn't help herself. She laughed.

"I am in obvious disarray, sirrah. Forgive me, but if you would allow me to quit your very nice castle, I will be on my way and you won't have to bear my noxious smell or my company further."

"Don't move," Dienwald said, raising his hand as she moved to climb over the side of the wagon. "Now, answer me. Who are you?"

It was the man with the mean deep voice, and her brief bout of laughter died a quick death. She was in a very dangerous situation. It didn't occur to her to lie. She was of high birth. No one with any chivalry would hurt a lady of high birth. She threw back her wild bushy head, straightened her shoulders, and shouted, "I am Philippa de Beauchamp, daughter of Lord Henry de Beauchamp."

"A witch! A lying crone!"

"I am not!" Philippa shouted, furious now. "I might look like a witch, but I'm not!"

Dienwald gazed at the hideous apparition, and it was his turn to laugh. "Philippa de Beauchamp, you say? From my vantage, 'tis barely female you appear, and such an unappetizing female that my dogs would cringe away from you. In addition, you have likely spoiled some of my wool."

"She will curse us, Papa!"

"*Your* wool? Ha! 'Tis my father's wool and you are nothing more than a common thief. As for you, you loud crude boy, I am mightily tempted to curse you."

Edmund shrieked, and Dienwald began to laugh. His people looked at him, then at the female creature, and they began to laugh as well, their chuckles swelling into a great noise. Philippa saw a misshapen fellow standing near the steps to the great hall, and even he was cackling wildly.

She wished now she'd lied. If she'd claimed to be a wench from a village, perhaps he'd simply have let her leave. But no, she'd told the truth — like a fool. How could she have imagined chivalry from a man who'd stolen two wagons of wool? Well, there was no hope for it. Up went her wool-clumped chin. "I am Philippa de Beauchamp. I demand that you give me respect."

The moment the creature had opened her mouth, Dienwald realized she wasn't an escaped serf or a girl from the village of St. Erth. She spoke like a gentlewoman — all arrogant, and loud, and haughty — like a queen caught in the jakes with her skirts up, yelling at the person who'd seen her. What the devil was this damned female doing hidden in a wool wagon, stinking like a hog's entrails, and covered with slime?

"I have long thought Lord Henry to be a red-nosed glutton whose girth makes his horses neigh in dread of carrying his bulk, but even he couldn't have been cursed with such as you. Now, get you down from the wagon." Dienwald watched her weave about, gain her balance, and climb down. She was very tall, and his villeins moved away from her, especially those unfortunate enough to be downwind of her. She stood on the ground, watching him, looking so awful it would curdle the blood of the unwary. He let Philbo back away from the fright and shouted at her, "Don't move!"

Dienwald dismounted, tossed the reins to his master-at-arms, Eldwin, and strode over to the well. He filled a bucket, then returned to the wagon. Without hesitation, he threw the bucket of water over her head. She wheezed and shrieked and jerked about, some of the wool rolled off her body and tunic. He could see her face now, and it wasn't hideous, just filthy. "More water, Egbert!"

"Water alone won't get me clean," Philippa said, gasping from the shock of the cold water. But she was grateful; she could now sniff herself without wanting to gag. She licked her lips and gratefully swallowed the drops of water that remained.

"I can't very well strip you naked here in my inner ward and hand you a chunk of lye soap. I mean, I could, but since you claim to be a lady, you would no doubt shriek were your modesty defiled."

A howl of laughter met this jest, and Philippa tried not to react. She said, calm as a snake sunning itself on a warm rock, "Couldn't I have the soap and perhaps go behind one of your outbuildings?"

"I don't know. My cat has just had kittens back there, and I hesitate to have her so frightened that her milk dries up." Dienwald felt the laughter billowing up again. He yelled for lye soap; then added, "Egbert, take the creature behind the cookhouse and leave her be. Look first for Eleanor. If she and her kittens are there, take the creature behind the barracks. Agnes, fetch clean clothes for her and attend her. Then bring her to me — but only when she no longer offends the nose."

"But, Papa, she's a witch!"

"Officious little boy," Philippa said as she turned on her bare heel — her boots were buried somewhere in the wool — and followed the man with the wonderful bucket of water.

"Careful what you call the creature, young Edmund," Crooky said, hobbling up. "It might cast a foul spell on you. Thass a relic from Hades, master." He threw back his head and cleared his throat. Dienwald, recognizing all too well the signs, yelled, "Keep your lips stitched, fool! No, not a word, Crooky, not a single foul rhyme out of your twitching mouth.

"As for you, Edmund," he continued to his son, "the creature isn't a relic. Relics don't turn your stomach with their stench, nor have I ever seen a relic that talked back to me. Now, let's have our wool begin its progress into cloth and into tunics. Prink! Get your fat arse out here!"

# 3

"The well will go dry before the creature is clean enough for mortal viewing and smelling," Dienwald said, rubbing his jaw as he spoke.

"Aye, thass the truth," said Northbert, who was sniffing the wool. " 'Tis not a virtuous smell, my lord," he added, picking up a clump of wool and bringing it to his nose, an appendage flattened some ten years before by a well-aimed stone.

"We'll let Old Agnes deal with it," Dienwald said.

"There she comes!" Edmund shouted.

Dienwald looked up at his son's yell. Indeed, he thought, staring at the female vision striding toward him, barefoot, the rough gown nearly threadbare and loose everywhere except her breasts. Her hair was a damp wild halo around her head, hair the color of dark honey and fall leaves and rich brown dirt, and growing curlier by the minute as it dried.

She walked up to him, stopped, looked him squarely in the eye, and said, "I am

Philippa de Beauchamp. You are a thief, but you also appear to be master of this castle and thus my host. What is your name?"

"Dienwald de Fortenberry. Aye, I am lord of this castle and master of all those herein, including you. Now, I have much to say to you, and I don't wish to speak in front of all my people. Follow me."

He turned without another word and strode across the dusty inner bailey toward the great hall. He was tall, she saw, following in his wake, some three or four inches taller than she was, and straight as a lance and just as solid. She couldn't see a patch of fat on him. He was also tough-looking and younger than she'd first thought when she heard him giving orders after his theft of the wool wagons. He wasn't all that much older than she, but he was treacherous — he'd already proved that. He was naught but a thief without remorse. She had still to see if he had the slightest bit of chivalry.

*Dienwald de Fortenberry.* She turned pale with sudden memory and was grateful he wasn't looking at her to see her face. She'd heard tales of him since she was ten years old. He was known variously as the Rogue of Cornwall, the Scourge, and the Devil's Blight. When de Fortenberry chanced to plunder or rob or pillage close to Beauchamp lands, Lord Henry would shake his fist in the air, spit in the rushes, and scream, "That damnable bastard should be cleaved into three parts!" Why *three* parts, no one at Beauchamp had ever dared to ask. She should never have told him who she was. She'd been ten times a fool. Now it was too late. He was master of this castle.

The great hall was shadowed and gloomy, with smoke-blackened beams supporting the high ceiling, and only a half-dozen narrow windows covered with hides. The floor rushes snapped and crackled beneath her bare feet, and several times she felt one of the twigs dig into her sole — a twig or mayhap a discarded bone. There wasn't much of an odor, just a stale smell. She watched the man wave away poorly garbed servants, several men-at-arms, the crooked-backed fellow, and the small boy whom she assumed was his son. Where was his wife? He had a son; surely he had a wife. On the other hand, what woman would want to be wedded to a scourge or a blight or a bastard? Philippa watched him sit down in the lord's chair, a high-backed affair of goodly proportions that had been made by a carpenter with some skill and a love of ornamentation. "Come here," the Scourge of Cornwall said, and crooked his finger at her.

No one had ever crooked a finger at her in such a peremptory way. Not even Lord Henry in his most officious moments.

Philippa forgot for a moment where she was and who it was who'd commanded her. She straightened her shoulders with alarming force. Her breasts nearly split the center seam of her gown. She nearly wailed with humiliation as she quickly hunched forward.

Dienwald de Fortenberry laughed.

"Come here," he said again.

Philippa walked forward, keeping her eyes on his face. It wasn't a bad face. She would have thought a scourge's face would be pitted by the pox, that he'd be wild-eyed and black-toothed, not hard and well-muscled and with eyes of light brown ringed with gold, with hair and brows the identical shade. There was a deep dimple in the center of his chin. Mayhap that was a mark of the devil. But if it were a devil's mark, why didn't he wear a beard to hide it? Instead he was clean-shaven, his hair worn longer than was the current fashion, with tight curls at his nape. He didn't look like a rogue or a devil's blight, but hadn't he stolen her father's wool without a by-your-leave?

"Who are you?"

"I am Dienwald de Fortenberry —"

"I know that. I mean, are you truly a devil's tool? Or perhaps one of his familiars?"

"Ah, you have realized my identity. Have you heard mind-boggling tales of me? Tales that have me flying over treetops with my arms spread like great wings to escape Christian soldiers? Tales that have me traveling a hundred miles from Cornwall in the flash of an eye to kill and butcher and maim in the wilds of Scotland?"

"No, I have heard my father curse you mightily when you have raided near Beauchamp, but you are always just a man to him, even though he roars about scourges and blights and such."

" 'Tis true. I am of this earth, not above it or below it. I am but a simple man. Do you, Philippa de Beauchamp, consider this earthbound man of sufficient prominence to sit in your august presence?"

"I don't think you care at all what I think. Moreover, I'm lost."

Dienwald sat forward in his chair. "You are in my castle, St. Erth by name. As to your exact whereabouts, I believe I shall keep that to myself for a time. Sit you down. I have questions for you, and you will answer them promptly and truthfully."

Philippa gazed about. There was no other chair.

He pointed downward at his feet. "On the floor."

"Don't be absurd! Of course I won't sit on the floor."

Dienwald stood up, still pointing to his feet. "Sit, now, or I will have my men fling you down. Perhaps I shall plant my foot on your neck to keep you down."

Philippa sat down on the floor, folding her long legs beneath her. She tried to straighten the skirt of her borrowed gown, but it was too narrow and too short and left her knees bare.

Dienwald resumed his seat, crossing his arms over his chest, negligently stretching his long legs in front of him. She noticed for the first time that his tunic and hose were in shameful condition.

She looked up at him. "May I please have something to drink? I am very thirsty."

Dienwald frowned at her. "You aren't a guest," he said, then in his next breath bellowed, "Margot!"

A thin young girl scurried into the hall, managed a curtsy, and waited, her eyes on the now-clean creature barely covered by a tattered garment of dull green belonging to one of the cookhouse wenches.

"Ale and . . ." He eyed the seated female, whose knees were showing. Nice knees connected to very nice legs. "Are you hungry as well?"

Her stomach growled loudly.

"Bread and cheese as well, Margot. Be speedy, we don't want our guest to collapse in the rushes."

Philippa could have hugged him at that moment. Food, at last. *Food!*

"Now, wench —"

"I am not a wench. I am Philippa de Beauchamp. I demand that you treat me according to my rank. I demand that you . . . well, you could begin by getting me a chair and then a gown that isn't so very rough and worn and old."

"Yes? What else? That isn't all you wish, is it?"

She ignored his sarcasm. "I know I am tall, but perhaps one of your wife's gowns would fit me."

"I have no wife. I had a wife once, but I don't have one now, nor have I had one for many a year, thank the saints. The gown Old Agnes found for you is doubtless precious. There isn't a single hole in it. It deserves your thanks, not your disdain."

"I meant no insult and I do thank you and the gown's owner. May I please borrow a horse? A nag, it matters not. I will see that it is returned to you."

"Why?"

To lie or to speak more foolish truths? Philippa settled for the middle ground. "I was traveling to see my cousin, who lives near St. Ives. I was riding in the wool wagon to the fair and then I planned to walk the rest of the way to my cousin's keep. Now, of course, I am here, and 'tis probably still too far away for me to walk."

Dienwald looked at the female and realized she was quite young. The wild hair and the ill-fitting gown had deceived him. The hair was now dry and a full glorious fall down her back. There were more shades than he could count, from the palest flaxen to dark ash to deepest brown. He frowned at himself. "All right, I believe you are Philippa de Beauchamp. Why were you hiding in a wool wagon?"

Margot appeared with a wooden tray that held ale, bread, and a chunk of yellow cheese. Philippa's mouth began to water. She stared at the food, unable to tear her eyes away, until Dienwald, shrugging, rose and pointed her toward the long row of trestle tables that lined the eastern side of the great hall.

He kept further questions to himself and

merely watched her eat. She tried to be dainty and restrained, but her hunger overcame her refined manners for a few minutes. When she chanced to look up, her mouth full of bread, to see him watching her, she quickly ducked her head, swallowed, and fell into a paroxysm of coughing.

Dienwald rose and leaned over the trestle table, and pounded her back. He handed her a cup of ale. "Drink."

Once she'd gotten her breath back, he was sitting again, silently watching her. If she'd been in that damned wool wagon all the way from Beauchamp, she hadn't eaten or drunk anything for nearly two days. It also seemed to Dienwald that she'd acted without much thought to any consequences, a usual feminine failing.

"You have a lot of hair."

She unconsciously touched her fingers to the tumbled curls. "Aye."

"Who is this cousin you were traveling to see?"

"I can't tell you that. Besides, it isn't important."

"How old are you?"

"Nearly eighteen."

"A great age. At first I had believed you older. Why were you running away from Beauchamp?"

"Because my father wanted me to marry a —" Philippa stopped cold. She dropped a piece of cheese onto the trestle table, then jumped to retrieve it. She fought with all her better instincts not to stuff it into her mouth. She bit off a big chunk.

"You were so against this marriage that you jumped into the moat, then buried yourself in my wool, making both it and you stink like a marsh hog?"

She nodded vigorously, her mouth full of the wonderful cheese. "Truly, I had to. If you don't mind, I should like to keep running."

"It won't work, you know. A lady of your tender years and wealth doesn't go against her father." He paused, giving her a long, brooding look, a look Philippa didn't like a bit. "A daughter should never go against her sire. As for marriage, 'tis to increase the family's wealth and lands and political influence. Surely you know that. Weren't you raised properly? What is wrong with you? Have you taken the minstrels' silly songs to heart? Did you fall in love with some silly fellow's eyebrows? Some clerk who read you romantic tales?"

She shook her head, thinking about her family gaining lands and wealth. Marrying her to William de Bridgport wouldn't bring any of those benefits. "Truly, sir, I can walk, if you'll just tell me the direction to St. Ives."

Dienwald continued brooding and looking. Finally he rose and returned to his chair, saying over his shoulder, "Well, come along. Sit on the floor."

Philippa grabbed the last piece of bread and the last morsel of cheese and followed. When she sat, the tunic slid up above her knees. She chewed on the bread, watching him, praying he wouldn't ask anything until she'd swallowed the rest of her food. But his next words nearly made her choke again.

"There are many things to consider here. I could ransom you. Your father is very wealthy, from what I've heard. Beauchamp is a formidable holding, and has been since William gave it to Rolfe de Beauchamp two hundred years ago. And your father has some influence at court, or so I heard some years ago." He paused, looking away, and Philippa's gaze followed his. He said, "Ah, I believed myself too lucky to be alone. Come here, Crooky, and join in my musings. What do you think the wench would bring in ransom?"

Crooky hobbled up, looked Philippa up and down, and said. "Thass a tall wench, master, even sitting, a strapping big wench.

Those legs of hers just don't stop. By Saint Andrew's nose, 'tis yer height she be, or nearly, I'll wager ye."

"No, no," Philippa said, "he is taller than I, by at least four inches."

"Yes, that's true," Dienwald said, ignoring her. "This is Crooky," he added after a moment to Philippa, "my fool, my ears, and a great piece of impertinence a good deal of the time. But I suffer his presence." He saw her nose go up. It was a nice narrow nose. It was also an arrogant and supercilious nose.

Fitting for a Philippa de Beauchamp.

To Philippa's surprise, Crooky suddenly broke into song.

> What be she worth?
> This wooly-haired wench?
> Jewels for a ransom?
> Not with her stench.
> She looks like a hag
> She brays and she brags —

"You're blind, clattermouth," Dienwald interrupted. "She's clean and wholesome and I've even fed her so her ribs are no longer clanking together. Come here so I can kick you in the ribs."

Crooky cackled and backed quickly away.

"A bath did her good, sweet lord. Aye, ransom the wench. She'll bring you coin, much-needed coin. Mayhap we'll need more weavers for all that wool. Let de Beauchamp pay dear to fetch the little partridge back into his fold. God gi' ye grace, madam." And the strange little man who bellowed off-key gave her a crooked-toothed grin.

"That was a horrid rhyme," Philippa said. "You've no talent at all. My mare neighs more agreeably than you sing."

"Slit her throat," Crooky said to his master. "She's got a bold tongue and she's naught but a pesky female. Of what earthly good is she?"

"You're right, Crooky. A deadly combination, surely, and of no use." Dienwald reached for the dagger at his belt.

Philippa gasped, sudden fear causing her to jump to her feet and back away. With her hunger and thirst slaked, she'd let herself forget who this man was, had let down her guard and behaved as she would have at home, and now look what her tongue had gotten her into.

Dienwald drew his dagger and fingered the sharp edge. He rose slowly. "Have a care, lady. This is not your domain. You have no power here, no authority. Moreover, you are naught but a female, a big strapping female with more wit than most, but nonetheless you are to keep your mouth closed and your tongue behind your teeth. Aye, I will ransom your hide, now that it is white again and sweet-smelling. I will have my steward write to your father telling him of your status. Have you an idea of what he'll pay for your return? A clean and hearty wench he'll get, I will promise it, a wench ready for him to flail with his tongue and his belt. Both of which you deserve."

Philippa shook her head. Fear clogged her throat. Fear of this unpredictable man and fear of the truth. Perchance the truth in this instance would serve her well. On the other hand, perhaps it wouldn't. She didn't know what to do. She said finally, "My father doesn't want me back. He won't pay you anything. He will be pleased never to see my face again in this life. He didn't want me. That's why I ran away."

"That's not hard to believe, what with the face you had when I first beheld you. He would have believed himself in hell, faced by the devil's mistress."

"I told you that I jumped into our moat and that I ran away. It was foolish, I admit, but I did it and I can't now undo it."

Philippa heard a gasp and saw a plump

big-breasted girl staring at them, her face pale. Then she saw the direction of the girl's eyes, and saw the girl was staring at the man's dagger. He was still holding it, caressing the blade with the pad of his thumb. Philippa had forgotten the dagger. Would he slit her throat? Wasn't he possessed of any chivalrous instincts? She very quickly returned to the floor, folding her legs under her as far as she could manage.

"It begins to rain, my sweet lord," Crooky said. "I'll see the wool is kept dry. Come along, Alice, the master is busy counting coins in his head. He'll make you happy later, once he's rid himself of this extra wench."

"Aye," Dienwald said, not looking toward the big-breasted girl. "Go. Leave me. I will make you happy tonight."

Philippa stared. Her father had mistresses; she and all at Beauchamp knew it. But he pretended otherwise; he was discreet. Of course this man had no wife to shriek at him. She turned back and saw that Dienwald was speaking to an old woman.

"Aye, master, that old fool Prink has sickened suddenly, taken to his bed, he has, yelling that he's dying."

Dienwald cursed, then said, "I'll wager Father Cramdle is at his bedside even now, just in case. His list of sins is long enough for three days."

Then the little boy strode up and bellowed, "Hers a witch, kill her, Papa, stick your dagger in her gullet!"

Philippa looked at the boy standing out of her reach, legs apart, an expression on his face that was remarkably like his father's.

"Not *hers* a witch," Philippa said. "Can't you speak properly? It's *she's* a witch." Of the boy's father she asked, "Have you no privacy here? And I'm not a witch."

"Very little privacy," Dienwald said, and waved Edmund away. "Go see to our wool. And keep out of mischief. Aye, and speak properly!"

Philippa added her coin. "Why don't you go visit the water and the lye soap?"

"I shan't. You're a lanky spear with a wooly head!"

"Officious little clodpole!"

"Enough! Edmund, get thee gone now. You, lady, keep your tongue behind your teeth or you will surely regret it." Again he pointedly fingered his dagger, and Philippa, not liking the sharpness of that blade, nor the tone of his voice, lowered her head and shut her mouth. She'd been a fool, but she didn't have to continue being one.

"I had great need of the wool," Dienwald

said, looking down at his frayed hose. "I lost forty-four sheep before shearing, and all of us are ragged. That's why I took the two wagons." He glanced up, straight at her, and seemed startled that he'd explained his theft.

"Your need is quite evident. But thievery will bring you only retribution from my father, doubt you not."

"Ah, you think so? Let me tell you something, Lady Lackwit. Those dauntless farmers with the other wagon will continue to the fair at St. Ives. They will sell the wool and hide well their profits. Then they will go bleating to Lord Henry about the theft of all three wagons. Moreover, they have no idea who robbed them. Now, in addition, you are my prisoner, as of this minute. If I decide to ransom you, I can always say I found you creeping along a road. And if you, wench, tell your sire the truth, think you those brave farmers will say they lied and robbed your father and were cowards? Now, I was considering treating you like a guest, but I think that isn't what you need. You are too bold, too brazen for a female. You want mastering and proper manners. Perhaps I shall take on the chore. You will remain at St. Erth until I decide what to do with you. You will leave me now."

"I would like to leave you forever! My father will discover the truth and crush you like the pestilence you are!"

Dienwald smiled. "It will make a jongleur's tale that will cause the beams of the hall to creak with mirth."

"You are the only lackwit here. I told you, my father wants nothing more to do with me."

"Then perhaps I can instead discover the name of the man he wished you to marry. I can send a message to the clothhead and *he* can ransom you."

"Nay!"

She'd actually turned white, Dienwald observed. Let her skin creep with the thought. He wondered who the man was.

"Arrogant fool," Philippa said as she looked out the narrow window of her cell down into the inner ward. The sky was leaden in the late afternoon, and fog rolled over the castle walls. It had stopped raining some minutes before.

Dienwald de Fortenberry was striding across the now-muddy ward toward the stables, three dogs at his heels, followed by two small children and a chicken with sodden feathers. He'd ordered her taken by Northbert, a man with a very flat nose, to a tower chamber and locked in. Chamber, ha! 'Twas a cell, nothing more. At least he hadn't locked her down in the granary. Philippa watched him until he disappeared into the stables. Only the chicken followed him inside. The children and dogs were stopped by a yelling stable hand with the blackest hair Philippa had ever seen. Although he spoke loudly, calling the children little crackbrains, she could barely hear him over all the other people in the inner bailey. So many people, and so noisy, each with an opinion and a loud voice. The men yelled and shouted, the women yelled and shouted, and the children and chickens squawked and shrieked. It was a cacophony of head-splitting noise and Philippa turned away from the window slit and surveyed her room. It was narrow and long and held only a low bed with a rank-smelling straw-stuffed mattress and a coarse blanket. There was no pillow, no water to drink; there was a cracked pot under the cot in which to relieve herself, but nothing more.

It was heaven-sent compared to her residence in the wool wagon, but it still wasn't at all what she was used to. She'd always taken Beauchamp and all the luxuries it had afforded her for granted. It had been her home, and all the people there were known to her and trusted. Now she was nothing more than a prisoner. All her wondrous escape had netted her was a dank cheerless room in the keep tower of a man more unpredictable than the Cornish weather and, by reputation, a thoroughly bad lot.

"Thass good quality, master," Old Agnes was saying to the thoroughly bad lot, her gnarled fingers caressing the wool. "Jes' lovely."

"Aye," Dienwald agreed. "Pick what wenches you need to help you clean and weave the wool and tell Ellis. I'll have Alain hire weavers immediately. The first new tunic is for Master Edmund — aye, a new tunic and new hose."

Old Agnes looked sour at that order but didn't say anything. "What about the creature, master?"

"The what? Oh, her. She'll be gone before you can give her a new gown. Let her return home in what we gave her. 'Tis a gift."

"Thass a lady, master, not a scullion."

Old Agnes sometimes forgot herself, Dienwald bluntly informed her. Old Agnes gave him a toothless grin and a mirthless cackle and returned to picking filth from the wool. Dienwald left the stables, nearly stumbling over a chicken. The bird squawked, deftly avoiding the kick of a foot.

Dienwald sniffed the heavy air. White fog hung over his head in patches. It would shower again soon. There was time enough to practice with the quintains, since today was Tuesday, but he felt unsettled and restless. He made his way to the solar, where there were three small rooms, one used for St. Erth's priest and Edmund's tutor, Father Cramdle. He eased open the door to the sound of his son's penetrating voice: "Thass naught but silly tripe for peasants!"

# 4

Father Cramdle's voice, normally the model of patience and tolerance, was a bit frayed. "Master Edmund, peasants can't read, much less cipher. Listen, now, 'tis what your father wants. If I add eleven apples from this barrel to the seven bunches of grapes in this barrel, what is the result?"

"Purple apples!"

Dienwald's first response was to laugh at his son's wit, but he saw the pained look on Father Cramdle's homely face. Edmund not only looked like a villein's child, he was as ignorant as any of them.

"Answer Father Cramdle, Edmund. Now."

"But, Papa, thass a foolish problem, and —"

"*That is,* not *thass.* I don't want to hear that from you again. Answer the problem. Speak properly." He remembered Philippa's correction, made without thought. Had his son become so ill-managed? He wanted Edmund to read at least enough so he wouldn't be cheated by merchants or his own steward in the future. He wanted him to cipher so that he would know if he'd gotten the correct measure of flour from the miller. Dienwald could sign his name and make out words if he spoke them aloud slowly, but little more. It wasn't something he regretted very often, just at times like this when he saw the proof of ignorance in his son.

It required all of Edmund's fingers and toes and painstaking counting, but finally the correct answer came from his mouth.

"Excellent," Dienwald said. "Father, if the boy needs the birch rod, tell me. He will learn."

"Papa!"

"Nay, little gamecock. You will remain here studying with Father Cramdle until he sees fit to release you. It is what I wish of you, and you will obey me."

Dienwald left the room knowing that the kindly and very weak-willed Father Cramdle didn't have the spirit to control a nine-year-old boy. Dienwald would have to involve himself more. As for Alain, the steward, he could control the boy, but Edmund hated Alain. Though he would never say why, he avoided him, slinking away whenever Alain came into the vicinity.

As Dienwald left the solar, he glanced

over to the east tower. He saw Philippa de Beauchamp at the narrow window, looking down. He hoped she was scared out of her wits wondering what he was going to do to her. He would give her until the following afternoon to become appropriately submissive. She was too proud. She was also too big, too tall, too curly-haired. He had no complaint about her legs, which seemed to go on until they reached her throat, just as Crooky had pointed out. Her breasts seemed more than ample as well. But she wasn't . . . He forced his thinking away from that channel. Kassia de Moreton was delicate and small and sweetly soft. And she would never belong to him. It wasn't fated to be. Pity that he liked her hulking warrior husband nearly as much as he cared for her, else he would be tempted to slit Graelam's throat some dark night and relieve him of his wife.

Dienwald sighed. He admired everything about Kassia — her gentleness, her shy humor and guileless candor, her fierce loyalty to her husband, her daintiness, even the smallness of her bones and her delicate wrists . . . Ah, well, it was hopeless. At least she was his friend, delighting in his company, though now she was determined to find him an heiress — to save him from mold and damp and ruin, she'd say, and pour him some of her father's precious wine from Aquitaine. She wanted Dienwald to become respectable, a concept that thoroughly irritated and frightened him. But not for long. After all, what family would want to be allied with a rogue like him? It was just as well. The Scourge of Cornwall liked life just as it was. With the acquisition of the wool, the days would continue to be as entertaining as they'd been before the mindless sheep had plunged off that cliff.

It occurred to him a few moments later why he was so restless. He needed a woman. He didn't delay, simply asked to have Alice sent to his chamber. When she arrived, plump and smiling, her arms held forward a bit to further push out her breasts, Dienwald waved her closer. When she stood in front of him, he started to sweep her onto his lap. But her smell stopped him cold. "When did you last bathe?"

Alice flushed. "I forgot, master," she said, eyes cast down. She knew to avert her eyes, because if she looked at him, he just might see the amazement on her face. All this insistence upon rubbing her body with water and soap! It was beyond foolish.

Dienwald wanted her, but even her breath smelled of the stuffed cabbage she'd eaten the previous night.

"I won't have you again in my bed until you wash yourself — all of you, do you understand, Alice? With soap. Even between your legs and under your arms. And cleanse your teeth."

He sent her away, calling out, "Use the soap!" He'd first herded her into his bed only two weeks before. She'd learn, he hoped, that he liked a woman's body to be free of odor and her breath sweeter than that of his wolfhounds.

He waited, tapping his fingertips impatiently on the arms of the single chair in his chamber. When Alice appeared thirty minutes later, her hair wet from its washing but smooth from a good combing, and her breath pure as a spring breeze, he smiled and patted his thighs.

She came to him willingly, and when he brought her to stand between his thighs, she again pressed her breasts forward. He wondered who'd taught her to do this. Normally it amused him. Now, however, he wanted only release, and quickly. He slipped her coarse gown over her head, to find her naked beneath. She hadn't dried herself completely, and his hands slid over her moist flesh.

He clasped her hands down to her sides

and looked at her. She was white and plump and smooth as an egg. She would also be quite fat in no more than five years, but that didn't disturb him one whit. She was merely pleasingly bountiful now, the flesh between her legs soft and damp, and she was nearly the same age as his long-legged prisoner in the east tower.

He kissed Alice's mouth, tentatively at first, until he knew that she'd cleansed her teeth; then he became more enthusiastic. When at last he eased her down onto his manhood, groaning at the feel of sinking deep into her body, he leaned back his head, closing his eyes. Finally he played with her hot woman's flesh until she squirmed and arched her back and cried out. Then he allowed himself relief, and it was sweet and long and good.

He left her asleep on his bed and quit his solar, stretching and contented, every restless feeling stilled. Night had fallen and the evening meal was late, as usual. Dienwald thought about his prisoner, alone and probably so hungry she was ready to gnaw on the cot in her chamber. He decided he was feeling benevolent and told Northbert to have her fetched. She would doubtless be grateful to him for feeding her.

When she appeared beside Northbert, he

motioned her to the chair beside his.

"Thass the witch," Edmund said, waving a handful of bread toward the approaching Philippa.

"She's not a witch. And it's *that is,* not *thass.* Mind your manners, Edmund. She's a lady, and you will treat her politely."

Edmund grumbled, and Dienwald, giving him a very pointed look, added, "One insult, and you will spend your evening with Father Cramdle reading the holy writ."

The threat brought instant obedience. Dienwald studied his prisoner again. She didn't look like a lady, of course, in that shapeless coarse gown, bare feet, and thick curling hair loose around her head.

"God's greetings to you, lady," he said easily to Philippa. "Sit thee here and take your fill."

"What? The master offers me a chair rather than the dank floor?"

He eyed her. Some show of gratitude. He should have guessed. She wasn't one whit broken; not a shadow of submissivenes. She was still insolent. He should have held to his original plan and left her in that chamber alone for twenty-four hours. He continued, still tolerant, lounging back in his chair, "There are no females at St. Erth as great-sized as you, lady, so moderate your appetite accordingly, for there are no more gowns for you."

"God bless your sweet kindness, sir," Philippa said with all the gratitude of a nun who'd just been made an abbess. "You have the charitable soul of Saint Orkney and the pious spirit of a zealot."

"There is no Saint Orkney."

"Is there not? Why, with your example, kind lord, there should be. Yes, indeed."

Philippa smiled at him, her dimples deep, so pleased with herself that she couldn't help it. Then she smelled the food. Her stomach growled loudly. She forgot Dienwald de Fortenberry, forgot that her situation was fraught with uncertainty, and looked down at her trencher, on which lay a thick slab of bread soggy with rich gravy and decorated with large chunks of beef.

Dienwald watched her attack the meal. A bold wench with a ready tongue. No wonder she thought her father didn't want to ransom her. Who would want such a needle-witted wench in his keeping? Unaccountably, he smiled. When she mopped up the trencher with her last chunk of bread, he said, "Will you eat all my mutton and pigeon as well? Every one of my boiled capons, with ginger and cinnamon, and all of my jellied eggs?"

"I don't see the jellied eggs." There was stark disappointment in her voice.

"Perhaps you ate them without seeing them. Your hands and your mouth toiled very diligently."

She turned to him. "And surely you wouldn't have mutton, would you? Didn't you lose all your sheep?"

Dienwald had to pause a moment on that one. He saw her dimples deepen again, and realized she was enjoying herself mightily at his expense. One could not allow a woman to have the last word. It was against the laws of man and God. It was as intolerable as a kick to the groin.

He shook himself. "What wear you beneath that gown?"

A man, Philippa thought, used whatever weapons available to him. Her father was a master at bluster. His nose turned red, his eyes bulged, and he raged long and loud. Her cousin Sir Walter de Grasse, if she remembered aright, turned sarcastic and cold when he was in a foul temper. Her father's master-at-arms never thought, just struck out with his huge fists. As for this man, at least his dagger still lay snug in its sheath at his belt, so a show of violence wasn't on his mind. It relieved her that he wished to best her with words, even though they were meant to shrivel her with embarrassment. Unfortunately, she'd taken a sip of the strong ale when he'd spoken, and now she choked on it. He slapped her on the back, nearly sending her face into a wooden platter of boiled capon.

"I can feel nothing," Dienwald said as he leaned down close to her. His fingers splayed wide over her back. "No shift? No pretense at modesty?"

Philippa felt the urge to violence — after all, she was her father's daughter — and she acted instantly. Quick as a snake, she reached for his dagger. She felt his hand lock around her wrist until her fingers turned white from lack of blood.

"You dare?"

She'd thought with her feet again, and the result had brought his anger on her head. She shook her head.

"You *don't* dare?"

But there was no anger in his tone, not now. He seemed amused. That was surprising, and vastly relieving as well. He loosened his grip on her wrist and pressed her hand palm-down against his thigh. Her eyes flew to his face, but she didn't move.

"I have decided to give you a choice, lady," Dienwald said.

Philippa wasn't at all certain she wanted

to hear of any choices from him.

"Not a word? I don't believe it." He paused a moment, cocking a brow at her. She remained silent.

"You tell me your father won't ransom you. You also refuse to tell me the name of your unpleasant suitor. You balk at telling me the name of this cousin you were running to. Very well, if you aren't able to bring me pounds and shillings and pence, the very least you can do is repay my hospitality on your back. It is doubtful, but perhaps I'll find you acceptable in that role, at least for a limited time."

She'd been right: she *hadn't* wanted to hear his choices.

"You don't care for the thought of me covering you?"

Surely a man who allowed children, dogs, and a chicken to follow him about couldn't be all that bad. There were still no words in her mind.

"Wrapping those long white legs of yours around my flanks? They're so long, mayhap they'll go around me twice. And plucking your virginity? Doesn't that give you visions of delirious pleasure?"

"Actually," she said, looking out over the noisy great hall at all the men and women who sat at the trestle tables eating their fill, laughing, jesting, arguing, "no."

"No, what?"

Philippa reached for a capon wing with her left hand and took a thoughtful bite. She couldn't let him see that he'd stunned her, demolished her confidence, and made her nearly frantic with consternation. Wrapping her legs around his flanks? Plucking her . . . Philippa wanted to gasp, but she didn't; she took another bite of her capon wing. Dienwald was so surprised at her nonchalance, her utter indifference, that he released her wrist. She shook her hand to get the feeling back, then reached for another piece of capon. Before she brought it to her mouth, she dipped it deep in the ginger-and-cinnamon sauce.

Dienwald stared at her profile. More thick tendrils had worked loose from her braid, a braid as thick as Edmund's ankle, and curled around her face.

She turned back to him finally, dipping her fingers into the small wooden bowl of water between their places. " 'Tis very good, the capon. I like the ginger. No, my father won't ransom me. I should have lied and told you he would, but again, I didn't think, I just spoke."

"True. Your point, lady?"

"I don't want to be your mistress. I don't

want to be any man's mistress."

"That won't be up to you to decide. You are a woman."

"That is a problem I share with half the world. What will you decide, then?"

"Must you persist in your picking and harping? Must you nag me with questions until I am forced to put my dagger point to your white neck?"

"Nay, but —"

"Swallow your tongue! I shall have the name of your betrothed, and I shall have it soon. I will even demand less ransom if he will have you back."

"No!"

Dienwald picked up her long braid and wrapped it around his hand, drawing her face close to his. "Listen, wench —"

"I am not a wench. My name is Philippa de —"

"You will do my bidding in all things, no matter you're the Queen of France. Now, what is the poor crackbrain's name?"

Philippa swallowed. She smelled the tart ale on his breath, felt its warmth on her temple. His eyes were darker, the flecks of gold more prominent. "I won't tell you."

"I think you will. You lack proper submissiveness and obedience. You need training, as I told you earlier. I think I should begin your lessons right now." He looked quite wicked as he said, "Take off your gown and dance for my people."

She stared at him. "Your priest would not approve."

Dienwald took his turn at staring. " 'Tis true," he said. "Father Cramdle would flee to meet his maker."

"Very well. If my choices are between being your mistress and telling you the name of that awful man my father wished me to wed, and if you then plan to ransom me to that horrid old man and make me suffer his presence for the rest of my life, then my answer is obvious. I will be your mistress until you don't want me anymore."

It took a moment for her flow of words to make sense. When they did, he refused to let her see how stunned he was. Was her intended husband that repulsive? Or had she simply no womanly delicacy? No, she was just toying with him, first telling him nay, then changing her tune.

"I could give you over to my men," he continued thoughtfully. "You are really not to my taste, with your big bones and your legs as long as a man's. Have you also feet the size of a man's?"

Philippa was frightened; she didn't understand this man. Unlike her father, who would have been purple-faced with rage and yelling his head off by now, this man's agile tongue cavorted hither and yon, leaving her mind in disarray. She didn't want to have to prance atop the trestle table naked. She didn't want Father Cramdle to clutch his heart with shock. All the power she'd felt whilst they fenced with words had been an illusion at best. The fact that this man didn't kick children or dogs or chickens didn't automatically endow him with an honorable nature. Now he was showing his true colors. Now he was getting down to serious business. She opened her mouth, but what came out was unbidden and unsanctioned.

"You make me sound like an ugly girl."

She was appalled that such errant vanity could come from her brain, much less from her mouth. But his insults, piled up now as high as the stale and matted rushes on the cold stone floor, had cut deep.

He laughed, an evil laugh. "Nay, but a gentle soft lady you are not. Now, let me see. There must be something about you that is . . . You do have very nice eyes. The blue is beyond anything I have ever seen, even beyond the blue speckles on robins' eggs. There, does that placate your female vanity?"

Philippa managed to say nothing. To her surprise, she saw the fool, Crooky, who'd been crouched beside Dienwald on the floor beside her chair, leap to his feet and sing out a coarse lyric about the effect a woman's blue eyes could have on a man's body.

Dienwald burst into loud laughter, and at the sound, the remaining fifty people in the great hall guffawed and thumped their fists on the tables until the beams seemed to shake with their raucous mirth.

"Come here, Crooky, you witless fool," Philippa called out over the din, caution again tossed to the four winds, "I want to kick your ribs."

Dienwald looked at the girl beside him. She was laughing, and she'd mimicked him perfectly.

Philippa, basking in her temporary wit, failed to notice that utter silence had fallen. She further failed to notice how everyone was gazing from her to Dienwald with ill-disguised consternation.

Then she noticed. If he didn't cut her throat, he'd throw her to his men. She didn't doubt it. He hadn't a shred of honor, and she'd crossed the line. Without a word, she quickly slipped out of the chair, jumped back, and ran as fast as she could toward the huge oak doors of the great hall.

# 5

*Windsor Castle*

Robert Burnell, Chancellor of England and King Edward's trusted secretary, rubbed a hand over his wide forehead, leaving a black ink stain.

" 'Tis time to take your rest," King Edward said, stretching as he rose. He was a large man, lean and fit, and one of the tallest man Robert Burnell had ever seen. Longshanks, he was called fondly by his subjects. A Plantagenet through and through, Burnell thought, but without the slyness and deceit of his sire, Henry, or the evil of his grandfather, John I, who'd maimed and tortured with joyous abandon anyone who chanced to displease him. Nor was he a pederast like his great uncle, Richard Coeur de Lion — thus the string of children he and his queen, Eleanor, had assembled to date. And that brought up the matter at hand. Robert wondered if his broaching the topic would call forth the Plantagenet temper. Unlike his grandfather, Edward wouldn't fall to the floor and bash his fists and his heels in bellowing rage. No, his anger was like a fire, perilous one moment cold ashes the next, a smile in its place.

"I work you too hard, Robbie, much too hard," Edward said fondly, and Burnell silently agreed. But he knew the king would continue to use him as a workhorse until he met his maker, thanks be to that maker.

"Just one more small matter, your highness," Burnell said, holding up a piece of parchment. "A matter of your . . . er, illegitimate daughter, Philippa de Beauchamp by name."

"Good God," Edward said, "I'd forgotten about the girl. She survived, did she? Bless her sweet face, she must be a woman grown by now. Philippa, a pretty name — given to her by her mother, as I recall. Her mother's name was Constance and she was but fifteen, if I remember aright. A bonny girl." The king paused and his face went soft with his memories. "My father married her off to Mortimer of Bledsoe and the babe went to Lord Henry de Beauchamp to be raised as his own."

"Aye, sire. 'Tis nearly eighteen she is, and according to Lord Henry, a Plantagenet in looks and temperament, healthy as a stoat, and he's had her educated as you instructed all those years ago. He reminds us 'tis time to see her wedded. He also writes that he's already been beleaguered for her hand."

The king muttered under his breath as he strode back and forth in front of his secretary's table.

"I'd forgotten . . . ah, Constance, her flesh was soft as a babe's . . ." The king cleared his throat. "That was, naturally, before I became a husband to my dear Eleanor . . . she was still a child . . . also, my daughter is a Plantagenet in looks . . . not a hag then . . . excellent, but still . . ." He paused and looked at his secretary with bright Plantagenet blue eyes, eyes the same color as his illegitimate daughter's. He snapped his fingers and smiled.

"My dear Uncle Richard is dead, God rest his loyal soul, and we miss the stability he provided us in Cornwall. For a son-in-law, Robbie, we must have a man who will give us unquestioning loyalty, a man with strength of fist and character and heart, but not a man who will try to empty my coffers or trade on my royal generosity to enrich himself and all his brothers and cousins."

Burnell nodded, saying nothing. He wouldn't remind the king that he, his faithful secretary, hadn't received an increase in compensation for a good five years now. Not that he'd ever expected one. He sighed, waiting.

"Such a man is probably a saint and in residence in heaven," the king continued, giving Burnell another Plantagenet gift — a smile of genuine warmth and humor that rendered all those in his service weak-kneed with the pleasure of serving him. "I don't suppose Lord Henry has a suggestion?"

"No, sire. He does write that suitors for his other daughter tend to look upon Philippa instead, as likely as not. He tires of the situation, sire. Indeed, he sounds a bit frantic. He writes that Philippa's true identity becomes more difficult to keep a secret as the days pass, what with all the young pups wanting her hand in marriage."

"A beauty." Edward rubbed his large hands together. "A beauty, and I spawned her. All Plantagenet ladies are wondrous fair. Does she have golden hair? Skin as white as a sow's underbelly? Find me that man, Robbie, a man of strength and good heart. In all of Cornwall there must be a man we can trust with our daughter and our honor and our purse."

Robert Burnell, a devout and unstinting laborer, toiled well into the dark hours of the night, burning three candles to their stumps, examining names of men in Cornwall to fit the king's requirements. The following morning, he was bleary-eyed and stymied.

The king, on the other hand, was blazing with energy and thwacked his secretary on the shoulders. "I know what we'll do about that little matter, Robbie. 'Tis my sweet queen who gave me the answer."

Was this another little matter he didn't know about yet? Burnell wondered, wishing only for his bed.

"Yes, sire?"

"The queen reminded me of our very loyal and good subject in Cornwall — Lord Graelam de Moreton of Wolffeton."

"Lord Graelam," Burnell repeated. "What is this matter, sire?"

"Lackwit," Edward said, his good humor unimpaired. " 'Tis about my little Philippa and a husband for her fair hand and a sainted son-in-law for me."

Burnell gaped at the king. He'd discussed his illegitimate daughter with the queen, with his *wife?*

He swallowed, saying, "Lord Graelam's wedded, sire. He was atop my list until I remembered he'd married Kassia of Belleterre, from Brittany."

"Certainly he'd wedded, Robbie. Have you lost your wits? You really should get more rest at night. 'Tis needful, sleep, for a sprightly brain. Now, Lord Graelam is the one to ferret out my ideal son-in-law. You will readily enough wring a list of likely candidates out of him."

"I, sire?"

"Aye, Robbie, certainly you. Whom else can I trust? Get you gone after you've had some good brown ale and bread and cheese. You must eat, Robbie — 'tis needful to keep up your strength. Ah, and write to Lord Henry and tell him what's afoot. Now, I must needs speak to you about the special levy against those cockscomb Scots. I think that we must —"

"Forgive me, sire, but do you not wish me to leave for Cornwall very soon? To Wolffeton? To see Lord Graelam?"

"Eh? Aye, certainly, Robbie. This afternoon. Nay, better by the end of the week. Now, sharpen your wits and recall for me the names of those Scottish lords who blacken the Cheviot Hills with their knavery."

# 6

*St. Erth Castle*

Philippa heard shouts behind her. One great bearded man grabbed at her, ripping the sleeve from her tunic, but she broke free. She heard a bellow of laughter and a man shouting, "Ye should have grabbed her skirt, rotbrain! Better a pretty bare ass than an arm!"

It was as dark as the interior of a well outside the great hall. Philippa dashed full-tilt across the inner bailey toward the stables, hoping to get to a horse and . . . And what? The gates were closed. There were guards posted on the ramparts, surely. The night was cold and she was shivering in nothing but a ragged one-sleeved gown to cover her.

Still, her fear kept her going. The stables were dark and warm and smelled of fresh hay, dung, and horses. They were also deserted, the keepers, she supposed, in the great hall, eating their evening meal with all the rest of the denizens of this keep. She stopped, pressing her fingers to the stitch in her side. She was breathing hard, and froze in her tracks when she heard her captor say from nearby, "You are but a female. I accept that as a flaw you can't remedy — God's error, if you will — yet it would seem that you never think before you act. What were you planning to do if you managed to get a horse?"

Philippa slowly turned to face him. Dienwald de Fortenberry was standing in the open doorway of the stable, holding a lantern in his right hand. He wasn't even breathing hard. How had he found the time to light a lantern?

"I don't know," she said, her shoulders slumping. "You have so many people within the keep, I hoped mayhap the gates would be open, with people milling in and out, that mayhap the guards and porters wouldn't notice me, but they all appear to be in the great hall eating, and —"

"And mayhap the moon would make an appearance and guide you to London to court, eh? And thieves would salute you and blow you sweet kisses as you rode past them, your gown up about your thighs. Stupid wench, I would not have gained my twenty-sixth year if I'd been so heedless of myself and my castle. We are quite snug within these walls." He leaned down and set the lantern on the ground. Philippa backed up against a stall door as he straightened to look at her.

"If you don't begin to think before you act, I doubt you will gain your twentieth year. You ripped off a sleeve."

"Nay, one of your clumsy men did that." She remembered another man's coarse jest and felt suddenly quite exposed, standing here alone with him, her right arm hanging naked from her shoulder. "Please, my lord, may I leave? I'm thinking clearly now. I should be most grateful."

"Leave? Tread softly, lady. Your position at present is not passing sweet. I think it more fitting that I should beat you. Tie you down and beat you soundly for your audacity and disrespect — something your father never did, I suspect. Do you prefer a whip or my hand?"

"Stay away!"

"I haven't moved. Now, you told me that you didn't want to be my mistress. Then, like a female, you danced away to a different tune and said you would prefer my using you as my mistress rather than wedding the man your father selected for you. Have I the sequence aright?"

She nodded, her back now flat against the stall door. "I should prefer Satan's smiles, but that doesn't seem to be an available choice. You told me you would give me choices but you didn't."

"Don't keep pushing against that stall door, wench. Philbo, my destrier, is within. He isn't pleased with people who disturb him, and is likely to take a bite of your soft shoulder."

Philippa quickly slid away from the stall door and looked back at the black-faced destrier. He had mean eyes and looked as dangerous as his master.

"Are you a shrew?"

"Certainly not! 'Tis just that de Bridg—" She broke off, stuffed her fist in her open mouth, and gazed at Dienwald in horror.

"William de Bridgport?" Interest stirred in Dienwald's eyes. He got no response but he saw that she'd terrified herself just by saying the man's name. He imagined anyone could eventually get everything out of this girl. She spoke without thinking, acted without considering consequences. She was a danger to herself, a quite remarkable danger. He wondered if she would yell in passion without thinking. "He is a repulsive sort," Dienwald said. "Fat and rotten-toothed, not possessed of an agreeable disposition."

"Nay, 'tis someone else! I just said his

name because he looks like . . . your horse!"

"My poor Philbo, insulted by a wench with threadbare wits." He became silent, watching her, then said, "You would prefer my using your fair body to wedding him. I know not whether to be flattered or simply amazed. Are you certain Lord Henry won't ransom you? I really do need the money. I would prefer money to your doubtless soft and fair — but large — body."

Philippa shook her head. "I'm sorry, but he won't. You must believe me, for I don't lie, not this time. I overheard him tell my mother and a suitor for my sister's hand who tried to ravish me that I would have no dowry at all."

"Your sister's suitor tried to ravish you? How was this accomplished?"

" 'Twas Ivo de Vescy. He's a sweet boy, but he fancied me and not my sister. My father pulled him off me before I hurt him, which I would have done, for I am quite strong."

Dienwald laughed; he couldn't help it. He'd come after her with violence in mind, but she'd disarmed him, first with her pale-faced fear, then with her artless candor. He looked at the long naked white arm. She was so young . . . Nay, not so young. Many girls were married with a babe suckling at their breast by her age.

"Your father told de Vescy that he was marrying you to de Bridgport?"

She nodded. "I didn't know — he'd never said a word to me about de Bridgport. At first I couldn't believe it, wouldn't believe it, but then . . ."

"And then you didn't think, just acted, and jumped in the moat, then into the wool wagon. Well, 'tis done. Come along, now. You've gooseflesh on your naked arm, and it's powerfully unappetizing. I think I'll take you to my chamber and tie you to my bed. I will be careful not to rip your gown further, since it is the only piece of clothing you have."

*Beauchamp Castle*

"She's a deceitful bitch and I hope she falls into a ditch! I hope she's been set upon by pillaging soldiers. I hope she's imprisoned in a convent. At least dear Ivo doesn't want her — at least, he'd better not."

"Bernice, quiet!" Lord Henry roared. "I must write to the king immediately . . . again. God's nails, I will lose Beauchamp, he will tear my limbs from my body."

Lady Maude quickly ordered Bernice from the solar. Her daughter whined and balked, for her curiosity was at high tide, but her mother's hand was strong and she was determined. Bernice would not find out her supposed sister's true parentage, not if Lady Maude had any say about it, which she did.

"My lord," she said upon returning to her spouse, "you must moderate your speech. Aye, you must write to the king again, but don't tell him the girl is missing. Nay, a moment." Lady Maude stared toward the ornate *prie-dieu* in the corner of the chamber. "We must think. We mustn't act precipitately. Philippa must have overheard our talk of marrying her off to de Bridgport."

Lord Henry groaned. "And she fled Beauchamp. Why did I think of that whoreson's name, much less spew it out to de Vescy like that? God's eyebrows, the man's a braying ass, and I've proved myself a fool."

Lady Maude didn't disagree with his assessment of himself, but said loudly, "I think William de Bridgport a man to make a girl a fine husband."

Lord Henry stared at his thin-lipped wife. When, he wondered, had her lips disappeared into her face? He seemed to remember years before that she'd had full, pouting lips that curved into sweet smiles. He stared down her body and wondered where her breasts had gone. They'd disappeared just like her lips. Through her endless prayers? No, that would just make her bony knees bonier. He thought of little Giselle, his sixteen-year-old mistress. She had magnificent breasts, and *her* lips hadn't disappeared. She also had all her teeth, which nipped him delightfully.

He groaned again, recalling his current problem. The king's daughter was gone; he had no idea where, and he was terrified that she would be killed or ravaged. His mind boggled at the possible fates that could befall a young, beautiful girl like Philippa. More than that, Lord Henry was quite fond of her. For a girl, she was all a father could wish. Nay, she was more, for she was also his steward.

She wasn't filled with nonsense like her sister. She wasn't particularly vain. She could read and write and cipher, and she could think. The problem with Philippa was that she didn't think when things were critical. Oh, aye, set her to solving a dispute between two peasants and she'd come up with a solution worthy of Solomon. But face her with a crisis and she turned into a whirling dervish without a sensible thought in her head. And she'd heard de Bridgport's name and panicked.

Where had she run?

Suddenly Lord Henry's eyes widened.

He'd been stupid not to think of it before. The wool wagons bound for the St. Ives Fair. Philippa wasn't altogether stupid; she hadn't merely thrown herself out on the road and started walking to God only knew where. He grinned at his wife, whose nostrils had even grown pinched over the years. Would they eventually close and she'd suffocate?

"I know where Philippa went," he said. "I'll find her."

*St. Erth Castle*

Dienwald hadn't completely lost his wits. Unlike Philippa de Beauchamp, he tended to think things through thoroughly before acting — if he had the chance, that is — and in this matter he had all the time he wanted. And he did want to punish the wench for dashing out of the great hall the way she had, making him look the fool in front of all his people. He held firmly to her naked white arm as he walked her back across the inner bailey. A donkey brayed from the animal pen behind the barracks; two pigs were rutting happily in refuse, from the sound of their squeals; and a hen gave a final squawk before tucking in her feathers and going to sleep.

Philippa was frightened now, and he felt

her resistance with every step. It was a chilly night and she was shivering. "Hurry up," he said, and quickened his pace, then slowed, realizing her feet were bare. She was going to try to escape him on bare feet and in a flimsy torn gown? She was an immense danger to herself.

Silence fell when he strode into the great hall with her at his side. He yelled for his squire, Tancrid. Tancrid, a boy of Philippa's years, was skinny and fair, with soft brown eyes and a very stubborn jaw. He ran to his master and listened to his low words, nodding continuously. Dienwald then turned on his heel and left. He pulled Philippa up the outside stairs to the solar.

"You're not taking me back to that tower cell?"

"No. I told you, I'm taking you to my bed and tying you down."

"I would wish that you wouldn't. Cannot you give me another choice?"

"You have played your games with me, wench —"

"Philippa. I'm not a wench."

Dienwald hissed between his teeth. "You begin to irk me, you wench, harpy, nag, shrew . . . The list of seemly names for you is endless. No, keep quiet or I will make you very sorry."

As a threat it seemed to lack unique menace, but Philippa hadn't known him long enough to judge. She bit her lip, kept walking beside him up the solar stairs, and shivered from the cold. His fingers were tight about her upper arm, but he hadn't hurt her. At least not yet.

They passed three serving maids and two well-armed men, bound, evidently, for guard duty. Dienwald paused, speaking low to them, then dismissed them. He took Philippa to a large bedchamber that hadn't seen a woman's gentling touch in a long time. There was a large bed with a thick straw mattress and a dark brown woolen spread atop it. There were no hangings to draw around it. There were two rough chairs, a scarred table, a large trunk, a single wool carpet in ugly shades of green, and nothing else. No tapestries, no wall hangings of any sort, no bright ewers or softening cushions for the chair seats. It was a man's chamber, a man who wasn't dirty or slovenly, but a man to whom comforts, even the smallest luxuries, weren't necessary. Or perhaps he simply hadn't the funds to furnish the room properly. Still, whatever the reason, Philippa didn't like the starkness of the chamber at all.

She wished now that there weren't any

privacy. She wished there was an army camping throughout the solar. She wished there was a chapel in the chamber next to this one filled with praying priests and nuns. But the chamber was empty save for the two of them. He released her arm, turned, and closed the chamber door. He slid the key into the lock, then pocketed the key in his tunic. He lit the two tallow candles that sat atop the table. They illuminated the chamber and had a sour smell. Didn't the lord of St. Erth merit candles that were honey-scented or perhaps lavender-scented?

"There is little moonlight," he said, looking toward the row of narrow windows, "as you'd have noted if you'd paused to do any planning at all in your mad dash for escape."

Philippa said nothing, for she was staring. There was glass in the windows, and that surprised her. Lord Henry had glass windows in the Beauchamp solar, but he'd carped and complained at the cost, until her mother had threatened to cave in his head with a mace.

Dienwald smiled at her then and strode toward her. "No," Philippa said, backing away.

He stopped, as if changing his mind. "I asked Tancrid to bring us wine and more food. I assume you're yet hungry? Your appetite seems endless."

To her own surprise, Philippa shook her head.

"You dashed out of the hall before you ate any boiled raisins. My cook does them quite nicely, as well as honey and almond pastes." He was prattling on and on about food, and all she could do was stand there looking petrified. He smiled at her, and if possible she looked even more alarmed.

There came a knock on the door. She nearly collapsed with relief, and Dienwald frowned. "You like having someone besides my exalted self with you? Well, 'tis just Tancrid with wine and food. Don't move."

The boy entered bearing a tray that was dented and bent but of surprisingly good craftsmanship. He set it upon the table and fiddled with the flagons.

"Go," Dienwald said, and Tancrid, with a curious look at Philippa, took himself off.

"They all wonder if I'm going to ravish you," Dienwald said with little show of interest, and sat at the table. "That, or poor Tancrid is afraid you'll stick a knife between my ribs." He didn't sound at all concerned. He poured himself wine, sat back in his chair, and sipped it.

"Are you?" She swallowed convulsively.

"Are you going to ravish me?"

Dienwald stretched. "I think not . . . to-night. I have already lain with a very comely wench, and have not the urge to do it again, particularly with a girl of such noble proportions and such —"

"I'm not ugly! Nor am I oversized or ungainly! I have had three very fitting men want my hand in marriage. How dare you say that I'm not worth your energy or that I am not to your taste or to your —"

Dienwald burst out laughing. Here she was, heedless as a squeaking hen, taking exception to his refusal to ravish her. He continued to laugh, watching her face turn alarmingly pale when she realized finally what she was doing.

Very suddenly she sat down on his bed, covered her face with her hands, and started crying. Not dainty feminine tears, but deep tearing sobs that racked her body and made her shoulders jerk.

"By god! I have done nothing to you! Stop your tears, wench, or I'll —"

She jerked up at his words and said through hiccups, "I am not a wench, I'm Philippa de —"

"I know, you're Goddess Philippa, Queen Philippa, Grand Templar Philippa. Be quiet. You'll sour my stomach. Now, no more crying. You have no reason to cry. I have done nothing to harm you. Indeed, I saved you from death. Thank me, Empress Philippa."

"Thank you."

Dienwald hadn't expected that. Perhaps she wasn't such a little tartar after all. He rose and watched her jump from the bed and scurry back against the far wall. He smiled and leaned down to unwrap the stout cross garters that wrapped securely about his calves.

When he rose to face her again, he waved the long cross garters. "Come here and let me tie you down. I won't tie you tightly."

"Nay!" she whispered.

Dienwald merely smiled and reached for her, a length of cross garter in his hand. She ducked away from him, stumbled and fell to her hands and knees on the floor. He winced for her, knowing that the rough stones were hard as a witch's kettle.

He grabbed her around her waist, realizing as he hauled her up that he liked the feel of her. Her waist was narrow and . . . He had no more time for female appraisal because Philippa turned on him. She screamed, making his ears ring, and her fist caught his jaw, sending his head snapping backward with the force of her blow.

He released her and she fell onto her back. He came over her, ready to thrash her, but her dirty foot caught him squarely in the belly, kicking him a good three feet back. He grunted and landed in a heap on the bed. Dienwald had blood in his eyes. He managed to stop himself, managed to remind himself that he, unlike this raving wench, thought before he acted. Slowly, very slowly, he sat up on the bed and looked at her.

Philippa scurried up to her knees, jerking the gown back into place. She stared back at him, her breath hitching, her breasts heaving deeply.

"Come here."

"Nay."

Dienwald sighed and smiled an evil smile at her. "Come to me now or I will tell Tancrid, who is doubtless outside my chamber door, his ear pressed against the oak, to fetch me three of my most foul men. They, wench, will strip you and have their sport with you. In front of me, I think. I should enjoy watching."

His threat this time was quite specific, and Philippa, without another contrary thought or word, struggled to her feet. She stiffly walked over to him, afraid, but still wanting to smash her fist into his face. He motioned her closer, and she stood between his spread legs, her head down.

"Put your hands together."

She shook her head, but at his look she slapped her palms together, watching as he wrapped the long narrow leather cross garter around her wrists.

"I can't take the chance you will be stupid enough to try to escape me again. Now, don't struggle."

He clasped his hands beneath her hips and lifted her onto the bed, dropping her on her back. He wrapped the other cross garter through the knot at her tied wrists and tethered her to a post at the top of the bed. Her arms were pulled above her head, but not tightly. She stared up at him, and he saw that she was very afraid. He didn't blame her, she was completely helpless.

Her gown had tangled up about her thighs, and the expanse of white flesh was annoying his groin. He pulled a blanket over her, bringing it to her chin. "Now, keep quiet."

It was an unnecessary command. She was silent as a tomb.

Within moments the bedchamber was as silent as she was. Dienwald snuffed out the single candle, then quickly undressed. He stretched out naked beside her. She could hear his breathing. He'd made no move to touch her. She gave the leather strap a tentative tug; nothing happened. She lay there trying to decide what she could do.

Dienwald said, "Were William de Bridgport here, he would have tied you down as well. The difference is, he would have pulled your white legs wide apart and pinched you with his dirty fingers and leered at you, whereas I, wench, will stroke your white flesh with clean fingers and a warm mouth and —"

"I have to relieve myself!"

"I'm powerfully comfortable and you've quite tired me out. Do you really have to relieve yourself or are you again lying to me?"

"Nay, please."

He cursed, lit the single candle again, then released her wrists. "The pot is beneath the window, yon. I will leave you for a minute or two. Don't dally." He pulled on his bedrobe as he spoke.

Philippa didn't look at him. She didn't move until he'd closed the chamber door behind him. She raced from the bed to the chamber pot without bothering to light the tallow candle. She could see well enough.

The chamber door opened some minutes later, and for a moment Dienwald was silhouetted in faint light. He closed the door behind him. "Get back into bed and stretch your hands above your head so I can tie you again."

He heard a deep hitching breath close to him, far too close, but he wasn't fast enough. The chamber pot hit him squarely atop the head and he dropped like a stone.

Philippa stared down at him. He looked dead, and she felt the shock of fear and guilt. She dropped to her knees and pressed her palm against his chest. "Don't you dare die, you scoundrel!" His heartbeat was steady and slow. She got to her feet and stood over him. Her mind began to function again as she stared down at the unconscious man.

Now what was she to do?

She'd thought with her feet again, only this time her actions could well prove to be worse than jumping into the Beauchamp moat.

Tancrid. She had to get the squire out of the way. Perhaps she could take him as a hostage. Yes, that's what she'd do. And she could take his clothes and his shoes and . . . Her mind squirreled madly about.

A hand curled around her ankle and pulled hard. Philippa's legs went out from under her and she went down hard on her bottom. Dienwald, his head spinning, threw himself on top of her, pinning her down with his weight.

She was larger than most women, but she couldn't push him off her. His eyes accustomed themselves to the dim candlelight and he stared down into her face.

"I didn't hit you hard enough."

"Aye, you did. I'm seeing four of you, and believe me, wench, even one of your sort is too many."

Dienwald became suddenly aware of her full breasts and her soft body beneath him. His lust sprang full-blown into life, and with it his manhood. Without thinking, he pressed himself against her.

"You're a menace," he said, hating the fact that he wanted to jerk up her gown and ride her until she was yelling with the pleasure of it and his own pleasure was washing over him. Instead he said, "You're a foolish girl who hasn't a thought for consequences, and I'm tired of it."

"What are you going to do to me?"

Dienwald didn't answer. His vision cleared, as did his lust. Cleansing anger took its place. He pulled himself off her and hauled her up with him. He strode to the bed, dragging her behind him, then pulled her down over his thighs. He held her down with one arm and lit the candle with the other. Then he yanked up her gown, baring a very lovely bottom. And brought the flat of his hand down as hard as he could on the white flesh.

For an instant, Philippa froze. No, he couldn't be spanking her, not like this, with her buttocks as bare as the day she'd come from her mother's womb. He struck her again, and she shrieked in rage and pain and tried to rear up.

He smacked her again, harder this time, then again and again. She was sobbing with pain and impotent fury, struggling with all her strength, when she felt his fingers pressing inward, pushing her legs more widely apart, touching her. She let out a small terrified cry.

Just as quickly, Dienwald flung her off him, onto her back on the bed. He wrapped her wrists again, tying her more securely this time.

She gave a pitiful sob.

"Don't you dare accuse me of hurting you. Edmund would laugh at a hiding that tender." He hated that word the moment it came from his mouth. It brought to mind the violent lust he'd felt for her moments before.

Her sobs died in her throat. "Your hand is hard and callused. You did hurt me."

"You can't even lie convincingly. Would you prefer a chamber pot on your head, you stupid wench? Thank St. George's lance you hadn't relieved yourself in it first!"

"Of course I hadn't used it! I'm not a —"

"Quiet! You will drive me to lunacy and back! Enough. Go to sleep."

Philippa's bottom felt hot and her flesh was stinging. Her tears were drying on her cheeks and itching. There was nothing she could do about it.

Dienwald was so irritated he couldn't remain silent. "I don't know why I don't simply take you. Why don't —"

"My father would see to it that you were sent as a eunuch to Jerusalem if you forced me."

"What know you of eunuchs and the Holy Land?"

"I am not an ignorant girl. I have learned much. I've had lessons since my eighth year."

"Why would your father waste good coin to educate you, a silly female? That makes no sense at all."

"I don't know why," Philippa said, having wondered the same thing herself. Bernice fluttered about with her ribbons and clothes and her extravagantly pointed slippers, given no opportunity for learning with Father Boise — not, of course, that she'd ever desired to read the *Chanson de Roland*. "Perhaps he thought I could be of use to him. And I have been of use to him. Our steward died nearly two years ago, and I have taken his place."

"You're telling me that you, a female, did the duties of your father's steward?"

"Aye. But my mother also insisted that I learn to manage the household. She didn't enjoy my instruction, but she did it — as an abbess would with an indigent nun."

This entire evening was odd in the extreme, Dienwald decided, exhausted by her nonsense, her violence, her female softness. He snuffed out the candle beside him, and turned onto his back.

"What am I going to do with you, wench?"

"I'm not a wench, I'm —"

Dienwald turned on his side away from her and began snoring very loudly.

"I'm Philippa de Beauchamp and —"

Philippa got no further. He rolled over atop her and kissed her hard. She felt his manhood swell against her belly, felt the heat of him, and opened her mouth to protest. His tongue was her reward, and without thought, she bit him.

He yelped, drawing back.

"I should have known you'd try to make me into a mute. Damned stupid wench, I . . .

No, don't you dare say it, lady, else I'll pull up your gown and —"

"You already did! And you looked at me and you hit me!"

He stopped, and even though she couldn't see his face clearly, she knew his expression was filled with evil intent.

He rolled off her and pulled up her gown. She was naked to the waist, her hands tied above her head, as helpless as could be.

"Now," Dienwald said, sounding quite pleased, "let's continue this conversation. What is it you wanted to say to me, *wench?*"

She shook her head, but he couldn't see it, and that infuriated him. All he'd done this night was to light and snuff candles, protect himself, curse her, and have his rod swell with lust.

He lurched over to the far side of the bed and lit the tallow candle again. It had nearly burned down to the mottled brass holder. He rested on his knees, the candle held high, and looked down at her. For a very long time Dienwald didn't say anything. He was pleasantly surprised, that was all, nothing more. This was to be her punishment, not his, damn her. He stared at her flat belly, then lower, at the profusion of curls that covered her woman's flesh. Curls the color of her head hair, rich and dark, with gleaming browns mingling with strands of the palest blond and . . .

". . . dirt, rich dark dirt."

His words took her so much by surprise that she forgot her terror of him, forgot he was staring at her, seeing her as no man had ever seen her before.

"What is like dirt?"

"Your woman's hair," he said, and cupped his hand over her, pressing his fingers inward.

She yelped like a wounded dog, and he lifted his hand and sat back.

He reached out and splayed his fingers over her flat belly. He stretched out his fingers, watching them nearly touch her pelvic bones. "You're made for birthing babes." He felt something within him move, and lifted his hand as if from a scalding pot. He looked at her face and schooled his expression into a cruel mask. "Remember what I can do to you, wench. Are you such an innocent that I must explain it to you? No? Good. Now, have you anything more to say to me? Any more carping? Any more nagging?"

She shook her head.

"You finally show some wisdom. Good night, wench."

He snuffed the candle yet again, burning

his fingers, since the candle had burned down to a wax puddle, then rolled onto his back. He forgot his burning fingers, still seeing her lying there, naked to the waist, those long white legs spread; he could still feel the softness of her flesh, feel the tensing of the muscles in her belly beneath his splayed fingers.

He cursed, grabbed the blanket, and pulled it over her.

When he was nearing the edge of sleep, he heard her whisper, "I'm Philippa de Beauchamp and I will awaken and this won't really be happening."

He grinned into the darkness. The wench had spirit and fire. A bit of it was interesting; too much, painful. He rubbed the back of his head. He hoped it hadn't cracked the chamber pot. It was the only one he owned.

# 7

The next morning, Dienwald wasn't grinning. His weaver, Prink, was very seriously ill with the ague, and much of the wool had already been cleaned and prepared and spun ready for weaving. Dienwald stomped about, cursing, until Old Agnes plucked at his worn sleeve.

"Master, listen. What of the fine young lady ye've tied to yer bed, eh? Be she really a lady or jest enouther of yer trollops?"

Dienwald ceased his ranting. He'd left Philippa asleep, but he'd untied her wrists, frowning at himself as he brought her arms down to her sides and rubbed the feeling back into her wrists. She'd never even moved. He imagined her bottom was still soft and white, without the mark of his palm, whereas his head ached abominably from her blow with the chamber pot.

"You mean, old hag, that she could weave mayhap? Direct the women, instruct them?"

Old Agnes nodded wisely. "Aye, master, she looks a good girl. Thass what I mean."

Dienwald remembered Philippa's words

about her household instruction. He took the solar stairs two at a time. When he opened his bedchamber door it was to see Philippa standing in the middle of the room staring around her.

"What's the matter?"

She pointed toward the corner of the bedchamber. "The chamber pot. I broke it when I struck your head with it. I need to . . ." She winced, then burst out, "I must relieve myself! You locked me in and —"

His only chamber pot, and she'd destroyed it. "Satan's earlobes! Get you here, wench." He directed her to a much smaller chamber, waving her inside. " 'Tis Edmund's room. Use his pot, then come down to the hall. 'Tis not a lovely hand-painted pot, merely a pottery pot, but it will do. After this, use the jakes. They're in the north tower; you won't get lost, you'll smell them. Don't tarry."

Why did he want her in the great hall? She dreaded it, knowing there would be snickering servants looking at her and knowing that she was now their master's mistress. When he'd burst into the chamber she'd momentarily forgotten what he'd done to her the previous night — smacking her, toying with her, stripping her, *looking* at her. She didn't understand him and was both relieved and afraid because she didn't. It was a good thing that she wasn't to his liking; otherwise she would no longer be a maid and no longer worth much to her father. That thought brought forth the vision of William de Bridgport, and she prayed that all her maneuvers and ill-fated stratagems wouldn't lead to marriage to him. When she left Edmund's small chamber and made her way down the outside solar stairs, her ears were nearly overcome by the noise. There were men and women and children and animals everywhere. All were shouting and squawking and carrying on. It seemed louder than the day before; it was, oddly, comforting.

"Come wi' me, lady."

She turned to see Gorkel the Hideous, the fiercest-looking and ugliest man she'd ever beheld, obviously waiting for her. Odd, though, he didn't seem quite so gruesome of mien as he had yesterday.

"I'm Gorkel, iffen ye remember. Come wi' me. The master wants ye."

She nodded, wishing she had shoes on her feet and cloth covering her naked right arm. She'd combed her fingers through her hair, but she had no idea of the result. Gorkel could have told her that she was as delicious a morsel as a man could pray for, if she'd asked. The master was lucky, he was, and about time, too. A hard winter, but they'd outlasted it, and now it was spring and there was wool and the master had this lovely girl to share his bed. Gorkel left her at the entrance to the great hall, his task completed.

Dienwald saw Philippa, nodded briefly in her direction, and went back to his conversation with Alain, his steward. The man who'd given her dirty looks the evening before. He looked at her now, and there was contemptuous dismissal in his eyes.

Philippa waited patiently, although her stomach was growling with hunger.

It was as if Dienwald had heard her. "Eat," he called out, waving toward the trestle table. "Margot, fetch her milk and bread and cheese."

Philippa ate. She wondered what was going on between Dienwald and the steward Alain. They seemed to be arguing. As she studied the master of St. Erth, she wondered at herself and her reaction to him. She felt no particular embarrassment upon seeing him this morning. In fact, truth be told, she'd rather been looking forward to seeing him again, to crossing verbal swords with him again. She felt a tug on her one sleeve and turned to see the serving maid, Margot, looking at her with worry.

She lifted an eyebrow.

" 'Tis the master," Margot said as low as she could.

"He's a lout," Philippa said, and took a big bite of goat cheese.

"Mayhap," Dienwald said agreeably, dismissing Margot with a wave of his hand. "But I'm the lout who's in charge of you, wench."

That was true, but it didn't frighten her. He hadn't ravished her last night, and he could have. She'd been completely helpless. She thrust her chin two inches into the air and fetched forth her most goading look. "Why do you want me here?"

Dienwald sat in his chair, noted her look, sprawled out to take his ease, and watched her eat, saying nothing for some time.

"You told me your mother taught you household matters. Is this true?"

"Certainly. I'm not a liar. Well, not usually."

Dienwald had a flash of memory of another lady speaking to him candidly, without guile. Kassia. That was absurd. This girl was no more like the gentle, loyal Kassia de Moreton than was a thorn on an apple tree.

"Can you weave?"

Philippa very nearly choked on the cheese in her mouth. No ravisher or ravening beast here. "You want me to weave my father's wool that you stole?"

"Yes. I want you to oversee the weaving and train the women, although several of them already know a bit about it, so Old Agnes told me."

Philippa grew crafty, and he saw it in her eyes and was amused by it. He was also impatient and on tenterhooks. He needed her help, but he couldn't afford to let her see that. She said with the eye of a bargainer at the St. Ives Fair, "What will you do for me if I help you with the wool?"

"I will allow you the first gown, or an overtunic, or hose. Just one, not all three, though."

Philippa looked down at the wrinkled, stained woolen gown that hung about her body like an empty flour bag. The bargain seemed like an excellent one to her. "Will you let me go if I do it for you?"

"Let you go where? Back to your father's household? Back into the repulsive arms of de Bridgport?"

She shook her head.

"Ah, to this other person, this alleged cousin of yours. Who is it, Philippa?"

She shook her head again.

"The gown or the overtunic or the hose. That's all I offer. For the moment, at least."

"Why?"

"Yea or nay, wench."

"I'm not a — !"

"Answer me!"

She nodded. "I will do it." She looked him straight in the eye. "How will you behave toward me?"

He knew exactly what she wanted him to say, but he was perverse and she irritated him and amused him and she'd nearly felled him with a chamber pot.

"I will keep you in my bed until I tire of you." He spoke loudly, and Alain looked up, his contempt now magnified.

Philippa grabbed Dienwald's arm and pinched him, hissing, "You make it sound as if I'm already your mistress, damn you!"

"Aye, I know. In any case, you will remain in my bed. I can't trust you out of my sight. Now, 'tis time for you to earn your keep."

He yelled for Old Agnes and brought her over to Philippa. Old Agnes was older than the stunted oak trees to the north of the castle, and mean as the dung beetles that roamed about the stables. He stood back, crossing his arms over his chest.

Philippa ate another piece of cheese, slowly, as she looked the old woman over.

To Dienwald's amazement, Old Agnes fidgeted.

Philippa drained her flagon of milk, then

said, "I shall see the wool after I've finished my meal. If it isn't thoroughly cleaned and treated, I shan't be pleased. The thread must be pure before it's woven. See to it now. Where is your weaving room?"

Old Agnes drew up her scrawny back, then sagged under Philippa's militant eye. " 'Tis in the outbuilding by the men's barracks . . . mistress."

"I will need you to pick at least five women with nimble fingers and with minds that rise above the thoughts of useless men and, can learn quickly. You will assist me, naturally. Go now and see to the quality of the thread. I will come shortly."

Old Agnes stared at this young lady who knew her way quite well, and said, "It will be as you say, mistress."

She shuffled out, her step lighter and quicker than it had been in two decades. Dienwald stared after her. This damned girl had wrought a miracle — and she'd not been nice, she'd been imperious and arrogant and haughty and . . .

He became aware that Philippa was looking at him, and she was smiling. "She needs a strong hand, and more, she wants a sense of worth. She now has both." Then Philippa began whistling.

Dienwald turned on his heel and strode

from the great hall, bested again by a girl who'd already smashed his head. He cursed.

Philippa silently thanked her mother, whose tongue was sharper than an adder's when it suited her purpose. But, Philippa remembered, her mother's tongue was also sweet with praise when it served her ends. Old Agnes would do more work than all the others combined, and she'd drive them in turn. Philippa turned back to her place, only to see a slight shadow hovering over her.

"Philippa de Beauchamp. I am Alain, Lord Dienwald's steward."

He was speaking to her. She hadn't expected it, given the dislike she'd felt coming from him. She raised her head and kept her face expressionless.

"If you will but tell me this cousin's name, I will see that you are quickly on your way out of this keep and away from Dienwald de Fortenberry."

"Why?"

His good humor slipped. "You don't belong here," he said, his voice loud and vicious. He immediately got hold of himself. "You are an innocent young lady. Dienwald de Fortenberry is a villain, if you will, a rogue, a blackguard, a man who owes loyalty to few men on this earth. He makes his own rules and doesn't abide by others'. He raids and steals and enjoys it. He will continue to hurt you, he will continue to use you until you are with child, and then he will cast you out. He has no scruples, no conscience, and no liking for women. He abused his first wife until she died. He enjoys abusing women, lady or serf. He cares not. He will see that you are cast out, both by him and by your family."

His venom shocked her. She'd smashed a chamber pot over the lord's head the previous night, but that had been different. That was between the two of them. Dienwald hadn't ravished her, and he could have. He hadn't abused her, even when she'd angered him to the point of insensibility. She'd hurt *him*. She thought suddenly of the thrashing he'd given her, but then again, what would she have done to him had he smacked her over the head with a chamber pot? But this steward of his, who should be praising his master, not maligning him — it was beyond anything she'd ever seen.

"Why do you hate him, sirrah?"

Alain drew back as if she'd struck him. "Hate my master? Certainly I don't hate him. But I know what he is and how he thinks. He's a savage, ruthless, and a renegade. Leave, lady, leave before you die or wish to. Tell me this cousin's name and I will get you away from here."

"Yes," she said slowly. "I will tell you."

She watched him closely, and saw immense relief flood his face. His eyes positively glowed and his breath came out in a whoosh. "Who?"

"I shan't tell you today. First of all I must earn a new gown for myself. That was my bargain with your master. I cannot go to my cousin as I am now. You must understand that, sir."

"I think you are a stupid girl," he said. "He will grunt over you and plow your belly until you carry a bastard, then will kick you out of here and you will die in a ditch." He turned on his heel with those magnificent words and strode away, anger in every taut line of his body.

Philippa brooded a moment. This was a peculiar household, and the lord and master was the oddest of them all. She rose from the wooden bench, replete with cheese and bread, and made her way to the weaving building.

Old Agnes had assembled six women, and silence immediately fell when Philippa entered the long, narrow, totally airless room. There were three old spinning wheels and three looms, each of them more decrepit-looking than its neighbor. Philippa looked at each of the women, then nodded. She spoke to each of the women, learned their names and their level of skill, which in all cases but two was nil. Then she tackled the looms. A shuttle had cracked on one; a harness had come loose on another; the treadle had slipped out of its moorings on yet another. She sighed and spoke to Old Agnes.

"You say that Gorkel knows how to solve these problems?"

"Aye, 'tis a monster he is to look at, but he has known how to repair things since he was a little sprat."

"Fetch Gorkel, then."

In the meanwhile Philippa inspected the spinning wheels and the quality of thread the women had produced from the wool. Given the precarious balance of two of the spindles and the wobbling of the huge wheels, the results were more than satisfactory. She smiled and praised the women, seeing her mother's face in her mind's eye.

Two hours later, the women were at their looms weaving interlacing threads into soft wool. They worked slowly and carefully, but that was to the good. As they gained confidence and skill, the weaving would quicken. Old Agnes was chirping over their shoulders, carping and scolding, then turning to

Philippa and giving her a wide toothless grin. "Prink — he were the weaver, ye know, milady — well, a purty sod he were, wot with his proud ways. Said, he did, that females couldn't do it right, the weaving part, only the spinning. Ha!" Old Agnes looked toward the busy looms and cackled. "I hope the old bugger corks it. Thass why none of the females knew aught — the old cockshead was afraid to teach them. Make him look the fool, they would have done."

Philippa wanted very much to meet Prink before he corked it.

All was going well. Philippa de Beauchamp, lately of Beauchamp, was busy directing the weaving of her father's wool into cloth for the man who'd stolen it. She laughed aloud at the irony of it.

"Why do you laugh? You can't see me!"

"I should have known — how long have you been watching, Edmund?"

"I don't watch women working," Edmund said, planting his fists on his hips. "I was watching the maypole!"

"Nasty little boy," she remarked toward one of the looms, and turned her back on him.

"I'll tell my papa, and he won't let you use my chamber pot again!"

Philippa whipped around, pleading in her

eyes and in her voice as she clasped her hands in front of her. "Ah, no, Master Edmund! I must use your chamber pot. Don't make me use the jakes, please, Master Edmund!"

Edmund drew up and stared. He was stymied, and he didn't like it. He assumed a crafty expression, and Philippa recognized it instantly as his father's. She whimpered now, wringing her clasped hands.

"My papa will make you sorry, and thass the truth!"

*"That's,* not *thass."*

She'd spoken without thinking, and watched the little boy puff up with fury like a courting cock. "I'll speak the way I want! No one tells me how to say things, and thass —"

*"That's,* not *thass."*

"You're big and ugly and my papa doesn't like you. I hope you get back into a wagon and leave." He whirled about, tossing back over his shoulder, "You're not a girl, you're a silly maypole!" — and ran straight into his father.

"I should expire with such an insult," Dienwald said, staring down at his son. "Why did you say such a thing to her, Edmund?"

"I don't like her," the boy said, and

scuffed at the dirt with a very dirty foot.

"Why aren't you wearing shoes?"

"There's holes in them."

"Isn't there a cobbler here in the castle?" Philippa asked, wishing she could have shoes on her own very dirty feet.

Dienwald shook his head. "Grimson died six months ago. He was very old, and the apprentice died a week after, curse his selfish heart. I haven't hired another."

Philippa started to tell him to send his precious steward to St. Ives and hire a cobbler, when she remembered he didn't have any coin. She searched for a solution. "You know," she said at last, "it's possible to stitch leather if your armorer could but cut it to size for the boy. Also, I'll need very sturdy thick needles."

Dienwald frowned. Meddlesome, female. Edmund was right: she didn't belong here. He looked again at his son's filthy feet and saw a small scabbing sore on his little toe. He cursed, and Edmund smiled in anticipation of his father's wrath.

Philippa said nothing, merely waited.

"I'll speak to my armorer," Dienwald said, and took Edmund by the arm. " 'Tis time for your lessons, Edmund, and don't carp!"

Edmund looked at Philippa over his

shoulder as his father dragged him from the room. His look was one of astonishment, fury, and utter bewilderment.

# 8

Philippa was sweating in the airless outbuilding. All the weavers were sweating as well, their fingers less nimble, their grumbling louder now than an hour before. Swirls of dust from the floor hung in the hot air, kicked up by the many feet. Even Old Agnes looked ready to drop in the corner and hang her scraggly head.

The master had demanded too much too quickly, a habit, Philippa learned from one of the main grumblers, that was one of his foremost traits. Philippa finally called out, "Enough! Agnes, send someone for water and food. 'Tis the afternoon. We all deserve it."

There were tired smiles from the women as they flexed their cramping fingers. The morning couldn't have gone much worse, Philippa was thinking as she walked around praising the cloth that had been woven. If Philippa had believed in divine retribution for sins she might have been convinced that the morning's calamities stemmed from some mortal act of heinous proportions on her part. The wretched looms, ill-cared-for by the infamous Prink, kept breaking, their parts were so old and worn. She'd become closer to Gorkel the Hideous than to anyone else during the long morning. He'd worked harder than she had, tinkering with the ancient treadle, tying together the spindle whose wood kept cracking from dry rot, balancing the loom when it kept teetering. Even Gorkel now looked ready to tumble to the ground. But even at his worst scowls, Philippa was no longer afraid of him or repelled by his face.

Excellent quality wool, though, Philippa thought as she examined the cloth woven by Mordrid, the only woman Prink had taught anything. Mordrid, Old Agnes had whispered to Philippa, had let the old cootshead into her bed, and thus he'd had to teach her something as payment.

Philippa could see that the woven wool was stout and strong enough to last through winters of wear, and would have fetched a good price at the St. Ives Fair. She didn't want to wait for the wool to be dyed before she set other servants to making a gown for herself. Perhaps an overtunic as well, one with soft full sleeves and a fitted waist. Dienwald wouldn't have to know.

Then she saw Edmund in her mind's eyes.

The little ruffian dressed and spoke like the lowest villein. She sighed. His tunic was a rag.

Then she saw Dienwald, the elbow poking out of his sleeve, and sighed again.

It occurred to her only then that he was her captor and that she owed him nothing. He could rot in the worn tunic he was wearing. Her clothing came first. Then she would escape and make her way to Walter, her cousin.

After everyone had eaten bread, goat cheese, and some cold slices of beef, Philippa reluctantly herded the women back to the looms. Nothing improved. The fates were still against her. The remainder of the day passed with agonizing slowness and heat. The looms continued to break, one part after another. Gorkel was taxed to his limits and was looking more bleak-browed as the afternoon wore on. The lord and master didn't show himself again. He'd set her the task and the responsibility and then proceeded to absent himself, curse him.

It was late, and Philippa was so tired she could barely stand. She rose from the loom where she was working, told the women to be back on the morrow, nodded to Old Agnes, then simply walked out of the weaving building. Long shadows were slicing across one-third of the inner bailey. She spoke to no one, merely walked toward the thick gates that led to the outer bailey. She weaved her way through squawking chickens, several pigs, three goats and a score of children. She just looked straight ahead, as if she had an important errand, and didn't stop.

She'd nearly reached the inner gates when she heard his voice from behind her. "Do my eyes deceive me? Does my slave wish to flee me again? Shall I tether you to my wrist, wench?"

So, now she knew. He must have set up a system whereby he would be told immediately if she did something out of the ordinary. Walking to the inner-bailey gates must meet that requirement. Well, she'd tried. She didn't turn around, merely stood there staring at the gates. She said over her shoulder, still not turning, "If you tether yourself to me, then you must needs sweat until you want to die in that dreadful weaving room. I doubt you wish to do that."

"True," Dienwald said, regarding her thoughtfully. Her face was flushed, but not, he thought, from his threat, but from the heat in the weaving room.

"And I'm not your slave."

He smiled at her defiance. Her hair was

bound loosely with a piece of leather and lay thick and curling between her shoulder blades almost to her waist. Her shoulders weren't straight and high, but slumped. She looked weary and defeated. He didn't like it, and frowned, then said, "I will have the pieces of leather for you soon. My armorer is cutting them. He will measure your feet as well."

"I doubt he has so much leather in single pieces."

"I did ask him to be certain. I wouldn't want him to measure your feet, only to discover that he couldn't cover them after all. I don't wish you to be humiliated."

"My feet aren't that large!"

"But they are dirty, nearly as dirty as my son's. Should you like to bathe now? The day is nearly done. Actually, I was on my way to the outbuilding to see to your progress. How goes it? Prink is trying his best to overcome his ague. He's furious that *women* are doing the weaving and that a woman is directing the proceedings. He is accusing poor Mordrid of base treachery."

"Old Agnes said he was about to cork it," Philippa said, so diverted that she turned to face him, smiling despite herself.

He was garbed in the same clothes as yesterday, and he looked hot and tired. His hair was standing a bit on end. Perhaps he'd had reason not to see to the work during the day. Then she happened to look at his long fingers, and she closed her eyes over the vision of his hands on her body.

This was absurd. He'd looked at her but hadn't wanted her. If he had tried to ravish her, she would have brought him low — naturally, she would have fought him to her dying breath. "You don't need me anymore. Old Agnes is adept at battering the women. Mordrid is capable of teaching them. Gorkel can repair the looms, even when they break every other breath. Your wonderful Prink is a sluggard and a fool. The looms should have been burned and new ones made ten years ago, and . . . Oh, what do you care?" Philippa threw up her hands, for he was simply looking at her with casual interest, the sort of look one would give a precocious dog. "Truly, all the women can weave passably now. I want my gown, and then I want to leave and go to my cousin."

"What did you say his name was, this so-called cousin of yours?"

"His name is Father Ralth. He's a dour Benedictine and will garb me as a choirboy and let me have a small cell of my own. I plan to meditate the rest of my days, thanking God for saving me from de Bridgport and villains like you."

"You will be known as Philippa the castrato?"

"What's a castrato?"

"A man who isn't a man, who's had his manhood nipped in the bud, so to speak."

"That sounds awful." Her eyes went inadvertently to his crotch, and he laughed.

"I would imagine it isn't a fate to be devoutly sought. Now, wench, come with me to my bedchamber. The both of us can bathe. I tire of my own stench, not to mention yours. I shall consider letting you scrub my back."

Philippa, as much as she wanted to exercise an acid tongue on his head, couldn't find the energy to do it. A bath sounded wonderful. Then she looked down at the old gown, dirty and sweat-stained, and sighed. Dienwald said nothing. He turned on his heel, firmly expecting her to follow afterhim like a faithful hound, which she did, curse his eyes.

They passed Alain. Philippa saw the steward give Dienwald an approving nod and wondered at it. Why had he so openly attacked his master to her just this morning? Something was decidedly wrong. Philippa had never before considered herself to be of an overly curious nature, even though her parents had accused her of it frequently, but now she wanted very much to shake Master Alain and see what fell out of his mouth.

It didn't occur to her to wonder how the bathing ritual would take place until Dienwald had locked the bedchamber door, tossed the key into the pocket of his outer tunic, and turned to say, "I'll exercise some knightly virtue and let you bathe first. You see, chivalry still abounds in Cornwall."

"I'm so dirty you'll need another tub. Also, you can't stay in here. Will you wait outside?"

"No." Frank enjoyment removed the tiredness from Dienwald's eyes. "No, I want to see you naked. Again. Only this time, all of you at one time, not just parts."

Philippa sat on the floor. She eyed the copperbound wooden tub with steam rising from it and felt a nearly murderous desire to jump in, but she didn't move. She wouldn't move, even if she had to rot here. She wouldn't allow him to humiliate her anymore. She wouldn't play the partial trollop. To her surprise, Dienwald didn't say anything, didn't threaten her with dire punishments. He rose from the bed and calmly stripped off his clothes.

She didn't look at him, but after several

minutes had passed and she heard no further sound, no movement, she couldn't stand it anymore. When she raised her head, it was to see him standing by the tub, not three feet away from her. She'd seen naked men before; only girls who had been raised by nuns in convents hadn't. But this was different; *he* was different. He was hard and lean and hairy, his legs long and muscled, his belly flat and sculptured. She looked — and couldn't look away. His manhood swelled from the thick bush of hair at his groin, and she stared with open fascination as it grew thicker and longer.

She felt something quite odd and quite warm low in her belly. Philippa knew this wasn't right; she also knew she was losing control of a situation she somehow no longer wanted to control. She swiveled about and faced away from him.

Dienwald laughed and climbed into the tub. He'd seen her stare at him, felt his sex rise in concert with her interest, seen her interest rise as well and her confusion. He reveled in her reactions — when they didn't irritate him.

He lathered himself, feeling the grime soak off, and said, "Wench, tell me of your progress. And don't whine to me about all your problems or of the heat in the outbuilding or of Old Agnes' carping. What did you accomplish?"

Philippa turned back, knowing the height of the tub would keep her from further inappropriate perusal of his man's body. His hair was white with lather, as were his face and shoulders. She couldn't see any more of him.

"It has been nearly nothing *but* problems, and I'm not whining. I may skin Prink alive if the ague doesn't bring him to his grave first. Oh, we now have wool, curse you. I was thinking, mayhap the first tunic should be for Edmund. He looks ragged as a villein's child."

Dienwald opened his eyes, and soap seeped in. He cursed, ducking his head under the water. When he'd cleansed his eyes of the soap he turned to her and nearly yelled, "Nay, 'tis for you, foolish girl. That was our bargain. I am an honorable man, and though you, as a woman, can't understand bargains or honor, I suggest you simply keep your ignorance behind your tongue. I dislike martyrs, so don't enact touching gestures for me. And you simply haven't looked at the villeins' children. They're nearly naked."

"You're taking your anger out on me because you were clumsy with the soap! You're naught but a tyrant and a stupid cocks-head!"

"Not bad for a maiden of tender years. Should I improve upon your insults? Teach you ones more spiteful and less civil?"

He saw her jump to her feet and knew what was in her mind. He said very calmly, even though his eyes still burned from the soap and he wasn't through with her, "Don't, Philippa. Leave the key where it is. You're not using your brain. Tancrid is outside the door. If you managed to trip him up and smash his head with something, there would still be all my men to be gotten through. Sit down on the bed and tell me more of your day. If you must, you may whine."

She sat down on the bed and folded her hands in her lap. He resumed his scrubbing. She looked at his discarded outer tunic, the one that held the bedchamber key. She sighed. He was right.

"We will begin dyeing the wool tomorrow."

He nodded.

"If there are skilled people, then the first of the cloth will be ready for sewing into garments the next day."

He was washing his belly. Philippa knew it was his belly — or flesh even more southerly

— and she was looking, she couldn't help herself. She wondered what it would feel like to touch him, to rub soap over him . . . He looked at her then and smiled. "I will order clean water for you. I have blackened this."

"Will you stay to watch me?"

Dienwald imagined that she'd choose to remain dirty if he said yes. He shook his head. "Nay, I'll leave you in peace. But if you try anything stupid I will do things to you that you will dislike intensely."

"What?"

"You irritate me. Close that silly mouth of yours and hand me that towel. 'Tis the only one, so I will use only half of it. Thank me, wench."

"Thank you."

*Wolffeton Castle, near St. Agnes*

"That damned whoreson! He *knew*, damn him, the scoundrel *knew* full well that wine was bound for Wolffeton from your father. I'll break all his fingers and both his arms, then I'll smash his nose, stomp his toes into the ground —"

Graelam de Moreton, Lord of Wolffeton, stopped short at the laughter from his wife. He eyed her, then tried again. "We have but two casks left, Kassia. 'Tis a present from your sire. It costs him dear to have the wine brought to Brittany from Aquitaine, then shipped here to us. Care you not that the damned whoreson had the gall to wreck the ship and steal all the goods?"

"You don't now that Dienwald is responsible," Kassia de Moreton said, still gasping with laughter. "And you just discovered today that the ship had been wrecked. It must have happened over a sennight ago. Mayhap it was the captain's misjudgment and he struck the rocks; mayhap the peasants stole the goods once the ship was sinking; mayhap everything went down."

"You're full of mayhaps! Aye, but I know 'twas he," Graelam said, bitterness filling his voice as he paced away from her. "If you would know the truth, I made a wager with him some months ago. If you would know more of the truth, our wager involved who could drink the most Aquitaine wine at one time without passing out under the trestle table. I told him about the wine your father was sending us. When we'd gotten the wine, Dienwald and I would have our contest. He knew he would lose, and that's why he lured the captain to his doom, I know it. And so do you beneath all that giggling. Now he has all the wine and can drink it at his leisure, rot his liver! Nay, don't defend him, Kassia!

Who else has his skill and his boldness? Rot his heathen eyes, he's won because he stole the damned wine!"

Kassia looked at her fierce husband and began to laugh again. "So, this is what it is all about. Dienwald has bested you through sheer cunning, and you can't bear being the loser."

Graelam gave his wife a look that would curdle milk. It didn't move her noticeably. "He's no longer a friend; he's no longer welcome at Wolffeton. I denounce him. I shall notch his ears for him at the next tourney. I shall carve out his gullet for his insolence —"

Kassia patted her hair and rose, shaking the skirts of her full gown. "Dienwald is to come next month to visit, once the spring planting is undertaken. He will stay a week with us. I will write to him and beg him to bring some of his delicious Aquitaine wine, since we are neighbors and good friends."

"He's a treacherous knave and I forbid it!"

"Good friends are important, don't you agree, my lord? Good friends find wagers to amuse each other. I look forward to seeing Dienwald and hearing what he has to say to you when you accuse him of treachery."

"Kassia . . ." Graelam said, advancing on

his wife. She laughed up at him and he lifted her beneath the arms, high over his head, and felt her warm laughter rain down upon his head. She was still too thin, he thought, but her pregnancy was filling her out, finally. He lowered her, kissing her mouth. She tasted sweet and soft and ever so willing, and he smiled. Then he hardened. "Dienwald," Graelam said slowly, evil in his eyes, "must needs be taught a lesson."

"You have one in mind, my lord?"

"Not yet, but I shall soon. Aye, a lesson for the rogue, one that he shan't soon forget."

*St. Erth Castle*

At least she was clean, Philippa thought, staring about the great hall, a stringy beef rib in her right hand. The dirty tunic itched, but she would bear it. She wouldn't be a martyr; Dienwald was right about that. She wanted clean soft wool against her flesh; it was all she asked. She didn't even consider praying for silk. It was as beyond her as the moon. Her eyes met Alain's at that moment and she nearly cringed at the malice she saw in his expression. She didn't react, merely chewed on her rib.

She heard Crooky singing in a high falsetto about a man who'd sired thirty children and whose women all turned on him when they discovered he'd been unfaithful to them, all nine of them. Dienwald was roaring with laughter, as were most of the men in the hall. The women, however, were howling the loudest as Crooky graphically described what the women did to the faithless fellow.

"That's awful," Philippa said once the loud laughter had died down. "Crooky's rhymes are a fright and his words are disgusting."

"He's but angry because Margot refused to let him fondle her and the men saw and laughed at him."

Philippa chewed on some bread, saying finally to Dienwald, "Your steward, Alain. Who is he? Has he been your steward long?"

"I saved his life some three years ago. He is beholden to me, thus gives me excellent service and his loyalty."

"Saved his life? How?"

"A landless knight had taken a dislike to him and was pounding his head in. I came upon them and killed the knight. He was a lout and a fool, a local bully I had no liking for in any case. Alain came to St. Erth with me and became my steward."

Dienwald paused a moment, gazing

thoughtfully at her profile. "Has he insulted you?"

She quickly shook her head. "Nay, 'tis just that . . . I don't trust him."

She regretted her hasty words the moment they'd escaped her mouth. Dienwald was staring at her as if she had two heads and no sense at all.

"Don't be foolish," he said, then added, "Why do you say that?"

"He offered to help me get away from you."

"Lies don't become you, wench. Tell me no more of them. Don't ever again attack a man who's given me his complete fealty for three years. Do you understand?"

Philippa looked at Dienwald, saw the banked fury in his eyes, making his irises more gold than brown, and read his thought: A woman couldn't be trusted to give a clear accounting, nor could she be trusted to be honest. She calmly picked up another rib from her trencher and chewed on it.

Dienwald was reminding himself at that moment that only one woman in all his life hadn't been filled with treachery and guile, and that was Kassia de Moreton. For a while he'd been unsure about Philippa. She had seemed so open, so blunt, so straightforward. He shook his head; even a woman as young as Philippa de Beauchamp was filled with deceit. He should simply take her maidenhead, use her until he wearied of her, then discard her. It mattered not if she was ruined; it mattered not if her father kicked her into a convent for the remainder of her days. It mattered not if . . . "Perhaps Alain distrusts you, perhaps he fears you'll try to harm me. That is why he wishes you gone from St. Erth, if, of course, he truly said that to you."

Philippa found she couldn't tell him of the steward's venom. Perhaps he was right about Alain's motives. But she didn't think so. She merely shook her head, then turned to Edmund.

"What color would you like your new tunic to be?"

"I don't want a new tunic."

"No one asked you that. Only whether you wish a certain color."

"Aye, black! You're a witch, so you can give me a black tunic."

"You are such an officious little boy."

"You're a girl, and thass much worse."

*"That's,* not *thass."*

Dienwald overheard this exchange, smiling until he heard her correct Edmund. He frowned. Meddlesome wench. But even so, he didn't want his son speaking like the butcher's boy.

"You will not have a black tunic. Do you like green?"

"Aye, he'll have green, a dark green, to show less dirt."

His father's voice kept Edmund quiet, but he stuck his tongue out at Philippa.

She looked at him with a wondering smile. " 'Tis odd, Edmund, but you remind me of one of my suitors. His name was Simon and he was twenty-one years old but acted as if he were no more than six, just like you."

"I'm nine years old!"

"Are you truly? My, I was certain you were no more than a precocious five, you know, the way you act, the way you speak, the —"

"Do you want more ale, wench?"

So Dienwald had some protective instincts toward his son. She turned and smiled at him. "Aye, thank you."

She sipped at the tart ale. It was better than her father's ale, made by the fattest man at Beauchamp, Rolly, who, Philippa suspected, drank most of his own brew.

"How much more ale do you need?"

She took another sip before asking, "Why do you think I need more? For what?"

"I think, wench, that I will take your precious maidenhead tonight. It taunts me, wench, that maidenhead of yours, just being there. And you do belong to me, at least until I tire of you. But who knows? If you please me — though I doubt you have the skill to do so — I will let you stay and see to the sewing of all the woolen cloth into clothing. What say you to that?"

Philippa, without a thought to the precariousness of her position, tossed the remaining ale from her flagon into his face.

She heard a gasp; then the hall suddenly fell silent as one by one the men and women realized something had happened. Oh, dear, Philippa thought, closing her eyes a moment. She'd thought with her feet again.

Dienwald knew he'd taunted her to violence, and actually, the ale in his face was a minor violence — nothing more or less than he'd expected of her. He supposed he should have waited until he had her in his bedchamber to mock her. Now he would have to act; he couldn't be thought weak in front of his villeins and his men. He cursed softly, wiped his palm over his face, then shoved back the heavy master's chair. He grabbed her arm and dragged her to her feet.

He saw the fear in her eyes, saw her chin

go up at the same time, and wondered what the devil he should do to her for her insolence. For now, he needed a show worthy of Crooky. He turned to his fool, who'd come to his feet and was staring avidly at his master like all the others in the great hall.

"What, Crooky, is to be her fate for throwing ale in her master's face?"

Crooky stroked his stubbled jaw. He opened his mouth, looking ready to burst into song, when Dienwald changed his mind. "Nay, do not say it or sing it."

" 'Tis not a song, master, not even a rhyme. I just wanted to ask the wench if she would make me a new tunic as well."

"Aye, I will sew it myself," Philippa said. "Any color you wish, Crooky."

"Give her another flagon of ale, master. Aye, 'tis a good wench she be. Don't flog her just yet."

"You're not to be trusted," Dienwald said close to her ear. "You'd promise the devil a new tunic, wouldn't you, to keep me from your precious maidenhead?"

"Where *is* the devil tonight?" Philippa asked, looking around. "In residence here? There are so many likely candidates for his services, after all."

"Come along, wench. I have plans for you this long and warm night."

"No," she said, and grabbed the thick arm of his chair with her left hand. She held on tight, her fingers white with the strain, and Dienwald saw that he'd set himself a problem. He looked at the white arm he held, then at the hand holding the chair arm for dear life. "Will you release it now?"

She shook her head.

Dienwald smiled, and she knew at once that she wasn't going to like what followed.

"I will give you one more chance to obey me."

She stared up at him, knowing all the people in the hall were watching. "I can't."

She didn't have to wait long. He smiled again, then lifted his hand, grasped the front of her gown, and ripped it open all the way to the hem.

Philippa yelled, released the chair arm, and jerked at the ragged pieces, trying to draw them over her body.

Dienwald locked his hands together beneath her buttocks and heaved her over his shoulder. He smacked her bottom with the flat of his hand and strode from the great hall laughing like the devil himself.

# 9

"You note, wench, I'm not breathing hard, even carrying you up these steep stairs."

Philippa held her tongue.

She felt his hands on her buttocks, caressing her, and felt him press his cheek for a moment against her side.

"You smell nice. A big girl isn't such a bad thing — there's a lot of you for me to enjoy. You're all soft and smooth and sweet-smelling."

She reared up at that, but he smacked her buttocks with the flat of his hand.

"Hold still or I'll take you back into the great hall and finish stripping off that gown of yours."

She held still, but thought that his priest would surely die of shock were he to do that. When Dienwald reached his bedchamber, he carried her inside and dropped her onto the bed, then strode across the room and locked the thick door.

When he turned, Philippa was already sitting on the side of the bed, clutching the frayed material together over her breasts.

She fretted with the jagged edges, not looking at him. "I must sew it. I have nothing else to wear."

"You shouldn't have thwarted me. You forced me to retaliate. It was a stupid thing to do, wench."

"I was supposed to let you tread on me like rushes on the floor? I'm not a wen—"

"Shut your annoying mouth!"

"All right. What are you going to do?"

He kicked a low stool across the bedchamber. One of its three legs shuddered against the wall and broke off. He cursed. "Get into bed. No, wait. I must tie you up first. I'll wager you'd even try to escape nearly naked, wouldn't you?"

Philippa didn't move. "I want to sew my gown."

"On the morrow. Hold out your hands." When she didn't, he merely stripped off his clothes. He shrugged into his bedrobe, and when he turned back to her, he was holding a leather cross garter in his right hand.

"No, I won't do it. It's like demanding a chicken to willingly lay its neck on the chopping block. I'm not witless."

"I'm not at all certain of that, but you're right about one thing. Remove the torn gown first."

"Please . . ." she said, and swallowed. "I've

never done anything like that before. Please don't make me do it."

"I've already seen you," he said slowly, the man of patience and reason. "I don't suppose you've perchance grown a new part to interest me?"

She shook her head.

He stared down at her bent head. He wanted her very much, but he wasn't about to give in to his appetite for her. It would do him in, mayhap irreparably. It would be stupid — and extremely pleasant. As much as Dienwald hated the notion of denying himself something because an outside authority would disapprove, he wasn't completely witless. If he ravished her, her father would sooner or later hear of it and come to St. Erth and besiege him until there was nothing left but rubble. Also, Dienwald didn't want to get a bastard on her. There were some things he simply couldn't bring himself to do. He wouldn't dishonor her and he wouldn't end up ruined. What he felt was only lust. Lust, he understood. Lust, like a thirst, could be quenched from any available flagon. He said nothing more. He wanted no more than to simply lock her in, but that would allow her to believe she'd gained the upper hand.

He took her off-guard, knocking her backward on the bed. He was fast and he was determined. Within moments the torn gown was on the floor and Philippa was naked beneath him. He saw that she was terrified and, oddly, seemingly curious. He saw it in her eyes. She was curious because she was a maid and he was the first man to treat her in this way. He knew she could feel his increasing interest. Well, let her feel it. It didn't matter. He rolled off, grabbed her wrists, and bound them together.

After he'd tethered the other cross garter to the bed, he stood beside her and looked down at her dispassionately. "You're quite beautiful," he said after a long study, and it was the truth. "You have large breasts, full and round, and your nipples are pale pink. Aye, I like that." He looked down at the curling triangle at the base of her belly. He'd like to sift his fingers through that hair and hear her cry out for him . . . He forced his eyes downward to those magnificently long legs, sleek with muscle and white as pale snow and of a shape to make a man groan with pleasure. Even her arched feet were elegant and graceful. He leaned down and lightly flicked a finger over her nipple. She tried to jerk away but couldn't move out of his reach. "Has a man ever looked at you this way before, wench?"

Philippa was beyond words. She'd watched him look at her, watched his eyes narrow. She could only shake her head, staring at him like a trapped animal, a trapped animal nearly incoherent from the strange sensations flooding its body.

"Have you ever had a man suckle your breast?"

She shook her head again, but he could see in her eyes not only the shock of his words but also the possible effect of the action.

He leaned down and took her nipple in his mouth. She tasted sweet and female and he felt her nipple tighten as he caressed her with his tongue, then suckled her more deeply. He felt his sex throbbing and pressing against his bedrobe. He had to stop this, or . . . "Do you like that?"

He expected a vehement denial — an obvious lie — mayhap a hysterical denial, but to his surprise, she said nothing. He felt a quiver go through her before he forced himself to rise. He tried desperately to keep his look dispassionate. "Has no man ever before touched his fingers to the soft woman's flesh between your thighs?"

"Please," she whispered, then closed her eyes, turning her head away from him.

He frowned. Please *what?* He didn't ask,

but merely grabbed a blanket and covered her. He'd tortured himself quite enough.

"I will go relieve myself now with a willing woman," he said, and strode toward the door of the bedchamber.

"You make a woman sound like a chamber pot!"

"Nay, but she is a vessel for my seed." To his surprise, his own words made him all the randier. He was aching, his groin heavy. He wanted Margot or Alice — it didn't matter which — and he wanted her within the next three minutes.

"I hope your male parts rot off!"

He paused, not turning, and grinned. "I will find out soon enough if your curses carry more than the air from your mouth," he said, and strode back down the solar stairs and into the great hall. He saw Margot sitting close to Northbert. He frowned at the same moment she saw him, for he realized he was wearing naught but his bedrobe. A wondrous smile spread over her round face, making her almost pretty. She jumped to her feet and hurried over to him.

"I want you now," he said, and Margot smiled a siren's smile. She followed him outside, then bumped into his back when he came to an abrupt halt. Dienwald didn't know where to take her. Philippa was bound to his bed. He quivered. Damned female. Where, then?

"Come," he said, grabbed her hand, and nearly ran to the stables. He took her in the warm hay in a far empty stall. And when she cried out her pleasure, her fingers digging into his back, he let his seed spill into her, and in that moment he saw Philippa, and could nearly feel her long white legs clutching his flanks, drawing him deeper and deeper. "Curse you, wench," he said, and fell asleep on Margot's breast.

She woke him nearly three hours later. She was stiff and sore, bits of hay sticking into her back and bottom, and he'd sprawled his full weight on top of her, flattening her.

Dienwald straightened his clothes and took himself to his bedchamber after giving Margot a perfunctory pat on the bottom. He'd left the single candle lit and it had burned itself out. He could make out Philippa's form on the far side of the bed as he stripped off his bedrobe and eased in beside her. He untied the cross garter that tethered her to the bed and lowered her arms and pulled her to him. With a soft sigh, she nestled against him. Fortunately for his peace of mind and Philippa's continued state of innocence, he fell asleep.

When Philippa awoke the following morning, she was alone, which was a relief, and her wrists were free. Her ripped gown was gone, and in its place she found a long flowing gown of faded scarlet, the style from her childhood, its waist loose and its sleeves tight-fitting to the wrists. With it was an equally faded overtunic with wide elbow-length sleeves and a fitted waist. She felt a jolt when she realized that the faded clothing must have belonged to Dienwald's long dead wife.

The gown was too short and far too tight in the bosom, but the material was sturdy despite its age, and well-sewn, so she needn't fear the seams splitting.

Her ankles and feet were bare, and she imagined that she looked passably strange in her faded too-small clothes, the skirt swishing above her ankles.

It was thoughtful of Dienwald to have had the clothes fetched for her, she thought, until she remembered that it was he who had ripped the other gown up the front, rendering it an instant rag. She hardened her heart toward him with ease, though the rest of her still felt the faint tremors of the previous night, when he'd looked down at her, then kissed her breast. Those feelings had been odd in the extreme, more than pleasant, truth be told, but now, alone, in the light of day, Philippa couldn't seem to grasp them as being real.

She made her way to the great hall, drank a flagon of fresh milk, and ate some gritty goat's cheese and soft black bread. It didn't occur to her not to go to the weaving shed to see to the work. Old Agnes, bless her tartar's soul, was berating Gorkel the Hideous for being slow to repair one of the looms. Philippa watched, saying nothing, until Old Agnes saw her and exclaimed as she shuffled toward her, "Gorkel's complaining of wood mold, but I got him at it again. Prink is threatening to come upon us today and whip off our hides. He didn't cork it! Mordrid said he ate this morning and was up on his own to relieve his bowels. May God shrivel his eyeballs! He'll ruin everything."

"No, he won't," Philippa said. She wanted a fight, and Prink sounded like a wonderful offering to her dark mood. She discovered when she called a halt for the noonday meal that Dienwald and a half-dozen men had left St. Erth early that morning, bound for no-one-knew-where. That, or no one would tell her.

*Now was the time to escape.*

"Ye look like a princess who's too big fer

her gown," said Old Agnes as she gummed a piece of chicken. "That gown belonged to the former mistress, Lady Anne. Small she were, small in her body and in her heart. Aye, she weren't a sweetling, that one weren't. Master Edmund's lucky to have ye here, and not that one who birthed him. She made the master miserable with her mean-spirited ways. When she died of the bloody flux, he was relieved, I knew it, even though he pretended to grieve."

Old Agnes then nodded as Philippa stared openmouthed. "The master'll fill yer belly quick enough. Then he'll wed ye, as he should. Yer father's a lord, and that makes ye a lady — and all will be well, aye, it will." Old Agnes nodded, pleased at her own conclusions, and shuffled away to where Gorkel squatted eating his food.

Philippa walked outside the shed, Old Agnes' words whirling about in her mind. Wed with the master of St. Erth? The rogue who'd stolen her father's wool and her with it? Well, it hadn't quite been that way, but still . . . Philippa shook her head, gazing up at the darkening skies. Evidently he had to get her with child first before such notions as marriage would come to him. She didn't want him; she didn't want his child. She wanted to leave, to go to . . . Where? To Walter's keep, Crandall? To a virtual stranger? More of a stranger than Dienwald was to her?

"It'll rain and we'll have to rot inside."

She turned to see Edmund, his hands on his hips, looking disgruntled.

"Rain makes the crops grow. The rain won't last long, you'll see. We'll survive it." She grinned down at him. "And aren't you supposed to be at your lessons?"

He looked guilty for only an instant, but Philippa saw it. "Come along and let's find Father Cramdle. I haven't yet met him, you know."

"He won't want to see you. He'll go all stiff like a tree branch. My father ripped off your gown last night and carried you off. You're only my father's mis—"

"I don't think you'd better say it, Edmund. I am not your father's mistress. Do you understand me? I'm a lady, and your father doesn't dare to . . . harm me."

Edmund seemed to think this over for a halfdozen steps before finally nodding. "Aye," he said, "you're a big lady. And I don't need lessons."

"Of course you do. You must know how to read and to cipher and to write, else you'll be cheated by your steward and by anyone else who gets the chance."

"Thass what my father says. *That's!*" he said before she could.

Philippa smiled. "Tomorrow you'll have a new tunic. Also study new shoes and hose. You'll look like Master Edmund of St. Erth. What do you think of that?"

Edmund didn't think much of it. He scuffed his filthy toes against a rock. "Father went a-raiding. He's angry at a man who hates him and who struck last night and burned all our wheat crop near the south edge of St. Erth land."

"Who is this man?"

Edmund shrugged.

"How long will your father be away?"

"He said mayhap a week, longer or shorter."

"How did your father find out about the burned crops?"

"Crooky. He sang it to him at dawn. Father nearly kicked his ribs into his back."

"I can imagine. How does Crooky find out things so quickly?"

"He won't tell anyone how he does it."

"If he provides useful information, I suppose one can forgive his miserable rhymes."

"Aye, but Father said that only he could kick Crooky because Crooky was *his* fool and no one else's and had his protection. So no one touches Crooky." Edmund shrugged. "Crooky always finds out everything first. I think mayhap he's a witch, like you, except he's not a silly girl."

So much for a little peace talk, Philippa thought.

"There's Father Cramdle," Edmund said as they came in sight of the priest.

Philippa made his acquaintance, and was pleased when he looked her squarely in the eye and was polite to her. She gave him Edmund with the admonition, "You will do as Father Cramdle tells you, Edmund, or you will answer to me."

"Maypole! Woolly head! Witch!"

Philippa didn't turn around when she heard Edmund's fierce whispers; she merely smiled and kept on going. She met with the armorer, a ferocious old man whose name was Proctor and who had only one eye and that one rheumy. He'd cut leather for many pairs of shoes, including a pair for her. She delivered the leather to Old Agnes, and she, in turn, set others to stitching the leather into shoes.

It was late afternoon when Philippa thought again of escape. Why not? She stopped cold. She'd acted all through the day, she realized suddenly, as if she were chatelaine here at St. Erth, and that was absurd. She was a prisoner; she was as good as a serf; she was a *wench*.

She stopped her ruminations at the sight of Alain. He was speaking with a man she hadn't noticed before. The conversation looked furtive to her sharp eyes, and the steward gave something to the man. She watched silently until the man melted away behind the soldiers' barracks. Alain then mounted a horse and rode out of St. Erth. Most curious, she thought. Without hesitation Philippa went into the great hall, through the side chambers, until she found the steward's small accounting room.

There were wooden shelves built against the walls, and in the small cubicles were rolled parchments tied with bits of string. There were also larger sections in which bound ledgers were kept. Quills and ink pots and a thick pile of foolscap lay atop the table, as well as large dust particles. There were books stacked on the floor in front of the shelves, a narrow cot against one wall, and a low trunk at the foot of the cot. Nothing more. Evidently Alain both worked and slept in this room.

Philippa took one of the large ledgers from a shelf, moved to his desk, and opened it. It was a record of the past three years' crops — what was planted in which section of land, the price of the grain, the sale of the product, and a log of the villeins who'd worked each section, including the number of hours and days. Another bound book contained birth and marriage records of St. Erth. Philippa returned to the first book and read it through. She sought out another book that held all the records of building and repairs done at St. Erth in the past three year — the tenure of Alain's stewardship.

It took Philippa only an hour and a half to discover that Alain was a thief. No wonder Dienwald had had to steal the wool: there was no coin available because Alain had stolen it all. Why didn't Dienwald know this? Didn't he go over his steward's records?

Philippa rose and rearranged all the steward's materials the way she'd found them and left the small airless room. He still hadn't returned. Where had he gone? Who was the man to whom he'd been speaking? What had he given the man? She had no answers.

Philippa went back to the weaving shed, saw that all work was progressing satisfactorily, then went in search of Crooky. She found him curled up in a corner of the great hall — sleeping off a huge meal, Margot told her, glaring down at the snoring fool.

Philippa walked over to him and lightly

stuck a toe in his ribs. He jerked up, his mouth opened, and he started singing:

> Ah, my sweet lord,
> don't cuff your loving slave;
> He slumbers rarely in your service,
> like a toothsome wench who —

"Don't finish that atrocious rhyme," Philippa said. "Stand up, fool. I'll have words with you."

Crooky blinked and staggered to his feet scratching his armpit. "What want you, mistress?"

"I suppose 'mistress' is better than 'wench.' "

"My sweet lord isn't here, mistress."

"I know it. I need your help, Crooky. I want to ask you several questions, but please don't sing your answers, just speak them like sensible people."

Crooky rubbed his ribs. "You've a sharp toe, mistress."

"It'll be sharper if you don't attend me."

"Oh, aye, I'm whetted."

Ten minutes later Philippa left the fool to resume his sleep. He'd given her more food for thought than she wished to consume. The greatest shock of all was the fact that the Lord of St. Erth could make out written words, but only slowly and with difficulty. He could write only his name and cipher only the most simple of problems. Not that all that many men could, and no more than a handful of women. She was foolish to be so surprised. She'd just thought that Dienwald, who, despite his stubbornness, his arrogance, was intelligent and seemingly learned . . . No wonder he was firm about Edmund's lessons with Father Cramdle. He knew it was important; he felt the lack in himself.

Philippa was very angry. She also realized when she saw Alain ride back into the inner bailey that she had less than no power at all. She was a prisoner, not the mistress of St. Erth.

She had to bide her time.

Unfortunately, Alain sought her out at the evening meal. He, she quickly discovered, played the master in Dienwald's absence, with Dienwald's permission, evidently. She knew she must tread warily. He sat beside her in the master's highbacked chair, ignored her for a good long while, then turned and gave her a leer a man would give a worn-out trollop of no account at all. She said nothing, didn't change her expression, merely sank her white teeth into a piece of pigeon pie, a delicious concoction that included carrots and turnips and potatoes.

"I see you stole the dead mistress's clothes."

So, Philippa thought, the steward wanted to bait her. He couldn't keep his dislike of her to himself. He really wasn't very good at the game. Not nearly so accomplished as his master. She smiled. "Do you see that, really? I'd thought you here only three years, *Master* Alain. The mistress, I'd heard, died shortly after Edmund's birth."

His right hand crushed a piece of bread. "Don't think you to insult me, whore. Dienwald will plow your belly, but he will show you no favors. You are but one of many, as I told you before. He will toss you to his men when he's through with you. You look a fool in the gown — 'tis far too small for you. Your breasts look absurd, flattened like that. And your legs stick out like two poles, it is so short."

" 'Tis better than wearing nothing."

"Aye, all of us saw him rip your clothing off you, then carry you to his bed. You must have angered him mightily. Did he ravish you until you screamed? Or did you enjoy his plunging member inside you?"

"Nay," Philippa replied, as if considering the matter.

Alain laughed, sopped up some gravy

from his trencher with the large piece of bread he'd crushed in his hand, and stuffed it into his mouth.

"You really don't look good in his chair," Philippa said, looking at his bulging cheeks. "It is too large for you, too substantial, too important. Or perhaps 'tis you who are just too meager, too paltry, for Dienwald's place." She thought he would spit out the bread in his anger at her, but he managed to keep chewing and swallow.

It was then she saw the shift in his expression. He'd realized that what he was doing wouldn't get him what he wanted. He was prepared to retrench. She waited. "We argue to no account," he said finally, and he sounded the reasonable man, not the furious brute who wanted to strike her. "Truly, Philippa de Beauchamp, you must leave St. Erth while there is still time. I will help you return to your father. You must go before Dienwald returns."

He wanted her gone, and very badly. Why? She was a threat to him now that she knew him for a thief, but he couldn't know that she'd discovered the truth about him. Why, then? "I've a notion to stay here and wed the Lord of St. Erth. He is a man of worth, and comely. What think you, steward?" The moment the words were out,

Philippa was appalled at herself. But she wouldn't take them back. She watched, fascinated, as his face mottled with rage — and something else, something sly and frightening. His hand shook.

"I'll have you whipped, whore," he said very quietly. "I've a fancy to wield the whip myself. God, how I'd enjoy it. I'd see those breasts of yours heave up and down when you scream and try to escape the whip, and I'd mark that back of yours with bloody welts."

Edmund suddenly slipped out of his place at the trestle table and quickly moved to her side even as Philippa said, "No you won't, Master Alain. You have no power here either. If Dienwald only knew that you —" She bit her lower lip until she felt the sting of her own blood. She'd very nearly spit at him that he was a liar and a thief and a scoundrel and probably even worse.

At that moment Crooky rose from the floor beside Alain's chair and moved to stand on Philippa's other side. He yawned deeply, stared blankly at the steward, then sprawled back onto the rushes.

Alain didn't look pleased. He eyed Edmund who looked for all the world like a mangy little gamecock. "The boy can't protect you, whore, nor can the fool, who's an idiot, a half-wit. He's naught of anything, and Dienwald keeps him here only because he finds it amusing to endure him. Now, what were you going to say, whore? You were going to accuse me of something? Make up lies about me?"

"My name is Philippa de Beauchamp. I am a lady. You're naught but offal."

"You're no more a lady than the fool is a poet. You're a silly vain trollop." Without warning, the steward raised his hand and struck her hard across the face. Her head snapped back from the force of it and she felt tears burn her eyes. Oddly, she noticed ink stains on his fingers, and wondered when he'd last bathed.

"Damned slut!" He raised his hand to strike her again, but suddenly, to Philippa's bewilderment, his chair began to shake, tip backward, then go crashing to the floor, the steward with it, landing on his back, his head striking the carved chair back.

Philippa, her hand pressed to her flaming cheek, could only stare at the fallen steward. Edmund stood over him, rubbing his hands together and crowing with laughter. The hall had fallen silent.

Alain scrambled to his feet, his face blotchy with rage, his thin body trembling. He waved his fists toward Edmund, yelling,

"You damned little cockscomb! I'll hide you for that!"

Philippa was out of her chair and standing in front of Edmund in a flash. "You touch the boy and I'll kill you. Doubt me not."

The steward drew up short, looking at the woman who was at eye level with him. She was strong, but she wasn't strong enough to do him damage. Her words meant nothing; she'd cringe away at the first threat of violence, like every other woman he'd known. He wanted to spit on her, he wanted to wring her neck. No, he had to keep control. "Stand aside, whore."

He raised his hand when Philippa didn't move. There came a deep grumbling sound from behind the steward. Slowly, very slowly, Alain lowered his arm, turning toward the sound as he did so. Philippa stared at Gorkel the Hideous. He was the most terrifying sight she'd ever seen. His bony face, with its pocked surface and puckered scars, its stubbled jaw and thick beetle eyebrows that met over his nose, looked like a vision from hell. And there was that low growl coming from his throat, like an animal warning its prey.

"Get ye gone, little man," Gorkel said finally, and his lips barely opened.

Alain wanted to tell the codshead take

himself to hell, but he was afraid of Gorkel; the man could easily break his spine with but little effort of his huge hands. He looked at Philippa, then at the boy, who was standing there with his hands on his hips, his chin thrust forward. He'd get her; then he'd punish the boy. The steward turned on his heel and strode from the hall.

Crooky suddenly jumped to his feet and burst into wild song, the words following the enraged steward from the hall:

A varlet he'll be to the end
A stench that rots in the walls
Next time he'll not have the gall
When the master's back in the hall.

Philippa looked down at Edmund. "Thank you."

"He's a bully. Father doesn't see it because Alain's always careful around him. Why does he hate you? You're naught but a girl. You've never done anything to him, have you?"

"No, I haven't. I truly don't know why he hates me, Edmund."

"You will stay away from him. I can't always be around to protect you."

"I know." She looked up and met Gorkel's eyes. She smiled at him and he nodded, a deep rumbling sound in his throat. He scratched his belly, turned, and strode back to his place below the salt.

Noise filled the hall again. Crooky sprawled once more to the rushes. Edmund crammed bread into his mouth, and Philippa, her cheek still stinging, merely sat back into her chair, wondering what she was to do now.

For the next three days she kept close to Gorkel. He didn't seem to mind, and his presence kept Alain well away from her. He even disdained to sit beside her at the lord's trestle table. Gorkel didn't tell her that it was the master's order that he keep close to her. It would be Gorkel's head were the wench to escape St. Erth. In those three days Philippa learned more about St. Erth, met all its inhabitants, sewed Edmund a tunic of forest-green wool, and began one for Dienwald. Hers could wait a bit longer. Philippa became so used to all the noise that she could even identify what squawks came from what chicken. One pig in particular chose her as its mother and followed her everywhere, making Gorkel laugh. Philippa named the pig Tupper.

On the morning of the third day, Philippa, her step buoyant and carefree, entered the weaving shed to be greeted by pandemonium. A gaunt middle-aged man with tufts of gray hair sticking straight up on his head was screaming at Mordrid. He was quaking with rage, shaking so violently that his clothes, hanging loosely around him, were in danger of leaving his body.

He yelled, "Bitch! Slut! Treacherous cow! I lie on my deathbed and ye take my job. I'll kill ye!"

# 10

Philippa stared at the man, then shouted, "Hold! Who are you? What do you do here?"

The man whirled about. He looked Philippa up and down and sneered, and his eyes seemed to turn red. "Aye, so ye're t' witch who's beleaguered t' master. Ye're t' one who's made him think of naught but plungin' into yer belly and givin' ye wot's mine!"

"Ah," Philippa said, crossing her arms over her breasts. "You must be Prink. Fresh from your deathbed. I see you are still with us."

Her bright, very polite voice stalled Prink, but only for a moment. He felt ill-used, betrayed, and he wanted to leap on the wench and tear the hair from her head. It was her size that held him back. He didn't have his full strength back yet. He drew himself up. "I'm here t' do my work. Ye're not welcome, wench. Out wi' ye, and take all these stupid women wi, ye." He grabbed Mordrid's arm and twisted it. "I'll keep this one — she deserves a hidin', she does, and I'll gi' it to her."

"Prink," Philippa said very slowly, "you will release Mordrid, now."

The weaver looked fit to spit. His hold tightened on Mordrid's arm until the woman moaned with pain.

Philippa wondered where Gorkel was. During the past three days he'd been where she'd been. Well, he wasn't here and she had no one but herself to handle this predicament. Even mouthy Old Agnes was hiding behind a huge woven piece of cloth newly dyed a bright yellow. Philippa stepped up to the furious weaver, saw his pallor, saw the spasms that shook his muscles, and knew him still to be very ill. She said calmly, her voice pitched low, "You aren't well, Prink. Here, allow me to help you back to your bed."

He squealed like Philippa's worshipful pig, Tupper, but he did drop Mordrid's arm. He gave Philippa his full attention. "Ye're naught but t' master's slut, and ye've taken wot's mine and —"

"Your face is gray as the sky this morning, Prink, and sweat drips off your forehead. Do you wish to remain here and fall on your face in a faint, in front of all the women?"

Prink didn't know what to do. He'd exhausted himself with his rightful indignation. He wanted to wring the wench's neck, but he hadn't the strength. He mumbled curses at Mordrid and walked slowly, his muscles cramping, toward the door of the outbuilding. At that moment Gorkel appeared, looking from the weaver to Philippa.

"Do help him back to his bed, Gorkel, and see that he remains there until he's completely well again. I will speak to you later, Prink."

The instant the weaver disappeared, Old Agnes bounded out of her hidey-hole, squawking with fury. "Old codshead! How dare he try to ruin everything, the stinking poltroon!"

Philippa ignored Old Agnes. "Mordrid, are you all right? Did he hurt your arm?"

The woman shook her head. "Thank you, mistress." She fretted a moment, then said, "Prink's a good man, he is, a proud man. The cramping illness makes him feel less than a man."

Would a woman forgive a man absolutely anything? Philippa wondered as she watched the work settle back into its placid routine. When Gorkel reappeared, he merely nodded to Philippa and took his post by the door.

The following afternoon, Philippa was

hot and tired and feeling lonely. She was walking across the inner bailey, the pig, Tupper, squealing at her bare feet in hot pursuit, when the porter, Hood, called out to her that a tinker was coming. Did she want him to enter? Excitement flowed through Philippa as she yelled back that, yes, she wanted him to come. A tinker meant trinkets and ribbons and thread and items the keep sorely needed. Perhaps the tinker even had gowns, sold or bartered to him on his travels. She didn't stop to think that it was odd for her to be asked permission by the porter.

Men and women were gathering in the inner bailey, buzzing with excited conversation. Children, feeling their parents' anticipation, stayed close. Even the animals quieted as the stranger came through the huge gates. Philippa greeted the tinker and her eyes glistened with enthusiasm at the sight of the two pack mules he led, each one carrying more packages than she'd ever seen.

It was when she was fingering two long lengths of pink ribbon that she realized she had no coin.

She had nothing, either, with which to trade.

She wanted to cry.

A soft voice sounded in her ear. "You agree to leave St. Erth, and I'll buy you all the ribbons you want. Mayhap even a gown and some shoes. The tinker has everything. Ah, yes, you silly girl, those ribbons would go very nicely with your hair. Do you want them?"

She expelled her breath, turning to see the steward standing close beside her, his leer as pronounced as ever.

Anger filled her and she very nearly screamed that she knew he was a thief and that was why the master had no coin. She stopped herself in the nick of time. She had to keep quiet. She had to wait until Dienwald returned. She tilted her head back so that she was looking down her nose at him. "Nay, sir steward, there is nothing I wish."

"Liar."

She stepped back then and watched the people of St. Erth buy and trade goods with the tinker.

She wanted to weep when she handed him back the ribbons. It was foolish, but she wanted them desperately. They were as pale a pink as the sunrise in early May, and matched a gown she owned back at Beauchamp.

The tinker remained the night and Crooky proved to be in fine fettle, singing until he was hoarse, the words of his songs so colorfully crude that Father Cramdle was forced to clear his throat several times. When Philippa finally left the great hall, Gorkel beside her, she was still smiling.

"I told the tinker to circle back this way when the master is here," Gorkel said as he left her beside her bedchamber door.

"It truly doesn't matter," Philippa said, and swallowed a bit hard.

"Keep the door locked," Gorkel said as he'd said each preceding night. She did as he'd said, then turned with her candle to set it down. Standing in front of her was Alain, holding a knife.

Philippa rushed back to the door and turned the large brass key in the lock, yelling, "Gorkel! Gorkel! *A moi! A moi!*"

The steward was on her in a second, his arm closing around her throat as he jerked her back against him. His right hand rose and the sharp point of the knife pointed down at her breast. Philippa couldn't scream now; his arm was cutting off her breath. She clawed at his arm with her nails, but he was strong — and strong with purpose.

He didn't slam the knife into her breast. She realized that he didn't want to kill her here. It would be far too dangerous for him.

The knife was to ensure her obedience. His arm tightened and she felt the chamber spinning as white lights burst before her eyes. She jerked at his arm and felt the tip of the knife prick into her throat. She felt a cold numbing followed by the slick wetness of her own blood.

"Hold still, whore, or I'll gullet you now. As for Gorkel, that cretinous idiot can't hear you. The doors are thick. But you'll keep quiet or all that will come from your mouth is a bloody gurgle."

Philippa held still as a stone, dropping her arms to her sides.

"Good. Now, come here."

He half-dragged her over to Dienwald's bed and shoved her down onto her back. He came down next to her, holding the knife over her throat. She swallowed, looking up at him.

" 'Tis past time for you to escape from St. Erth. Aye, you'll be long gone by the time the master returns. And he'll blame Gorkel, the hulking fright. Not me. He'll never even think about me."

She said nothing, letting her brain work rather than her mouth. It was a novel approach.

"You wonder why I want you gone so badly from St. Erth — I can see it in your silly female's eyes. Those eyes of yours . . . they're familiar, the shape and the color, aye, that shade of blue has bothered me . . . I have seem them before, somewhere . . . but no, I have no time for such nonsense. I wouldn't have killed you had you left before, but now you give me no choice. Stupid sow, you should have left when I first offered you the chance.

"But you didn't, did you? You wanted the master, wanted to believe his lies. Did he tell you that he wanted you more than any other female? He deceives women well. You should have left. But now 'tis too late, far too late."

He was rambling on and on, bragging and insulting Dienwald, and it seemed to Philippa that he must be mad.

"Why?" she whispered, not moving because the knife was still pressed so deep, its tip already bathed in her blood.

"Why? Should I tell you, I wonder? Well, soon you'll be dead and gone, so it matters not. I know who you are."

That made no sense. She said slowly, "I'm Philippa de Beauchamp. Everyone knows that."

"Aye, but you see, I sent my two men after the third wagon of wool, the one my foolish master left to the farmers because he felt pity for them. Aye, my men got them, and before they killed the luggards, they found out all about you. The farmers didn't know you'd been hiding in one of their wagons, but they were ready to talk all about you once knives were at their hearts. My men found out you were your father's favorite, that you were his steward in fact and in deed, that it was you who had set the price of the wool and sent them to the St. Ives Fair to get that price. Which means that you can read and write and cipher, unlike my master, who believes whatever I tell him.

"So you must die. You wonder why Dienwald trusts me, don't you? Aye, I can see it in your eyes. Dienwald saved me from a knight I'd swindled, and then he killed my master, who'd sided with the knight, after I told him how I'd been cheated and beaten. Then he brought me to St. Erth, where I've become a rich man. He believed he had earned my gratitude, the pathetic fool.

"Dienwald believes himself a rogue, a scoundrel, a rebel who can wave his fist in the face of higher authority, but deep in his soul he holds beliefs that can and will do him in. So you see, I can't let you remain, for I also know you visited my chamber. You left papers and documents just the way you found them, but one of my spies saw you.

Aye, he saw you leaving, looking furtive and wary. So you found out the truth, did you, and were just waiting for the proper moment to tell Dienwald.

"And he set Gorkel to keep you from escaping, not realizing that he was at the same time protecting you from me. You didn't know that, did you? Gorkel has stayed close, and I didn't know how to get you until tonight. Then it came to me, and I knew I must be bold. You know, Philippa de Beauchamp, I hated you the moment I first saw you. I knew your purpose to be contrary to mine."

Before she could say a word, before she could draw another breath, Alain brought the bone handle of the knife down against her temple, hard. She saw a burst of lights, felt a sharp pain, and then there was blackness.

Philippa awoke with the earthy smells of the stables filling her nostrils. Her hands were bound tightly behind her, but her legs were free. She lay perfectly still, waiting for the dizziness to clear. When it did, she realized she couldn't breathe easily. A blanket covered her. She gripped an edge with her teeth and pulled it off her face. She seemed to be alone, but it was very dark in the stables and she couldn't be certain. She couldn't hear anyone moving about or speaking. Where was Alain?

Now, she thought, now was the time to think. Not with her feet, though they were the only free part of her, but with her brain. What to do? Alain had nothing to lose; he had to remove her from St. Erth. Snatches of songs sung by the jongleurs paraded through her mind in those moments, songs about mighty heroes rescuing fair maids from degrading and frightful situations. There wasn't a mighty hero anywhere to be found. The fair maid would have to save herself.

She tried to loosen the ropes at her wrists, but the effort did nothing but shred her skin. She rolled over and managed to rise to her feet, peering from the stall where she'd been left unconscious. She nearly fainted from the pain in her temple where the knife handle had struck, but she held on. She had no choice but to hold on. She couldn't have much time left now. Alain would be coming back for her soon. And he'd kill her; she didn't doubt it for an instant.

Philippa managed to free the latch on the stall and push the door open. It squealed on its rusted hinges, and she froze. Where was the steward?

It was at that moment that she heard two

men speaking in low voices in the stable-yard. The steward's men. Standing guard until he returned. From where?

Philippa drew a deep breath of relief. She'd been on the point of rushing out of the stables at full tilt, screaming for help. She'd been fully ready to think with her feet again. She looked around carefully, her eyes now used to the darkness, and saw an old scythe, sharp and deadly, hanging from a hook on the wall.

Her bonds didn't take long to cut through, but the edge of the scythe was sharp and she felt her own blood, sticky and slippery, covering her palms before she was free. Once she was loose, she stooped down and eased back to the stable door. The two men were still there, still speaking in low voices.

Now, she decided, she could take them by surprise and run as far as the great hall before they caught up with her.

"Well? Heard you aught out of the whore? she still unconscious?"

Alain had returned. Philippa shrank back, her heart pounding so loudly they must hear it. No matter. Let them come. She pulled the scythe from the wall and clutched it to her breast.

She heard one of the men say, "Nay, t'

wench is still quiet. T' blow will keep her unconscious until we cut her throat. Can we split her afore we kill her?"

Philippa swallowed convulsively. She realized suddenly that her bloody hands were making the scythe handle slick. She picked up some hay at her feet and rubbed it over the handle and over her palms. The pain was fierce, but she welcomed it. As long as she felt pain, she was alive. And as long as she had the scythe, she had a chance.

"You can do whatever you wish to her. But you must kill her afterward, make no mistake about it, and make certain her body's never found. The wench is conniving, so take care if she comes to herself again. Now, I've spoken to Hood, the porter, and told him that I'm sending some supplies to the master. The man's not stupid, so be careful. You'll load the girl on a pack mule and take her away from St. Erth. When you return, you'll be paid. Now, go."

Then Alain was leaving; she heard his retreating footsteps. Only his two accomplices remained, then.

All she had on her side was surprise.

She raised the scythe over her head and waited. One of the men was coming into the stables, saying to the other, "Wait here and I'll fetch t' wench."

The other man protested, "Nay, ye'll take her in t' stall, ye bastid!"

They were fighting over who was going to ravish her first. Her hold on the scythe handle tightened. Filthy villains. One appeared in the doorway, moonlight framing his head. Philippa drew a sharp breath and brought the scythe down hard. It was only the blunted, curved edge of the blade that hit him, but the force of her blow cracked the man's head open and he didn't even cry out, but fell, blood spewing everywhere, to the hay-strewn floor.

The man behind him cried out, but Philippa, like a blood-spewed vision from hell, screamed and came at him, the scythe raised over her head.

The man bellowed in fear, his eyes rolling in his head, and turned on his heel. Philippa drew up for an instant, her mouth gaping in surprise. The man had run from her, terrified. She quickly ran across the inner bailey and up the steps of the great hall. She flung the doors open and rushed in. As always, there was the loud noise of general conversation. Then a few people noticed her standing there, the scythe in her hands, covered with blood, her hair wild about her pale face.

There was an awesome silence. Then

Alain jumped to his feet and yelled, "Kill the whore! By the devil's knees, she's butchered our people! Look at her, covered with blood! Murderess! She's stolen the master's jewels! Kill her! Strike her down quickly!"

Philippa looked around her and raised the scythe. The silence was deafening and paralyzing. No one was moving yet. Everyone was staring as if at a mummers' scene. "Gorkel," she said, her voice just above a croak, "help me."

Alain, seeing that no one had moved, bounded to his feet, screaming as he ran toward her, "Kill the damned witch! That's what she is, a cursed witch!"

He grabbed one of the men-at-arms' swords and ran straight toward her.

"Kill her!" another man's voice roared with the steward's. "Aye, she's a witch who steals men's jobs!" It was Prink, still pale and sweaty but ready to do her in. "Slay her where she stands!"

Eerily, Philippa now heard each voice separately. Every sound came singly and loudly and obscenely. She heard Father Cramdle praying loudly, she heard Edmund screech like one of her mother's peacocks as he dashed toward her. "No, Edmund, stay back!" But her words were just an echo in her mind. Northbert, Proctor, the armorer,

Margot, Crooky, Alice — all of them were rushing at her. To aid her? To kill her?

She shuddered and backed away. She knew Alain's other henchman was out there in the inner bailey somewhere, just waiting to kill her if she came out. And here was Alain, fury and hatred burning him, ready to kill her even as she stood here in a hall filled with people.

She wasn't a coward. She raised the scythe.

"Nay, mistress."

It was Gorkel and he was moving slowly toward her, a look of abandoned joy on his terrifying face. His teeth were bared in a smile, and in that instant Philippa felt a bolt of pity for Alain.

Gorkel caught the steward's arm just above the elbow and simply squeezed. Alain's sword clanked harmlessly to the floor.

Then the steward was screaming and begging and pleading. Philippa saw that Gorkel was twisting the steward's elbow back and up, even as Alain's screams grew louder and louder.

Finally, seemingly without emotion, Gorkel closed the thick fingers of his other hand about the steward's neck. He raised him with one arm, the fingers tightening, and the steward dangled above the floor. He couldn't scream now; his voice was a mere liquid gurgle in his throat, as Gorkel shook him until his neck snapped — an indecently loud noise in the silent hall.

Gorkel grunted and flung the quite-dead steward to the rushes.

Philippa dropped the scythe, covered her face with her bloody hands, fell to her knees, and burst into tears.

She heard voices, felt hands touching her gently.

Then she heard a little boy's voice, Edmund's voice, and it brought her face out of her hands, for he said, "Stop those silly female tears."

She looked at him, and, surprising herself, smiled. "You are a mean little boy, with no more sympathy than a bug, but the sight of you right this moment pleases me."

"Aye," Edmund said. "That's because you're a female and need to be protected. You're filthy and covered with blood. Come along."

"Go with the boy," Gorkel said. "You did well, mistress, very well."

"There's another man, Gorkel. I killed his partner — he's in the stables — but the other man ran. I don't know who he was, but I would recognize his voice."

"It was probably the cistern keeper, a scurvy ruffian," Gorkel said. "He's been hanging about the steward. Aye, I'll have him fetched, and the master can see to his punishment when he returns."

"What about him?" Old Agnes screeched, pointing at Prink. "He's a filthy traitor!"

The weaver was swaying on his feet, looking sick and afraid as Gorkel advanced on him.

"Leave him be," Philippa called. "Don't kill him, Gorkel. He's just stupid and foolish from his illness. Leave him be."

"I'll give him a taste of pain," Gorkel said. "Just a little taste of pain so he'll remember not to make another mistake like this one."

Philippa watched him lift the weaver high above the floor and shake him like a mongrel. Then he sent his fist into the weaver's stomach, dropping him, kicking his ribs, and saying softly, "Ye touch the mistress again, ye say one word out of the side of yer mouth to her, and I'll kick ye until yer ass comes out yer ears."

Philippa turned away. Edmund took her hand. "Come along, Philippa. I'll take you to your chamber."

Edmund was whistling as he walked beside her up the solar stairs.

*Wolffeton Castle, Cornwall*

Graelam de Moreton wiped the sweat from his brow and greeted his visitor. "Aye, Burnell, 'tis a pleasure to see you again. Is our king well? And Eleanor? Is our kingdom healthy?"

The two men spoke as Burnell, weary to the tips of his worn leather boots, trudged beside the lord of Wolffeton Castle. He was met by Graelam's wife, Lady Kassia, a charming, slight lady with large eyes and a laughing mouth. He found her delightful but wondered how such a small female dealt with the huge warrior that was her husband.

"What brings you here, Burnell?" Graelam asked finally, waiting for their guest to refresh himself with a bit of the remaining excellent Aquitaine wine.

"Actually, my lord, 'tis a mission for the king. He wishes your advice."

Graelam's dark brows shot upward. "Edward wants *me* to advise *him?* Come, Burnell, 'tis nearly May and the king must want to march against the Welsh or the Scots, and I imagine he wants more men and more money for a campaign. Come, now, and tell me the truth —"

" 'Tis true, my lord. The king has a daughter and he wants to find her a husband, one here in Cornwall."

"But Edward's daughters are far too young, and the king couldn't want an alliance with only a baron," Lady Kassia protested.

"His daughter isn't a princess, my lady," Burnell said to Kassia, who was sitting in her husband's vast chair. Graelam was standing beside her. It was then that Burnell noticed that she was heavy with child.

"What is she, then?"

"Kassia, my love," Graelam said, grinning down at her, "methinks I scent a royal indiscretion. Edward must have been quite young, Burnell."

" 'Tis true. Her name is Philippa de Beauchamp. She's nearly eighteen and 'tis past time for her to be wedded."

"De Beauchamp! But Lord Henry's daughter —"

"She's the king's illegitimate daughter, my lord, raised by Lord Henry as his own."

Both Graelam and Kassia were staring with fascinated eyes at the king's secretary. Slowly Robert Burnell gave them all the facts and the king's request. ". . . So you see, my lord, the king wants a man who won't try to bleed him, but also a man of honor and strength here in Cornwall."

Graelam was frowning. He said nothing.

Burnell, hot and tired, said with some desperation, "He wants you to give him a man who would be worthy of his daughter's hand, my lord, so —"

"I may know the man the king seeks," Graelam said with his first spark of enthusiasm, and Kassia saw the evil intent in her husband's eyes.

"You do?" she asked, staring at him.

"Aye, mayhap I do."

"His present rank isn't important, my lord. The king will make him an earl."

"An earl, you say? 'Tis something to think about. You will remain until tomorrow, Burnell?"

Robert Burnell would have happily remained in a soft feather mattress for a week. After visiting Lord Graelam, he would have to stop at Beauchamp and speak to Lord Henry and tell him, hopefully, that there would be a groom for Philippa shortly.

"Good. I will tell you my opinion on the morrow. Aye, advice for the king."

That night, Graelam was laughing heartily in bed beside his wife. Kassia was chiding him sharply. "You cannot, Graelam! Truly, you cannot!"

"I told you I would bring that whoreson down, Kassia. This will do it." And Graelam continued to laugh, finally holding his belly.

"But Dienwald despises authority — you know that. His father-in-law would be the King of England! Dienwald wouldn't accept it. He'd travel to the Pope to plead for his freedom, or escape to the Tartars, or even pray to the devil if need be. And to be made an earl. Dienwald disdains such trappings. He hates respectability and responsibility and tending to his name and his holdings and his *worth*. Oh, my lord, he bested you, but this revenge would make him miserable forever. He could no longer raid when it pleased him. He could no longer brag about being a rogue and a scoundrel. He is proud of his reputation! And what if the girl is a hag? What then?"

Graelam laughed harder.

Kassia just looked at her husband and thought about the casks of Aquitaine wine that Dienwald had probably stolen from the wrecked ship. She thought of Dienwald as an earl, his father-in-law the King of England himself. Hadn't Burnell mentioned that the girl, Philippa, looked every inch a Plantagenet?

Kassia started laughing herself. "He'll murder the both of us," she said, "if Edward takes your advice."

It was the middle of the night and Philippa was dreaming that she felt a warm hand lightly stroking through her hair, rubbing her scalp, and it felt wonderful. Then a man's mouth was touching her cheek, her jaw, nipping at her throat, licking over her lips; then a man's tongue was stroking rhythmically over her lower lip. She sighed and stretched onto her back. She loved the dream, cherished it, held it tightly, now feeling the man's fingers caressing her breasts, his callused fingertips stroking her nipples.

When the man's fingers rubbed over her ribs, curved in with her waist, then stroked her belly, her muscles contracted with pleasure. Then he was pressing her legs open and delving through her hair to find her, and she sighed, then moaned deeply, wanting more, lifting her hips, and wanting, wanting . . .

She opened her eyes to see the man wasn't a dream. It was Dienwald, and she looked at him until she could make out his features in the darkness. He looked tired and intent and he was breathing hard as he stared down at her.

"It wasn't a dream," she said.

"No, wench, it wasn't a dream. You feel like the softest of God's creatures." She felt his fingers caressing her flesh and knew she was wet beneath his fingers and swelling, her flesh heating. Then he eased his middle finger inside her, and she cried out, jerking up, feelings she'd never before imagined welling up inside her.

"Hush," he said, and pressed his palm against her belly to push her down again, and then his finger eased more deeply within her, and more deeply still. "Does that pain you, wench? I can feel you stretching for my finger. Ah, there it is, your badge of innocence. Your precious maidenhead. Intact, ready for my assault." He shuddered, his whole body heaving, and for a moment he laid his face against her, his finger still inside her, not moving now, soothing and warm. "You almost died tonight, Gorkel told me. I'm sorry, Philippa. I thought you well-protected — from yourself, truth be told — yet my trusted man was an enemy of the worst sort. I'm so sorry." He kissed her belly, licked her soft flesh, and his finger pressed more deeply into her, testing the strength of her maidenhead. He moaned, a jagged raw sound, and withdrew his finger.

He came over her and his mouth covered her, and Philippa, excited and quiescent in the dark of the night, yielded completely to him.

His tongue was inside her mouth, tasting her, savoring her, and she touched the tip of his tongue with hers. Then, once again, without warning, he rolled off her, leaving her abruptly.

"Please," Philippa whispered, holding her hand toward him. She felt nearly frantic with longing — for what, she knew not.

"Nay, wench," he said, sounding as though he'd been running hard. "Nay, 'tis just that I've been without a woman for a week and my loins are fit to burst with lust. Get you back to sleep."

She cried out at his words, hating them, hating him for making her realize yet again that she was nothing to him, nothing but a vessel, nothing more. She heard him leave the chamber and slam the door.

She turned onto her side and wept, her sobs a faint sound in the quiet darkness.

When Dienwald returned some time later, she pretended to be asleep. He made no move to touch her when he climbed into the bed beside her. She listened to his breathing even into sleep and knew she had to leave him and St. Erth.

As soon as she could find a way.

# 11

The next morning, Philippa awoke to the slap of a hand on her naked buttocks and lurched up.

"You're awake. 'Tis time I had some answers from you, wench. I leave my castle in fine fettle, only to return and find my steward dead and everything in an uproar. Get you up and come into the great hall."

Dienwald smacked her bottom one more time and left her alone. She lay there wondering what would happen to her if she cracked his head open with a scythe. The cockscomb.

She rolled onto her side and tried to go back to sleep, but it was impossible.

In the great hall, Dienwald was staring at his fool, stretched on his side on the floor. "Tell me again what happened, Crooky, and say it in words that make sense. No rhymes, no songs."

Crooky looked at Dienwald. His master was tired, ill-tempered, and had obviously ridden back to St. Erth in haste. Why? To see the mistress? He'd missed the girl?

Crooky hadn't seen him the previous evening when he'd stormed into the hall yelling his head off because the porter had screeched about Philippa being covered with blood and dead bodies everywhere.

Crooky grinned at his master. "Methinks you grow cockhard, master."

"I grow what? Listen, you damnable mule offal, I don't —"

"You caught the bastards who burned the crops?"

Dienwald tore into a piece of bread with his strong teeth. "Aye, three of them, but curse their tongues, they were already dead and couldn't tell me who'd sent them."

" 'Twas Walter de Grasse, the slimy serpent."

"Aye, in all likelihood." Dienwald chewed another piece of bread, not speaking again until he'd swallowed. Then he bellowed, "Margot! Bring me ale!"

"Let the mistress tell you of her adventures, master. 'Twill make your hair stand up in fright."

"You dare to call the wench 'mistress'? It's mad! I should kick you —"

Crooky quickly rolled away from his master's foot and came up onto his knees. "She's good for St. Erth," he said. "And stouthearted. She saved herself."

Margot brought the ale, giving Dienwald a wary look as she served him. "What's the matter with you?" he demanded, then waved an irritable hand when she paled at his words.

He turned back to the hapless fool. "You were here, damn your ears! I want to hear what happened."

"Oh, leave him alone," came Philippa's irritated voice from behind him. "The last thing I want to listen to is Crooky singing at dawn."

Dienwald turned about and eyed her. It required all his will not to smile at her. It took him only a few moments more to tamp down on the wild relief he felt upon seeing her whole and ill-tempered. " 'Tis about time you deign to come to me," he said. "You look like a snabbly hag."

Actually, she looked tousled and soft and very, very sweet. He eased back into his chair, stretching out his legs in front of him, folding his hands over his chest. He'd fetched her another old gown worn by his first wife, this one a pale gray, frayed and baggy. It stopped a good three inches above her ankles.

"Thank you for the gown. There is no overtunic?"

"I didn't even have the chance to see you

in the other gown I gave you. This one doesn't fit you at all, but there was nothing else. And don't whine. Why haven't you yet sewn yourself a new gown and overtunic?"

"I should have," she said, wanting to kick him. He'd touched her and caressed her and kissed her, then left her to find himself another female vessel. And now he was baiting her and insulting her. But she also remembered how he'd laid his head on her stomach and told her how he'd been afraid when he'd heard what had happened. Had she dreamed that? He didn't seem at all concerned about her this morning, just bad-tempered. She raised her chin. "I think I shall begin immediately." She picked up a piece of bread and began to chew it with enraging indifference.

"Tell me what happened, wench. Now."

She chanced to look down at her wrists. They were bruised and raw but there wasn't much pain now.

Dienwald hadn't yet noticed her wrists; now he did, and sucked in his breath. His irritation rose to alarming heights. "I don't believe this," he bellowed at her. "I leave my keep, and look what happens. Have Margot wrap up your wrists." He added several lurid curses, then sat back, closing his eyes. "Tell me what happened whilst I was gone."

Philippa looked at him closely, decided he'd calmed himself sufficiently, and said, "Not all that much happened at the beginning. We spun nearly all the wool into cloth, and now we've gotten most of it dyed. The sewing has begun, just yesterday. Oh, just one small happening out of the ordinary — Gorkel had to break your steward's neck, but Alain deserved it. I have determined that you are the most pious of saints when compared to the loathsome departed Alain."

"I see. Now, before I take you to my chamber and thrash you, you will tell me why my loathsome steward wanted you dead."

Philippa just shrugged. She knew it infuriated him, and, unable to stop herself, she shrugged again.

He rose swiftly from his chair, walked to her and grabbed her beneath the arms, and lifted her off the bench. He held her eye-to-eye. "Tell me what happened, else you'll be very sorry."

"What will you do? Will you continue what you did to me in my sleep during the night?"

A spasm of some emotion Philippa couldn't identify crossed his face; then his expression was closed again. "Give over,

Philippa, give over. I am weary and wish to know what happened."

His serious voice, empty of amusement, brought her eyes open. "I'll tell you. Put me down."

Dienwald very slowly lowered her to her bare feet. He walked back to his chair, pressing his hand against the small of his back. "Your weight strains even my strength," he remarked to the black-beamed ceiling, and sat down again, waving his hand at her.

She told him of what she'd found in the steward's chamber. "I didn't trust him, even from that first day I was here. He hated me, and there was no reason I could see. Well, my lord, he's been cheating you all the time he's been here, and when he held the knife to my throat in your chamber, he admitted it and insulted you and me and said he was going to kill me."

He made a strangled sound but said nothing. Philippa, swallowing against the remembered fear, spoke in a clipped and precise voice, emotionlessly telling him of coming to in the stables, of killing one of the men with the scythe, of running into the great hall, and of Gorkel's killing of the steward. "Alain also sent his men out to take the other wool wagon. He had the farmers killed. It was from them that he learned that

I could read and write and that I'd acted as my father's steward."

Dienwald said nothing for a very long time. He merely looked beyond her, over her right shoulder, she thought, as she waited tensely for him to say something, anything. To show concern perhaps for her safety, as he had in the dark of the night. To tell her of his undying gratitude. To tell her that he was glad she wasn't hurt, to tell her he was sorry it had happened. To exclaim over the perfidy of his steward. To thank her for her diligence, her concern for him and for St. Erth. To tell . . .

He exploded into her thoughts, nearly yelling, "What in the name of St. Andrew am I to do now? I have no steward because you ensured that he'd die, curse you! Poor Gorkel had no choice but to dispatch him, and 'tis all your fault!"

Philippa stared at him, nearly choking on the piece of buttered bread in her mouth. "He was *cheating* you! Didn't you attend me? He was a filthy knave! Didn't you hear me? Don't you care?"

Dienwald merely shrugged, causing her to leap to her feet and throw the remaining bread at his head. He ducked, but some of the sweet butter hit his cheek in a yellow streak.

"You ungrateful fool! You —"

"Enough!" Dienwald rose from his chair, wiping the butter from his face with his hand.

"I repeat, wench, what will I do for a steward?"

She stuck out her chin, squared her shoulders, and readied herself for his insults. "I will be your steward."

It didn't take him long to produce the insults she expected at her announcement. "You? A female? A female who has no more sense than to spy on a man and be caught and nearly butchered for her stupidity? Ha, wench, ha!"

"That's not true. I was careful when I searched through his chamber. I saw him ride away before I went into the room. It was just bad fortune that he had spies and one of them saw me. And what about his dishonesty? You, so astute, such a keen and intelligent male, didn't even begin to realize he was robbing you down to your last tunic, to your last hay straw, to your last . . . You, a brave male, didn't realize anything at all. You might even, now give a thought to the fact that Alain's spies are very likely still here. Ha!"

"Females don't have the brains to resolve problems and keep correct records of things."

Philippa just stared at him, her bile spent, her rage simmering down to weary resentment.

"Females," Dienwald continued, waxing fluent now, "don't know the first thing about organizing facts and making decisions. Females have one useful role only, and that is —"

"Don't you dare say it!"

"They should see to the weaving and the sewing and the cooking. They are useful for the soft things, the things a man needs to ease him after he's toiled a long day with both his body and his brain."

"You're a fool," Philippa said, and without another word, for she'd spent even her anger now, turned on her bare heel and strode toward the oak doors.

"Don't you dare leave, wench!"

She speeded up, and was through the door within moments. She raced across the inner bailey, dodging chickens and Tupper, who squealed with berserk joy at the sight of her. She felt his wet snout against her ankle as she ran. Children called to her, women stared, and men just shook their heads, particularly when the master emerged from the great hall, his face a storm, his temper there for all to see.

"Come back here, you stupid wench!"

Philippa turned to see him striding toward her. "By the saints, you are a miserable clod!" She ran now, holding the frayed gown to her knees. Her legs were long and strong and she ran quickly — right into Gorkel.

"Mistress," Gorkel said. "What goes?"

"I go," she said, and jerked away from his huge hands. "Release me, Gorkel!"

"Hold her, Gorkel. Then, if you wish, you can watch me thrash her hide."

Gorkel gave a mournful sigh and shook his ugly head. "Ye shouldn't prick t' master."

"He's a fool and I'd like to kick him hard."

Dienwald winced at that mental imagine. At the same time, he felt an unwanted sting of distress at her words, but shook it off. "Come with me," he said, and grabbed her arm.

"Nay."

He stopped, looked from Gorkel back to Philippa, who was pale with fury. "You'll but hurt my back if you force me to carry you again."

Philippa drew back her right arm and swung with all her strength. Her fist struck his jaw so sharply that his head snapped back. He lost his balance and would have gone down in humiliation into the dirt had not Gorkel grabbed him and held him until he regained his balance.

Dienwald looked at Philippa as he stroked his sore jaw. "You're strong," he said at last. "You're really very strong."

She raised her fist and shook it at him. "Aye, and I'll bring you down again if you try anything."

Dienwald looked beyond her, his eyes widening. He shook his head, and Philippa snapped about to see what or who was behind her. In the next instant, she was flung over his shoulder, head down, her hair nearly trailing the ground as she yelled and screeched like hens caught in a rainstorm.

He laughed, and strode back toward the great hall. He took the solar stairs, aware that all his people were watching and talking about them and laughing, and the men, ah, they were shouting the most explicit and wondrous advice to him.

When he reached the solar he tossed her on her back onto his bed. "Now," he said. "Now."

"Now what?"

"I suppose you expect me to give you wages?"

She stared at him, her brain fuzzy from hanging upside down.

"Well?"

"Wages for what?"

"For being my steward, of course. Have you no brain, wench?" Suddenly he smacked his palm to his forehead. "I cannot believe what I'm saying. A female who has so little sense that she escapes in a gown reeking of a moat in a wagon of wool. And this female wants to control all that happens at St. Erth."

"My father trusted me." Philippa came up onto her elbows. She looked wistfully toward the empty chamber pot on the floor beside the bed. Old Agnes had seen that it was mended.

Dienwald said absently, "Don't do it, wench, else you'll regret it. Now, just be quiet. I must think."

"The pain it must cause you!"

He ignored her remark, saying finally, "I suppose you will demand to sleep in the steward's chamber as well as do the work there."

"Aye, of course. Certainly. To be free of you is —"

He grabbed her arms and kissed her hard. She didn't fight him. It didn't occur to her to do anything but ask him to kiss her again.

"Did you not beg me last night, wench?" he said when he raised his head. "Beg me to take you? You wanted me to relieve you of your maidenhead, didn't you? Well, sleep in your cold bed by yourself. You'll miss me, you'll want my hands and mouth on you, you know it. But enough. I won't miss you. I will sleep sweetly as a babe. Now, straighten yourself and sew yourself something to wear. I can't abide the way you look." He dropped her back onto the bed and strode from his bedchamber.

Nearly an hour later, her hair combed and fastened at the nape of her neck with a piece of cloth, bathed and sweet-smelling, Philippa visited the steward's chamber — now her chamber, she amended to herself. She arranged papers and moved the table some inches to the right. She asked Margot to bring fresh rushes for the floor, then returned to Dienwald's bedchamber. He was in bed, asleep, snoring loudly. On the floor beside the bed were her blood-stained clothes. She'd looked at them briefly, hoping they could be saved, but saw now that it was impossible.

Then she looked at Dienwald. He was sprawled on his stomach, one arm hanging over the side of the bed. Clutched in his hand was the nearly finished tunic she'd sewn for him. Philippa slowly eased it out of his fingers and shook out the wrinkles.

"I should burn it," she said, and left the

chamber, needle and thread in her other hand.

*Crandall Keep, near Badger's Cross, Cornwall*

Lord Henry wiped his hand across his sweating brow and listened to his destrier blow loudly. The trip had been long and hot and wet and altogether miserable. Three days to get to this damned keep, and what if he were wrong? What if Philippa hadn't run here to her cousin? He took a deep drink from the water skin and handed it back to his servant. His men had just spotted Crandall Keep, where his nephew Sir Walter de Grasse was castellan. All appeared calm. Lord Henry motioned his men forward again.

Crandall was a prosperous keep, he saw, noting the green fields that surrounded the low thick walls. But its defenses were meager, the reason being that Crandall paid obeisance to Lord Graelam de Moreton of Wolffeton. An attack on Crandall would mean swift and awful retribution from Lord Graelam.

Philippa had to be here, she simply had to be. Lord Henry wiped his brow again. There was no other place for her to escape to. She was either here or she was dead. His farmers had been found dead, all the wool wagons disappeared, the guards gone — fled or dead, he didn't know. No sign of his daughter. He'd put off Burnell, the king's tenacious chancellor and secretary, but the man wasn't stupid and would want to see Philippa. He would want to give a personal report to the king. He would want to tell Lord Henry the name of the man the king had selected to be Philippa's husband. Lord Henry raised his eyes to the heavens. Philippa had to be here with her cousin, she had to be.

Sir Walter de Grasse was playing draughts in the hall with his mistress, Britta. She knew the game well, as well as she knew him. She always managed to lose just when he became frustrated, a ploy that pleased Sir Walter. He was informed that his uncle, Lord Henry de Beauchamp, was approaching Crandall. What was his uncle doing here? He thanked the powers that he'd returned two days before from the raid on the southern lands of that whoreson Dienwald de Fortenberry. He'd lost three men, curse the luck. But he'd burned the crops and razed peasants' huts and killed the villeins. All in all it had been worth the price the three men had paid. De Fortenberry must be grinding his teeth by now. The bastard was helpless; he would know who was behind the attack. Oh, he could guess, but Lord Graelam wouldn't act against him, Walter, unless there was proof, and Walter was too smart for that. Luckily the three men had died before Dienwald could question them.

Sir Walter frowned and lightly patted Britta's cheek in dismissal. She removed the draught board and herself, giving him a look over her shoulder designed to excite him. Walter frowned after her. He wished he'd had some warning of his uncle's visit. The keep could be in better condition, fresh rushes strewn on the floor and the like, but it was well enough. It wasn't his overlord, Lord Graelam, thank the saints.

The two men greeted each other. Lord Henry had never been particularly fond of his wife's nephew. Walter was thin and tall and his nose was very long and narrow. His eyes were shrewd and cold and he had no sense of humor. He hated well, but to Lord Henry's knowledge, he'd never loved well.

As for Walter, he thought his uncle by marriage a fat buffoon with more wealth than he deserved. He should have been Lord Henry's heir, but there were the two stupid girls instead. When they were finally alone, Lord Henry wasted no more time. "Your cousin Philippa has run away from Beauchamp. Is she here?"

Now, this was a surprise, Walter thought, staring at his uncle. Slowly he shook his head. "Nay, I haven't seen Philippa since she was a gangly girl with hair hanging to her knees."

"She's no longer gangly. She's nearly eighteen, long since ready to be wedded."

Suddenly, to Walter's surprise, Lord Henry lowered his face into his hands and began to sob. Not knowing what to do, Walter merely stared at his uncle's bowed head, saying nothing.

"I fear she's dead," Lord Henry said once he'd regained control.

"Tell me what happened."

Lord Henry saw no reason not to tell Walter the entire truth. After all, it hardly mattered now. He spoke slowly, sorrow filling his voice.

"She's *what?*"

"I said that Philippa is the king's illegitimate daughter. He is at this moment selecting a husband for her."

Walter could only stare. Damn! What had happened to the girl?

Lord Henry soon enlightened him about the rest of it.

"I know not who killed the farmers or who stole the wool, but Philippa is now likely as dead as the farmers."

Lord Henry wiped his eyes. His sweet Philippa, his stubborn-as-a-mule Philippa. Dead. He couldn't bear it. He'd lost a daughter, a steward, and, most terrifying, he'd lost the king's illegitimate progeny. It wasn't to be borne.

"I shouldn't be too certain, Uncle," Walter said, stroking his rather pointed chin gently. "I hear things, you know. I can find out things too. Return to Beauchamp and let me try to discover what happened to my dear little cousin. I will send you word immediately, of course, if I find her."

Lord Henry left Crandall the following day, Sir Walter's assurances ringing hollow in his ears. Walter had already dispatched men to scout out information. Empty words, Lord Henry thought, but they had lightened his burden, if just for a little while.

As for Sir Walter, he was rubbing his hands together by the following afternoon. The cistern keeper of St. Erth had escaped to Crandall, arriving just that morning with news that Walter's steward, Alain, was dead, unmasked by a big female with lavish tits and bountiful hair whose name was Philippa. Walter nearly swallowed his tongue when he realized how very close Philippa had been to dying by the steward's order.

Now he knew where his dear cousin was, his dearest cousin, the girl he would wed as soon as he got his hands on her. Oh, aye, she'd want him. After all, in all likelihood she'd been on her way to him when she'd been captured by that miserable Dienwald de Fortenberry. Walter could just imagine how Dienwald had treated the gently bred girl — ravishing her, humiliating her, shaming her . . . But why and how had she uncovered the steward's perfidy if she'd been thus shamed?

It didn't matter. The cistern keeper had probably confused things. Walter would marry the king's illegitimate daughter. She was his gift horse and he would have her. He prayed she wasn't carrying de Fortenberry's bastard in her womb. Perhaps he could rid her of the brat — if there was one — when he got his hands on her.

Walter sighed with the pleasure of his contemplations. At last he would be somebody to reckon with. He would starve out de Fortenberry and have him torn limb from limb. He would regain St. Erth, the inheritance he should have had, the inheritance his father had lost to Dienwald's father so many years before. He would spit on Lord Graelam — behind his back, of course — and leave this pigsty Crandall. He would be overlord of all Cornwall and Lord Graelam would be his vassal, with his father-in-law's agreement and assistance. He would almost be a royal duke! He would then look south to Brittany. Aye, his grandfather had held lands there, now stolen away by that whoreson de Bracy of Brittany. Aye, with the king's help, with the king's money, with the king's men, he would take back what was his, all of what should have been his in the first place. And he could add to it if he were wily and cunning.

Sir Walter hummed as he made his plans. He wondered briefly what Philippa looked like. If she were a true Plantagenet, he thought, she must be beautiful. The cistern keeper spoke of her tits and hair. What color? he wondered. He liked big breasts on a woman. He couldn't let himself forget, though, that she was a bastard, after all, and thus tainted, despite her royal blood. He wouldn't forget that, nor would he allow her to forget it. Aye, she would welcome him, her dear cousin. After her doubtless brutal treatment at de Fortenberry's hands, she'd come leaping into his waiting arms.

Philippa sat in the steward's chamber, her head bowed, entering inventories of the crops in a ledger. Her back hurt from sitting so long, but there was much to be done, much to be corrected and adjusted. Alain had created fiction, and it must be set aright, and quickly.

Dienwald's new tunic of deep blue, so soft that it slithered over the flesh, was finished and lay spread smooth over the back of the only other chair in the small chamber. She was a fine needlewoman, and the thread, thankfully, was stout.

She looked up then and smiled upon the tunic. He would look very nice wearing it, very nice indeed, fit to meet the king thus garbed. She hoped she'd made the shoulders big enough and tapered the waist inward enough, for he was lean. She hoped he thought the color nice and . . .

She stopped herself in mid-thought. Here she was thinking like the mistress of St. Erth again. As if this were her home, as if this were where she belonged. She'd entertained no thought of escape in more hours than she cared to reckon.

She laid down the quill and slowly rose, pushing back from the table. She was nothing more than his servant. For the past two days she'd worked endless hours in this small airless chamber, and for what?

For the joy of wearing an ill-fitting gown belonging to his long-dead first wife? For the joy of helping him, the man who'd lain atop of her, his finger easing into her body, making her hot and frantic and . . .

"Stop it, you stupid wench!"

"I thought your name was Philippa."

She could have gladly removed her own tongue at that moment. Dienwald stood in the doorway, amusement lighting his eyes.

" 'Twas a private exhortation," she said. "It had naught to do with you."

"As you will, wench. How goes the work?" He waved toward the stacks of foolscap on the table.

"It is an abominable mess."

"I imagined as much."

"You do not read," she said, and unknowingly, her voice softened just a bit.

"Nay, not very much. 'Twas not deemed important by my sire. Few read or cipher — you know that. Why ask you?"

She shrugged. "I merely wondered. You insist upon Edmund's learning from Father Cramdle."

"Aye. The world changes, and men must change with it. It is something Edmund must know if he is to make his way."

Philippa had seen no sign of change in her brief lifetime, but she didn't disagree. She realized belatedly that she was staring at him, hunger in her look, and that he was already aware of it.

He grinned at her. "Come have your dinner. That is why I am here, to fetch you."

She nodded and rounded the table. He caught her hand and pulled her against him. "You miss me, wench?"

She more than missed him. She lay awake at night, thinking of how much she wanted him lying beside her.

"Of course not. You are arrogant and filled with conceit, my lord."

"You don't miss my hands stroking you?"

One arm kept her pressed against his chest. She felt his other arm lower, his fingers parting her, pressing inward. She tried to draw away — a paltry effort, they both knew.

Her breathing hitched. She felt the heat of his fingers, the heat of herself, and there was only the thin wool of her gown between the two.

Then he released her, turned, saying over his shoulder, "Come and have your dinner now, wench."

"I'm not a —" she yelled, then stopped.

He was gone, the door closed quietly behind him.

That evening she learned from Northbert that the cistern keeper had escaped but that several men were out searching for him.

"Alain worked not by himself, so thinks the master," Northbert said, then wiped his bread in the thick beef gravy on his trencher.

" 'Tis a varmint named de Grasse the cistern keeper has run to," Crooky announced, his mouth bulging with boiled capon.

Philippa grew instantly still. "Walter de Grasse?" she asked slowly. Her heart was pounding, her hand squeezing a honey-and-almond tart.

Dienwald heard her and turned, saying, "What know you of de Grasse?"

"Why, he's my cousin," she said without thinking.

# 12

Dienwald's face was pale, his eyes dark and wild. "Your *cousin?* Lord Henry's *nephew?*"

He didn't sound angry, merely incredulous, and Philippa felt emboldened to add freely, "Nay, Walter is my mother's nephew. My father doesn't like him, but I do." She raised her chin, knowing that Dienwald wouldn't be able to keep his opinion to himself, and that it would be contrary to hers.

"I don't believe this," was all he said. He rose, slamming his chair back, and left the great hall.

Crooky looked at Philippa and shook his head.

"He is always slamming out of here like a sulking child!"

"Nay," Gorkel said. "He leaves because he is angry and he doesn't wish to strike you."

"Strike me? I have done nothing. What is wrong with him this time? I cannot help that Sir Walter is my kin."

"It matters not," Crooky said. "You, mistress, you say that you like this serpent, this vicious brute . . . well, what do you expect the master to do?"

"But —"

Crooky cleared his throat, and Philippa closed her eyes against the discordant sounds that emerged loud and clear from the fool's mouth:

> A villain, a coward,
> A knave without shame.
> De Grasse maims and he destroys
> And takes no blame.
> He lies and he steals
> And he slithers out to kill.
> My sweet master will slay him,
> Come what will.

"Why do you keep calling him 'sweet master'?" Philippa asked, irritated and frightened and wondering all the while what her cousin had done to earn such enmity.

Crooky gave her a small salute with a dirty hand and said with a wink, "Think you not that he is a sweet master? The females hereabouts think him more than sweet. They like him to bed them, to push apart their thighs and —"

"Hush!"

"Forgive me, mistress. I forget you are yet a maid and unknowing of the ways of men and women."

Edmund, hearing this outpouring from Crooky, frowned at Philippa and said, "Are you truly a maid? Still? I know you were before, but . . . You still aren't my father's mistress, even after all the times he's carried you off to his chamber? You said that —"

"I'm not his mistress. I'm naught but his drudge, his captive . . ." Philippa ground to a halt. She was also St. Erth's steward. "Why aren't you wearing your new tunic? You don't like it? I know that it fits. Margot told me it did. 'Tis well made, and the color suits you. And the hose and shoes. Why don't —"

"I don't like them. Besides, my father doesn't wear anything new. Until he makes me, then I'll stay the way I am."

"You are such a stubborn little irkle."

" 'Tis better than being a maypole."

"Edmund, if you do not wear your new tunic on the morrow, I will come to your chamber, hold you down, and put it on you. Do you understand me?"

"You won't!"

She gave him a look to shrivel any male. He ducked his head, and she saw that he was quite dirty, his fingers and fingernails coated with grime. He looked like a villein's child; he looked like he'd been wallowing in mud with Tupper. She had to speak to Dienwald about this. He forced his son to learn to read and write and cipher but allowed him to look like a ragged little beggar.

"Yes," she said, "yes, I will. And you will bathe, Master Edmund. When was the last time your hands were in soap and water?"

"There ban't be any soap, mistress," Old Agnes shouted to Philippa. The old woman had amazing hearing when it suited her. "No one thought to make it," she added, quick to defend herself should the need arise. "The master said aught."

Philippa called back, "But that is absurd. I have used soap in the master's chamber."

"Aye, thass the last of it. The master likely didn't realize it was the last of it."

"We will make soap on the morrow," Philippa said. "And you, you pigsty of a boy, will be the first to use it."

"Nay, I won't!"

"We'll see."

Philippa had much to consider that night when she closed the door to her small chamber. She'd just pulled the frayed tunic over her head and laid it carefully over the back of the single chair when she heard his voice say softly, "Put it back on. I don't wish to enjoy you here. I want you in my bed, where you can warm me when it grows cold near dawn."

"I'm not your mistress! Go away, Dienwald!"

"I've already enjoyed a woman this night. I have no pressing need for another, be she even as soft and big and, in truth, as eager as you. Come along, now."

Her eyes had adjusted to the dimness of the chamber and she saw him now, holding her discarded gown, his hand stretched out to her. She was standing there quite naked, just staring at him. Philippa grabbed the gown and pulled it over her head. In the next moment he had her hand and was pulling her after him, out of the steward's chamber.

There were still a dozen or so people milling about the great hall, and two score more sleeping on pallets lining the walls. "Hush," he said, and pulled her after him. Everyone saw. No one said a thing. Not a single man yelled advice. Philippa wanted to kick him, kick *all* of them, hard.

She tugged and pulled and jerked, but it was no use. He turned on her then, frowning, and said, "No more carrying you. You come willingly or I will drag you by the hair."

"You will pay for this, Dienwald, you surely will." She gave him an evil smile. "I will send word to my dear cousin Sir Walter — aye, and I'll tell him what a cruel savage you are, a barbarian, a —"

"I'm already paying, wench. But I beg of you not to tell your precious cousin that I'm a ravisher of innocent maids. Nay, do not, even though it would please you mightily were I to take you." It was at that instant she realized he'd drunk more ale than usual. He didn't slur his words like Lord Henry did, nor was his nose flaming red. He walked very carefully, like a man who knows he's drunk but doesn't want anyone else to know. She wasn't at all afraid of him, drunk or sober. She found that she was rather anticipating what he would do.

Once inside his bedchamber, Dienwald went through the now-familiar routine of pushing her onto the bed. "Now," he said, looking down at her, "now you can remove the gown. It is ugly and offends me. Haven't you yet finished something for yourself?"

She lay there staring up at him, not moving, marshaling her strength. "I made you a tunic. 'Tis down in my chamber."

He paused. "Did you really finish it? It disappeared, and I believed you'd destroyed it in your ire at me."

"I should have." She began inching away to the far side of the bed. "You have drunk too much ale."

"Philippa," he said quietly, "there are no

more gowns, not another stitch of anything for you to wear. Take care of the only one you have, else you will be naked. Aye, I have drunk more than I usually do, but 'tis done. Take off the gown now."

"Blow out the candle first."

"All right." He snuffed the candle, throwing the chamber into gloom. Moonlight came through the one window, slivering clear light directly across the bed. There was nothing she could do about it. Still, she wasn't at all afraid of him or of what he could do to her if he so chose. Philippa eased out of the gown and laid it at the foot of the bed. Then she slid beneath the single blanket.

"It's deep spring now," Dienwald said, and she knew he was taking off his clothes as he spoke, even though she wasn't looking at him. His voice deepened, grew absent and thoughtful. He didn't sound at all drunk. "That's what we call it here. Deep spring. Very late April and early May. My grandmother told me of deep spring when I was but a boy, told me this was what men called it a very long time ago when priests ruled the land and everyone worshiped the endless force of spring, the timeless renewal of spring. She said they saw the wheat shoving upward, ever upward toward the blazing gold of the sun, all the while deepening its roots into the soil, into the darkness. Opposites, this light and darkness, yet bound together, eternal and endless.

"She called it by the old Celtic words, but I cannot remember them. Whenever I say 'deep spring' now, I think about how a woman takes in a man and holds him, then empties him and yet renews him and herself with his nourishment, just as spring is infinite yet predictable in its sameness, just as spring always renews the earth, and the light and the dark exist together and complement each other." He turned to face her now. "I like thinking about you in that way — how you would empty me and renew me and yourself with my seed.

"But you are Walter de Grasse's cousin, and that makes you my enemy, not just my slave or my captive or my mistress. Nay, my enemy. I loathe the very thought of the man. I wonder, wench, should I punish you for his evil? For his wickedness? Does the foulness of his blood run in you? In your soul?"

Philippa was shaken. He'd shown her another side of himself that drew her and made her want to weep, but it had also called forth his hatred, his bitterness. Was he speaking so freely only because he'd drunk too much to keep his thoughts to himself?

"What did he do to you that you hate him so?"

"I lost much with the burning of my crops. And not just the crops, but all the people who worked them, *my* people. All of them butchered, the women ravished, the children piked on swords, the huts destroyed, burned to the raw earth. And it was your cousin who ordered it done."

"But you are not certain? You could catch no one to tell you?"

"Sir Walter de Grasse was once a landless knight. He still is, though Lord Graelam de Moreton made him castellan of Crandall, one of his keeps to the southwest of St. Erth. It is not enough for Sir Walter; he believes it his right to have more. The man hated me before I even knew of his existence. My father won St. Erth from his father in a tourney in Normandy when I was a small boy. Walter screams of dishonor and trickery. He demands back his supposed birthright. King Edward wouldn't give him heed, yet he still seeks my death and my ruin. He nearly succeeded once, not long ago, but I was saved by a beautiful artless lady who holds my loyalty and my heart, aye, even my soul. So there it is, wench. Sir Walter will do anything to destroy me, and you are his kin."

Philippa felt a lance of pain go through her. She swallowed, and licked her dry lips. "Who is this lady? How did she save you?"

Dienwald strode toward the bed then and laughed, a drunken laugh, one that was sharp yet empty, raw yet thick. She saw his body in the shaft of clear moonlight and she thought him beautiful — a strange word surely to describe a being who was sharply planed and angled and shadowed and hard, but it was so. He stood straight and tall and lean, and still he laughed, and it hurt her to listen.

Yet she wanted to hear his story, and he, free-speaking from the ale, said, "You wish her name? She is a lady, a sweet, loving, guileless lady, and her name is Kassia. She hails from Brittany. I cannot have her, though I tried."

"Why can't you?"

"She is wedded to a powerful man who is also my friend and a mighty warrior — the same overlord of your precious Walter, Lord Graelam de Moreton."

"You . . . you love her, then?"

Dienwald eased down onto the bed, lifting the blanket. She could feel the heat from his body, hear the steady rhythm of his breathing. She didn't move. He was silent for a very long time, and she believed him asleep, finally insensate from the ale he'd drunk.

"I know not of love," he said, his voice low and slurred now. "I just know of feelings and passions, and she took mine unto herself and holds them. Aye, she holds them gently and tenderly because she could do aught else. She is like that, you see. You are very different from her. She is small and delicate and fragile, yet her spirit is fierce and pure. Her smile is so sweet it makes you want to weep and protect her with your life. Aye, she came to womanhood, but she went to him — her body and her heart both went to Graelam. Go to sleep, wench. I grow weary of all this talk."

" 'Tis you who have done all the talking!"

"Go to sleep."

"I am not your enemy. I am merely your captive."

"Perhaps. Perhaps not. I will think about it. God knows, I think of little else. You are a problem that irritates like an itch that can't be reached. Perhaps I will send word to Lord Henry that I have you and will return you if I am given Sir Walter in your place. Perhaps I will demand his head upon a silver platter, like that of St. John, though Walter is about as righteous as a dung beetle. What think you? Would your esteemed father send me Sir Walter's head to have you returned?"

"My esteemed father won't even dower me. My esteemed father seeks to wed me with de Bridgport. My esteemed father probably doesn't even care that I am gone. I have told you this before. I didn't lie."

"It seems the answer is no, then. I am to be cursed with the eternal itch. What am I to do with you?"

"I am your steward."

He laughed again, low and deep, and she wanted to strike him, but didn't move. Only then did she realize she hadn't demanded that he release her and let her go free.

"Well, I suppose you cannot do a worse job of it than Alain. You will ruin me in your ignorance and innocence just as he was doing in his dishonesty and thievery. Or will you cheat me as well for your own revenge, since I stole from your father?"

"I'm not ignorant. Nor will I cheat you."

"So you say. Come here, wench. I'm cold and wish your big body to warm me."

When she didn't move, Dienwald rolled against her, drawing her to his side. "Hush and sleep," he said, his breath warm against her temple as he pressed her cheek against his chest. She smelled the sweet ale on his breath as he said, his words low and indistinct, "Do not berate me further. My brain is calm for the moment."

Nay, she thought, there was nothing she had to say now.

Philippa didn't sleep for a very long time. She thought of a lady whose name was Kassia, a lady who was small and delicate and sweet and loyal. A lady who had saved Dienwald's life.

And Philippa was a naught but an irritant that made his brain itch.

He, the drunken brute, was asleep almost at once, his snores uneven rippling sounds, like his dreams, she thought, aye, like his ale-filled dreams. She hoped monsters visited him that night. He deserved them.

*Wolffeton Castle*

Robert Burnell wrote industriously as Graelam de Moreton spoke of the man he believed would be the ideal husband for King Edward's bastard daughter.

"He is strong and young and healthy. He is comely and has excellent teeth and all his hair. He's an intelligent man who cares for his villeins and his lands. He was wedded once and has a son, Edmund, but his wife died many years ago. Is there aught else, Burnell?"

Robert accepted a flagon of milk from

Lady Kassia, smiling up at her. "The day brightens now that you are here, my lady," he said, and nearly choked on his words, so unlike him they were. But something deep inside had leapt to speak to her poetically. Mayhap it was the sweetness of her look, the soft curve of her lips as she smiled. Burnell quickly recovered his wits and sent an agonized look to Lord Graelam, but that intimidating warrior merely cocked his head at him, his look ironic.

"I thank you, sir," Kassia said. She moved slowly because of her swollen stomach, and sat down. "You are telling Robert of Dienwald's excellent qualities?"

"Aye, but there are so many, my head buzzes with the sheer number of them. What say you, Kassia?"

"Dienwald de Fortenberry is loyal and trustworthy and kind. He enjoys a good jest and loud talk, as do most men of spirit. He has wit and is facile with words. He fights well and protects what is his."

"He begins to sound like a possible saint," Burnell said, "and a man you perhaps praise more than he deserves."

"Ha!" Graelam said. "I have many times wanted to trounce him into the ground and crush his stubborn head beneath my heel and give the imbecile a kick in the ass —"

"But always," Kassia interrupted easily, "my lord and Dienwald are grinning at each other and slapping each other's shoulders in great friendship after they've decided not to kill each other. We do not overpraise him, sir, for Dienwald is a good man, sir, a very good man."

"Despite all his shortcomings," Graelam said.

"I must needs hear some of these shortcomings, my lord. Edward is sure to be suspicious if I give him only this glowing praise."

Graelam grinned, and Burnell saw the answering smile on his lady's face.

"He is stubborn as a mule, grandiose in his gestures, poor in his material belongings, and doesn't care. He revels in danger and enjoys treading the narrow path. He is crafty and sly and cunning as a fox. He isn't greedy, however, so Edward need have no fear of his coffers. As I said, he doesn't lust after earthly things. Further, there is no family, so Edward need have no worry that he will be pressed for endless favors. Dienwald is also a shrewd, ruthless, occasionally disgraceful man who will do anything to gain what he wants."

"Ah," said Burnell, writing again. "He becomes human at last, my lord."

"The lady, Philippa de Beauchamp," Kassia said. "Is she a pretty girl? Sweet-tempered?"

"I know not, save what I have been told, my lady. That is, she is a Plantagenet and thus must be considered beautiful. Since his majesty said that, it is a matter of close-held opinion and not be contested."

Kassia laughed. "And her disposition?"

"I know not. She was raised by Lord Henry and she still believes him her father. I know aught about the Lady Maude. The king, very young then, ordered that if the child survived her infancy, she be taught to read and write and cipher. She does these things well, I was told. She is perhaps too well-learned for Dienwald de Fortenberry — or mayhap for any man, no matter his rank or his leanings toward kindness and tolerance. She is possibly too set in her own ways of thinking to be content with a master's heavy hand, but truly, I know not for certain."

"Dienwald needs a woman of strong character," Graelam said. "A woman who can kick his groin one minute and salve his wounds the next."

"I travel to Beauchamp upon my return to London. I will see the girl then and report all to the king. De Fortenberry sounds like a man the king might wish for his daughter. Does the king know de Fortenberry?"

"I don't think so," Graelam said. "Edward hasn't been long in England yet, nor has he come to Cornwall to see his vassals. Dienwald is not a man to travel to London to wait upon his majesty. He is a man who holds to himself."

"I suppose that could show that he is not a leech. It is also true that his majesty has not long been home, but Edward is so overwhelmed with all the needs of England."

"Aye, and there are Wales and Scotland to be ground under the royal foot."

Robert Burnell gave Lord Graelam a thin smile. The lord was criticizing, though his tone was light and his sarcasm barely touched the ear, but Burnell wouldn't tolerate it. He harrumphed as his eyes narrowed, and said, "Did I tell you, my lord, that it was the queen herself who suggested that you be consulted? The *queen!* She advised him on his illegitimate daughter."

"The queen," Graelam said, "is a lady of honest and gracious ideals. Edward gained another part of himself when he wedded with her. Mayhap the best part."

At these last words, Lord Graelam smiled yet again at his wife as Burnell sipped his milk and looked on.

Dienwald avoided his prisoner. He remembered, the next morning, what he'd said in his drunkenness. God's ribs, had he truly gone on and on about deep spring? What nonsense! Had he truly told her of Kassia and of his feelings for her? What idiocy! He despised himself so much that he'd welcomed the violent retching. He'd been a blockhead and a loose-mouth. The next thing he knew he'd be singing to her in rhyme like his fool.

Thinking of Crooky, Dienwald wondered where he was and went in search of him. He asked Hood, the porter, but he hadn't seen the fool. He asked the armorer, who merely spat and shrugged. It was Old Agnes who told him.

"Aye, the little mistress is fitting him for a tunic, master. She told him she would have two sewn for him if he would but promise not to sing to her for a month."

"She's not little," Dienwald said, and strode away. Damn the wench's eyes, he thought, interfering in everything, sticking her big feet in where they didn't belong. If his fool's elbows stuck out of his clothes, it wasn't her mission to give him a new tunic. He looked down at his own nearly worn-through tunic. He had yet to see the one she'd made for him, sewed it herself, he remembered, and for an instant he softened. But only for that brief moment. He'd told her about Kassia, blathered on about a pagan belief that, in his mind at least, fitted cleanly with Father Cramdle's heaven and its multitude of saints. Then he'd gone on and on about Walter de Grasse, a man he'd sworn to kill, a man who'd given him no choice but to try to kill him. He'd made an ass of himself. It wasn't to be borne.

Everywhere he looked these days, the women were sitting in small groups, gossiping whilst they sewed. They'd see him and giggle, and he wanted to bellow at them that Philippa wasn't their damned mistress.

How had things gotten so twisted up? She'd jumped out of the wool wagon looking like a fright from hell itself, and then she'd proceeded to take over. It wasn't to be tolerated, despite the fact that she slept in his bed and he touched her and caressed her whenever he wished to — but it was harder now, because it was no longer the game it had started out to be. He wanted her, wanted her more than he'd ever wanted any of the women who'd always welcomed him when he'd had the need. But because the witch was still a maid and because he had somehow come to regard her as more than just another female to be treated according to his whims, he couldn't, wouldn't, suffer the obvious consequences of taking her maidenhead. He wasn't that great a fool.

His thoughts were interrupted by a shriek from his son, near the cistern by the weaving shed. Dienwald didn't worry about it until he heard Philippa yell, "Hold still or I'll break your ear! Edmund, hold still!"

Interfering again, and this time with his son. What was she doing now? He broke into a trot.

"You rancid little puffin! Hold still or I'll cuff you!"

Dienwald rounded the corner of the weaving outbuilding to see Philippa holding Edmund's arm and dousing him with a bucket of water. She quickly picked up a block of soap once she'd gotten him wet, and now she was scrubbing him with all her strength, which was considerable. Edmund was squirming and fighting and yelling, but he couldn't break away. He was also naked, his ragged clothes strewn on the ground.

Philippa wasn't unscathed, however. She was sopping wet, her hair loose from its tie at the nape of her neck and flying out in a wild nimbus around her head. Her frayed gown was plastered against her breasts. She and Edmund were standing in a growing mud puddle from all the water she was throwing on him.

Dienwald watched Philippa pull Edmund back against her, and now she scrubbed him with both hands — his face, his hair, even his elbows. He was shrieking about his burning eyes, but she just kept saying over and over, "Edmund, stop fighting me! It will go easier with you if you just hold still."

Edmund went on howling like a gutted hog.

Dienwald came closer but kept out of range of the deepening mud puddle. His people were wandering by, not paying much attention, but there was Father Cramdle, his arms crossed over his chest, looking pious and quite pleased. The pig, Tupper, was squealing near Philippa, coming close to her, then retreating quickly when threatened with flying streams of water from the bucket.

Dienwald kept quiet until Philippa had doused Edmund with another bucket of water to rinse him off. Then she wrapped him in a huge towel — one newly cut, he realized — and lifted him out of the mud and rubbed him until he was dry.

She kept him wrapped up, then lifted him onto a plank of pine and hunkered down to her knees in front of him. "Listen to me, you wretched little spittlecock. 'Tis done, and you're clean. Stay away from all this mud and filth. Now, you will go with Father Cramdle and garb yourself in your new clothes. Do you understand? And then you will have your lessons."

Dienwald heard a muffled shout of, "I hate you, Maypole!" coming from beneath the towel that covered Edmund's head.

"That's all right. At least you're clean and I don't have to watch you stuff food in your mouth with filth under your fingernails. Go, now."

Edmund's head emerged from the towel. He glowered at Philippa, but she didn't change expression. Edmund was about to retire from the field when he saw Dienwald.

"Father! Help me, look what the witch did to me!" And on and on it went as Dienwald just stood there, wanting to laugh, yet furious that Philippa had forced cleanliness upon his son, and wondering how she'd enlisted Father Cramdle in her task, for the priest was surely on her side.

Meanwhile Edmund kept shrieking and complaining, dancing about on his clean feet. Finally Dienwald, seeing that the result was to his liking, even if Philippa's pushing ways were not, said in a voice that brought his son to instant silence, "Edmund, I fancy that I hear your mother in you, which is distressing. You will go with Father Cramdle and clothe yourself. I had no idea you had become such a filthy little villein. Keep your shrieks behind your teeth or you will feel my hand."

Edmund, head down and silent as a pebble, trailed after Father Cramdle, the towel wrapped around him like a Roman toga.

"Thank you," Philippa said to Dienwald. He said nothing for a moment, just watched her try to straighten her hair, pulling it back, away from her face.

He strode up to her. "Hold still yourself, wench."

She did. He smoothed her hair and retied it with the bit of leather. He frowned at the dirty strip of hide. She needed a proper ribbon, a ribbon of bright color to complement her hair, something . . .

"You look worse than Edmund. Much worse. Like a dirty wet rag. Do something with yourself." With those pleasing sentiments duly expressed, Dienwald turned on his heel. He heard a loud whoosh, but not in time. A half-filled bucket of water struck him squarely between the shoulder blades and he went flying forward from the force of it, hitting a goat. The goat reared back and kicked Dienwald on the thigh. He cried out, grabbing his leg, which caused him to lose his balance and fell sideways into a deep patch of black mud. He came up on his hands and knees, but for a moment he didn't move. He had no intention of moving until he'd regained complete control of himself. Slowly, very slowly, he rose and turned to see Philippa standing there like a statue yet to be finished, a look of mingled horror and defiance on her face. People had stopped their conversations and were converging and staring. Then Gorkel, with a low rumbling noise, came forward, stepped squarely into the mud, and began to brush off his master.

" 'Twere an accident," Gorkel said as he grabbed gobs of mud from Dienwald's clothing and flung them away. "The mistress acts, then thinks — ye know that, master. Aye, but she's —"

"You damnable monster, don't defend her! Be still!"

Gorkel obligingly shut his mouth and continued scraping off mud.

Dienwald shook himself free of his minion's help and strode over to Philippa, who took one step back, then stopped and faced him, squaring her shoulders.

"You struck me!" The incredulity in his voice equaled the outrage. "You're a *female*, and you struck me. You threw that damned bucket at me."

"Actually," Philippa said, inching a bit further back, "it was the bucket that struck you, not I. I didn't realize I was such a marksman, or rather, that the bucket was such a marksman." Then, to her own astonishment, she giggled.

Dienwald drew several very long, very deep breaths. "If I throw you into that mud, you will have nothing to wear. You haven't yet sewed anything for yourself, have you?"

She shook her head, not giggling quite so loudly now.

He looked at her nipples, taut against the wet tunic. The material also clung to her thighs.

He smiled at her, and Philippa felt herself shrivel with humiliation. "Throw me in the mud," she said. "Do that, but please don't do what you're thinking."

"And what is that, pray? Ripping off that rag and letting my people see the shrew beneath it?"

She nodded and tried to cover her breasts with her hands. "I'm not a shrew."

"All right," he said, and without another word, moving so quickly she had only time to squeak in surprise, Dienwald grabbed her about the hips, lifted her, and strode to the black puddle and dropped her. She landed on her bottom, arms and legs flying outward, and mud spewed out in thick waves, hitting him and Gorkel. She felt it squishing over her legs, felt it seep through the gown, and she wanted to laugh at the consequences that she'd brought upon herself, but she didn't. She now had nothing to wear, nothing save this now-ruined gown.

She looked up at Dienwald, who stood in front of her, his hands on his hips. He was laughing.

Philippa saw red. Tears clogged her throat, but her fury was stronger by far. She managed to come to her feet, the mud clinging and making loud sucking noises. She flung herself at him, clutching his arms and yanking him toward her. She locked her foot behind his calf and he fell toward her, laughing all the while. Together they went down, Dienwald on top of her, Philippa flat on her back, the mud flying everywhere.

Dienwald raised himself on his hands, his fingers clenching deep into the muck. He slowly raised one mud-filled hand and opened it against her face and rubbed. She gasped and spat, but then he felt her knees against his back and he was falling sideways as she rolled against him, knocking him onto his back, pounding her fists at him, her muddy hands sliding over his face, slapping him with it.

He dimly heard people laughing and shouting and cheering for him, cheering for Philippa. Wagers were screamed out, and even the animals were dinning, for once louder than the children. Then Tupper leaped into the mud, not three inches from Dienwald's head, snorting loudly, poking his snout into Dienwald's face.

It was too much for a man to suffer. Dienwald spread his arms in surrender and yelled at the bouncing fury astride him, "I yield, wench! I yield!"

Tupper snorted and squealed and kept the mud churning.

Philippa laughed, and as he looked up at her, he wanted her right then — muddy black face, filthy matted hair, and all.

"Master, pray forgive me." Northbert stood on the edge of the mud puddle, consternation writ on his ugly face.

Dienwald cocked an eye at him. "Aye? What is it?"

"We have visitors, master."

"There are visitors at St. Erth's gates?"

"Nay, master. The visitors are right here."

# 13

Philippa was shocked into numb silence. She didn't move, but of course, she had no drier place to move to. Dienwald looked behind Northbert and saw Graelam de Moreton striding toward them, tall and powerful and well-garbed and clean, and he was staring toward Dienwald as if he'd grown two heads. And then he was staring at Philippa.

"God give you grace, Graelam," Dienwald said easily. His eyes went to Kassia, standing now beside her husband, wrapped in a fine ermine-lined cloak of soft white wool. She looked beautiful, soft and sweet, her chestnut hair in loose braids atop her head. He saw she was trying very hard not to laugh. "Welcome to St. Erth, Kassia. I hope I see you well, sweet lady."

Kassia couldn't hold it back. She burst into laughter, hiccuping against her palm as she gasped out, "You sound like a courtier at the king's court, Dienwald, suave and confident, while you lie sprawled in the mud . . . Ah, Dienwald, your face . . ."

Dienwald looked up at Philippa, who'd turned into a mud statue astride him. "Move, wench," he said, grinning up at her. "As you see, we have visitors and must bestir ourselves to see to their comfort."

Kassia, Philippa was thinking, her mind nearly as muddy as her body. Kassia, the lady that Dienwald held so dear to his wretched heart. And Philippa could understand his feelings for the slight, utterly feminine confection who stood well out of range of the mud puddle. That exquisite example of womanhood would never, ever find herself sitting astride a man in a mud puddle. Philippa's eyes went to Lord Graelam de Moreton, and she saw a man who would never yield, a man both fierce and hard, a man who was Kassia's husband, bless his wondrous existence. She remembered now seeing him once at Beauchamp when she was very young. He'd been bellowing at her father about a tourney they were both to join near Taunton.

"Wench, move," Dienwald said again, and as he spoke, he laughed, circled her waist with his hands, and lifted her off him. He carefully set her beside him in the mud.

She felt the black ooze sliding up her bottom.

"Graelam, why don't you take your very

clean wife into the hall. I will scrub myself and join you soon."

" 'Twill take all the water in your well," Graelam said, threw back his head, and laughed. "Nay, Dienwald, sling not mud at me. My lady just stitched me this fine tunic." He laughed and laughed as he took his wife's soft white hand in his and led her away, saying over his shoulder, "All right, but I begin to cherish that black face of yours. It grows closer to the color of your heart."

Dienwald didn't move until Graelam and Kassia, trailed by a half-dozen Wolffeton men-at-arms, had disappeared around the side of the weaving shed. He could hear Kassia's high giggles and Graelam's low rumbles of laughter.

Philippa hadn't said a single word. She hadn't made a sound, merely sat there in the mud, a study of silent misery.

Dienwald eyed her, then yelled for another bucket to be brought. "Get up, Philippa," he said, and when she did, he continued, "Now, step out of the mud," and when she did, he threw a bucket of cold water over her head. Philippa gasped and shivered and automatically rubbed the mud off her face. The late-April air was chill, but she hadn't realized it until now.

After three more buckets she was ready for the soap.

"You will have to remove the tunic soon," he said, then called for Old Agnes to fetch two blankets. He looked at the score of people staring at them, laughing behind their hands, and roared, "Out of here, all of you! If I see any of you in two seconds, you'll feel the flat of my sword on your buttocks!"

"Aye," Crooky yelled, "but the wenches would much enjoy that kind of play."

Dienwald bellowed again, and soon he and Philippa were alone standing on the plank of lumber, scrubbing themselves with the newly made soap. Dienwald had simply stripped off his clothes. He looked up at Philippa, his face clean and grinning. "I've dismissed everyone, wench — you heard and saw. Take off the gown now."

She did, without comment, seeing no hope for it, and together they washed and scrubbed and threw water on each other. At one point Dienwald paused, looking at her, beautifully naked in the April sunshine, and pulled her against him. He didn't kiss her, merely soaped his hands. Philippa felt his large hands soaping down her back and over her buttocks. She felt his soapy fingers sliding between her legs and tensed, but his touch seemed impersonal.

It wasn't, but Dienwald wasn't about to let her know that. When he'd finished, Philippa cleaned his back, her touch more tentative than his had been. He stared at the mud puddle, then thought of the eyes that were probably watching them at this very minute.

Once dry, they wrapped themselves in the blankets. Dienwald looked at Philippa, her face scrubbed pink, her hair plastered around her head, and he thought her exquisite. He said instead, looking once again toward the mud puddle, "You made me feel very young with our play. Do you wish to come into the hall and meet our guests?"

Speak to Lady Kassia, Philippa thought. She would feel like a great bumbling fool, like a huge ungainly blanket-wrapped beggar gawking next to a snow princess in her white cloak. She shook her head and swallowed her misery.

"They are my friends," Dienwald said, not seeing the misery, only the stubbornness.

"Not yet, if it pleases you."

"Very well," he said, her respectful tone softening him. "But if you wish to meet them, I would ask that you not tell them your name or that you're my prisoner."

"Then what am I?" she asked, irritation

now writ clear in her voice.

Dienwald paused at that. So much for respect and deference from her. "My washerwoman?"

"No."

"My weaver?"

"Nay. I would be your steward."

"Graelam would burst his bladder laughing at that notion. No, you can be my mistress. You begin to look passable again, so that would not strain his credulity. Does that please you, wench?"

"Doesn't it worry you that I might beg Lord Graelam to return me to my father? That I might tell him you're naught but a miserable scoundrel and thief?"

"Why should it worry me? You'll not do that. You have no wish to return to your father. Don't forget that that toad William de Bridgport awaits you with widespread fat arms and foul breath."

That was true, damn him. She chewed on her lower lips. "I could ask him to send me to his vassal, Sir Walter, since I am his cousin and since that is where I was bound in the first place."

"Aye, you could do that, but it would displease me mightily. You know, Philippa, Sir Walter wouldn't treat you well. He is not the man you think him."

"Of course he would treat me well! I'm his cousin, his kin. I won't be your mistress."

He raised his hand and lightly touched his fingertips to her cheek. "You're a snare, Philippa. Of the devil? I wonder."

He said nothing more, merely turned on his bare heel and strode away from her. He should have looked ridiculous, walking. barefoot and wrapped in an ugly brown blanket, but he didn't.

Philippa followed more slowly, and she saw faces and heard laughter and knew that she and Dienwald had been observed whilst they bathed. Was there nothing private in this wretched castle? She knew the answer was no, just as it had been at Beauchamp.

How could Dienwald ask her to meet Kassia, the woman who was the most precious of all God's female flock? The woman who'd saved his life, the woman who was so lavishly guileless, the essence of purity and perfection?

Philippa wanted to be sick.

Instead, she walked up the solar stairs, the blanket wrapped close like a shroud, and locked herself in Dienwald's chamber. He'd already come and gone. His blanket was a heap on the rushes. She fretted about what he was wearing, wishing she'd given him the tunic she'd made for him. It looked every bit as fine as the one Lord Graelam was wearing, the one the beautiful Kassia had sewn for him.

In the great hall, Dienwald, garbed in a tunic and hose that were tattered and faded from their original gray to a dirty bile green, finally greeted his guests.

Graelam and Kassia were speaking with Northbert and Crooky, drinking ale and tasting the new St. Erth cheese that Dienwald had directed made from his own recipe, passed to him by his great-aunt Margarie, now long dead.

"Where is my wine, you whoreson?" Graelam asked without preamble upon Dienwald's appearance.

Dienwald looked at him blankly. "*Your* wine? What wine? That's not wine, it's ale, and made from my own recipe. I would have offered you wine had I some, but I don't. I have naught but ale, and no coin to purchase wine. God's bones, Graelam, I always bring myself to Wolffeton when I wish to reward my innards."

Graelam's dark eyes narrowed with suspicion. "You're a convincing liar when it pleases you to be so."

"What cursed wine?" Dienwald nearly shouted, flinging his arms wide.

Kassia laughed and placed her hand on

his forearm. "You don't remember the wager between you and my lord? The Aquitaine wine my father was shipping to us? The ship was wrecked on the rocks and all the cargo disappeared. You didn't do it? You didn't steal the wine?"

Dienwald just shook his head. "Of course not. Are you sure, Kassia, that your wondrous lord didn't do it? He feared losing the wager to me, you know, and was at his wits' ends to find a way out of humiliating himself."

"Nay, don't try to win her to your side, you sly-lipped cockscomb."

Kassia laughed. "The both of you be still. 'Tis obvious that another rogue stole the wine, my lord. Drink your ale and forget your wager."

"But who?" Dienwald said as he accepted a flagon from Margot.

"Roland is in Cornwall," Graelam said.

"I don't believe it! Roland de Tournay! He's really here?"

"Aye, he's here. I heard it from a tinker who'd traveled the breadth of Cornwall."

"Aye, the tinker was here not long ago, but I was not." More's the pity, he thought, that the fellow hadn't as yet returned. He was seeing that strip of dirty leather tying Philippa's hair back. A narrow ribbon of pale yellow would be beautiful with her hair color. "He told you of Roland?"

"It seems that Roland stopped him, brought him to his camp in the forest of Fentonladock, and instructed him to tell me of his coming — not the why of it, but just that he would be at Wolffeton. I do wonder what he wants. You and Roland were boys fostering together, were you not? At Bauderleigh Castle with Earl Charles Massey?"

"Aye, we were. Old Charles was a proper devil, mean and evil and hard, but we both survived to become mean and evil and hard. I've not heard from Roland in five years."

"He went with Edward to go crusading, as did I. I didn't see him much in the Holy Land, but he survived, thankfully."

"I wonder how he does and what he wants with you."

"I am to meet him at Wolffeton in two weeks' time. He will tell me then. I was told that he used his talents spying for Edward whilst in the Holy Land. A Muslim he was, becoming so like them they never guessed he was an Englishman. He was an intimate of the sultan himself, so it was said."

"He's a dark-skinned bastard, looks like a heathen."

Graelam shrugged. "Aye, and his eyes are

as black as a fanatical priest's and his tongue as smooth as an asp's."

Dienwald was thoughtful, then said without thinking, "I should like to see him. Mayhap I could bring the wench with me. She would enjoy —" The instant it was out of his mouth, Dienwald wanted to kick himself.

Graelam, a man of subtlety when he so wished, inquired mildly, "Who is the wench, Dienwald? She was the one astride you, I gather? Sporting in the mud with you?"

"Aye."

"No more? No explanations? Is she clean? Where is she now?"

"She has no clothes, not a stitch, the muddy gown was old — it belonged to my first wife — and it was the last one. The wench is wearing a blanket now, and is in my bedchamber."

Kassia cocked her head to one side. "Wench? What is her name?"

"Morgan," Dienwald said without hesitation, then nearly swallowed his tongue. Well, he'd said it. He said it again, looking Grae- lam right in his eye. "Her name's Morgan and she's my mistress."

"She's a villein?"

He shook his head vigorously, and said, "Yes."

Graelam snorted. "What goes on here, Dienwald? Don't try to lie to me, I'll know it. You're clear as a spring pond."

"You said I was a fine liar just a moment ago."

"I exaggerated."

"Both of you relieve your minds and shut your mouths! Now, the female we saw, her name is Morgan, you say. An odd name, but no matter. I shall go visit her. I have no extra clothing with me, but I can have gowns and other things sent to her."

"She is a maypole, a giant of a girl. Nothing you own would fit her big body."

Kassia merely frowned at him, shook out the skirt of her finely woven pale pink gown, smoothed the sleeves of the delicate white overtunic, and walked slowly from the great wall. It was then that Dienwald saw her big belly.

He was suddenly very afraid. He turned to Graelam and saw his friend nodding.

"I shield her as best I can. She is so small, and the child grows large in her belly. She insisted upon coming to St. Erth today. She grows bored and restless at Wolffeton — the women won't let her do a thing within the castle, and even my men hover about her when she is in the bailey — and I couldn't deny her. You should see Blount, my steward — he feels a quill is beyond her strength. She frets."

"How much longer before the babe comes?"

"Not until June. I die each day with the thought of it." Graelam then cursed luridly, and Dienwald, looking hopeful and thoughtful, said, "She appears well and is beautiful and laughing."

"Aye," Graelam said, and drained his flagon. He eyed Dienwald. "I wish you wouldn't speak of my wife as though you were her lover. It irks me. Now, 'tis true you didn't steal the wine from Kassia's father? You didn't have the ship wrecked with false warning lights from the point?"

"I wish I'd thought of it," Dienwald said, his voice gloomy with regret.

"Roland, then," Graelam said, nodding in satisfaction at his conclusion. "I'll break two of his ribs for his impertinence."

"That I should like to see," Dienwald said.

Kassia slowly climbed the solar stairs. She held to the railing, careful, as always, of the babe she carried. She felt wonderful and healthy and very alive. If only Graelam would but believe her and stop his worrying and his endless agitation. It was driving her to distraction. And there was her father, now threatening to come to Wolffeton and watch over her. Between the two of them she'd go mad, she knew it.

She reached Dienwald's bedchamber and knocked softly on the solid door. Then she turned the handle. It was locked. She called out, "Please, Morgan, let me in. 'Tis Kassia de Moreton."

Philippa stared at the door from her huddled spot in the middle of Dienwald's bed.

*Morgan!*

Who in the name of St. Andrew was Morgan? She rose, wrapped the blanket securely about her, and padded on bare feet to the door. She opened it and smiled.

"Come in, my lady."

"Thank you. Oh, dear, I see Dienwald was speaking true. You have no clothes."

Philippa simply shook her head.

"You are no villein's daughter, are you? What prank does Dienwald play now?"

"What did he tell you?"

"That you are his mistress."

Philippa snorted and tossed her head. Her hair was nearly dry now, and curled wildly down her back.

"Your hair is beautiful," Kassia said. "I've always wished for hair such as yours. Not long ago I was very ill and my head was shaved. My hair has grown back thicker, but not like yours. Do you mind if I sit down? My burden is heavy."

Philippa realized as the small lady walked across Dienwald's bedchamber that this female was very nice and probably hadn't a mean bone in her very feminine body. She was also heavy with child. She was married to that huge warrior. For an instant Philippa imagined that huge man covering this very small female. It didn't seem possible. But it didn't matter. This Kassia was safely out of the way; Dienwald was safe from her perfection.

It was an unspeakable relief.

"Forgive me," Philippa said. "Would you care for some milk perhaps? I don't imagine that Dienwald thought of that."

"Nay, I am fine as I am, and no, he didn't. He is a man much like my dear lord. Tell me, what is your real name?"

Philippa wanted to spit it out, all of it, but she paused. She realized that she didn't want Dienwald to be put upon or doubted or questioned, even by his friends. Nor did she want to go to her cousin Walter. She wanted to stay right here. "Morgan *is* my name," she said, and her chin went up.

Kassia thought: You're a truly awful liar. She merely smiled at the tall, very lovely girl who sat on Dienwald's bed, a blanket wrapped around her. What was she doing here? It was a mystery, and Kassia was quickly fascinated. Then she thought of Robert Burnell's visit and of Dienwald as the husband of Edward's illegitimate daughter and how she and her husband had praised Dienwald's very eyebrows to Burnell. She felt a frisson of worry, but shook it off. If Dienwald loved this girl, then he would simply say no to Edward if he offered him his daughter's hand in marriage. Dienwald would say no to anybody, even the Pope. He would laugh in the king's face if it pleased him to do so. No, Dienwald couldn't be coerced into doing anything he didn't wish to do. She wouldn't worry. Everything would work out as it was meant to.

"I have come to offer you clothes, Morgan. I have none with me, but if you will let me see your size, then I can have some sent to St. Erth on the morrow."

Philippa had sunk into guilt over the truly violent thoughts she'd harbored toward this elegant lady. "I have woven wool. I merely haven't had time to see to clothes for myself. There were Edmund and Dienwald, even the fool, Crooky. He was so worn and ragged and so . . . so *accepting* of it. I couldn't bear it. I will sew myself something this evening. But I thank you, truly. You are kind."

"This is very interesting," Kassia said, cocking her head to one side.

"What is, my lady?"

"You and Dienwald. He is not, in the usual course of everyday events, a man in the habit of giving much of his attention to ladies."

*That's because he's thinking of you.* "Is that true?" Philippa said, noncommittal.

"Aye. Don't mistake my words. He has always enjoyed women, that is true, but not for longer than it takes him to relieve his needs with them. He's a complicated man, and obstinate, yet loyal and true. He is also a rogue, sometimes quite a scoundrel, and he much enjoys being unpredictable."

"I know."

"You do? Well, that is even more interesting. Do you know him well, then? You've been at St. Erth a long time?"

Philippa raised her chin. Was this lady toying with her? Showing her that it was she, not Philippa, who held Dienwald? No covering it up with fresh rushes, she thought, and said with the most emotionless voice she could dredge up, " 'Tis you, my lady, who holds Dienwald's interest, not me. 'Tis you he worships and admires, not me. 'Tis you he bleats on about, not me. He finds me unwomanly, ungainly, clumsy. But he speaks of you as if you were a . . . a *shrine,* and he wishes to fall on his face and worship at your feet."

"By all the saints' waggery, that is wondrous stupid," Kassia said, and burst into laughter. "And not at all like Dienwald."

"Dienwald is a man," Philippa said when Kassia had subsided into only an occasional giggle.

"Aye," Kassia said slowly, "he is, is he not? He is just like my lord. A man who dominates, a man who must rule, a man who yells and bellows when one dares cross his will or challenge him, and a man who will cherish and protect those weaker then he with all his strength."

"I'm just barely weaker than Dienwald."

"I doubt that, Morgan."

"He doesn't cherish me at all. He knows not what to do with me. I am a thorn in his flesh." Philippa's chin went up yet another notch. "But I am also his steward, though he doesn't wish to tell anyone, the obstinate cockscomb. He said were your husband to know, he would burst his bladder with laughter."

"His steward? Tell me, please. What happened to Alain?"

Philippa's dam burst, and words poured out of her mouth. She didn't tell Kassia de Moreton who she really was or how she came to be at St. Erth, but she told her of Alain's perfidy and how he'd tried to kill her and how she had since taken his place because Dienwald had no one else of the *proper* sex to do it.

Kassia stared at this rush of confidences, but before she could speak, the door burst open and Dienwald catapulted into the chamber, yelling even before his two feet were firmly planted on the floor, "Don't believe a word she says!"

Philippa jumped to her feet. "Morgan!" she shouted. "Who the devil is this Morgan?"

Dienwald drew up, frowning. "I don't know. The name merely popped into my mind. I like it. It has a certain dignity."

"What is your name, then?" Kassia asked.

" 'Tis Mary," Dienwald said quickly. "Her name is Mary. A nice name, a simple name, a name without pretense or deceit."

"I wouldn't say that," Graelam de Moreton said as he came through the bedchamber door. He looked over at his grinning wife. "I once knew a Mary who was as cunning and devious as my former mistress, Nan. You remember, Kassia? Ah, perhaps you don't wish to. You wonder why I'm here, sweetling? Well, Dienwald feared what the girl was telling you and bolted out of the hall. What was I to do? All that was of interest was here, so I followed."

"This is the wench, Mary," Dienwald said, and he gave Philippa a look that would rot off her toes if she dared to disagree with him.

"You don't look like a Mary," Graelam said, coming closer. He studied Philippa, his dark eyes intent. Then he looked troubled, questioning. "You look familiar, though. Your eyes . . . aye, very familiar, the blue is brilliant, unique. I wish I could remember —"

"She doesn't look familiar," Dienwald said, stepping in front of Graelam. "She isn't at all unique. She looks only like herself. She looks like a Mary. Nothing more, just a simple Mary."

"She looks clean," Graelam said, and turned to his wife. "Kassia, have you learned all of Dienwald's secrets? Did he steal my Aquitaine wine?"

"Dienwald isn't a thief!" Philippa turned red the moment the words flew out of her mouth, but proceeded to make matters worse: "He isn't except when necessity forces him to be, and —"

"Ph . . . Mary, be quiet! I don't need you

to plead my innocence before this hulking behemoth. I didn't steal your puking wine, Graelam."

Kassia rose slowly to her feet. "This is quite enough. Now, I suggest that we have our meal up here, since Mary can't come to the hall wearing naught but a blanket. What say you, Dienwald?"

What could he say? he wondered, both his brain and belly sour, even as he nodded.

The evening meal, all cozy in Dienwald's bedchamber, passed off more smoothly than Dienwald could have hoped. Philippa held her tongue for the most part, as did Kassia. The men spoke of men's things, and though Philippa would have liked to join in, because she was, no matter what Dienwald said, St. Erth's steward, she kept still. She was afraid she would inadvertently give something away. Neither Graelam de Moreton nor his lovely wife was stupid.

Why had Graelam looked at her so oddly? Could he believe she looked familiar because he remembered seeing her very briefly at Beauchamp some years before?

Graelam sat back in his chair, a flagon of ale between his large hands. "Kassia and I will return to Wolffeton on the morrow. She wished merely to see that you were all right."

"Why? Nay, Graelam, your lie contains more holes than a sieve. You wished to see if I was drinking your wine."

"That as well." Graelam paused a moment, then continued easily, "Let us go for a walk, Dienwald. I have something to discuss with you."

Kassia shot him a questioning look, but he only smiled and shook his head.

What was going on here? Philippa wondered. She watched the two men leave the bedchamber. On the threshold, Dienwald turned, saying, "Mary, we will give our bed over to Graelam and Kassia tonight. Tell Edmund that he is to sleep with Father Cramdle. No, wait — we will sleep in your small bed in the steward's chamber." That taken care of to the master's satisfaction, Philippa was left sitting on the bed, her face red with anger and embarrassment.

"I will surely kill him, the miserable bounder," she said to no one in particular.

To her surprise, Lady Kassia laughed.

Graelam made a decision as he and Dienwald walked down the solar stairs and into the inner bailey. He wouldn't tell Dienwald of Burnell's visit. Kassia was right: leave things alone. Dienwald delighted in doing precisely what he wanted to do, and King

Edward at his most cajoling or his most threatening wouldn't change his mind once he'd set himself a course. The two men walked toward the ramparts and climbed the ladder to the eastern tower.

"Your steward stole everything?" Graelam asked, leaning his elbows on the rough stone.

Dienwald nodded. "Bastard. Gorkel the Hideous broke his neck. But Alain had a spy who managed to flee St. Erth. My fool, Crooky, somehow knows such things — his ways of finding out things both amaze and terrify me. He believes Alain was involved with Walter de Grasse and that one of the men who tried to kill Ph . . . Mary is even now at Crandall. He is the cistern keeper."

Graelam said nothing for several moments. Finally: "I know of the hatred between the two of you, needless to say! And yes, I heard about the burning of your crops on the southern border and the butchering of all your people. You have no proof that Sir Walter was behind it, though, do you?"

Dienwald admitted that he had none. Thus, he was surprised when Graelam said, "I have decided to remove Walter. I will tolerate no more discord. If we discover that he burned your crops and destroyed your people, I will kill him. Now, my friend, bring out my wine — I'm convinced you have it hidden."

Dienwald could but stare at Graelam; then he bellowed for Northbert. "Bring out the wine!"

It wasn't Aquitaine wine, but it wasn't vinegar either. There was but one cask, and it hailed from a Benedictine abbey near Penryn.

When Dienwald entered the steward's small chamber in the early hours of the morning, not at all drunk, for he hated wine, he smiled toward the lump on the narrow bed.

He walked silently to the bed and went down on his knees, setting his lit candle on the floor beside him. He said nothing, merely lifted the blanket that covered Philippa. She was naked, lying on her side facing away from him, one leg stretched out, the other bent, and all the beauty of her woman's flesh was there for him to see. He swallowed and didn't wait another moment. Lightly he touched his fingertips to her inner thighs, then moved them up slowly, very slowly, until he felt the warmth of her. He drew in his breath, aware that his sex was swollen and aching. Slowly, he eased his middle finger inside her. She was very tight and he loved the feeling of his finger stretching her and he imagined how it would feel to have her around his manhood, so tight, squeezing him until he wanted to die with the wonderful feelings. His finger deepened. Her body was responding, dampening, easing for his finger.

He leaned forward and kissed her hip even as he let his finger ease more deeply. He heard her moan and felt her tighten convulsively. He would spill his seed right here in this damned darkened room. He quickly withdrew his finger and tried to calm his frantic breathing. He rose and stripped off his clothes. He lay beside her, feeling her buttocks against his swelled sex. He began to knead her belly then let his fingers go once more where they ached to. He found her woman's flesh in the soft curls and moaned deep in his throat as he began to stroke her, gently exploring.

When her hips jerked and she moaned in her sleep, he rolled her onto her back and came over her.

# 14

Philippa was whimpering even as she opened her eyes. Then she shrieked into the shadowed face above her.

Dienwald cursed, bent down, and kissed her mouth. He gave her his full weight for an instant, then raised himself on his elbows, still kissing her wildly.

He was between her legs, his sex stiff and hot and hurting. He reared back onto his knees and parted her thighs with his hands, looking down at her. "You would make me debauch you," he said, his voice low and raw. "You're a witch, a siren, and you would take me and wring me out and make me feel things I don't want to feel."

Philippa's mind finally cleared. She was still throbbing, deep in her belly, but she saw him clearly now and heard his words and understood them and was enraged. All unwanted sensations quickly fled her body. "*I* make *you* debauch *me?* What about your grandmother's deep spring and all that religious nonsense of renewal and light and dark and how you thought of me as being deep and fulfilling and renewing you and . . . I am in my own bed, you insensate brute! 'Tis you who seek to dishonor me! I am a maid and not your wife. 'Tis you who make me feel things I shouldn't feel. 'Tis you who wish to desecrate me — a prisoner with no voice in anything, a wretched captive who has no clothing even!"

"A fine volley of words you fling at me — but naught but peevish rantings. You have no voice, you say? You beset me, wench, your mouth is nearly as bountiful as your ass!"

She saw red, fisted her hands, and smashed them against his chest even as he shouted, "You make yourself sound like a shrine, a relic to heedless virgins! Desecrate? You came to me through foul mischance, wench — that, or God sent you as my penance —" He was still holding her thighs when she hit him again as hard as she could.

Dienwald growled a half-dozen curses even as he teetered sideways and fell to the stone floor beside the bed. He didn't release her, and she came crashing down on top of him. When her head hit his as he was trying to rise, and he was plunged back, she heard the ugly thudding sound of his head against the leg of her steward's table.

His head lolled on the stone floor and he was still. Philippa was frozen for an instant, trying to comprehend what had happened; then she knew bone-deep fear, rolled off him, and flattened her palm against his chest. His heartbeat was slow and steady. She brought the single candle closer and examined his head. A lump was beginning to swell over his left temple. Well, it served the slavering ravisher right. He'd come to take her even as she slept, so she wouldn't fight him; then his wayward mouth had accused *her* of debauching *him,* or some such nonsense. She wanted to hit him again, but didn't. Instead she sat on the cold stone floor, crossed her legs, and eased his head onto her thighs. She didn't feel the chill of the stones against her flesh; rather she felt the heat from his shoulders, the warmth of him beneath her hands. She leaned against the bed and gently stroked his forehead. She was conscious only of him and her worry for him. After a while she also found that she was staring, and discovered he quite delighted her. His sex wasn't hard and throbbing now; quite the contrary. His long legs were sprawled out, slightly parted. She smiled and laid her hand on his belly. Slowly she traced the ridges of muscle, then let her fingers stray to the thick brush of dark hair at his groin.

"You are such a churlish knave," she said. "What am I to do with you?"

He didn't reply, nor did he stir. Philippa sang him a soft French ballad her mother had taught her when she was four years old. Then she stopped and sighed. More to the point of course was what *he* would do with *her.* She forced her fingers away from him. She couldn't begin to imagine how he would taunt her were he to know what she had done whilst he lay unconscious.

"St. Gregory's chilblains, wench, your voice sounds like a wet rag slapping against the side of a sleeping horse."

"You're awake," she said, her voice flat. "A minstrel who sojourned at Beauchamp just last year told my parents that my voice was dulcet and silvery, like a turtle dove's."

"Dulcet dove? The fellow lied, and is worse with words than Crooky." Dienwald fell into melancholy silence, for he'd realized that his head lay in her lap, that if he turned his face inward he could kiss the soft flesh between her legs. He didn't want to do that. Why must she offer him such wondrous fodder for his weakness? It wasn't to be borne. He turned his face against her, his lips seeking.

Philippa sucked in her breath and shoved

him away. He moaned, and immediately she felt guilty. "You shouldn't have done that. You'll hurt yourself again."

He moaned again, dramatically, and Philippa gritted her teeth against laughing. "Come, you must get up now. You're naked."

"I'm pleased you noticed. So are you, wench." Dienwald struggled to his feet, stood there weaving for a moment, then collapsed onto her narrow bed.

Philippa looked down at him. He gave a loud snore. She cursed and covered him with a blanket.

"I'm cold and will die of watery lungs brought on by your cruelty if you leave me."

"I like the sound of your snores better," Philippa said even as she eased down beside him. "Nay, I shan't let you touch me again. It isn't right you should do that, and well you know it. I'm not your mistress. I shan't ever be your mistress." She grabbed another frayed blanket and wrapped it about herself. "Go to sleep, master, else I'll fling you off my bed again."

Dienwald sighed. "Big wenches are difficult."

"I know," she said, her voice nasty. "You'd much prefer your precious *little* Kassia, your so perfect *little* princess who doubtless sighs and swoons all over you — a *big* warrior."

He laughed.

"Well, you can't have her, you ass! She's well-wedded and she's with child and she's not for you, so you might as well forget her."

"How well you extol her person," he said. "Mayhap you are right. I will think about it. Big wenches are even more difficult when they're jealous." He began snoring again and soon, much sooner than Philippa, he was truly asleep.

Jealous, was she? He turned onto his side away from her and soon she was snuggled against his back. She wondered what he'd do if she bit him. Probably just laugh at her again. She fell asleep finally, feeling warm and secure, damn him.

Graelam stood in the open doorway of the steward's chamber early the next morning, staring toward the narrow bed that held his host and the wench whose name wasn't Mary. The girl's face was pressed against Dienwald's naked back, but the rest of her was protected from him by an old blanket, a blanket that, he saw, separated the two of them. An eyebrow cocked upward. So the girl whose name wasn't Mary also wasn't Dienwald's mistress either. Kassia would find this fascinating.

Suddenly Dienwald groaned and turned

onto his back, flinging his arm over his head. Philippa, jerked from a sound sleep, was nearly thrown off the narrow bed onto the floor. Dienwald groaned again, muttering, "My God, you've nearly killed me, wench. My head, it's swollen and hurts and —"

"And has put you in particularly good humor," Graelam said, stepping into the chamber.

Philippa's eyes flew open and fastened in consternation upon the intruder. He merely smiled. "God give you a good morrow, Mary. I am sorry to disturb your slumber, but my wife and I must take our leave soon. This door was open and I did tap my fist upon it, but there was no reply."

Dienwald opened an eye, and complaints issued rapidly from his mouth. "The wench nearly killed me. I've a lump on my skull the size of my foot."

Philippa was less than sympathetic. "You deserved it, you disgusting lout!"

"Lout? God's knees, you randy wench, all I did was think about letting you debauch me, nothing more." He smiled guilelessly up at her.

Philippa reared up, quickly jerked the blanket over her breasts, and sent her fist into his belly. "My lord," she said, turning immediately toward Graelam, "I cannot rise to see to you and your perfect wife's needs. But this attempted defiler of innocent maids can, and he will, once he stops acting like he's been flayed by a band of Saracens."

"I've never known him for a coward, thus it must be your superior strength and cunning, Mary. Dienwald, rise now, and pay your homage to my lady. Kassia wishes to bid you adieu." Graelam's eyes suddenly widened. "*Perfect* wife?" He guffawed. "I shall tell Kassia, it will amuse her. *Perfect!*" He shook his head. "The little witch — *perfect!*" Still laughing, Graelam left the steward's chamber, closing the door behind him.

"*You* think she's perfect," Philippa said.

"Feel the lump on my head. Tell me if I will survive rising from this bed."

Philippa leaned over and gently examined his head. "The lump will grow if you stay in this bed. You will survive it, so get thee gone, I tire of you."

He sighed and rolled over her, coming to his feet beside the bed. He was naked and quite unconcerned about it. He grinned down at her and said, "Don't stare, wench, else my manhood will rise like leavened bread." He gave a heartfelt sigh. "And 'twill make my hose uncomfortable. It will also bring the stares of all your gentle rivals — in short, most of the wenches here at St. Erth. What say you?"

"I grant you good morrow," Philippa said, then turned away from him and stared at the wall.

Dienwald knew well enough that his body pleased her. Although he wasn't a massive warrior like Graelam, he was big enough, well enough made, muscled and lean and hard, not a patch of fat on him. He leaned down and quickly kissed her cheek, then straightened, began whistling, and dressed himself. He was out of the steward's chamber in but a moment, still whistling.

Philippa spent her morning sewing herself a gown from soft wool dyed a light green that Old Agnes had brought to her; she hummed to herself as she sewed. She jumped at the knock on her door, then smiled when Edmund burst into the room. He drew to a halt, planted his hands on his hips, and said, "What think you, Maypole?"

She studied him silently for several minutes, until he began fidgeting about. "Very nice, Master Edmund. Come here and let me inspect you more closely."

Edmund swaggered over to where

Philippa sat draped in her blanket. He was proud, that was clear to see, he'd even combed his fingers through his hair, and Philippa was pleased. "What says your father?"

"He just looked at me and rubbed his chin. Lord Graelam thought I would become a fine knight, and Lady Kassia asked that I carry her favors when I am in my first tourney."

Perfect Kassia had done it again, Philippa thought, had said just the right thing at the right time. Curse the woman.

"Father said that soon I will go to Wolffeton to foster with Lord Graelam. I will be his page, then, soon, his squire. I will prove myself and my loyalty."

"Do you wish to go to Wolffeton?"

Edmund nodded quickly, but then he fell silent. " 'Tis not far from St. Erth, no more than a half-day's hard ride. I shall go and I shall earn my spurs very soon."

"You will not, however, be an ignorant knight, Edmund. Few pages can read or write, but you will. Few men of any class can read or write, save priests and clerks. Lord Graelam will thank God the day you come to Wolffeton. Now, Father Cramdle awaits you. Go and leave the maypole to sew something to cover herself."

It wanted only Edmund's father, Philippa thought, watching Dienwald come into the small room after his son had left. She nearly filled it, and with him in here as well, it was suffocating. "What do you want?"

"I wish to tell you that my son is mightily pleased with himself."

Philippa merely nodded.

"Thank you, wench."

She swallowed a lump in her throat and said in an offhand manner, "Shall you also be pleased with your new tunic? 'Tis finished." Before he could answer her, Philippa eased out of her chair, her blanket firmly in place around her, and handed him the tunic she'd sewn for him.

Dienwald took it from her outstretched hand and stared down at it, running his fingers over the tiny stitches, feeling the soft wool, marveling that she had made it for him and that it was so fine, the most excellent tunic he'd ever owned. It was too special to wear on this ordinary day, but he said nothing, merely pulled off his old tunic and pulled this one over his head. It felt soft against his flesh, and it fitted him perfectly. He turned to face Philippa and she smiled at him. " 'Tis very well you look, Dienwald, quite splendid." She reached out her hand and smoothed the cloth over his chest. Her breathing quickened and she suddenly stilled.

Dienwald stepped back quickly. "I'm leaving and I wanted to tell you to stay close to St. Erth."

Her stomach cramped tight. "Where go you? Not into danger?"

He heard the forlorn tone and the fear, and frowned at it. "I go where I go, and 'tis none of your affair. You will stay here and not move one of your large feet from St. Erth. When I return, I will decide what to do with you."

"You make me sound like entrails tossed out of the cooking shed."

Dienwald merely smiled at that, touched his fingertips to her cheek, then leaned down and kissed her mouth. Still smiling, he jerked the blanket from her breasts, gazed down at them, kissed one nipple, then the other.

"Don't do that!"

He straightened, gave her a small salute, and strode from the room.

He began whistling again as the door closed firmly behind him. Philippa just stood there, the blanket bunched around her waist. He'd worn his new tunic.

Dienwald didn't think of her as anything remotely close to "entrails," but he didn't know what to do with her. What he wanted to do, in insane moments, was take her again and again until he was sated with her. And the insane moments seemed to be coming more and more often now; in fact, were he to count his errant thoughts, the moments would melt together.

He cursed and gave Philbo a stout kick in the sides. The destrier snorted and jumped forward. Northbert, surprised, kicked his own destrier into a canter, as did Eldwin, who rode on his left side.

Dienwald could remember the fragrance of her sweet woman's scent, and something else more elusive — perhaps 'twas the essence of gillyflowers, he thought, dredging the scent from his childhood memories.

The wench had bewitched him and beset him, curse her for the guileless siren she was. And somehow she'd made him like it and want more of it, more of her. He'd very nearly taken her maidenhead the previous night, and he hadn't even drunk enough ale to account for such stupidity. No, he'd just thought of her, seeing her in his mind's eye sleeping in her narrow bed in the steward's chamber, and he'd left Graelam to stare after him, their chess game still undecided. He would have taken her had she not awakened with that loud shriek in his face.

What was he to do with the damned wench? He sighed, now picturing his son strutting about in his new clothes, bragging about the Maypole. His son, who just this morning hadn't carped and crabbed quite so much about being sacrificed to studies with Father Cramdle.

The wench was taking over St. Erth. Everywhere he saw her influence, her touch. It was irritating and disconcerting. He didn't know what to do about it.

It was Northbert who pulled him from his melancholy thoughts. "Master, what do you expect to find?"

"We didn't search before. We buried the dead and came back to St. Erth. I wish to find something to prove that Sir Walter ordered the burning and the killings. That or find someone who mayhap saw him or recognized one of his men."

Northbert chewed on that for several miles. Finally he said, "Why not just kill the malignant bastard? You know he's responsible, as do all the rest of us. Kill him."

Dienwald wanted to kill Walter, very much, but he shook his head. He wanted things done right. He wanted to keep Graelam's trust and his friendship. "Lord Graelam needs proof; then we will argue together to determine who gets to scatter the bastard's bowels."

"Ah," said Northbert, nodding his ugly head. "Lord Graelam includes himself now. 'Tis good, methinks."

They reached the southern acres of St. Erth late that afternoon. The desolation was shattering. There was naught but emptiness and black ruins. There was only the occasional caw of a rook. Curls of smoke still rose from some of the burned huts. There were a few peasants prodding the burned remains in leveled hovels, and Dienwald drew up and began to ask his questions.

Philippa was bored. More than bored, she'd discovered what Dienwald's errand was and she was worried, despite the fact that he was a trained fighter and no enemy was supposed to be where he was going.

She accepted without question that her cousin Sir Walter de Grasse was a black villain. She just wished there was something she could do.

She wore her new gown that afternoon and she looked proud and very pretty, so Old Agnes told her, very much the proper mistress. Then Agnes sought confirmation from Gorkel, who looked at Philippa and grunted, his hideous face achieving a repellent smile. She'd cut a narrow piece of wool and tied it around her hair. As for Crooky, he was feeling expansive in his own new clothes, which were still very clean, and praised her to her eyebrows. Philippa expected the worst and wasn't disappointed:

She sweetly sews for all of us, this lovely
maid whose name's not Mary.
Our sweet lord who stole her wool aches to
drink from her sweet dairy.
She made him a tunic and kissed it pure
Our sweet lord wonders what to do with her.

Philippa cheered loudly and the other servants in the hall quickly joined her. "It rhymed, truly," she said, wiping her eyes with the back of her hand. "Though your sentiments don't do the master justice."

Crooky, in a new mood of self-doubt, merely said, "Nay, mistress, 'twas hideous. I must do better, aye, I must tether my wayward thoughts and bring them to smoothness and pleasure to the ear. Aye, I will beg Father Cramdle to write it down for me."

Philippa said, "You have lightened me for a few moments, Crooky, and I thank you. Now, before you go to the priest, tell me when the master will return."

"No one knows," Gorkel said, stepping

forward. "He's gone to the southern borders."

She knew that, and sat there worrying her thumbnail. She paced the great hall. In a spate of feverish activity to distract herself, she had lime dumped down the privy hole in the guardroom. She spaded the small garden near the cistern, willing the few vegetables to grow. She watched the women sewing, always sewing, and she praised them, and joined in herself for an hour, making another tunic for the master. Old Agnes ran her arthritic fingers over it and gave her a sly smile. Philippa went to the cooking shed and spoke with Bennen, a stringy old man who knew more of herbs than anyone she had ever known and presided over the cooking with what Philippa's mother had called the "special touch." He got along well with St. Erth's withered cook, which was a good thing, because no one else seemed to get along with him. She spoke of several dishes she herself liked, and Bennen committed them to memory, and called her "mistress" and smiled at her, his toothless mouth wide. If Dienwald wanted to feel trapped, he needed only listen to his own people. She even visited Eleanor the cat and her four kittens, all healthy and mewing loudly.

The night was long, and Philippa wished Dienwald were there, kissing her, fighting with her, trying to fit himself between her legs even as he fought himself.

The next morning, Edmund said to her after watching her crumble a particularly fine hunk of cheese and toss it to one of the castle dogs, "You didn't sleep well, Maypole. You look sour and your eyes are all dark-circled. My father has a nice palfrey that should be big enough for a female your size. Come riding, Philippa. You won't miss my father so much." He added after a little thought, "Aye, I miss him as well. We will both ride."

"I don't miss him, but I should like to ride."

The palfrey's name was Daisy and she was docile and well-mannered. Philippa, her gown hiked up to her knees, her legs and feet bare, sat her horse, smiling down at Ogden, the head stableman. He was wildly red-haired and so freckled she couldn't make out the tone of his flesh beneath.

Gorkel approached and said, "You'll want men with you, mistress. The master ordered me to . . ." He faltered, and Philippa could only stare, it was so unexpected of the man who'd without hesitation snapped the steward's neck.

"I understand," she said. "The master doesn't want me perchance to lose myself in the wilds of Cornwall."

Gorkel beamed at her. "Aye, mistress, thass it. I don't ride well, but I'll fetch men who will accompany you."

The afternoon was sunny, only a light breeze stirring the air, and the countryside was wild and hilly, trees bowed from the fierce winds and storms that blew from the Irish Sea just to the north — but not now, not during Dienwald's fanciful deep spring.

Edmund allowed that she looked less testy upon their return to St. Erth some three hours later.

"You must take care with your flattery, Master Edmund, else I may mistake your sweet words for affection."

To which Edmund snorted in disgust and said with a dignity that sat well on his boy's shoulders, "I am not a churl."

"Not today, at least," she said, and grinned at him.

Edmund didn't retort to that because they'd just crossed into the inner bailey and he was staring at a pack mule loaded with bundles, three men in Wolffeton colors lolling around the mule.

Perfect Kassia, the little princess, the glorious little lady, had sent clothing, just as she'd promised. An entire muleload of clothing. Philippa gasped as she unwrapped the coarse-wool–wrapped garments. Gowns, overtunics, fine hose, shifts of the softest cotton and linen, ribbons of all colors, even soft leather slippers large enough for her, the toes pointed upward in the latest fashion from Eleanor's court. It was too much and it was wonderful and Philippa felt like the most sour-natured of wretches. She read the letter from Kassia, handed to her by one of the men. Mary was thanked for the hospitality of St. Erth, and Philippa could practically see Kassia smiling as she penned the words. The close of the letter made her frown a bit: ". . . do not worry if things transpire somewhat awry. Dienwald makes his own decisions and he is strong and unswerving. Don't worry, please do not, for all will be as it should be."

Now, what did that mean? Philippa wondered as she rolled the sheet of foolscap and retied it. She looked at the clothing spread out on the trestle table in the great hall. So much, and all for her. Odd how she'd forgotten how much she'd owned at Beauchamp, and how dear one simple gown had now become to her.

She hummed and arranged the clothing

in the steward's room. Then she began to work, quickly and happily, still humming. She sent Gorkel to direct the children to collect fresh rushes after she measured him for a new tunic. She asked Bennen for rosemary to scent it. More lime was dumped down the privy, for the easterly winds were strong.

The following morning, she and Edmund rode out from St. Erth again, this time with three men in attendance. Gorkel was master in Eldwin's absence, and he was directing the remaining men in the practice field. As they rode out, she could hear the men's shouts and yells and the dull thuds of the lances as they rode against the quintains. She wanted to see the cattle in the northern pastures, to make a count so she could be certain that her steward's ledgers were correct. She was garbed anew and felt like a very fine lady surrounded by her courtiers. Then it rained and she worried and fretted that her new clothing would be ruined. The cattle counted, they returned to St. Erth, Philippa to her steward's books.

On the third morning, she wore the gown she'd sewed for herself and left her legs bare. It didn't matter, for the day was warm and the master wasn't here to see her and perhaps smile at her with lecherous intent. Ah, but she missed him and his hands and his mouth and the feel of his hard body. She missed his smile and his volley of words. She missed arguing with him and baiting him. She thought suddenly that debauching him was an interesting notion — folly, to be sure, but seductive folly. Her fingers flexed as she remembered holding his head on her lap that morning and how he'd turned his face inward and kissed her. She doubted she would have time to debauch him before he'd already done the debauching. She laughed aloud, and Edmund stared at her.

As to her future, she refused to think about it. As to St. Erth's future, it looked much brighter. With luck, there would be some cattle to sell and coins in Dienwald's coffers. She would need to check on the pigs just as she had on the cattle. She wanted nothing left to chance or hearsay. Her entries in her steward's ledgers grew longer, by the hour, it seemed, and she felt pleasure for St. Erth's master as she worked. Repairs were needed in St. Erth's eastern wall. Soon, perchance this fall, there would be enough coin to hire them done. She whistled and worked faster.

She turned her attention back to Edmund as he demanded to know why she, a heedless maypole of a girl, could read and write and cipher. "Because my father wished it, I suppose," she said, frowning as she spoke the words, the same reply she'd given Edmund's father. "I do wonder, though, why he wished it. My sister, Bernice, has naught but space in her head, that and visions of chivalrous knights singing praises to her eyebrows. Aye, she's a one, Master Edmund."

"Is she a maypole like you?"

Philippa shook her head. "She's short and plump and has a pointed chin and very red lips. She pouts most virtuously, having practiced before a mirror for the past six years."

"And she had all your suitors?"

"Must you keep asking me questions? All right, there was Ivo de Vescy, and he was wildly in love with me."

"His name sounds shiftless. Did he truly wish to wed with you? Was he a giant? You're almost as tall as my father." Edmund paused, then shook his head. "Mayhap not."

"You're naught but a little boy. How can you possibly tell from down there? I come nearly to your father's nose."

"He likes small women, *short* women. Just look at Alice and Ellen and Sybilla —"

"Who are Ellen and Sybilla?"

Edmund shrugged. "Oh, I forgot. Father

married Ellen to a peasant when he got her with child, and Sybilla sickened with a fever and died. But Alice is small, not like you."

Philippa wanted to cuff his ears and stuff one of her new leather slippers into his mouth. She wanted to scream so loud that it would chase the cawing rooks away. Edmund's flowing child's candor had smitten her deep, very deep, with pain; she wanted to weep. Of course Dienwald had made no secret of his couplings. He'd said merely that they saved her maidenhead. And she'd not cared then because he was a stranger she hadn't come to know yet. But now she had and she wanted to send her fist into his belly and hear him bellow with pain. She wanted . . .

"Father will send you back to Lord Henry. He has no choice. He doesn't want to wed, ever. Thass what he tells everyone."

*"That's,"* Philippa said automatically. "Why do you believe that?"

Edmund shrugged. "I heard him tell Alain once that women were a man's folly, that if a man wished more than a vessel, he was naught but a windy fool and an ass."

"Your memory rivals a priest's discourse in its detail."

This was greeted with another shrug. "My father knows everything. Thass . . .

*that's* why he doesn't use you as he does the others. He'd be ashamed, perchance worried that he would have to wed you. Is your father very powerful?"

"Very powerful," Philippa said. "And very mean and very strong and —"

It was then that Edmund grunted and jerked at his pony's reins. "Look yon, Philippa! Men, and they're coming toward us!"

# 15

Philippa saw the men and felt her heart sink to her toes. They were riding hard, and even from a distance they looked determined. Who were they?

"Your father, Edmund?"

"Nay, I don't recognize Father or Northbert or Eldwin, and they ride the most distinctive destriers. I don't know who they are. We must flee, Philippa."

The man-at-arms, Ellis, turned to Philippa, consternation writ clear on his face. "There are too many of them, mistress. Ride! Back to St. Erth. We can't fight them."

Philippa, without a word, jerked on her palfrey's reins and dug her bare heels into the mare's sides. She looked sideways at Edmund and realized that his pony didn't have the endurance to keep pace with the rest of them. Their pursuers' horses were pounding toward them, ever closer, their hooves kicking up whorls of dust into the clear air. Who were they?

It didn't matter. Philippa lowered her head and urged her palfrey faster. When

Edmund's pony faltered, she'd simply bring him onto Daisy's back with her, Daisy was strong and stout of heart. Philippa gently tugged Daisy's reins to the right and drew closer to Edmund.

Sir Walter de Grasse looked toward the fleeing men, the girl and young boy protected in the midst of them. His destrier, a powerful blooded Arabian, couldn't be outrun, particularly by that muling mare Philippa was riding. He really didn't care about the others. Walter was pleased; he smiled and felt the wind tangle his hair and make his eyes tear. At last. He'd waited and planned and waited. Finally she'd ridden this way, and that whoreson peasant Dienwald wasn't with her. He was back scrounging about in his burned southern acres, finding nothing because Walter never left anything to find. Dead bodies were the only witnesses. Walter urged his destrier faster. If only Philippa knew that it was he, her own cousin, in pursuit, she would wave and flee from Dienwald's men. He noticed the little boy beside her on his laboring pony and wondered who he was.

He wished he could make out her face, but from this distance all he could see for certain was her wildly beautiful hair rippling out behind her head, atop the slenderness of her body. It was enough. If she had no teeth, he would still crave her above all women, this king's daughter who would shortly be his wife. He thought of St. Erth and how it would be his within the year, he doubted not. How could King Edward deny his son-in-law his own castle, stolen from his father by Dienwald's thieving sire?

Philippa could hear the pursuing horses. They were very close now. She knew all was lost. They were still a good two miles from St. Erth. The countryside around them held only a few peasants' huts, low pine trees and scrubby hawthorns and yews, and indifferent cattle. No one to help them. She saw the fierce look on Ellis' face, attesting to his impotent rage. Their pace was frantic and the horses were blowing hard, their flanks lathered white. She saw Edmund's pony stumble and she acted quickly, jerked Daisy close, dropped the knotted reins, and grabbed Edmund even as his pony went down. He was heavy, heavier than she'd imagined, but she pulled him onto Daisy's back. "My pony!" he yelled, nearly hurtling himself off Daisy's back.

Philippa fought to steady him. "The pony will make its way back to St. Erth. Worry not for the pony, but for us."

Edmund quieted, but he was breathing in

quick sharp gasps, his small body shuddering.

"Your pony will go home," she said again, this time in his ear, hoping he heard her and understood.

He made no sign. His small face was white and grim.

She held him close and urged her mare faster.

Suddenly, without warning, Ellis screamed, a tearing raw-throated sound. Philippa saw an arrow bedded deep between his shoulder blades, its feathered shaft still vibrating from the force of its entry. Ellis lurched forward, gasping, then fell sideways, his foot catching in the stirrup. He was dragged along, blood spewing from his back onto his maddened horse. Philippa tried to hide Edmund's head, but he watched until Ellis' foot worked free of the stirrup and he fell to the hard ground, rolling over and over, the arrow's shaft going deeper into his body.

Edmund made no sound; Philippa held him tighter, swallowing convulsively.

The other two men closed around her, and one of them yelled at her to keep down, to hug her mare's neck, but even as the words left his mouth he slumped forward against his horse's back, an arrow through his neck.

Philippa knew it was no use. "Flee," she shouted to the third man, whose name was Silken. "Go whilst you can. 'Tis I the men want, not you. Go! Get help. Get the master."

The man looked at her, his eyes sad and accepting. He drew his horse to a screaming halt, whipped him about, and drew his sword. "I won't die with a coward's arrow in my back," he yelled at Philippa. "Nor will I die a coward's death in my soul by escaping my fate. Ride hard, mistress. I'll hold them as long as I can. Keep the boy safe."

"Nay, Silken, nay!" Edmund shouted, and Philippa knew that she couldn't leave the man, knew that even if she rode away, she would manage to save neither herself nor Edmund. She pulled Daisy to a halt. "Stay back behind me, Silken," she yelled at him. "Keep your sword to your side!"

The men were upon them in moments. Dust flew, blurring the air, making Philippa cough. She couldn't have been more horrified or surprised when one of the men yelled, "Philippa! My dearest cousin, 'tis I, Walter, here to save you!"

Silken whirled on Philippa, his face gone white, his mouth ugly with sudden rage. "*You*, mistress! You brought this bastard cur upon us! You got word to him!"

"Find the master, Silken. Here, take Edmund with you, quickly!"

But Edmund wouldn't budge, shaking his head madly and clutching at the mare's mane. Silken waited not another moment, but rode away as only a desperate man can ride, and Walter, intent for the moment upon the object of his capture, allowed the man to gain distance. Then he yelled for two of his men to bring him down. Philippa prayed hard, as did, she imagined, Edmund. Silken was their only chance. He disappeared over a rise, the two men in pursuit.

"Philippa," Walter said as he rode up to her. "Ah, my dearest girl, you are safe, are you not?"

Philippa stared at her cousin Walter, a man she hadn't seen for some years. He wasn't a handsome man, but then, neither was he ill-looking. But he did look different to her. She had remembered him as very tall and thin. He wasn't thin now; he was gaunt and wiry, his face long, his cheekbones high and hollow, his eyes more prominent. She remembered thick dark brown hair fashionably clipped across his forehead. His hair was thinner now but still clipped across his forehead. She hadn't remembered his eyes. They were dark blue, and they looked hot with triumph, with success. She quickly assessed matters and got control of herself. He believed he'd rescued her, saved her. She whispered to Edmund, "Hold your peace, Edmund. Do as I do."

The boy was white with fear, but he nodded. She squeezed him comfortingly.

"Walter, 'tis you?"

"Aye, Philippa, 'tis I, your dearest cousin. You have changed and grown into a woman and a beautiful creature. You are most pleasing to mine eyes. And now you are safe from that knave." Walter paused a moment, noticing Edmund, it seemed, for the first time.

"Who is this? The bastard's whelp? Shall I dispatch him to heaven, Philippa? Surely that is where the angels would carry him, for he is yet too young to have gleaned the foul wickedness from his sire."

"No, leave him be, Walter. He is but a child, too young for heaven, unless God calls him. Leave him to me. He cares not for his sire, for he foully abuses him." She prayed Edmund would keep his small mouth firmly closed. He started, stiffening against her, but said nothing.

"Aye, that I can believe. The cruel traitor not only abused his own child, but you as well, I doubt not. You are both safe with me, Philippa, at least until I decide what to do with the boy. Aye, I'll ransom him. His father is coarse of spirit, but the boy is of his flesh and his heir. Aye, we'll all return to Crandall now."

"I'll tear out his lying tongue!"

"Shush, Edmund, please, say nothing untoward!"

Philippa turned Daisy about, saying as she did so, "What is the distance to your keep, Walter?"

"Two days hence, fair cousin."

"My palfrey is lathered and blowing."

"Leave the beast and take that one. Dienwald's man needs it no more." And Walter laughed, pointing to Ellis' body sprawled in a ditch beside the dusty road.

"Nay, leave me the mare, just keep our pace slow for a while."

Walter felt expansive. Everything had come about as he'd planned. Philippa was beautiful and she was gentle and yielding, her expressive eyes filled with gratitude for him. "I'll grant you that boon, Philippa." He rode forward to speak to one of his men. Philippa whispered in Edmund's ear, "We must pretend, Edmund, and we must think. We must exceed Crooky's most talented fabrications."

"I will kill him."

"Perhaps I shall be the quicker, but hold

your tongue now, he returns. Say naught, Edmund."

"We will ride until it darkens, sweet cousin. I know you are tired, but we must have distance from St. Erth." He turned and looked behind them, and she knew he was at last worried that his men hadn't returned to report Silken's death. She prayed harder.

"We will do as you wish, Walter," she said, her voice soft and low. "You're right — we're too close to the tyrant's castle." He seemed to expand before her eyes, so pleased was he at her submissiveness.

"Shall I carry the boy before me?"

"Nay, he is afraid, Walter, for he knows you not. He can't abide me — he follows his sire's lead and insults me and abuses me — but at least I am a known adversary. Leave him with me for the moment, if it pleases you to do so."

It evidently suited Walter, and he turned to speak to a man who rode beside him.

"You act the flap-mouthed fool," Edmund said, his child's voice a high squeak. "He cannot believe you, 'tis absurd!"

"He doesn't know me," Philippa said. "He wants to believe me soft and biddable and as submissive as a cow. Fret not, at least not yet."

It wasn't until late that afternoon that the

two men who had followed Silken caught up with them. Philippa held her breath as they pulled their mounts to a halt beside Walter. She waited, still with apprehension. To her wondrous relief, Walter exploded with rage. "Fools! Inept knaves!"

"Silken escaped," Philippa said into Edmund's ear. "Your father will come. He will save us."

Edmund frowned. "But he is your cousin, Philippa. He won't harm you."

"He's a bad man. Your father hates him, and for good reason, I think."

"But you mocked my father about him and —"

" 'Tis but our way — your father and I must rattle our tongues at each other, goad and taunt each other until one wants to smash the other's head."

Edmund said nothing to that, but he was confused, so Philippa just hugged him, whispering, "Trust me, and trust that your father will save us."

It came to dusk and the sky colored itself with vivid shades of pink. They rode inland a bit and stopped at the edge of a forest whose name Philippa didn't know. It was dark and deep, and she watched silently as two men immediately melted into the trees in search of game. Two other men went to collect wood.

Walter lifted Edmund down and paid him no more attention. Then he wrapped his hands around Philippa's waist and lifted her from Daisy's back. He grunted a bit because she wasn't a languid feather to be plucked lightly. She grinned. When her feet touched the ground he didn't release her, but held her, his hands lightly caressing her waist. "You please me, Philippa, very much."

"Thank you, Walter."

He frowned suddenly. "Your feet are bare. The gown you wear, it is all you have? That wretched bastard gave you nothing to wear?"

She lowered her head and shook her head. "It matters not," she said, her voice meek and accepting.

Walter cursed and ranted. To her horror, he turned on Edmund, and without warning, backhanded the boy. The blow sent Edmund sprawling onto his back on the hard ground, the breath knocked out of him.

"Foul spawn of the devil!"

"Nay, Walter, leave the boy be!" Philippa was trembling with rage, which she prayed her voice didn't give away. She quickly dropped to her knees beside Edmund. She felt his arms, his legs, pressed her hand against his chest. "Oh, God, Edmund, is there pain?"

The boy was white-faced, not with pain but with anger. "I'm all right. Get back to your precious cousin and show him your melting gratitude, Maypole."

Philippa gave him a long look. "Don't be a fool," she said very quietly. She got to her feet. Walter was standing there, absently rubbing his hands together.

"Come to the fire, Philippa. It will grow cool soon, and your rags will not protect you."

Her new gown wasn't a rag, she wanted to yell at him, but she held her peace. She gave Edmund another look and walked beside Walter. One of his men had spread a blanket on the ground, and she eased down, her muscles sore, her back aching from the long ride. "Let the boy warm himself as well," she said after some minutes had passed.

It was nearly dark before the two men returned with a pheasant and two rabbits. After they'd supped and the fire was burning low and orange, Philippa wrapped herself in a blanket, pulled Edmund down to the ground beside her, and waited. It took Walter not long to say, "I heard that de Fortenberry was holding you prisoner. I planned and schemed to get you free of him."

"Where did you hear that?"

Walter paused a moment, then said with a rush of dignity, "I am not without loyal servants, cousin. St. Erth's cistern keeper told me of your position." Walter paused a moment, then leaned over to take Philippa's hand in his. His was warm and dry. She said nothing, didn't move. "The man told me how his master had mistreated you, molesting you, holding you against your will in his bedchamber whilst he ravished you. He even told how Fortenberry had ripped your gown before all his people, then dragged you from the hall to rape you yet again. Then he told me how Alain, the steward, had wanted you killed and how he and another were to do it. He didn't realize that you, dearest heart, were mine own cousin. I killed him for you, Philippa. I slit his miserable throat even as the words gagged in his mouth. You need never fear him again."

The cistein keeper had deserved death, she would have killed him herself had she been able, but to hear of it done in so cold-blooded a fashion . . . And Walter believed she'd been abused, violated. It was, she supposed, a logical conclusion. "Does my father know?"

"You mean Lord Henry? Nay, not as yet."

"What else did he tell you?"

"That his master had stolen Lord Henry's wool and forced you to oversee the weaving and sewing, that he treated you as a servant and a whore. How was Alain found out?"

Philippa said this cautiously, not wanting Walter to realize that she'd discovered his treachery because she worried and fretted about St. Erth and its master. She said only, "He was a fool, and one of the master's men broke his miserable neck."

"Good," Walter said. "I just wish I could have done it for you, sweetling. Of course, I know why the steward feared you and wanted you dead. It was because you read and write and cipher and he knew you'd find him out. A pity he tried to kill you, for he was a good servant and bled St. Erth nearly dry of its wealth, and much of the knave's coin found its way to my coffers."

Philippa felt Edmund stir, felt fury in his small body, and she quickly laid a quieting hand on his shoulder. "Walter, will you return me to my father?"

"Not as yet, Philippa, not as yet. First I wish you to see Crandall, the keep I oversee. And you need clothes for your station, aye, soft ermine, mayhap scarlet for a tunic, and the softest linen for your shifts. I long to see you garbed as befits your position. Then we will speak of your father."

She frowned at him. What was going on here? Why was Walter acting loverlike? Her position? She was his cousin, that was all. Surely he didn't want her, since he believed she was no longer a maiden, since he believed Dienwald had kept her as his mistress. Had perchance her father gone to him? Promised him a dowry if he found her, thus promising her in marriage to her cousin? It seemed the only logical answer to Philippa. No man could possibly want her if he believed she lacked both a maidenhead and a dowry.

"Do we reach Crandall on the morrow?"

He nodded and yawned. He smiled upon her, seeing her weariness. "I will keep you safe, Philippa. You need have no more fear. I will make you . . . happy."

Philippa was terrified, but she nodded, her look as pleasingly sweet as she could muster it. *Happy!*

*St. Erth Castle*

"What say you, Silken? She what? That whoreson Walter killed both Ellis and Albe? *Both* of them? He took Edmund as well?"

"Aye, master. He took both the mistress and Master Edmund. We fetched Ellis' and Albe's bodies, and Father Cramdle buried them with God's sacred words."

Dienwald stood very still, weary from a long hard ride, his mind sluggish; he couldn't take it in. Two days had passed since Sir Walter de Grasse had taken his son and Philippa and killed Ellis and Albe. He himself had just ridden into St. Erth's inner bailey and learned what had happened from Silken. Dear God, what had Walter done to them? Had he taken them for ransom? Fear erased his fatigue.

Silken cleared his throat, his gnarled hand on Dienwald's arm. "Master, heed me. I have been filled with murderous spleen since my escape, but have wondered if what I first believed to be true was true or was the result of blind seeing."

"Make sense, Silken!"

"This Sir Walter greeted the mistress as if . . . as if she'd sent for him and he'd rescued her as she wished him to. As if he'd known she would be riding and he'd had but to wait for her to come in his direction. He was waving at her, smiling like a man filled with joy at the sight of her."

Dienwald stared blankly at the man, and his gut cramped viciously.

"Aye, she'd ridden out three days in a row, master, and that last day, only three men attended her and the young master."

"And was that her demand?"

"I know not," Silken said. "I know only that Ellis and Albe lie rotting in the earth."

The heavens at that moment opened and cold rain flooded down. Thunder rumbled and the sky darkened to night. Dienwald, his tired men at his heels, ran into the great hall. It was silent as a tomb. There were clumps of women standing about, but at the sight of him they became mute. Then Gorkel came to him, his hideous face working. With anger? With betrayal?

"Ale!" Dienwald bellowed. "Margot, quickly!"

He ignored Gorkel for the moment, his thought on his son, now a prisoner of Sir Walter de Grasse, his greatest enemy, his only avowed enemy. His blood ran cold. Would Walter run Edmund through with his sword simply because the boy was of his flesh and blood? Dienwald closed his eyes against the roiling pain of it, against the helplessness he felt. And Philippa . . . Had she betrayed him? Had she taken Edmund riding with her on purpose so that Dienwald wouldn't follow for fear his son would be killed?

He was tired, so tired that his mind went adrift with frantic chafing, with uncertainty. Philippa was gone . . . Edmund was gone, his only son . . . two of his men were dead . . .

Gorkel drew nearer to speak, but Dienwald said, "Nay, hold your peace, I would think."

It was Crooky who said in the face of his master's prohibition, "The mistress left her finery. Surely if she'd wanted to be rescued by her loathsome cousin, if somehow she'd managed to send him word, she would have taken the garments sent her by Lady Kassia, nay, she would have worn them to greet her savior."

"Mayhap, mayhap not."

"She knew you hate the man and that he hates you."

" 'Tis true, curse the proud-minded wench."

"She would not endanger Master Edmund."

"Would she not, fool? Why not, I ask you. Edmund calls her maypole and witch. She held him by his ear and scrubbed him with soap. He howled and scratched and cursed her. Surely she can bear him no affection. Why not, I ask you again."

"The mistress is a lady of steady nature. She has not a sour heart, master, nor did she allow herself to be vexed with Master Edmund. She laughed at his sulky humors and teased him and sewed him clothes, aye, and held him firm to bathe him, as a mother would. She would never seek to harm the boy."

"I don't understand women. Nor do you, so pretend not that you possess some great shrewdness about them. But I do know their blood sings with perversity. They become peevish and testy when they gain not what they want; they become treacherous when they believe a certain man to be the framer of their woes. They see only the ends they seek, and weigh not the means to achieve them. She could perceive Edmund as only a minor obstacle."

"You are the one who sees blindly, master."

"That is what Silken said. Oh, aye, I hear you. Get you gone, fool. Thank the heavens above that you did not sing your opinion to me. My head would have split open and my thoughts would have flowed into oblivion."

"I have known it to happen, master."

"Get out of my sight, fool!" Dienwald made a halfhearted effort to kick Crooky's ribs, but the fool neatly rolled out of reach.

"What will you do, master?"

"I will sleep and think, and think yet more, until the morrow. Then we will ride to Crandall to fetch my son and the wench."

"And if you find she deceived you?"

"I will beat her and tie her to my bed and berate her until she begs God's forgiveness and mine. And then . . ."

"And if you find she deceived you not?"

"I shall . . . Get out of my sight, fool!"

*Windsor Castle*

"Dienwald de Fortenberry," King Edward said, rubbing his jaw as he looked at his travel-stained chancellor. "I know of him, but he has never come to my court. Not that I have been much in evidence before I . . . But never mind that. I have been on England's shores for nearly eight months now and yet de Fortenberry disdains to pay his homage to me. He did not attend my coronation, did he?"

"Nay, he did not. But then again, sire, why should he? If all your nobles — the minor barons included — had attended your coronation, why then London would have burst itself like a tunic holding in a fat man."

The king waved that observation aside. "What of his reputation?"

"His reputation is that of knave, scoundrel, occasional rogue, and loyal friend."

"Graelam wishes an occasional rogue and a scoundrel to be the king's son-in-law?"

Robert Burnell, tired to his mud-encrusted boots, nodded. He'd returned from his travels but an hour before, and already the king in his endless energy wanted to wring him of all information. "Aye, sire. Lord Graelam wasn't certain that you knew Dienwald, and so he recited to me this man's shortcomings as well as his virtues. He claims Dienwald would never importune you for royal favors and that since he has no family, there are none to leech on your coffers. Lord Graelam and his lady call him friend, nay, they call him good friend. They say he would cease his outlaw ways were he the king's son-in-law."

"Or he would continue them, knowing I could not have my son-in-law's neck stretched by the hangman's noose!"

"Lord Graelam does not allow that a possibility, sire. I did question him closely. Dienwald de Fortenberry is a man of honor . . . and wickedness, but his wickedness flows from his humors, which flow from the wildness and independence of Cornwall itself."

"You turn from a shrewd chancellor into a honeyed poet, Robbie. It grieves me to see you babble, you a man of the church, a man of disciplined habits. De Fortenberry, hmmm, Graelam gave you not another name? You heard of no other man who would become me and my sweet Philippa?"

Burnell shook his head. "Shall I read you what I have writ as Lord Graelam spoke to me, sire?"

Edward shook his head, his thick golden hair swinging free about his shoulders. Plantagenet hair, Burnell thought, and wished he could have seen if Philippa was as gloriously endowed as her father.

"Tell me of my daughter," Edward said suddenly. "But be quick about it, Robbie. I must needs argue with some long-nosed Scots from Alexander's court, curse his impertinence and their barbaric tongue."

"I didn't see her," Burnell said quickly, then waited for the storm to rage over his head.

"Why?" Edward asked mildly.

"Lord Henry said she was ill with a bloody flux from her bowels, and thus I couldn't meet her."

"St. Gregory's teeth, will the girl live?"

"Lord Henry assures me the de Beauchamp physician worries not. The girl will live."

"I wish you had waited, Robbie, until you could have spoken with her."

Burnell merely nodded, but his soul was mournful. The king had abjured him to return as soon as he could. And he had obeyed his master, as he always did.

"Lord Henry showed me a miniature of the girl."

The king brightened as he took the small painting from Burnell's hand. He studied the stylized portrait, but saw beyond the white-faced expression of bland purity and the overly pointed chin to the sparkling Plantagenet eyes, eyes as blazing bright as a summer sky, eyes as blue as his own. As for her hair, it was nearly white, it was so blond, and her forehead was flawless, high and white with but thin eyebrows to intercede, but then again, an artist strove to please. He tried to remember the color of Constance's hair but couldn't bring it to mind. He couldn't recall that she'd had such flaxen white hair; no woman had hair that color. That much, he thought, was the artist's fancy. He placed the miniature in his tunic. "Let me think about this. I will speak to the queen. She will translate the artist's rendering, and her counsel rings true. I suppose if I agree, I must bring de Fortenberry here to Windsor to tell him of his good fortune." King Edward strode to the door, then turned back to say, "The damned Scots! Harangue me they will until my tongue swells in my mouth! You must needs rest, Robbie, 'twas a long journey for you, and wearying." The king turned again, his hand on the doorknob, then said absently over his shoulder, "Fetch your writing implements, Robbie. I must have you record faithfully their muling complaints. Then we shall discuss what is to be done with them."

Burnell sighed. He walked to a basin of cold water and liberally splashed his face. He was back in the royal harness, he thought, and smiled.

# 16

*Crandall Keep*

"You are beautiful, Philippa. The soft yellow gown becomes you."

"I thank you, Walter, for your gifts. The gowns and overtunics please me well." They were of the finest quality, and Philippa had wondered where her cousin had gotten them. Obviously from a woman who was short and had big breasts. Evidently she also had rather big feet for her height, for the soft leather slippers pinched Philippa's toes only slightly. Who and where was the woman? Surely she couldn't be pleased to have Philippa wearing her clothing.

"Crandall is a well-maintained keep, Walter, and since you are its castellan, it is to your credit alone. How many men-at-arms are there within the walls?"

"Twenty men, and they are finely trained. Lord Graelam does not stint on our protection, but of course 'tis I who have trained them and am responsible for their skills."

Philippa nodded, wishing there were only

two, and those old and weak of limb. It didn't bode well for her and Edmund getting out or for Dienwald getting in. She hadn't spoken to any of the men, but she had spent a bit of time with several of the keep servants, and discovered that her cousin wasn't a particularly kindly master nor much beloved, but he did appear fair — when he wasn't brandishing his whip. "He's fast wi' t' whip," one of the servants, a bent old woman, had told her in a low voice. "Ye haf t' move fast when he's got blood in his eye and t' whip in his hand." Philippa had but stared at her. A whip! She remembered how several of the women had looked at her when they thought she wasn't paying heed, and they'd spoken behind their hands and looked worried, even frightened. Even now she could feel the female servants looking at her, judging her perhaps, and she wondered at it.

She said now to Walter as she accepted a hunk of bread from his hands, "These lovely garments, cousin — from whence did they come?"

" 'Tis not your concern, sweetling. I had them, and now they are yours. That is all you must needs know."

And Philippa could only wonder, and wonder yet more. He'd given her until yesterday to rest and be at her ease, and then he'd begun to woo her. Philippa couldn't be mistaken, particularly after enduring Ivo de Vescy's outpourings of affection. Walter was playing the besotted swain. Only he wasn't besotted; his words bespoke all the right sentiments, but his eyes remained cold and flat. At first Philippa couldn't credit it. There was no reason — no dowry, in short — for a man in Walter's position to be interested in marriage with her. And it was impossible that he could have fallen deliriously in love with her; he'd known her for but two days. No, her father was behind it; he had to be. But just how, Philippa couldn't imagine.

She toyed with the cabbage stuffed with hare and decided it was time to test the waters. "Walter, does my father know I am here?"

His eyes narrowed on her face, eyes that were always cold and flat when they looked at her. "Not as yet, Philippa. You care so much to return to Beauchamp?"

She shook her head, smiling at him, not chancing an argument because there was something in him that frightened her, something elusive, yet it was there, and she wanted to keep her distance from it.

Walter chewed thoughtfully on mashed chestnuts encrusted with boiled sugar, his favorite dish. Philippa wasn't what he'd expected. He saw flashes of contradiction in her, and although they surprised him, they didn't worry him unduly. Despite her hardy size, he could control her easily should the need arise. He would wed her by the end of the week. He had the time; he could afford to go gently with her, to bend her slowly to his will. Three days was enough time to bend the most rebellious woman to his will. He thought now that he could tell her some of the truth. Perhaps it would make her trust him all the more quickly, and it didn't really matter one way or the other to him.

"Your father was here, Philippa," he said, and watched her twist in her chair, her expression stunned. "He thought perhaps you had come to me when you escaped in the wool wagons, as you would have if that bastard hadn't captured you and taken you to St. Erth.

"At the time of Lord Henry's visit, I didn't know where you were. Lord Henry told me, Philippa, that he'd promised you to William de Bridgport in marriage. He was most adamant about it, even when I argued with him. I could not, nay, still cannot, imagine you wedded to that testy old lecher. But Lord Henry needs the coin de Bridgport will pay for you. You see, Philippa, as much as it hurts me to wound you, you must know the truth. Lord Henry holds his possessions more dear than he ever held you."

Philippa could only shake her head. So her father had come here. She'd shown surprise to Walter, guessing it was the correct response, but she'd already guessed her father's presence. Her insides felt cold and cramped. She wanted to scream that her father couldn't have told Walter that, he couldn't have, it wasn't true.

But it was true. Philippa had overheard him say it himself. It wasn't Walter's fault.

"You must still send a messenger to my father to tell him I am here. I would not wish you to be my father's enemy."

Walter started to shake his head, then thought better of it. He'd just been offered his best opportunity. "I think we still have some time, sweetling, before I do that. Three days, perhaps four." He saw her revulsion, her fear, and he moved swiftly to take advantage of it. He gently took her hand in his. There were calluses on the pads of her fingers, attesting to the labors Dienwald had forced her to, the mangy scoundrel. He felt her tense, but she didn't pull away. "Listen, Philippa," he said, his voice low and soft, "if you wed me, there is naught Lord Henry can do. You cannot be forced to wed de Bridgport. You will be safe as my wife, you will be secure. No one — not even the king himself — could take you from me."

There it was, Philippa thought, staring at her cousin. He wanted to marry her, but it made no sense. He believed her already ravished by Dienwald, so he couldn't expect a virgin's blood on the wedding sheets. More important, there was no coin forthcoming from her father. What was going on? She must continue her deceit until she discovered his plot. She kept her head modestly lowered and let her fingers rest against his.

"You offer me much, Walter, more than I deserve. You must allow me time to compose my thoughts. All this comes as a surprise, and my thoughts have gone awry." She raised her head and saw the frown of impatience in his eyes. She added quickly, "I am slow of reason, Walter, being but a woman, and your generosity, though a gift from God, leaves me tongue-tied, but just for a brief time. Until tomorrow, dear cousin — then I will speak to you of my feelings."

He gave her a grave nod and squeezed her fingers again before releasing her hand. Her tongue was smooth, her words gently flowing, respectful, filled with deference, but something bothered him. Perhaps it was that she hadn't asked of their close kinship, thus requiring special permission by the church. But she was but a woman and probably ignorant of such things. Aye, just a woman, but she could read and write and cipher. He didn't wish to tell her that he shared not one drop of her blood, that he knew her conceived of another man's seed, a seed most royal, but he wasn't at all certain of her reaction. No, he must hold his tongue. She was biddable, soft and comely, and she was endowed with beauty aplenty. She was too tall for his taste, but then again, there was Britta, hidden away now, but waiting for him, and he would continue with her when it pleased him to do so. Tonight, he thought, his loins tightening at the thought of her. He gave a small shudder. Were it not for Philippa, he would leave this instant and go to Britta. He saw that Philippa was looking about the hall, and said, "What troubles you, sweet cousin?"

"Naught, 'tis just that I see not the boy, Walter. Although I do not hold him dear, I have a responsibility for him, since he was with me when you rescued me. Have you yet sent a demand of ransom to Dienwald?"

Walter shook his head. He wouldn't send anything to anyone until he was her husband. Not even to his overlord, Graelam de

Moreton. "The whelp keeps company with my stable lads. I do him a good service. 'Twill humble him to see how those beneath him live, and make him more stouthearted. He will learn what it is like to serve."

At least he wasn't locked away somewhere in the keep, but she worried that the villeins would abuse him. She said nothing, merely forced herself to eat another bite of the cabbage. It needed some of the wild thyme she'd just planted in her garden at St. Erth. *Her* garden. Philippa wanted to cry, odd in itself, but it was true: St. Erth had become home to her in a very short length of time and its master had become the man she wanted. But he didn't want her, had never lied about it, had even kept his manhood out of her body because he feared having to keep her, having to take her to wive because she was too wellborn to use at his whim.

She pushed Dienwald and his perversity from her mind. She had to escape Walter, and she had to take Edmund with her. She had not many more days before Walter pushed her into wedlock. She doubted not that he would bed her to force her hand. She was sleeping by herself in a tiny chamber off the great hall, a chamber, from the smell of it, that had held winter grain but days before her arrival. It was airless, but she didn't mind; the stuffiness kept her awake, and that allowed her to think. And she thought of St. Erth and its master and wondered if he were close even now. But she knew she couldn't simply wait for Dienwald to do something; she had to act to save herself and Edmund.

Walter kept her with him that evening, playing draughts, and when she won, forgetting that she was but a woman and thus inferior to male stratagems, he was sharp with her.

"You were lucky," he said, his voice edged with anger. "I allowed you too much time with your moves because of your sex. You deceived me, cousin, but . . ." He paused, and the light changed in his eyes. He shook his head, wagging a playful finger in her face. "Ah, Philippa, you won because of your sweet nature and your softness. You took me in with your gentle presence, your glorious eyes. You see me slain at your dainty feet. All my thoughts were perforce of you, my dearest. Would you sleep now, sweetling?"

He wasn't stupid, Philippa thought as she rose from her chair. He'd been furious because she'd beaten him, but quickly adjusted himself to a more favorable position in her eyes. He was still her gallant suitor.

But for how much longer? She shuddered as she walked beside him to the small room. Before he left her, he grasped her upper arms and pulled her against him. "Beautiful cousin," he said, and kissed her ear because she jerked her head to one side. It was a mistake. She felt his fingers dig into her flesh, heard his breath sharpen with anger.

"Please, Walter," she said softly, "I wish . . ." Words failed her. She wanted to scream at him to remove his slimy person.

He drew a false conclusion. "Ah, 'tis because he abused you, because he forced you. I won't hurt you, cousin, never will I touch you amiss. I will always be your gentle master. You must trust me, and I will make you forget the knave's violence toward you." He leaned down and lightly touched his mouth to her forehead and released her arms. "Sleep well, my heart."

Philippa nodded, her head down, but she couldn't prevent the words that came spilling from her mouth. "Walter, you know me so little. You met me only as a child. Why do you wish to wed with me? You know I am no longer a maid. You know that my father will not dower me. Tell me, dear cousin, tell me why you so wish me as your wife."

She raised her head and knew that she'd

again jumped with her feet; she hadn't thought. What if he turned on her, what if . . . ? She waited, tense and still, hoping he would speak, yet fearful that he would simply rant at her and perhaps beat her with that whip of his.

Walter found himself at something of an impasse. Again he saw the contradiction in her. She was but a woman, full of softness and gentle smiles, and here she was questioning him, but, ah, so sweetly she questioned. He'd thought to slap her hard to show her that he wouldn't always tolerate inquiries from her, but now he thought better of it. That was doubtless how Dienwald had treated her. Aye, Dienwald had been violent and rough with her. Walter must prove to her that he was different. He would resort to more straightforward methods only if she pushed him to them.

"I have loved you since I first saw you five years ago, Philippa. I spoke to Lord Henry then, but he only shook his head and laughed and called me fool. I have corresponded with him over the years, but had almost admitted failure of my hopes when he came to me and admitted that you'd fled to escape the marriage with de Bridgport. I am a simple man, Philippa, with simple needs and only one desire that burns in my life, and that is you, to earn you for my wife."

"But I am used," she said, and looked at him straightly, wishing she could tell him his memory was faulty. He'd last seen her more than five years before. "He debauched me again and again. He used me unnaturally."

If only Dienwald had done a bit more debauching than he had, she thought now, watching Walter. He wasn't stupid, this cousin of hers, so when he leaned down and kissed her gently on the mouth, she wasn't overly surprised. Dismayed, but not surprised. "It matters not to me," he said in a richly sincere voice. He turned and left her, locking the door behind him.

"But you must needs lock me in," she said after him.

There was but one candle to light the chamber. She felt the shadows surround her, and they were comforting. She made her way to the narrow bed, stripped off her soft yellow overtunic and the gown beneath. She stretched out on her back, staring up into the darkness.

What, after all, could he have said to her? she wondered now. But why did he wish to wed her? *Why?* Sir Walter was a dangerous man, and she recognized the threat in him. She saw the intensity in him, the will to drive himself, to drive others. The last thing that would be his main desire was a woman, any woman.

She must go very carefully. She must give him false security. She must hang around his neck until he wished her to leave him alone. Then, perhaps, she would find a way for her and Edmund to escape Crandall. If they didn't escape, she feared what would happen to them. She would refuse to wed Walter and he would rape her endlessly. She knew it. But *why?*

She dared not wait for Dienwald, for the way things were progressing, he might well be too late. But why, she wondered again and again, did Walter want to wed her so badly?

Over and over she tortured her brain with possible motives Walter could harbor. Had her father changed his mind and offered Walter money if he found her and wedded her? Land? She shook her head on that possibility. Her father never changed his mind. Never. There were no answers, only more questions that made her head ache badly.

*Near Crandall Keep*

Dienwald scratched his chest. He was hot and dirty and disliked the fact. He hated the waiting but knew there was naught else to be done. He rose and began pacing the perimeter of his camp. They were withdrawn into a copse of thick maple trees, well-hidden from the narrow winding road that led to Crandall. His men were lolling about, bored and restless, arguing, tossing dice, recounting heroics and tales of their male prowess.

Where were the fool and Gorkel?

What of Philippa and Edmund? Worry gnawed at him, paralyzed his brain. What was the truth? Had Philippa betrayed him, or had she been caught as certainly as Ellis and Albe had been slain?

Only she could give him the answer. She or that whoreson peasant, Walter. Dienwald sat down and leaned against an oak tree older than life itself, and closed his eyes. What he wanted, damn her soft hide, was Philippa. He saw her sprawled in the mud, laughing, her eyes a vivid blue in her blackened face; then he saw her naked as he threw buckets of water on her and soaped her body with his hands. His loins were instantly heavy, his rod hard and hurting. He knew in that moment that he would have to return her to her father the moment he got his hands on her again. If he kept her with him, he would take her, and he wouldn't allow himself to do that. If he did, it would be all over for him.

He wouldn't allow himself to be caught. Allying himself to de Beauchamp — he couldn't bear the thought of it. Lord Henry was a pompous ass, arrogant and secure in his own privilege, in his immense power and dignity. No, Dienwald would remain free, unencumbered, answerable to no one other than himself, responsible for no one but himself and his son. If he needed wool, he'd steal it. He wished now he hadn't forgotten about the wine arriving from Kassia's father. He would have gladly planned the shipwreck and the theft of every cask. He would have laughed in Graelam's face, and taken a pounding if Graelam had pushed him on it. He wanted to be free.

He wondered what was happening at Crandall, and he fretted, bawled complaints to the heavens, and paced.

*Crandall Keep*

In Crandall's inner bailey, Crooky smiled and sang and capered madly about, drawing everyone's attention. He held Gorkel on a chain leash fastened about his huge neck with a leather band, and tugged at him, carping and scolding at him as though he were a bear to be alternately baited and cajoled. "Nod your ugly head to that fair wench yon, Gorkel!"

Gorkel eyed the fair wench, who was staring at him, fear and excitement lighting her eyes. He nodded to her and smiled wide, showing the vast space between his front teeth. He felt the fool tugging madly at his leash and growled fearsomely, making the females in the growing crowd scream with fear and the men step back a pace. The bells on his cap tinkled wildly.

The fool laughed and pranced around Gorkel, kicking out but not quite touching him. "Fret not, fair maids. 'Tis a brute, and ugly as the devil's own kin, but he's a gentle monster and he'll do as I bid him. Hark now, yon comely maid with the soft smile, what wish you to have the creature do?"

The girl, Glenda by name and pert by nature, angled forward, preening in the center of all attention, and sang out, "I wish him to dance. A jig. And I want him to raise his monstrous legs high."

Crooky hissed between his teeth, "Canst thou jig for the maid, Gorkel?"

Gorkel never let his wide grin slip. His expression vacuous, his eyes blank, he began to hop and jump. He ponderously raised one leg and then the other and clambered about gracelessly. Quickly Crooky began to sing and clap his hands to a beat Gorkel didn't need. His eyes scanned the crowd as he bellowed as loudly as he could:

All come to see the beastie prance
He'll cavort and jump, he'll do a wild dance
He's a heathen and a savage, ugly and black,
But withal he's merry, no matter his lack.

Crooky wanted to shout with relief when he saw Edmund slip between two men and gape at Gorkel. The boy was ragged and bruised and filthy, but at the sight of him and Gorkel, he looked happy as a young stoat, his eyes gleaming. Thank St. Andrew that he was alive. Where was the mistress? Was she imprisoned? Had Sir Walter harmed her? Crooky's blood ran cold at the thought.

Crooky jingled Gorkel's chain, and he ceased his clumsy movements and stood quietly beside the fool, breathing hard and still grinning his frightening grin. He eyed Edmund and nodded, his eyes holding a warning. "Ah," yelled Crooky suddenly, "methinks I see another fair wench. A big fair wench with enough hair on her head to stuff a mattress! Come hither, fair maid, and let my gargoyle behold your beauty. He'll not touch you, but let him behold what God created after he made a monster."

Philippa's heart was pounding madly. She'd watched Gorkel do his dance, not at first recognizing him in his wildly colorful and patched garments, the fool's cap on his head and the mangy beard that covered his jaws. It had been Crooky's bellowing verses that had brought her, nearly running, to the inner bailey. Dienwald was here, close, thank God. And she saw Edmund, filthy but well-looking, and quite alive, thank God yet again. "I come," she called out, voice filled with humor. "Let the monster gawk at the fair wench."

She picked up her skirts and raced toward them. She saw Crooky's relieved smile stiffen and go flat. She didn't understand. She drew to a halt, thinking frantically. "I am here. I bid you good morrow, monster." She curtsied. "Behold me, a maid who frets and who wishes for the moon but sees naught but a melting sun that holds her in bondage and gives her to chaff endlessly."

Crooky beheld her closely, all the while Gorkel loped in a clumsy gait around her, stroking his big bearded jaw.

She was beautiful, Crooky thought, finely dressed as a maid should be, as a *beloved* maid should be. She was no prisoner, Sir Walter no warden. Had he rescued her at her wish? He thought through her words, elegant words that twisted and intertwined about themselves. Had she meant that she wanted to escape her cousin? Crooky knew the matter wasn't his to decide. Since his tenth year, when the tree had broken and fallen on him, he knew that he wouldn't survive unless it was by his wits. He learned that his memory was his strength. He now committed her every word to his memory.

"Well, lovely maid," he said after a moment, "God grant you no ingratitude or bitter wrongs. If you will seek the moon, I will tell you that like the sun, the moon must hide in its hour, then burst forth, when least expected, to glow fairly yet in stark truth upon the face that seeks it forth. The moon awaits, maid, ever close as its habit, waits till tide and time issue it out."

"What is this, cousin? A cripple and a beast to be held by its leash?"

Philippa smiled at Walter, beckoning him to her side. "Aye, Walter, a team that brings shrewd humor and light laughter to Crandall. The little crooked one here tells me of the moon and the sun and how each must await its turn, and the monster there, he bellows and dances for all your fair maids."

Walter cared not a whit for the two who

stood facing him. "If they please you, dearest heart, then so let them frolic and rattle their tongues to rhymes that bring good cheer."

Crooky said loudly, "Fair and hardy maid, what wish you for Gorkel the Hideous to do?"

"Why, I believe I wish to write him a love poem, not rhymed, for I have not your talent, but one to tell of beauty and love that ravaged the heart. What say you, beast? Wish you to have a love poem from me?"

Gorkel scratched his armpit, and Crooky, yanking hard at his leash, yelled, "Will you, monster? Nod aye, beast!"

Gorkel nodded and bellowed, and the crowd cheered.

Philippa nodded. "I shall hie me to my paper and write the poem for the monster. Give the crowd more laughter, then."

"I don't understand you," Walter said, and he sounded impatient and fretful.

"I amuse myself, Walter, as the beast has amused me. It pleases you not?"

She gave him that sweet, utterly diffident look that made him feel more powerful than a Palatine prince. It was on the tip of his tongue to tell her to write an immense tome, but he changed his mind. He mustn't give in to her female whims each and every time.

"It doesn't please me this time, sweetling. Fret not." And before he left her, he raised his hand and lightly touched her cheek. As she looked at him, her smile frozen in place, his fingers fell to her throat, then to her breast, and before all of his people, he caressed her with his fingertips. He laughed and strode away.

*Near Crandall Keep*

"Tell me, and be quick about it."

Crooky, silent for once, looked at his master, uncertain how to begin.

"Did you see Edmund? The wench?"

"Aye, they're both alive," Gorkel said as he pulled off his belled cap. "The young master was dirty, his clothes rags, but he looked healthy."

"And the mistress?"

"She was finely garbed," Crooky said, looking over Dienwald's right shoulder. "Very finely garbed, a beautifully plumed peacock, a princess."

Dienwald felt his gut cramp. She'd betrayed him, damn her, betrayed him and stolen his son.

"Tell me everything. Leave nothing out or I'll kick in your ribs."

And Crooky related everything that had

occurred. He recited faithfully what Philippa had said to him and to Gorkel. He paused, then ended, "She is no prisoner, at least it appeared not so. Sir Walter kissed her in full view of his people, and his hand caressed her breast."

Dienwald saw red and his fists bunched in savage fury. What had he expected, anyway? The wench had fled him, and that was that. "Tell me again her words." After Crooky had once more recited them, he said, "What meant she about the moon — am I the moon, silent and hidden, then bursting and malignant in her face? Bah! It makes no sense, the wench was playing with you, turning your own rhymes back on you, mocking you."

"She asked Sir Walter if she could pen a love poem to Gorkel, but he refused her. Mayhap she would have written of her plight, master."

Dienwald cursed with specific relish, saying in disgust, "She fooled you yet again! She would have penned her request for me to keep away, else she'd see Edmund hurt!"

Gorkel said, "Nay, master."

"What know you of anything!"

"Why did she keep the boy with her?"

"For protection, fool, what else? She isn't stupid, after all, for all that she's a female."

He shook his fist in disgust at both of them, ignored his other men who looked ready to speak their opinions, and strode away from them all, disappearing into the maze of maple trees.

"He is sorely tried," Galen said, shaking his head. "He knows not what to think."

"The mistress wants rescuing," said Crooky, "despite all the plumage and display."

"And the boy," Gorkel added. "I fear what that whoreson will do to the boy, for he sorely hates the father."

# 17

*Crandall Keep*

Late that night Philippa lay in her bed thinking furiously, an occupation that hadn't paled since Walter had brought her to Crandall. She thought of her excitement, her hope, when she'd burst into the inner bailey to see Gorkel cavorting about like a mad buffoon and Crooky twirling Gorkel's leash while singing at the top of his lungs. But what good had any of it done? Her attempt to tell Crooky of her plight, her plea to write Gorkel a love poem, all had been dashed when Walter had shown his possession of her in front of everyone by kissing her and caressing her breast. Crooky would tell Dienwald, of a certainty. But still they would attempt a rescue, if not for her, then for Edmund. But how? What could Dienwald do? He couldn't very well storm Crandall Keep. Walter would kill Edmund without blinking an eye. No, Dienwald would use guile and cunning; she doubted not that he would succeed, but still, the thought of him being hurt terrified her.

She knew well enough that Walter would kill him if but given a chance.

She had to do something, and she had to do it early on the morrow. She fell asleep, and her dreams, oddly enough, were of her first riding lessons at six years old on a mare named Cottie, a gentle animal Bernice had urged over a fence two years later, breaking the mare's leg.

Philippa came awake suddenly, tears still in her mind for the mare. She hadn't really heard anything, it was just a feeling that something wasn't right and she must pay attention now and wake up fully or she wouldn't like what happened to her.

Slowly, very slowly, Philippa turned her head toward the door. Walter had locked it as usual when he'd left her earlier, yet a key was turning in the lock and the door was opening slowly but surely.

It had to be Walter. He'd tired of waiting. He'd come to ravish her and be done with it. He didn't play the besotted swain very well.

So be it, Philippa thought, her muscles flexing to make her ready. She didn't move, just thought of what she would do to him to protect herself. She would fight him, and at the very least she would hurt him badly. She still wore her shift, one of soft linen that came to her thighs and left her arms bare.

She wished now she had on every article of clothing Walter had given her, to make his task of ravishing her all the more difficult. She listened and strained her eyes toward the door. Walter wasn't making any noise. Why? That made no particular sense. He wouldn't care, would he? He wouldn't care if she screamed or yelled. His men would do naught to help her.

The door widened, making no sound, the hinges not even creaking. From the dim light in the passage without, Philippa could at last make out the outline of the person.

It wasn't Walter. It was a woman.

Philippa didn't act immediately, as her nature urged her to. No, she held herself perfectly still, waiting to see what the woman would do, waiting to see what the woman wanted. Perhaps she wanted to free her. But how had the woman gotten the key to her chamber?

From Walter, of course. Walter was far too careful, far too possessive a man to allow others to keep something as important as the key to her chamber. So the woman must know him very well, must know him intimately. . . . Philippa gathered herself together and waited.

The woman was creeping across the narrow chamber now, and Philippa saw that she held a knife in her raised hand. The woman had come to kill her, not free her.

Philippa's astonishment was replaced by rage, and she jumped to her feet, yelling at the top of her lungs, "What do you want? Get away from me! Help! *A moi!* Walter . . . *A moi!*"

The woman lunged at her, extending her arm, bringing the knife down toward her chest. Philippa grabbed the woman's wrist, wrenching her arm back, but the woman was stronger than her meager inches would indicate. She was panting, gasping, fury making her as strong as Philippa, and she said, her voice vicious, filled with hatred, "You damnable slut! You devil's spawn! You'll not have him! Do you hear me? Nay, never! I'll kill you!" And she jerked away from Philippa, her breasts heaving, staring at Philippa with hatred. Philippa slowly backed away from the furious woman and that very sharp knife.

She held up her hand in supplication. "Who are you? I've done nothing to you. What are you talking about? You're mad, wanting to kill me for no reason!"

"No reason!" the woman hissed, the words so harsh that spittle flew out of her mouth. "You damnable trollop, Walter is mine, only mine, and he'll stay mine. You'll not get him. He'll not wed you, no matter what you bring him! He loves me, wants me more than all the filthy riches you would bring him!"

*But I wouldn't bring him anything,* Philippa started to say, just as the woman lunged again, bringing the knife down in a brutal arc, sure and fast, and Philippa whirled to the side, away from the maddened woman, but she wasn't fast enough and she felt the tip of the knife slice through the flesh of her upper arm. She felt the coldness of it, then a quick numbness.

"You won't escape me, whore!"

Philippa, knowing there was no choice now, jerked about and struck out, back-handing the woman, her palm flat, ringing hard against her cheek. The woman yelled in pain and rage but didn't falter. She flew toward Philippa, the knife extended to the fullest.

Philippa saw the knife coming into her heart, stabbing deep, killing her, before she'd known what it was to really live, to love and be loved, and she whispered, "Dien-wald . . ."

She could hear the air hiss as the knife sliced through it, and she dashed frantically toward the open door and into the arms of Walter de Grasse.

"What in God's name goes on here?"

Walter was shaking Philippa hard until he saw the blood flowing from her upper arm. He paled in the dim light, not wanting to credit it. Then he stared at the woman, half-crouched, the bloody knife dangling in her hand, and he whispered, "Britta . . . oh, no, why?" He pushed Philippa away from him and was at the woman's side, lifting her up, pulling her against him.

"Britta?"

She shook her head, her breath coming in painful gasps, her huge breasts heaving.

"She tried to kill me," Philippa said, watching with benumbed fascination as he caressed the woman. "Who is she? Why does she want me dead?"

She watched, silent now, as pain crossed Walter's face and it whitened, and she understood at last that this was the woman whose garments she wore, this was the woman who was her cousin's mistress, a woman who, incredibly, loved her cousin, and who couldn't, perforce, abide her. Philippa's mind clogged and she could but stare silently as Walter held the woman even more tightly, clutching her against him, speaking softly, so softly that Philippa couldn't make out his words.

Without further hesitation Philippa

picked up a small three-legged stool, held it high over her head, and brought it down with all her strength on Walter's head. The woman cried out as Walter slumped against her, bearing her to the floor with his weight.

"Don't yell, you stupid fool!" Philippa hissed at the woman. "Just stay where you are and hold your peace and your lover. I'm leaving you and him and this cursed keep forever. He's yours until the devil takes him." Before Britta could push her lover off her, Philippa had grabbed the knife from her hand and jerked the keys from the pocket in her tunic.

"Just be quiet, you silly bitch, if you want him here and me gone!"

Philippa grabbed her gown and pulled it over her head even as she dashed toward the door. She locked it, then froze on the spot. Just around the corner, not three feet from where she stood, she heard two men in argument.

"I'll tell ye, thass trouble! I heard them wenches yelling and t' master runs in."

"Leave t' master be an' get back to yer bed."

"Oh, aye, there's trouble and it's yer ears he'll slice off, that, or he'll take his whip to yer back."

"Ye go back and I'll look."

Philippa flattened herself against the cold stone wall. She heard the one man still grumbling as he shuffled away. As for the other man, in the next instant he came around the corner to see a wild-eyed female with a knife in her hand and blood running in rivulets down her arm. He had time only to suck in his breath before the knife handle slammed into his temple and he crashed to the floor.

Slowly Philippa got enough nerve to peer around the corner. She saw sleeping men and women spread over the floor in the hall, and snores rose to the blackened rafters above. She crept as quietly as she could, inching slowly along the wall toward the large oak doors. Slowly, ever so slowly, she moved, knowing at any second a man or woman could rise up and shriek at her and it would be all over and perhaps Walter would kill her if his mistress didn't do it first. A dog suddenly appeared from nowhere and sniffed at her bare feet.

She didn't move, her heart pounding, letting the dog tire of her scent, then move on, praying the animal wouldn't bark. Then, without warning, she felt a spurt of pain in her arm and looked at it. So much blood, and it was hers. She had to slow it or she would faint. She slipped outside into the inner bailey and looked heavenward. There was no moon this night, and the sky was overcast, with no stars, no light whatsoever. She flattened herself against the wooden railing and ripped off a goodly section of the lower part of the gown. She wrapped it around her arm, using her teeth to tie the knot tightly. She felt the pain, felt it deeply, but it didn't matter. She had to find Edmund and they had to escape this wretched keep. She couldn't allow the wound to slow her. She had to be strong.

Fortune turned, and Philippa found Edmund close to the stable door, atop a heap of hay, sleeping on his side, his legs drawn up to his chest, his face resting on his folded hands. Philippa knelt beside him. "Edmund, love, come wake up." She shook him gently, ready to slap her hand over his mouth if he awoke afraid and cried out.

But Edmund awoke quickly and completely and simply stared up at her. "Philippa?"

"Aye, I'm here, and now we must leave. We'll need horses, Edmund. What think you?"

"Is my father here to save us?"

Philippa shook her head. "No, 'tis just us, but we can do it. Now, about those horses."

Edmund scrambled to his feet, excitement and a goodly dose of fear churning in his belly, and he grinned up at her. Then he was thoughtful, and Philippa waited. "We need to croak the two stable lads. We need —"

Philippa raised the knife handle. "It works," she said.

Edmund's eyes glistened and Philippa wondered if all men were born with the battle cry of war in their blood, with the love of violence and battle bred into their bones. "Show me where they are and then I'll . . ." She paused, then added, "You get the horses, Edmund. Pick well, for they must carry us to your father. He awaits out there somewhere."

"He can't be far away," Edmund said. "But we will come to him and not have to lie like helpless babes for him to rescue us. There is a difficulty, though, Philippa. I can't get the horses for us."

She stared down at him and saw the chain and thick leather manacle clamped about his right ankle. Those miserable whoresons! She wanted to yell in rage, but she said calmly, "Who has the key to that thing?"

"One of the stable lads you're going to croak," he said, and gave her an impudent smile.

They were good together, Philippa

thought with surprised pleasure a few minutes later. She'd quickly found the key and released Edmund. She hadn't even paused before coshing the two stable lads on the head. They'd probably given Edmund his bruises, the malignant little brutes, and tethered him like an animal. No, she had no regrets that the both of them would have vile head pains on the morrow.

Edmund had brought out Daisy and the destrier that belonged to Walter. Should she dare? she wondered, then tossed her head. She dared. Her arm was paining fiercely now, and they weren't yet out of Crandall. She couldn't succumb to the pain, not yet, not for a very long while.

Edmund held the reins of the two horses, staying back in the shadows whilst Philippa sauntered like a whore in full heat and in need of coin toward the one guard who stood in a near-stupor near Crandall's gates. Three other sentries were patrolling, but they were distant now. She'd watched them, counting.

"Ho! Who are . . . ? Why, 'tis Sir Walter's mistress! What want you? Wh—"

She poked out her breasts and threw her arms around the man. He gaped and gawked and quickly grabbed her buttocks in his big hands, dropping his sword to fill his hands with her, and Philippa whipped out the knife and, leaning back, slammed the handle down on his head. He looked at her in mournful surprise but didn't fall. "You shouldn't ought to a done that," he said, and brought his hands up to her throat. He squeezed, saying all the while, "Ye're a handful, wench, but I'll show ye not to play wi' me." He squeezed harder and harder, and Philippa saw the world blackening before her eyes as the knife dropped from her slack fingers.

Then, as if from afar, she heard a voice saying, "You're a bloody coward, hurting a female like that . . . you whoreson, stupid lout with a mother who slept with infidels . . ." The fingers left her throat and she sagged to her knees, clutching her throat, gulping in air. She looked up to see the man turning, as if in a dream, turning toward Edmund, but Edmund was astride Daisy, and he was higher than the guard and brought a thick metal spade down as hard as he could on the guard's head. Philippa watched the man stare up at Edmund and shake his head as if to clear it. Then he made a small sound in his throat and fell in a heap to the ground.

Philippa staggered to her feet, grabbing the knife. Her throat felt on fire, and she croaked out, "Excellent, Edmund. Now we must go, quickly. The sentries will be returning in but moments now."

She raced to the keep gates and jerked at the thick beam levered from side to side of the large gate. It was heavy and she was getting weaker by the moment. She cursed and heaved, and finally the beam began to ease slowly upward until finally she managed to bring it fully vertical. "Now," she whispered, and pushed the gate open.

Philippa quickly mounted, grunting with effort, for there was no saddle and her right arm was now nearly useless. Suddenly she felt Edmund heaving her up, and she landed facedown against the destrier's neck, panting with exertion and pain.

Then Edmund was astride Daisy again and she cried, "Away, Edmund!"

The destrier was huge and fast and mean, and he quickly ate distance from Crandall. They needed to be fast. Philippa could imagine that Walter was already after them, unless she'd hit him so very hard that he was still unconscious and unable to give orders. The destrier pulled away even further, quickly outstripping Daisy. Philippa tried to pull him back, but her one strong hand wasn't enough. The destrier was in control.

"Edmund!" She turned back, her hair

flying madly in her face.

"Hold, Philippa. I'm coming!"

But it wasn't Edmund who stopped the great destrier. It was a man flying out of the darkness astride a huge stallion, his head bare, his face averted, all his attention on the frantically galloping horse.

Other men appeared, shouting out, and she heard Edmund yell, "Father! Father, quickly, help Philippa!"

And she felt the reins jerked from her hand and then the destrier lurched up on his hind legs, whinnying frantically, his front hooves flailing, and she heard Dienwald's voice, soothing, calming the frenzied animal.

Then it was over and Philippa was weaving on the horse's back, her gown torn and pulled to her thighs, and she smiled at the man who turned to face her.

"The horse was maddened because of my smell," Philippa said, just content to stare at his face.

"You make no sense, wench."

"The blood . . . the smell of blood," she said. "It maddens animals to smell a human's blood." She slumped forward against the animal's neck. Before she fell unconscious, his arms were around her, drawing her close, and she sighed deeply, content now to give it up.

The burning pain brought her back. She tried to jerk away from it, cursing it in her mind, begging the pain to release her for just a few minutes longer, just a moment longer, but it was there and it was worse and she moaned and opened her eyes.

"Hold still."

She focused on Dienwald, leaning over her. He wasn't looking at her face, but looking grimly down at her arm. "Hello," she said. "I'm glad to see you. We knew you had to be close."

"Hold still and keep your tongue behind your teeth."

But she couldn't. There was too much to be said, too much to be explained. "Am I going to die?"

"Of course you're not going to die, you heedless wench!"

"Is Edmund all right?"

"Yes. Now, be quiet, you try me sorely with your babble."

"I fainted, I suppose, and I've never before fainted in my whole life. I was scared until I saw you, and then it was all right."

"Be still. Why is your voice so rough?"

"The guard tried to strangle me after I struck him with the knife handle. His head was powerfully hard, but Edmund told him his mother bedded infidels to get his attention from me, and then hit him with a spade and he finally fell. We got away from him, we got away from all of them. I counted the minutes, you know, and the other sentries were elsewhere. You knew we were at Crandall. Silken reached you safely."

"Aye, be quiet now."

"I prayed he would reach you. It was our only hope. Walter was stupid — he gave Silken time to outrun his men. I knew he would reach you, knew you would come."

"Wench, shut your irritating mouth."

"Walter's mistress tried to kill me, you know. Isn't that strange? And she kept screaming that she didn't care that I would bring him riches, 'twas she who would have him. I gave him to her freely, and I told her that. I also wanted to tell her that there were no riches, nay, not even a single coin. And he came in when I yelled my head off and he saw the blood on my arm, yet he went to her and held her and her name was Britta and it was her clothes he'd given me to wear. I struck him with a stool and he went down like a stone. It was a wonder sound and he pinned the woman beneath him. I got her knife and the keys and locked them in."

"Philippa, you're weak from loss of blood

and you're babbling. Now, be still."

"She has huge breasts," Philippa said, then closed her eyes at a particularly sharp jab in her arm. "Walter had given me her clothes and they were much too short for me and much too loose in the chest. Her breasts are of a mighty size. Gorkel and Crooky were wondrous funny." Dienwald drew in a deep breath at that moment and poured ale over the wound. Philippa lurched up, crying out softly, then fell back unconscious.

Dienwald stilled for a moment, then quickly placed his palm over her heart. The beat was slow and steady. He bound up her arm, then turned to see Northbert's legs. He didn't rise, just looked up at his man and said, "She's unconscious again, but the wound is clean, and if there is no poisoning, she will be all right."

Northbert nodded. "Master Edmund is overexcited, master, his tongue rattling about. Gorkel told him to go to sleep, but he can't close his mouth."

"She was the same."

Crooky hobbled up then. "The mistress wasn't a betrayer wi' her cousin, master."

"I suppose she wasn't, yet it strikes an odd chord."

"Aye, it does," said Gorkel in his low, terrifying rumble. "The boy refuses to sleep until he sees that the mistress is all right."

Dienwald looked surprised at that. "He *what?* Oh, the devil! Nothing is aright here, nothing! I let the two of them out of my sight for the space of a week, and everything goes topsy turvy. Bring Edmund and let him see the wench, I don't care."

Gorkel and Crooky exchanged looks, and Northbert merely shrugged.

Edmund knelt next to Philippa, and said softly as he stared down at her face, "She was very angry when she saw the manacle around my ankle. Her face turned all red and her hands shook. She'll be all right, truly?"

"Aye, she's too hardy to let this bring her down," Dienwald said. "You must sleep now, Edmund. At dawn we'll ride."

"You're not worried that the whoreson will come upon us tonight?"

His father grinned. "He'd never find us in this dark. There's not even a single star to guide him."

It was the middle of the night when Philippa awoke again. Her arm hurt, but not too badly. She was surrounded by darkness, which she'd become accustomed to in the small chamber at Crandall, but this was different. Sweet air touched her face and filled her nostrils, and she could hear the rustle of tree leaves in the gentle night breezes, and the deep breathing of a man. She opened her eyes and saw Dienwald stretched out next to her, his hand holding her wrist. He was snoring lightly.

She smiled and said, "Edmund and I escaped. Are you not pleased?"

His hand on her wrist tightened. Dienwald was dreaming of an explicitly passionate scene in which Philippa was naked, lying pliant in his arms, her hand was stroking down his belly, closing around his swelled rod and she was kissing him, her tongue thrust deep in his mouth and she was moaning as she kissed him and her fingers were caressing him and . . .

"Are you not pleased?"

He opened his eyes, startled, disoriented, and saw her beside him, not naked as he'd believed, but lying on her back, a blanket pulled to her waist. She was speaking of pleasure, but a pleasure different from the one of his dream. Philippa was really there with him, and he hurt with need for her, hurt with the urgency of it, and the reality melded into his dream and he didn't question it or the dark night or her beside him on the floor of a copse of maple trees.

"Philippa . . ." he said, his voice low as he rolled over until he half-covered her with his body.

"I'm so glad to see you, Dienwald," she said, and raised her hand to stroke his hair, to touch his jaw, his mouth. His tongue stroked over her finger, and she shivered. "Dienwald," she said again, and parted her lips, staring up at him as if he were the only man on earth, and she was so close to him, but a breath away from his mouth, and he couldn't bear it and leaned down and kissed her, gently at first, then more deeply because it was what she wanted and what he'd done in his dream, yet now the dream was real and his tongue was stroking her mouth. He didn't think, didn't consider his actions. He wanted her, wanted her more than he ever had.

He'd been terrified that Walter would kill her, and at the same time he'd hated her because she had perhaps betrayed him. He couldn't have borne that, but now she was here and it was all that mattered, and she was his at last.

The night was still and she was here, beneath him, and she wanted him. Her dream was his, and they were together. He stroked her face with urgent fingers, easing himself over her. He felt her part her legs, and he lay between them, hard against her woman's flesh, and she was making soft noises deep in her throat and her arm was around his neck, pulling him down, bringing him closer and closer.

She'd been hurt. God, she'd been hurt. Dienwald, his senses restored for an instant, drew back, saying, "Philippa, your arm, I can't hurt you. If your arm . . ."

She simply smiled up at him and said, "I will hurt more if you leave me. Don't leave me now. Please, Dienwald, debauch me. I've wanted you to for so long."

He laughed, he couldn't help himself. Then his laugh turned to pain as she said, "I didn't want to die, because if I did I would never have you, never know what it was like to have you come inside me."

He groaned now, her words burning deep, and he was drawn back into the intense feelings that were conquering all of him. But he realized even in his delirious state that she was a maid and he didn't want to hurt her more than was necessary. He saw his sex tearing through her maidenhead, and he moaned with the excitement of it, the triumph in claiming her, of possessing her, finally. He eased himself up until he grasped the hem of her gown, and he pulled it up and felt her naked flesh beneath his hand. Until he reached her upper thighs. She wore a shift, and it stymied him for a moment, for in his dream she'd been freely naked and open for him. He worked in growing impatience until she was naked to the waist, then came over her again, wanting only to feel her body against his, but he couldn't, for he was still dressed. He cursed, softly and foully, and came up onto his knees.

She was watching him, her eyes large and vivid as he clumsily jerked off his tunic, his cross garters, his hose, and then he was finally naked and she found him beautiful.

He was covering her again, his male flesh against her, and she was kissing him wildly, her tongue probing until she found his. He held her head between his hands and kissed her face, his words fast and frantic between kisses, telling her of his need for her, how he loved the feel of her, how he was happy she was still a maid and he would be easy with her, and how he wanted to come into her and meld into her flesh and stay there even as he spilled his seed in her.

She watched his face as he looked down at her, and she felt his fingers parting her flesh, then his sex pressing against her.

He threw back his head, his eyes closed. "Don't move," he said, and his voice trembled, for he was coming very slowly into her, and despite his instruction, she was lifting her hips for him, wanting to feel all of him, now, this very moment. He came deeper and she whimpered as he stretched her and it hurt, but it was what she wanted because he was what she wanted. She could feel him so exquisitely, the hard smoothness of his member easing so gently, just a bit of himself at a time, pressing into her.

In the next instant he felt her maidenhead stretched against his sex. "Philippa," he said, his eyes on her face, "look at me!" He had wanted to be gentle at this moment, but he found he could not. He thrust deep. She cried out at the wrenching tear inside her. He fell over her, his mouth covering hers, and he soothed her with his tongue, even as he held himself still and deep inside her, saying again and again, "No more pain, my sweet Philippa, no more. Hold me and feel me and let me lie deep inside you. 'Tis where I belong."

Then slowly he began to move, his breath soft and warm against her mouth. "Nay, love, accept me now and hold me tight inside you. Aye, that's it, lift your hips for me and bring me deeper . . . ah, Philippa . . . no, don't move, I can't bear it, and —"

She watched his beloved face distort with the pain of his need, and he was heaving, delving deep, his breath sharp and raw and her body burned as he thrust again and again, his hands drawing her up to meet him. She couldn't help herself and cried out but he couldn't stop, wouldn't stop. He threw back his head and she felt his release, felt the wetness of his seed as he emptied himself deep inside her body.

He was limp and weak, torpid in mind and drained in body, and he came over her and she welcomed his weight and he lay with his head beside hers and he was still deep within her.

He said, his voice echoing from the dream, "I'm sorry, Philippa. I wanted you badly. Hold still and the pain will fade."

Philippa regained her breath and her equilibrium. He was still inside her but there was only stinging now, not the tearing pain of before. It was strange, this love-making. She'd wanted him, very much, felt desire for him that overcame the pain in her arm, that, actually, made the pain as nothing, and she'd been whipped about with wild, urgent feelings, wanting to touch him, feel him, urge him to come to her, but the incredible feelings had fallen away when he'd come into her and ridden her so wildly. She'd been left stunned, bewildered, and hurting.

Not hurting now, she thought, smiling as she lightly stroked her hand over his naked back. His flesh was smooth and warm and she felt the muscle beneath and she said quietly, "I love you." And she said it again and again and she knew he didn't hear her for he slept soundly. She felt his member sliding out of her, and the wet of his seed and her wetness as well, she supposed.

She kissed his ear and settled herself beneath his weight. Soon she slept.

It was nearly dawn when Dienwald opened his eyes and came abruptly and horrifyingly awake. He was lying naked, half covering Philippa and he was cold and shivering in the night air, and his rod was swelled again and pressing against her. He cursed his randy sex, and gently and slowly eased himself off her, his mind still not accepting what had happened, for the dream was still strong in his mind, and it had become more, that vivid dream. He shook his head. What he'd done he'd done and it hadn't been a dream, but it had been in the dark of the night and he'd cleanly lost his wits. The early morning in the copse was an eerie gray and thick white mist hovered overhead. He could see her clearly though, her beautiful body bare from the waist down and her parted legs, parted for him when he pushed them apart to come over her, and there was her virgin's blood mixed with his man's seed smeared on her thighs, and he closed his eyes and swallowed.

He'd done himself in. He cursed softly, then smiled, feeling yet again the tightness of her, her urging hand, how she'd lifted her hips to him, how he'd driven into the depths of her, touching her womb. He wouldn't worry about it now. He looked down at her and wanted her again, powerfully, but he saw her wounded arm and the wound he himself had inflicted inside her. He would wait. He pulled a blanket over both of them and pulled Philippa into his arms. He would think soon, once the sun was shining down on his face, warming his brain. He would think of something, he would save himself and somehow he would at the same time protect her from dishonor. How, he didn't know, but an idea would come to him; it was still very early, his brain foggy with sleep. He slept again, holding her close, breathing in the scent that was uniquely hers, but only for a few moments.

He was brought painfully and abruptly to his senses by his son's outraged voice.

"Father!"

Dienwald opened an eye and saw Edmund standing over him and Philippa, his hands on his narrow hips, his eyes wide and disapproving.

"Father, you've taken Philippa."

"Well, perhaps . . . but perhaps not. Perhaps I am simply holding her, for she is hurt, Edmund — aye, very hurt and cold in the night and —"

"I won't allow you to dishonor her. You are holding her too close to just warm her, Father. And just look at her! She's hurt and yet she's asleep and she's smiling!"

Dienwald, startled, looked at the still-sleeping Philippa. She *was* smiling, her lips slightly parted, and the sight made him feel wonderful.

"Edmund, get you gone for a time. I am weary and the wench here will awaken soon and I must think —"

"You will wed her, Father. Aye, you must wed her. You've no choice now."

Dienwald looked with horror at his son and forgot that his men were all within hearing distance. "Wed her! God grant me death instead. 'Tis possible that she betrayed me, Edmund, aye, that she told her cousin to save her from me and took you as a hostage."

Edmund just shook his head and looked disgusted.

"You don't even *like* her! She bullies you and corrects your every word. You call her witch and maypole and you stick out your tongue at her and —"

"Father," Edmund said with great patience, "Philippa is a lady and you have taken her virtue. You must wed her."

Dienwald cursed and looked back down at Philippa. She was awake and staring up at him, and there were tears in her eyes.

# 18

"Why are you crying? For God's sake, cease your wailing this minute! I hate a woman's tears. Stop it, wench. Do you hear me?"

"She's not making a sound," Edmund said, peering down at Philippa.

Dienwald made no reply to this, simply kept staring down at Philippa.

Her tears didn't immediately do his bidding, and he turned further onto his side and leaned over her, his nose nearly touching hers. "Why are you crying? Did you hear Edmund and me, curse the boy's interfering habits?"

She shook her head and wiped her eyes with the back of her hand.

"Then why are you crying?"

"My arm hurts."

"Oh." Dienwald frowned at that. Her revelation was believable, yet somehow he felt insulted, and perversely he said, "Well, did you hear what my son demanded we do?"

Philippa lay on her back, looking up at the man she'd willingly given her innocence to during the night. His jaw was dark with whiskers, his hair tousled, and his naked chest made her heartbeat quicken. He looked beautiful and harried and vastly annoyed. He also looked worried, hopefully about her, which pleased her.

She smiled up at him then and raised her hand to touch his cheek. He froze, then jerked back.

"You're besotted," he said, his voice low, "and you've no reason to be. For God's sake, wench, I took your maidenhead but three hours ago, and you're smiling at me as if I'd just conferred the world and all its riches upon you. You got no pleasure from our coupling, I hurt you, and . . . ah, Edmund, you are still here, then?"

"Will you marry Philippa?"

"You know but one song, and its words more tedious than Crooky's. By St. Anne's knees, boy, the wench couldn't wish to wed with me, for —"

That was such an obvious falsehood that Philippa laughed. "Good morrow, Master Edmund," she said, facing him for the first time, her tears dry now.

The boy grinned down at her. "We must soon be on our way back to St. Erth," he said. "Northbert sent me to awaken you. *Both* of you," he added, meaning dripping from his voice. "Philippa, does your arm pain you sorely?"

She shook her head. "Nay, 'tis bearable, and thus so am I, unlike your father here, who must bring himself to the morning with foul words."

Dienwald said nothing, merely stared off into the thick maple trees. "Go, Edmund, and strive to keep your opinions beneath your tongue."

Edmund frowned down at his father. "We are close to Crandall. Sir Walter could come this very very soon. Shouldn't we —"

Dienwald's expression changed suddenly. It was austere now, cold and forbidding, his eyes narrowed, and he said very softly, in such a deadly voice that Philippa could but stare at him, "I want the whoreson to come out from the safety of his walls. I owe him much, and the time has come to repay the debt. I've men carefully watching the road from Crandall. Aye, I want the bastard to come after you and Philippa, and 'tis I who will greet him."

Edmund grinned suddenly. "But Philippa struck him hard, Father. Perhaps he still lies in a heap."

Dienwald's expression lost its cruelty and he shook his head. "We'll see, but I doubt it. We will leave soon, Edmund, for St. Erth. The wench here needs to rest, and I can't very well wed her here in a forest. Search out Northbert and tell him that if Sir Walter hasn't shown his weedy hide within the next hour, we'll ride to St. Erth."

Edmund, swaggering with importance, took his leave. Dienwald stared after him, shaking his head, seemingly all thoughts of Sir Walter and his hatred of the man gone from his mind, for he said to Philippa, "I can't believe that my own son, a boy of good sense, would yell at me, and carp and bellow."

Philippa said nothing to that, and Dienwald, in a spate of ill-humor, flung back the blanket and jumped to his feet. For a moment it appeared he didn't realize he was naked, but not for a single instant was Philippa unaware of it. She stared at him in the gray light of dawn and was pleased with what she saw, very pleased. Before, she'd admired him, but this morning, now that she understood how men used their bodies to attach themselves to women . . . well, now she had a different way of looking at him, a softer way, a more intimate way.

He scratched his belly, stretched, looked down at himself and saw her blood on his member. He cursed then turned to frown down at her. "Open your legs."

"What?"

"Open your legs," he repeated, then dropped down to his knees beside her. He pulled the blanket to her ankles, then without asking her again, pulled her shift to her waist and pried her thighs open. His seed and her maiden's blood were on her inner thighs. Soft flesh, he saw, very soft, and he wanted to touch her, to ease his finger into her, feel her tighten about him. Curse her and curse his member that hadn't the good sense to remain calm and uninterested. Well, soon he wouldn't have to deny himself. He could have her again and again, as much as he wished and whenever he wished it until his member stayed quiet in exhaustion and his heartbeat stayed slow and steady. He drew in his breath and said, "By St. Peter's toes, there's no choice for me now. We'll wed upon our return to St. Erth."

His duty done, at least in his mind, Dienwald rose again and began pulling on his clothes. He frowned and said, turning to look down at her, "Don't fret about the blood, Philippa, 'tis your virgin's blood and all females are so afflicted their first time with a man. It won't happen again. Now, pull down your clothes else I'll be tempted to think you wish my rod between your thighs again."

She thought it was a fine idea but jerked

down her clothes. She could hear Dienwald's men moving about in the woods, very close to them. "Wouldn't you at least like me to tell you what happened at Crandall?"

"You did," he said shortly. "I couldn't force you to keep your woman's mouth closed last night and you babbled until you finally slept. I learned everything, finally. Are you very sore?"

"But I didn't get to sleep all that long, did I? You didn't wish me to! Sore where?"

He shook his head, giving her a sour look. "Nay, it wasn't all my doing. You wanted me and you had me, curse my man's weaknesses. Your soreness is in your female brain and between your female thighs. You are small, Philippa, at least inside you are." He paused a moment, frowning toward her. "I was dreaming about you, wench, empty-headed dreams they were, and then there you were, beside me, and holding out your arm to me, making me want to debauch you, and making all those whimpering noises in your throat —" He stopped, finished fastening his cross-garters and took his leave of her, not looking back.

"Well," Philippa said aloud as she slowly got to her feet. "He will wed me and he won't mind, once 'tis done." She could still see the appalled look on his face when his nine-year-old son had demanded that he marry her. Truth to tell, that had surprised her as much as it had Edmund's father.

The boy didn't seem to mind that she would be his stepmother. So be it. She clutched her arm and gently began to massage it. The pain was a steady throbbing now, but she could bear it. She looked down at herself and shook her head. Her single garment, the once beautiful yellow gown, was now fatally wrinkled, and rents parted its folds, material torn off to make a bandage for her wounded arm. But she had become so used to wearing rough clothing, even rags, that she gave it not much thought.

She was standing there wondering where she could go to relieve herself when Crooky appeared.

"God gi' you grace, mistress," he said, and sketched her a bow. "I hear from the lad that you will soon wed the master. 'Tis well done. I knew his lust for you would plant his body in his brain, and so it has. Strange that it struck him so swiftly and here in a wild forest, and with you hurt and all, but perhaps that's what pushed him, fear for you and seeing you hurt.

"But the master holds strong feelings for

you and missed you, though he cursed you more than he sang of your bountiful beauty. Father Cramdle will speak wondrous fine words for your ceremony." He paused and added, "Don't mind the master. He'll get used to the idea once it seeps into that thick head of his. Aye, 'twill be fine." Crooky gave her another bow and took himself off. She was left standing alone in the small clearing.

Crooky's words had sounded to her like an attempt to convince himself. Well, perhaps Crooky's master didn't love her, but at the moment Philippa didn't care. But she did feel discomfort that she was nothing more than a waif, not a coin in her possession, her only clothes those Lady Kassia had sent her. Once she and Dienwald were wedded, she would dispatch a message to her father. He would have no choice but to send her possessions to her. She knew little about marriage contracts, dowries, and the like, but it seemed that there had been none for her, so how could her father complain? He'd had no intention of forming a grand alliance with another house of Beauchamp's stature. She no longer brooded on his reasons. Indeed, she no longer cared. Beauchamp seemed a lifetime ago, and surely that was another girl who'd had servants attending her every whim and clothes to suit her every mood. That girl had had a mother who didn't like her and a sister who carped constantly at her. Both the pleasant and the unpleasant were gone, forever.

St. Erth. She liked the sound of it on her tongue, the feel of it in her blood. St. Erth would be her home and Dienwald would be her husband. Her father could bellow until all Beauchamp trembled and his nose turned purple, but it wouldn't matter. Sir Walter had told her that her father had needed coin. She didn't believe it for a moment. However, she didn't know what to believe, so she left off all thought about it and consoled herself with the fact that even that repellent toad de Bridgport wouldn't want a bride who'd been bedded by another man. She smiled and sang a tuneless song as she prepared to return to her home with the man who would be her husband.

Her smile remained bright even when she faced all Dienwald's men, for they knew now that she would be the lady of St. Erth and there would be no more vile cursing from the master because he wanted to bed the maid. Now that he had, he would do what was right. She smiled until she was riding in front of Dienwald. She didn't turn to face him, not because she didn't want to but because his destrier, Philbo, took exception whenever she moved, cavorting and prancing, sending shafts of pain up her arm. The miles passed slowly and her arm throbbed.

"You cry again and I'll kick you off my horse. God's teeth, wench, you have me now. What more do you wish?"

"I'm not crying," she said, and stuffed her fist into her mouth.

"Then what are you doing? A new mime for Crooky's benefit? I suppose you'll tell me your arm pains you again?"

"Aye, it hurts. Your horse likes not my weight."

He snorted and stared over her shoulder between Philbo's twitching ears. "It's true you're a hardy wench and an armful. Still, Philbo hasn't bitten you — aye, methinks even he approves you for the mistress — so cease your plaints. You wanted me and now you've got me. I suppose your woman's ears beg to hear rhyming verses to the beauty of your eyes? That's why you're crying."

She shook her head.

" 'Tis too late to woo you, wench. You'll be a wife before you can congratulate yourself on your tactics, and then 'tis I who will show you that I am master at St. Erth and your master as well. I will do just as I please with you, and there will be none to gainsay me."

"You've always done precisely as you wished with me."

That was true, but Dienwald said nothing. His ill humor mounted and he sang out his own grievances. "Aye, I will wed you, and with naught to your name or your body save the clothes that Lady Kassia sent you. Your damnable father will likely come to St. Erth and demand my manhood for the insult to the de Beauchamps, since I am not of his importance or yours. You'll cry and carp and wail, and he'll lay siege, and soon —"

"Be quiet!"

Dienwald was so startled that he shut his mouth. Then he grinned at the back of her head. He fought against raising his hand to smooth down her wildly curling hair, and merely waited to see if she would continue. She did, and in a very loud voice, right in his face as she whirled about.

"I never cried, never, until I met you, you wretched knave! You are naught but an arrogant cockscomb!"

"Aye," he said mildly, and tightened his arms about her to keep her steady, "but you want to bed the cockscomb, so you cannot continue to carp so shrewishly.

"Should you prefer to be my mistress

rather than my wife? Would you prefer being my chattel and my slave and my drudge?"

She jerked back against the circle of his arms and slammed her fist into his belly. Philbo snorted and reared on his hind legs. Dienwald grabbed Philippa, pulling her hard against him. He was laughing so hard that he nearly fell sideways, bringing her with him. He felt Northbert pushing against him, righting him once again.

"Take care, master," Northbert said. "The mistress isn't well. You don't wish her wound to open."

"God's bones, I know that. But the wound isn't in her arm, 'tis in her brain." He leaned against her temple and whispered, "Aye, and between those soft thighs of yours, deep inside, where I'll come to you again tonight. Think about that, wench."

She lowered her head, not in defeat at his words, but because she wanted to strike him again, but both of them would probably crash to the ground if she did so.

Dienwald said nothing more. He enjoyed baiting her, he admitted to himself. For the first time in his adult male life, he enjoyed talking, fighting, arguing — all those things — with a woman. Well, it was a good thing, since he would be bound to her until he shucked off his mortal coil.

He looked sideways at Northbert and saw that his man was frowning at him. Curse his interference! He said curtly, "No sign of de Grasse?"

Northbert shook his head.

Dienwald cursed. "You've got the men in a line behind us? At intervals, and hidden?" At his man's nod, Dienwald looked fit to spit. "The man's a coward." He cursed again. "I've wanted him for a long time now."

"Why?"

"Ah, you deign to speak to me again, wench?"

"Why?"

"I got a letter supposedly written to me by Kassia, but 'twas from him. He captured me when I went to see her, and I ended up in Wolffeton's dungeons. Kassia saved me, but not before the bastard had broken several of my ribs and killed three of my men. I owe him much. More than enough, since he took my son. Soon now I will repay him."

"And he took me."

"Aye, and you, wench."

So Kassia — perfect *small* Kassia — had saved him. Hadn't she other things to do? Like saving her own husband every once in a while? Curse the woman, she was a thorn in her side, nay, a veritable bush of thorns.

Well, there were those who'd wanted her as well, and she said now, "Why did Walter want to marry me?"

"Are you certain that he did?"

"Unlike you," Philippa said, her voice as bitter as the coarse green goat grass that grew beside the road, "he was most desirous of it. Indeed, he would have ravished me to ensure it, had I not escaped from him when I did. But it makes no sense to me."

"The man's mad."

Her elbow trembled, wanting to fling itself back into his belly. Finally she could bear it no longer and allowed her elbow to have its way.

He said nothing, merely grunted; then he closed his arms more tightly around her, higher now, his forearms resting under her breasts. He raised them a bit until they were pushing up her breasts, very high.

"Stop it, your men will see!"

"Then bait me not, wench."

She chewed thoughtfully on her lower lip, then said suddenly, "When the woman came to kill me, she screamed at me, something about how he — Walter — didn't want me, really, but the riches I would bring him. What could she have meant? My father must have visited Walter and promised him coin if he found me. I can think of no other reason."

"I don't know. We will find out soon enough. Your family must be told, once it is over."

"Then my father will come and cut off your manhood."

"Don't sound so vicious. 'Tis my manhood that endears me to you." To her surprise and to Dienwald's own astonishment, he leaned forward and kissed her ear. "I will give you pleasure, Philippa. And not only my manhood. The pain last night was necessary — 'twas your rite of passage into womanhood, 'tis said."

"Who says?"

"Women. Who else?"

"Some arrogant male."

"Acquit me, wench. I want only to give you pleasure and to teach you how to pleasure me."

"I didn't give you pleasure last night?"

He grinned at the hurt tone of her voice. "A bit, I suppose. Aye, a bit. At least you were willing enough."

He felt her stiffen, and very slowly he eased his hand upward to cup her right breast. He caressed her, his fingers circling her nipple until he could feel the slamming of her heartbeat beneath his palm. "Shall I call a halt and tell my men that my bride wishes to have me here and now? Would you like that, wench? Shall I slip my hand inside your gown to touch your warm flesh and feel your nipple tighten against my palm?"

Her breathing was ragged, her breasts heaving. She wanted to feel his hands caressing her body. She wanted his mouth too, and his manhood, and so, without thinking, she said on a soft sigh as she leaned back against his chest, "Aye, if you will, Dienwald, 'twould please me very much, I think."

He forgot all his baiting, forgot everything save his desire for her, his seemingly endless need for her. The more she yielded to him, the more he seemed to want her. It was disconcerting and it was vastly annoying and it was so enjoyable his brain reeled.

He very gently eased his hand into her gown and cupped her breast. He could feel her breathing hitch beneath his palm. He saw her lips part, and her eyes never left his face. He knew it was ridiculous, what he was doing. Any of his men could come upon the mat any time. Northbert could draw alongside to tell him something . . . his son . . . St. Peter's toenails!

He pulled his hand out of her gown and

slapped the wool back over her. "There'll be time for this later," he said, and turned her away from him. "Watch the trees and the hawthorns and the yew bushes. Colors are coming out now. Life is renewing." His words stopped abruptly, for he suddenly realized that he'd spilled his seed deep inside her but hours before — a new life could have already begun. An image flashed in his mind: a girl child with wildly curling hair streaked with many shades of brown and ash colors, tall and hardy, filled with laughter, her eyes a vivid summer blue.

He growled into Philippa's ear, "I suppose you'll give me more children than I can feed."

She just turned and gave him a beautiful smile.

*Windsor Castle*

King Edward nodded decisively. "Aye, Robbie, you must needs go and inform de Fortenberry of his immense good fortune. The fellow probably has gaps in his castle walls, he's so poor. His sire had not a coin to bless himself with either. Aye, I'll have St. Erth repaired. I don't want my sweet daughter in any danger, so mayhap I'll have more men sent."

Robert Burnell said, "But I thought you didn't wish to acquire a son-in-law who would drain your coffers, sire."

"Nay, not drain them, but we're speaking of my daughter, Robbie, the product of my youth, the outpouring of my young man's . . ." The king grinned. "He has but a young son? All Plantagenet ladies love children. She will take to the boy, doubtless, so we need have no worries there. After you've gotten de Fortenberry's consent and endured all his endless thanks and listened to all his outpourings of gratitude, have Lord Henry bring our sweet daughter here to Windsor. My queen insists that my daughter be wedded here. Philippa's nuptials will take place in a fortnight, no longer, mind you, Robbie."

The king moved away from his chancellor, flexing his shoulders as he paced. "Aye, you must go now, for there is much else to be done. God's teeth, so much else. It never ceases. Aye, we'll soon finish this business, and it will end happily."

Robert Burnell, accompanied by twenty of the king's finest soldiers, left the following morning for Cornwall.

Not two days later, the king was sitting with Accursi, plotting ways of wringing funds from his nobles' coffers for all the castles he wanted to build in Wales. Accursi, the son of a famous Italian jurist, was saying in his high voice, "Sire, 'tis naught to worry you. Simply tell the nobles to open their hearts and thus their coffers to you. Your need is greater than theirs. 'Tis *their* need you seek to meet! They are your subjects and 'tis to your will they must bow."

Edward looked sour. He stroked his jaw. Accursi would never understand the English nobleman despite all his years in service with him. He thought them weak and despicable, sheep to be told firmly to shed their very wool. Edward was on the point of saying something that would likely send Accursi into a sulk when he heard a throat clear loudly, and looked up.

"Sire, forgive me for disturbing you," his chamberlain, Aleric, said quickly, "but Roland de Tournay has come and he awaits your majesty's pleasure. You gave orders that you wished to see him immediately."

"De Tournay!" Edward laughed aloud, rising quickly. A respite from Accursi. "Send him hence. I wish to see that handsome face of his."

Roland de Tournay paused a moment on the threshold of the king's chamber, taking it all in, as was his wont, and Edward knew he was assessing the occupants, specifically

Accursi. Edward saw the very brief flash of contempt in Roland's eyes, an instinctual Englishman's reaction to any foreigner.

Edward said, grinning widely, "Come bow before me, de Tournay, you evil infidel. So our gracious Lord saw fit to save you to return to serve me again, eh?"

Roland strolled into the chamber as if he were its master, but it didn't offend Edward. It was de Tournay's way. It did, however, offend Accursi, who said in his high, accented voice, "See you to your manners, sirrah!"

"Who is this heathen, sire? I can't recall his face or his irritating manners. You haven't told the fellow of my importance?"

Edward shook his head. "Accursi, hold your peace. De Tournay is my man, doubt you not, and I'll not have him abused, save by me. 'Tis about time we see you in England, Roland."

"That is what I heard said of you, sire, you who wandered the world for two years before claiming your crown."

"Impudent dog. Come and sit with me, and we will drink to our days in Acre and Jerusalem and your nights spent wallowing in the Moslems' gifts. I hear Barbars gave you six women to start your own harem."

It was some two hours later when the king said to the man who'd done him great and loyal service in the Holy Land, "Why did you not come to my coronation October last? Eleanor spoke of your desertion."

Roland de Tournay merely smiled and drank more of the king's fine Brittany wine. "I doubt not the beautiful and gracious queen spoke of me," he said. "But, sire, I was naught but a captive in a deep prison, held by that sweetest of men, the Duke of Brabant. He, in short, demanded ransom for my poor body. My brother paid it, afraid not to, for he knew that you would hear of it if he didn't." Roland grinned wickedly. "Actually, I think it was his fair wife, lusty Blanche, who forced him to ransom me."

It took Edward only another hour before he slapped his knee and shouted, "You shall marry my daughter! Aye, the perfect solution!"

"Your daughter!" Roland repeated, staring blankly at the king. "A royal princess? You have drunk too much of this fine wine, sire."

The king just shook his head and told de Tournay about Philippa de Beauchamp. ". . . so you see, Roland, Robbie is on his way, as we speak, to de Fortenberry. I would rather it be you. You're a known scoundrel and de Fortenberry is an unknown one. What say you?"

"De Fortenberry, eh? He's a tough rascal, sire, a rogue, and worthy withal. I know naught ill of him as a man. But he's wily and likes not to bow to anyone, even his king. Why did you select him?"

" 'Twas Graelam de Moreton who suggested him. He's a force in Cornwall, a savage place still. I need good men, strong men, men I can trust. As a son-in-law I could trust his arm to wield sword for me. But you too could settle there, Roland. I would deed you property and a fine castle. What say you?"

"Will you make me a duke, sire?"

"Impudent cock! An earl you'll be, and nothing more."

Roland fell silent. It felt strange to be back in his own land, sitting with his king, discussing marriage to a royal bastard. He wanted no wife, truth be told, yet the truth hesitated on his tongue. Doubtless the king would regret his hastiness. The flagon of wine lay nearly empty between them. Roland would wait until the morrow.

" 'Twould enrage your brother, I vow," the king mused. "Himself the Earl of Blackheath, and to have his troublesome young brother be made an earl also and the king's son-in-law? Aye, 'twould make him livid."

That it would, Roland thought. But he

didn't particularly like to rub his brother's nose in dung, so he slowly shook his head.

" 'Tis a generous offer, sire, and one that must be considered conscientiously and in absence of your good drink."

"So be it, Roland. Tell me of your harem," King Edward said, "before my beautiful Eleanor comes to pluck us away."

# 19

*St. Erth Castle*

On the last day of April, under the flowering apple trees in the St. Erth orchard, Father Cramdle performed a marriage ceremony crowned with enough ritual to please even the Archbishop of Canterbury himself. The sweet scent of the apple blossoms, musk roses, and violets filled the air, the bride looked more beautiful than the yellow-and-purple-patterned butterflies that hovered over the scores of trestle tables laden with food and ale, and the bridegroom and master of St. Erth looked like he wanted to frown himself into the ground. Father Cramdle ignored the bridegroom. The ceremony was right and proper. All the people of St. Erth were happy. The master was doing his duty by the maid.

The soon-to-be-mistress of St. Erth looked as excited as any other girl at her own wedding, Old Agnes thought as she watched Philippa de Beauchamp become Philippa de Fortenberry, the master's helpmeet and steward and keeper of the castle. Aye, she was lovely in her soft pink gown with a dark pink overtunic — both garments among those sent to her by Lady Kassia de Moreton, a fact that had seemed, for some unknown reason, to annoy the mistress.

She wore her richly curling hair long and thick down her back, with flowers twined together into a crown on her brow. She was a maiden bride, and if anyone thought differently, he was wise enough to keep silent.

The master looked a magnificent animal as well, clothed in the new bright blue tunic the mistress had sewn for him, his long lean body straight and tall. But he also looked uncommonly severe and forbidding, something Old Agnes didn't understand but hadn't the courage to ask about. As for the young master, he was grinning like a fatuous little puppy after a big meal.

Since they were wedded here at St. Erth, no dowry or bridal gifts involved, Dienwald spared himself and his bride the ceremonial stripping. He knew his bride was very nicely formed and he knew that she thought well of his body as well. He chewed his thumbnail and wished Father Cramdle would finish with his array of Latin, words spoken so slowly that Dienwald didn't know where one word began and another left off. Nor did he understand any of the words, so it really didn't matter.

Neither did Philippa. She just wanted it over with. She wanted to turn and smile at her new husband and watch him smile back at her. They'd returned the evening before, and to Philippa's surprise and chagrin, Dienwald hadn't come near his own bedchamber. She'd slept alone, wondering at his sudden bout of nobility — if, indeed, it were a case of nobility.

Perhaps, she thought, as Father Cramdle droned on, he'd not found her particularly to his liking that first time. Perhaps he didn't . . .

The ceremony was over, and there was suddenly loud, nearly riotous cheering from all the people of St. Erth. Gorkel had set Crooky on his massive shoulders and the fool was leading the people in shouts and yells and howls of glee.

" 'Tis done."

Philippa, her brilliant smile in place, turned to her new husband, but she didn't get a smile in return. He was staring beyond her at nothing in particular as far as she could tell.

"Aye," she said with great satisfaction, "you are now my husband. What is it? Is something the matter? Something offends you?"

"All my people," Dienwald said, still staring about him, "are shouting their heads off. And it is because they believe you to be good for their well-being. They make me feel I've been a rotten tyrant in my treatment of them."

"Mayhap," she said with a grin, "they believe I'll temper you rottenness and make you as sweet and ripe as summer strawberries. As for me, husband, I shall try to be good for our people. Mayhap they also believe I'll be good for their master. I had much food prepared. Indeed, everyone wished to help. Look at the tables, I vow they are creaking with the weight of it. There are hare and pork and herring and beef and even some young lamb —"

"Aye, I know." He struck his fingers through his hair. "Edmund," he bellowed. "Come hither!"

The boy was still grinning even as he came to a halt in front of his father and announced with glee, "You are wedded to the maypole."

Philippa laughed and cuffed his shoulder. "You weedy little spallkin! Come, give me a kiss."

Edmund came up to his tiptoes and

hugged her, then raised his face, his lips pursed. She kissed him soundly. "Can you call me something a bit more pleasing, Edmund?"

Edmund struck a thoughtful pose. Crooky came up then and Edmund said, "A name, Crooky, I must have a comely name for my father's wife."

"Ah, a name." Crooky stewed a look at his master. "Mayhap Morgan? Or Mary?"

"Shut your teeth!" Dienwald bellowed, and cuffed Crooky, sending the fool tumbling head over arse to the ground in a well-performed roll.

"I think," Edmund said slowly, "that I wish to think about it. Is that all right?"

"That is just fine. Now, husband, would you like to partake of your wedding feast?"

There was enough feasting and consumption of ale to keep the people of St. Erth sick for a week. And that, Philippa thought, smiling, was probably the reason they'd cheered her so vigorously — enough food and drink and dancing to make the most sullen villein smile. Even the blacksmith, a man of morose habits, was laughing, his mouth stuffed with stewed hare and cabbage. Everyone was frolicking.

All but the master.

He danced with her; he picked at the

roasted hare and pork Philippa served on his trencher, but he didn't try to pull her away to kiss her or fondle her on his lap. And that, she knew, wasn't at all like Dienwald. His hand should have been on her knee, moving upward, or caressing her breast, a wicked gleam in his eyes. She wished she had the courage to stroke her hand up his leg, but she didn't.

When the time came, Philippa allowed Old Agnes and the other women to see her to the master's bedchamber. Margot combed her hair and the women took off her clothes and placed her in Dienwald's big bed. Then, with much giggling and advice that Philippa found interesting but quite unnecessary, they left.

"Aye," Old Agnes called back, "we'll send up the master soon, if he isn't too sodden to move!"

Margot laughed and shouted, "We'll tell him stories to stiffen his rod! Right now 'tis too full of ale to do more than flop about!"

Now that, Philippa thought, was an interesting image to picture.

The night was dark, and but one candle flickered in the bedchamber. Philippa waited naked under the thin cover, for it was warm this night, her wedding night. Her arm was still bound in a soft wool bandage, but it scarce bothered her. She wanted her husband to come to her, she wanted him to touch her with his hands, with his mouth, and she wanted his rod to come inside her and fill her. She wanted desperately to hold him to her as he moved inside her. She loved him and she wanted to give him everything that she was, everything that she had, which, admittedly, were only her love and her goodwill for him, his son, and his castle.

Time passed and the candle gutted. She fell asleep finally, huddled onto her side, her hands beneath her cheek.

The door crashed open and Philippa came instantly awake and lurched upright. Her new husband was standing in the open doorway holding a candle in his right hand. He was scowling toward her, and she saw that he wasn't happy.

He stepped into the chamber and kicked the door shut with his heel, then strode across the chamber and came to a halt beside the bed. He looked down at her. She pulled the blanket over her breast to her chin.

"Good," he said.

"Good what?"

"You're naked, wench — at least you had better be under that flimsy cover. The women were giggling enough about your fair and willing body, ready for me. Now that I've enslaved myself and all I own for you, now that you've gotten everything you wanted, I think I will take advantage of the one benefit you bring me."

He was pulling off his clothes as he spoke. Philippa stared at him, realizing that he was drunk. He wasn't sodden, but he was drunk.

She just looked at him. She wasn't afraid of him, but still she said, "Will you hurt me, Dienwald?"

That brought him upright. He was naked, standing with his arms at his sides, his legs slightly spread, and he was staring down at her. "Hurt you, wench?"

"I am not a wench, I'm your wife, I'm Philippa de Fortenberry, and —"

"Aye, I know it well . . . too well. Come, lie down and shut your woman's mouth and open your legs. I wish to take you, and if there is much more talk, I doubt I'll be able. Nay, I'll not hurt you if you obey me."

She didn't move for a very long time. Finally she said slowly, "You said you would give me pleasure."

He frowned. He had said that, it was true, but that was before he'd drunk so much ale he felt he'd float away with the Penthlow River. He felt ill-used, but he supposed it wasn't her fault, not really. No matter how he railed and brawled, he had taken her, and all because of that cursed dream of her he'd been having. That and the fact that he'd wanted her for longer than he could remember.

And so he said in a voice that was fast becoming sober, "I'll try, by all the saints' sweet voices, I'll try to bring you pleasure."

She smiled at that, all the while looking at him. He was tall and lean and hard, and so beautiful she wanted to cry. Her body was taut with excitement and soft with a need she knew lay buried within her, a need he would nurture into being. " 'Twill be fine, then, my husband."

She lay on her back and lifted her arms to him.

"Why must you yield to me so sweetly?" he asked as he lay down and pulled the blanket to her waist. He came over her naked breasts, and the feel of her so soft and giving beneath him made him shiver. "Ah, Philippa," he said, and kissed her. It was a gentle kiss until he felt her respond to him, and then he lightly probed with his tongue until she parted her lips and he slipped his tongue in her mouth. He felt her start of surprise and said into her mouth, "Touch your tongue to mine."

She did, shyly, as if she were afraid of what

would happen. Then she gasped with the wonder of it and threw her arms — both of them — around his back. He laughed at that, both amazed and pleased to his male soul at her yielding reaction. He taught her how to kiss and how to enjoy all the small movements he made with his tongue. He rubbed his chest over her breasts, and her response was beyond what he'd expected. She was panting and arching up against him, her hands fluttering over him.

"The feel of you," Philippa said, rubbing herself against his hairy chest. "I love the feel of you," and he felt her trying to open her legs for him. He fitted himself there, his sex against her belly, then raised himself and said, "Touch me, Philippa. I can't bear it anymore. Touch me."

She reached between their bodies and instantly clasped her fingers about him. "Oh," she said, and her fingers grew still. "I hadn't thought . . . 'tis wondrous how you feel . . . your strength." And she began to caress him, to stroke him, to learn him, and then she closed both hands about him and fondled him, and soon he couldn't bear it. He pulled back up onto his knees between her widespread thighs and looked down at her. Her sleek long legs were beautifully shaped and white and soft, and he wanted them around his flanks and wanted to come inside her, and he said only, "Now, Philippa, now."

There was in her expression only sweetness and anticipation, and it seeped slowly through his brain that he had become infinitely more sober than when he entered the room.

"Pleasure," he repeated slowly as he paused before guiding himself into her. "Pleasure." He stopped, drew a deep shuddering breath, and frowned down at her. "You're my wife." He eased down then between her legs, and his lips were on her stomach, his hands stroking her, his tongue wet and hot against her flesh. He was moving lower and lower, and Philippa, so surprised that she hadn't the chance to be shocked by what he was doing, yelled when his mouth closed over her.

He raised his head, staring at her in consternation. "Pleasure," he said. " 'Tis for your pleasure."

"Oh."

"Be quiet, wench. This is good."

And so it was, but it was also more, much more. When his mouth took her this time, she lurched upward but didn't yell. She felt the sensation of his mouth into the very depths of her, sensations she'd never before even guessed could exist. She whimpered, her fist in her mouth. His hands slipped beneath her buttocks, and he lifted her, his tongue wild on her and inside her, delving and probing, and she cried out, unable to keep still any longer. And it went on and on, gaining in urgency until she gave herself to it.

Dienwald felt the stiffening of her legs, the convulsions that tightened her muscles, and in those moments his mind was as clear as a cloudless summer day, and he saw her, really saw her, and felt her even as she stared at him, her eyes wide and wild, filled with surprise and passion, and she cried out and arched upward, giving herself to him fully. It was a woman's pleasure swamping her, and he was giving it to her and felt himself sharing it, deeply, and it dazed him. He wanted to shy away from it, to escape it, but he couldn't because he was held firm and close, a part of her, even though he had never known it could be so. Nothing had prepared him for this joining. When she quieted, he raced back, taut and wild and fierce, lifted her hips even higher — but again he looked down at her, and slowed himself. He came into her very slowly, for she was small. It was almost too much for him. She was wet from the pleasure he'd brought her, and the feel of her, the feel of himself inside her, made him shudder and moan until he couldn't bear it and he drove into her, coming over her then, even as he felt her womb. And he exploded then and groaned loudly, heaving into her as his seed filled her.

He didn't want to think, didn't want to feel anymore. It was all too new and too urgent. His head was spinning and he felt ripped apart, for she would see his soul and know that she'd taken him, all of him, and so he escaped her and slept.

Philippa stared at her husband's face beside hers on the pillow. He was breathing slowly and deeply, his fingers splayed over her breast, one muscled leg covering hers. She raised her hand and stroked his hair. He'd promised pleasure, but this had exceeded pleasure. Pleasure was a new gown whose color suited one perfectly. What he'd made her feel . . . It could make one mad, it was madness. And she wanted it every day of her life.

Light streamed onto Philippa's face and she opened her eyes and smiled even before she saw her husband's face. Dienwald was on his side, balanced over her, and he was looking very serious and intent. He appeared to be playing with her hair.

"What are you doing?"

"Counting the different shades in your hair. Here is a strand as dark a brown as my own, and next to it is one so pale I can scarce see it against my arm."

"My father once frowned at me and told me my hair wasn't golden."

"He's right. It isn't. It's far more interesting. Here's a strand that's an ash color. So far, I've counted ten different colors. Why did your father want you to have golden hair?"

"I don't know. I just remember that he was shaking his head about it. I was hurt, but then he didn't say anything more. Indeed, he seemed to forget about it."

He went on as if she hadn't spoken, "And the hair covering your mound —"

Instinctively Philippa closed her legs, and he laughed. "Nay, you're my wife now. I'll look my fill and you'll not gainsay me." He laid his open palm over her, cupping her. "You feel warm beneath my hand."

He closed his eyes as he spoke, and Philippa felt a surge of something much stronger than mere warmth beneath his palm. It was desire, and it felt powerful and compelling. Unconsciously she lifted her hips against his hand.

He opened his eyes and looked into hers. "I thought you'd be a greedy wench," he said, a good deal of male satisfaction in his voice, and leaned down to kiss her. She felt his long finger glide over her, slip between her thighs, and enter her slowly. She gasped, and he took the sound into his mouth and kissed her more deeply. Then his tongue moved into her mouth just as his finger was moving into the depths of her and she lurched up, crying out, so overwhelmed by the feelings his actions brought that she was helpless against them. He pressed her down. "Hush," he said. "Lie quietly and enjoy what I'm doing to you."

"It's too much," she said, and began kissing him urgently, frantically, his chin, his nose, his mouth. He laughed into her mouth but it turned quickly into a groan as her tongue touched his.

In a sudden move he rolled onto his back and brought her over him. He arranged her over him, saying, "Sit up, wife, come astride me." He lifted her, his hands around her waist. "Guide me into you."

Philippa was eager and more than willing, and she brought him into her and felt him slowly ease her down over him. She stared at him, not moving.

He smiled painfully and moved his hands

upward to cup her breasts. "Move," he managed to say. "Move as you wish to."

She was uncertain and tentative at first, then realized that she could make him insane with lust, moving quickly, then slowing until he thought he would die from sensations of it. She watched his face and quickly learned how far she could push him before drawing back. Then she drew back her head and thrust her breasts forward, her hands splayed on his chest and when his fingers found her, she yelled and jerked, beyond herself, seeking her climax and when it overwhelmed her it overwhelmed him as well.

"It's too much," she whispered a few moments later. She lay with her cheek on his shoulder, her legs stretched over him, his member still inside her.

Dienwald couldn't have said anything if the Saracens had been attacking St. Erth at that moment.

He was barren of wit. He heard Philippa's breath even into sleep. He'd worn her to a bone and he was pleased. He discounted his own feelings of utter contentment. He cupped her hips in his hands. Aye, his wife was a bountiful wench, her flesh soft and firm, and perchance 'twas a fine thing to have her here, at St. Erth, in his bed, for a very long time.

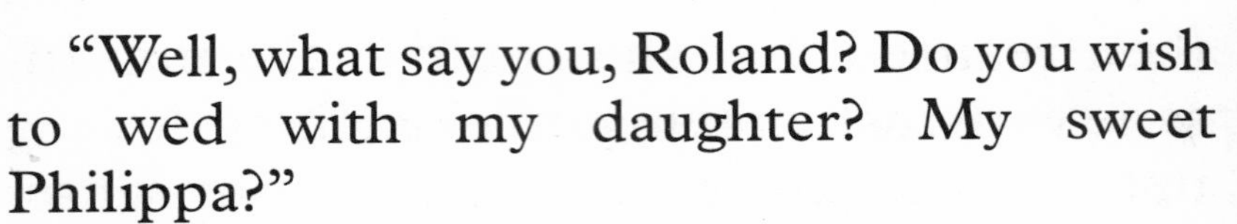

*Windsor Castle*
*May 1275*

"Well, what say you, Roland? Do you wish to wed with my daughter? My sweet Philippa?"

Roland chewed slowly on the honey bread. He didn't want to anger his king by saying frankly that the last thing he wanted in his life was a wife to hang around his neck.

The king frowned. "My man Cedric told me of two wenches who visited your chamber last night. I told him to keep his rattling tongue in his mouth."

"Two wenches," Roland repeated, his eyes widening in surprise. "Nay, sire, 'twas three, but I was too fatigued to do much with the third one. I let her assist."

The king stared at Roland de Tournay, his face darkening. Then he burst into laughter. "You make me a flap-eared ass, Roland. Aye, I will tell Cedric he miscounted your wenches. 'Twill serve the beetle-headed clod right. Now, what will you? Have you decided?"

Roland decided to postpone the inevitable anger that would take the king when he knew himself thwarted. "Why do I not travel to see this daughter, sire? Mayhap she will look at my churl's ugly face and shriek in despair."

"Aye, 'tis possible," the king said, stroking his chin as was his habit. "Very well, Roland, go to Cornwall and give the sweet maid your countenance and tell her to behold it with shrewdness. Tell her you are my trusted man. Nay, tell Lord Henry that."

Roland nodded. He didn't mind going to Cornwall. He needed to see Graelam de Moreton. He also trusted that something would happen to save him the fate of being wedded. He was lucky; his luck would hold without his having to insult the king or his bastard daughter. He doubted not that being a Plantagenet, she was beautiful. Edward sired only beautiful daughters, as had his father before him. But whenever Roland envisioned a beautiful face, it was Joan of Tenesby he saw, and he knew it would remain so until the day he died — the beautiful face of treachery that mirrored his folly.

*St. Erth Castle*

"Aye, 'tis besotted she is, and it's good." Old Agnes spat out a cherry seed, continuing to Gorkel, who was plaiting strips of leather into a whip, "I doubt t' mistress will be able to walk if t' master doesn't let her out of his bed."

Gorkel blushed and missed his rhythm with the plaiting.

Old Agnes brayed with laughter and wagged a gnarled finger at him. "Oh, aye, a beast like you turning red as a cherry pip! Aye, 'tis a wondrous thing to see. Look not sour, Gorkel, 'tis no pain t' master gives the mistress. Aye, 'tis she who plunders his manhood, I'll vow, and wrings him dry and limp."

She cackled until Gorkel, furious at himself, threw the half-plaited whip aside and strode to the well to drink. And there was the master himself, drinking from the well in the inner bailey.

Gorkel watched him straighten, then stretch profoundly. There was a smile on the master's face, a look of vanity perhaps, but in a man of the master's position, Gorkel forgave it.

"Aye, t' master has t' look of a man wrung out of all his seed," Old Agnes chortled close to Gorkel's ear, coming to a halt behind him.

Dienwald heard the old woman laughing and wondered at the jest. The sun was bright overhead, the air warm, and it was nearing midmorning. He became aware of all his people around him, looking at him from the corners of their eyes, smirking — one fellow, a shepherd, was slapping his hands over his heart and sighing loudly. Dienwald decided to sigh too. Then he saw Philippa in his mind's eye stretched on her back, her white thighs parted, her arms flung over her head. He felt a bolt of lust so great it made him reel. It vexed him to realize this effect she had on him, just thinking of her lying in his bed, naked and soft and warm. He cursed, turned on his heel, and rushed back up the solar stairs.

He heard laughter from behind him, but didn't slow. When he flung open the bedchamber door, it was to see his wife standing in the copper tub, naked.

Philippa, startled, brought the linen cloth over her breasts and covered her woman's mound with her hand. Her husband stood in the middle of the room and stared at her.

"You're too plentiful for such a small square of cloth, wench."

When she just stood there returning his stare, Dienwald strode to her, pulled the cloth from her fingers, leaned down, and took her nipple in his mouth. At her gasp, he straightened again and washed the cloth over her tautened nipple. "I think of you and my manhood is cock-sore for your attention. Now, stand still and I will finish your bath for you." He began to whistle as if he hadn't a care, bending over now, the cloth gliding down her belly and between her legs. "Wider, wench, part your legs for me." She opened her legs, her hands on his shoulders to balance herself. She threw her head back when she felt the cloth pressing against her, then his hands, slick with soap, stroking her buttocks. His whistling stopped. He was breathing heavily, and suddenly he was cupping water in his hands and pouring it over her, rinsing away the soap.

"Dienwald," she said, her fists pounding on his shoulders, "you make me frantic."

He looked at her. "Aye, wench? Is that true? This?" And his middle finger slipped inside her.

She looked at his mouth and he felt his blood churn and his member harden. She kissed him, moving against him, shuddering when his finger eased out of her, then plunged in deeply again.

"You're mine," he said into her mouth, and she moaned, kissing him frantically, biting him, her fingers digging into his back. His finger left her and he shoved his clothes aside, freeing his member. He looked at her and said, "I want you to come to me now. Clasp your legs around my flanks."

She stared at him, not understanding, but

he just shook his head and lifted her. Her legs went around him and then she felt his fingers on her, stroking and caressing her and parting her, and her breath caught sharply in her throat as he slid upward into her.

She gasped and wrapped her legs more tightly around him. Then he carried her to the bed and eased her down, not leaving her, driving furiously into her until she was crying out, nearly bucking him off her in her frenzy. When his climax overcame him, he yelled, his head thrown back, so deep inside her that he no longer thought of her as separate from him, as a vessel for his pleasure, as a wife to bear his children. She was his and a part of him and he accepted it and fell atop her, kissing her as she cried softly into his mouth.

Late that afternoon, as Dienwald was sitting in his chair drinking a flagon of ale, he looked up to see Northbert run into the great hall, shouting at the top of his lungs. "Someone comes, master!"

Dienwald rose immediately. "That peasant whoreson Sir Walter?"

"Nay, 'tis Lord Henry de Beauchamp. He has a dozen men, master," Northbert added. "All armed."

Dienwald straightened his clothes, mentally girded his loins, and went to greet his father-in-law. It hadn't taken Lord Henry long to reply to his message.

# 20

Dienwald watched two stout men-at-arms assist Lord Henry de Beauchamp from his powerful Arabian destrier. He was a portly man, not tall, but strongly built even in his late years.

He was huffing about, wheezing and cursing, and Dienwald soon realized it was with rage, not the result of his exertions. No sooner had Lord Henry seen him than he yelled to the four corners of St. Erth, "You lie, you filthy whoreson! You must lie! You cannot have wedded my daughter! 'Tis a lie!"

For a father who had planned to give his daughter to William de Bridgport without a dowry, Lord Henry seemed unaccountably incensed. Dienwald motioned him into the great hall. "It is not much more private, but the entire population of St. Erth will be spared your rage." He preceded him, saying nothing more. He could hear Lord Henry's furious breathing close to his back, and wondered if he should give Philippa's father such a good target for a dagger.

He motioned Lord Henry to his own chair, but his father-in-law wasn't having any niceties. He stood there facing his son-in-law, his hands on his hips. "Tell me you lied!"

" 'Twould be a lie to tell you that I lied. I wedded Philippa two days past."

Lord Henry actually spat in his fury. "I will have the ceremony proclaimed invalid! I will have it annulled! She had not her father's permission, 'tis a disgrace! Aye, 'twill be annulled quickly!"

"It is very possible that Philippa even now is carrying my babe. There will be no annulment."

Lord Henry's face, already red, now became purple. "Where is she? Where is that insolent, ungrateful —"

"Father! What do you here? I don't understand — why are you angry?" Philippa broke off. So Dienwald had written to her father telling him of their marriage, probably the very day of their wedding, to bring him here so quickly, and he had come and he wasn't pleased. But what matter was it to him? Why should he care?

Philippa walked quickly to her father and made to embrace him. To her surprise, he took several steps back, as if he couldn't bear the sight of her, much less her touch.

"You spiteful little wretch! You wedded this . . . this scoundrel?"

Philippa grew very still. She made no more moves toward her father. She saw Dienwald looking at Lord Henry, his expression ironic, and said simply, "I love him and I have wedded him. He is my husband, my lord, and I'll not allow you to insult him."

" 'Tis no insult," Dienwald said with a sudden grin. "I *am* a scoundrel."

Lord Henry turned on Dienwald. "You make jests about your foul deeds! You ravished her, didn't you? You forced her into your bed and then to a priest!"

"Nay, but you will doubtless believe what you wish to believe. However, if you believe any man could ravish Philippa and not sport a year's worth of bruises and broken limbs for it, you are wide of your mark."

"And you, you female viper, what know you of love? You who have been protected all your life from curs of this sort? How long have you known this poor and ragged cur? Days, only days! And you say you love him! Ha! He seduced you, and being a witless fool, you let him!"

"I do love him," Philippa repeated quietly. She laid her hand on her father's arm when he would have erupted further. "Listen to me, sir. He did not ravish me. He is chivalrous. He is kind and good. He saved me from Walter, and I love him. 'Twas *he* who finally consented to marry *me*."

Lord Henry shook off her hand as if it were something abhorrent. He stared hard at her. "You little harlot," he said slowly. "Just look at you, your hair wild down your back like a peasant girl's, your feet bare! I can even smell him on you. You little whore!" He pulled back his arm and struck her a blow hard across the cheek with the palm of his hand. The blow was unexpected, and Philippa went careening backward. She cried out as her hip struck a chair and she went sprawling onto the reed-strewn floor.

Dienwald was on his knees beside her, his face white with rage. "Are you all right?" He grabbed her arm and shook it. "Philippa, answer me!"

"Aye, I'm all right. I wasn't expecting a blow. It surprised me." She felt Dienwald's long fingers stroke over the bright red mark on her cheek. She watched him rise and stride to her father. Lord Henry's men stood still as statues, staring at their master and at their master's daughter and husband. They would, Philippa knew, protect Lord Henry with their lives, but they were uncertain now, afraid to move. It was a family matter and thus more dangerous than fighting a band of Irish thieves.

Dienwald stopped six inches from Lord Henry's nose. "You will listen to me, old man, and listen well. I sent you a message telling you of my marriage to your daughter as a courtesy. I didn't particularly wish to, but I deemed it proper to inform you. You didn't want her; you held her in no esteem; you planned to give her no dowry. You were going to wed her to de Bridgport! Now you have no more say in her life. Philippa is now mine. What is mine I protect. Because you happen to share her blood, I will not kill you, but be warned. My dagger is sharp and my rage grows stronger by the moment. You touch her again in anger and I will tear your worthless heart from your fat body. Heed me, old man, for I mean my words."

Lord Henry doubted not that this man meant what he'd said. He took a step back and dashed his fingers through his grizzled hair. He looked toward Philippa, standing now, her hand pressed against her side. She was very still, her face pale with shock. He'd never struck her in her life. "I am sorry to have clouted you, Philippa, but you have sorely tried me. You ran away, leaving me to believe you dead or murdered or —"

"You know I ran away because I heard you

tell Ivo that I was going to be wedded to William de Bridgport. I knew it must be the truth, because my mother was there as well. What would you expect me to do? Roll my eyes in thankfulness and joy and go willingly to that filthy old man?"

Lord Henry collapsed onto a bench, all bluster gone from him. He looked toward Dienwald — his treacherous son-in-law — and managed a bit more anger. "You stole my wool! You killed my men!"

"Aye, I did steal your wool. As for the other, acquit me. I am no murderer. 'Twas one of my people who killed your farmers without my knowledge, something that displeased me. The man responsible is dead. There is naught more I can do to avenge your people. As for the wool, this tunic I wear is a result of your daughter's fine skills. She sewed it, and many others for my people."

Philippa drew closer to her father. "Do you know naught of Sir Walter, sir? He kidnapped me and Dienwald's son and took us to Crandall. He wanted to marry me, Father, and I could find no reason for his ardor. I am a stranger to him, and beyond that, he had a mistress who . . . Never mind that. Did you perchance offer him a reward if he found me for you? Is that what made him want me for his wife?"

Lord Henry's eyes gave a brief renewed flash of rage. "That traitorous slug! Aye, I know why he took you, Philippa, and he would have wedded you . . . but why did he not? You are wedded to this man, are you not?"

"Edmund — 'tis Dienwald's son — he and I managed to escape Crandall and Walter."

"Ah. Well, no matter now. I offered Walter no reward, at least not in the way you think. I spoke truth to him, and the malignant wretch planned to gain his own ends. Ah, 'tis over for me. It matters not now. One husband is much the same as another, given that both are calamity to me. If you prefer this man to your cousin, so be it. At least this man wedded you without knowing about you. But I am dead, no matter your choice. 'Tis this man, then, this rogue, who will comfort you whilst you pray over your dead father's body. Will you strew sweet ox-lips on my grave, Philippa?"

Philippa wanted to shake him, but she held to her patience. "But, sir, this makes no sense. Why would Walter de Grasse want to marry me? Why?"

Lord Henry shook his head, mumbling, pulling at his hair. "It matters not; nothing matters now. I'm a dead man now, Philippa. There is no hope for me. My head will be severed from my body. I will be lashed until my back is but blood and bones. I will be drawn and quartered and the crows will peck at my guts."

"Crows? Guts? What is he babbling about?" Dienwald asked his bride. "Who would wish to kill him?"

Philippa again approached her father, but she didn't touch him. "What is it, Father? You fear reprisals from de Bridgport? He's an old man full of spleen, but he has no spine. You needn't fear him. My husband won't allow him to harm you."

Lord Henry groaned. He dropped his head in his hands and pulled his hair all the harder. He weaved back and forth on the bench, distraught, and wailed, "I am undone and spent, and my remains will be fodder for the fields. Beauchamp will be stripped from me and mine. Maude will be cast out to die in poverty, probably in a convent somewhere, and you know, Philippa, she hates that sort of thing, despite all her pious ravings. Bernice will not wed, for she will have no dowry, and the saints know that her humors are uncertain. She will become more sour-hearted and wasp-tongued —"

"You weren't going to give me a dowry."

Lord Henry paid no attention. "Dead, all because I tried to discourage that silly young peacock de Vescy. I lost my wits, and my tongue ran into the mire with lies."

"What lies? Tell me, Father. What does Ivo de Vescy have to do with this?"

"He is to wed Bernice. Rather, he was. Now he won't. He'll run back to York and seek an heiress elsewhere."

Philippa looked at Dienwald. She was no longer pale, but she was confused. He nodded at her silent plea for help.

"You make no sense, old man," Dienwald said. "Speak words with meaning!" It was the tone he used with Crooky, and it usually worked. But it didn't this time, not with Lord Henry. He merely shook his head and moaned, rocking more violently back and forth.

Northbert came into the hall and motioned to his master. He was panting from running and his face was alight with excitement and anticipation. "Master! There is another party here at our gates. The man claims to be Robert Burnell, Chancellor of England, here to see you, master, as a personal emissary from the king himself! Master, he has twenty men with him and they carry the king's standard! The Chancellor of England, here! From King Edward!"

Dienwald exploded in Northbert's face, "Chancellor, indeed! By St. Paul's blessed fingers, your brain becomes as flat as your ugly nose! More likely 'tis Lord Henry's precious nephew, Sir Walter, come to carp to his uncle."

Lord Henry was staring in horror at Northbert. His face had gone gray and his chin sagged to his chest. "It is the chancellor, I know it is. Accept it, Dienwald. 'Tis over now." He clasped his hands in prayer and raised his eyes to the St. Erth rafters. "Receive me into heaven and thy bosom, O Lord. I know it is too soon for my reception. I am not ready to be received, but what can I do? 'Tis not my fault that I spoke stupidly and Philippa was listening. Perhaps some of the blame can lie on her shoulders for creeping about and hearing things not meant for her ears. Must all the blame be mine alone? Nay, 'tis not well done of me. Aye, I will go to my death. I will perish with my dignity intact and will carry no blame for my sweet Philippa, who was always so bright and ready to make me smile. Many times she acted stupidly, but she is but a female, and who am I to correct her? 'Tis done and over, and I am nearly fodder for Maude's musk roses."

"A soldier carries the king's banner!" Edmund shrieked, flying into the hall. He stopped in front of his father's visitor and stared. Lord Henry had raised his head at Edmund's noise, and his face was white with fear. Edmund looked from Philippa to his father, then back to the old man, and said, "Who are you, sir?"

"Eh? Ah, you're the villain's brat. Get thee away from me, boy. I am on my way to die. A sword will sever my gullet, and my tongue will fall limp from my mouth. Aye, a lance will spike through my ribs and . . ." He rose slowly to his feet, shaking his head, mumbling now. Philippa ran to him. "Father, what is the matter? What say you? Do you know the king's chancellor? Why are you so afraid?"

He shook her off. "Boy, take me away. Take me to your stepmother's solar, aye, take me there to wait for my sentence of torture and death. Aye, I'll be thrown into a dungeon, my fingernails drawn out slowly, the hairs snatched from my groin, my eyeballs plucked from their sockets."

Edmund, wide-eyed, said, "Philippa, is this man your sire?"

"Aye, Edmund. Take him to your father's bedchamber. He seems not to be himself. Quickly."

"He pays homage to witlessness," Dienwald said, staring after his father-in-law. "What does this Burnell want, I wonder."

"The king's chancellor . . ." Philippa said, her voice filled with awe and fear. "You haven't done anything terribly atrocious, have you, husband?"

"Do you wonder if the king has discovered my plans to invade France?" Dienwald shook his head and patted her cheek, for he could see she was white with fear. "I shall go greet the fellow," he said. "I bid you to remain here until I discover what he wants. No, go to your father and let him continue his nonsense in your ears. Perhaps he will say something that will make sense to you. I want you kept safe until this matter is clear to me. Heed me in this, Philippa."

She frowned at his back as he strode from the great hall. He was her lord and master and she loved him beyond question, but for her to hide away whilst he faced an unknown danger alone?

"Come away from here, as the master bids, mistress."

"Gorkel, you shan't tell me what to do!"

"The master told me you would try to come after him. He says your loyalty is dangerous to yourself, for you're but a female with crooked sense. He told me to take you to your steward's room and keep you there until he was certain all was well and safe. He decided he doesn't want you near your father. He believes him mired in folly."

"I won't go! No, Gorkel, don't you dare! No!"

Philippa was an armful for her husband, but for Gorkel she was naught but an insignificant wisp, to be slung over his massive shoulder and carried off. She pounded his back, shrieking at him, but he didn't hesitate. Philippa gave it up for the moment, since there was nothing else for her to do.

In the inner bailey Dienwald waited, his arms crossed negligently over his chest as he watched England's chancellor ride through the portcullis into St. Erth's inner bailey. The man wasn't much of a rider; indeed, he was bouncing up and down like a drunken loon in the saddle. Suddenly the chancellor looked up and saw Dienwald. The man's eyes were intense, and Dienwald felt himself being studied as closely as the archbishop would study a holy relic.

Burnell let his destrier come apace, then turned to an armored soldier beside him and said something that Dienwald couldn't make out. He stiffened, ready to fight, but held his outward calm. He watched Burnell shake his head at the soldier.

Robert Burnell was tired, his buttocks so sore he felt as though he were sitting on his backbone, but seeing St. Erth, seeing this man who was its lord, he felt a relief so deep that he wanted to fall from the horse and onto his knees and give his thanks to the Lord. Dienwald de Fortenberry was young, strong, healthy, a man of fine parts and good mien. His castle was in need of repairs and many of the people he'd seen were ragged, but it wasn't a place of misery or cruelty. Burnell straightened in his saddle. His journey was over, thank the good Lord above. He felt hope rise in his blood and energy flow anew through his body. He was pleased. He was happy.

He said to the man standing before him, "You are Dienwald de Fortenberry, master of St. Erth, Baron St. Erth?"

"Aye, I am he."

"I am Robert Burnell, Chancellor of England. I come to you from our mighty and just king, Edward I. I come in peace to speak with you. May I be welcomed into your keep?"

Dienwald nodded. The day, begun promisingly with lust and passion and a bride who seemed to believe the sun rose upon his head and set with his decision, had become increasingly mysterious with an irate and mumbling father-in-law, and now a messenger from the King of England. He watched Robert Burnell dismount clumsily from the mighty destrier, then nodded for the man to precede him into the great hall.

He was aware that all his men and all his people were hanging back, staring and gossiping, and he prayed that no one would take anything amiss. He told Margot in the quietest voice she'd ever heard from the master to bring ale and bread and cheese. She stared at him, and Dienwald was annoyed with himself and with her.

"Where is the mistress?" Margot asked.

Dienwald wanted to cuff her, but he merely frowned and said, "Do as I bid you and don't sputter at me. The mistress is reposing and is not to be disturbed for any reason." He turned back to Burnell, praying that Margot wouldn't go searching for Philippa, and cursing the fact that the servants appeared more eager to serve his wife than him. If it was so after but two days of marriage, what would be his position a week from now?

"I have looked forward to this day, sir," Robert Burnell said as he eased himself down into the master's chair. "My cramped bones praise your generosity."

Dienwald smiled. "Take your rest for so

long as it pleases you."

"You are kind, sir, but my duty is urgent and cannot be delayed longer."

"I pray the king doesn't want money from his barons, for I have none and my few men aren't meant to swell the ranks of his army."

Burnell merely shook his head, forgiving the presumption of the speaker. "Nay, the king wishes no coin from you. Indeed, he wishes to present you with a gift."

Dienwald felt something prickle on the back of his neck. He was instantly alert and very wary. A gift from the king? Impossible! An inconsistency, a contradiction. Surely a danger. He cocked his head to the side in question, already certain he wasn't going to like what Burnell said.

"Let me peel back the bark and get to the pith, sir. I'm here to offer you a gift to surpass any other gift of your life."

"The king wishes me to assassinate the King of France? The Duke of Burgundy? Has the Pope displeased him?"

Burnell's indulgent smile faltered just a bit at the blatant cynicism. "I see I must speed myself to the point. The king, sir, is blessed with a daughter, not one of his royal daughters, not a princess, but, frankly, sir, a bastard daughter. He wishes to give her to you in marriage. She is nonetheless a

Plantagenet, greatly endowed with beauty, and will bring you a dowry worthy of any heiress of England to —"

Dienwald was reeling with surprise at this, but he still managed to remain outwardly calm. He held up his hand. "I must beg you to stop now, Lord Chancellor. You see, I am wedded two days now. You will thank the king, and tell him that as much as I wish I could hang myself for being unable to accept his wondrous offer, I am no longer available to do his bidding. I am already magnificently blessed." He hadn't realized that he would ever be blessing Philippa as his wife with such profound gratitude.

Wed the king's bastard? He wanted to howl aloud. It was too much. Such an offer was enough to make his hair fall out. But he was safe, bless Philippa and her escape from Beauchamp in a wool wagon.

Burnell looked aghast. He looked disbelieving. He looked vexed. "You're wedded! But Lord Graelam assured me that you were not, that you had no interest, that —"

"Lord Graelam de Moreton?"

"Naturally I spoke to men who know you. One cannot give the daughter of the King of England to anyone, sirrah!"

"I am already wedded," Dienwald repeated. He sounded calm, but now he had a target — Graelam — he wanted to spit on his lance. So Graelam would make *him* the sacrifice to the king's bastard daughter, would he! "Will you wish to stay the night, sir? You are most welcome. St. Erth has never boasted such an inspiring and important guest before. And do not beset yourself further, sir. I doubt this will gravely disappoint the king when he is told his first choice of son-in-law is not to be. Indeed, I venture to say that his second choice will doubtless be more to his liking."

Robert Burnell got slowly to his feet. He ran his tongue over his lips. This was a circumstance he hadn't foreseen, an event he hadn't considered as remotely possible. He felt weary and frustrated, bludgeoned by an unkind fate.

Margot made a timely entrance with ale, bread, and cheese. "Please," Dienwald said, and poured ale into a flagon, handing it to Burnell, who drank deeply. He needed it. He needed more ale to make his brain function anew. So much work, and all for naught. It wasn't just or fair. He couldn't begin to imagine the king's reaction. The idea made him shudder. He started to think of a curse, then firmly took himself in hand. He was a man of God, a man to whom devoutness wasn't a simple set of precepts or rules, but a way of life. But neither was he a man to rejoice when providence had done him in. He looked at the man he'd hoped would become the king's son-in-law and asked, "May I inquire the name of our lady wife?"

" 'Tis no secret. She is formerly Philippa de Beauchamp, her father Lord Henry de Beauchamp."

To Dienwald's astonishment, the chancellor's mouth dropped open; his cheeks turned bright red. He dropped the flagon, threw back his head, and gasped with laughter. It was a rusty sound, Dienwald thought, staring at the man, a sound the fellow wasn't used to making. Was the king so grim a taskmaster? What was so keen a jest? What had he said to bring forth this abundance of humor?

Dienwald waited. He had no choice. What in the name of the devil was going on?

Burnell finally wiped his eyes on the cuff of his wide sleeve and sat back down. He ignored the fallen flagon and poured himself more ale, taking Dienwald's flagon. He drank deeply, then looked at his host and gave him a fat, genial smile. He felt ripe and ready for life again. Fate was kind; fate gave justice to God's loyal subjects after all.

"You have saved me a great deal of

trouble, Dienwald de Fortenberry. Oh, aye, sir, a great deal of trouble. You have made my life a living testimony to the beneficence of our glorious God."

"I have? I doubt that sincerely. What mean you, sir?"

Burnell hiccuped. He was so delighted, so relieved that God still loved him, still protected him. "I mean, sir, that the Lord has moved shrewdly and quite neatly, mocking us mere men and our stratagems and our little fancies, and all has come to pass as it was intended." And he began to laugh again. He swallowed when he saw that his host was growing testy. "I will tell you, sir," Burnell said simply, "and I tell you true — you have wedded the king's daughter. I know not how it came about, but come about it did, and all is well now, all is as it should be, praise the Lord."

"You're mad, sir."

"Nay, Philippa de Beauchamp is the bastard daughter of the King of England, and somehow you have come to wed her. Will you tell me how it chanced to happen?" Burnell smiled a moment, and added under his breath, "So Lord Henry lied about her bloody flux. The girl wasn't at Beauchamp. Ah, this tempts me, this ingenious story he will soon tell me."

Dienwald's brain was a frozen wasteland. His belly was twisted with cramps. He couldn't feel his tongue moving in his mouth. He couldn't hear his own heartbeat in his breast. Philippa, the king's bastard? Philippa, who didn't have the golden hair of the Plantagenets but instead a streaked blond that was uniquely hers? Philippa, whose vivid blue eyes were as bright as a summer's sky — like the king's, like all the Plantagenets' . . . He shook his head. It was inconceivable, impossible. She'd leapt from a wool wagon and into his life, and now she was his wife. She couldn't be the king's daughter. She couldn't. She wasn't to be dowered by her father — by Lord Henry. Oh, God.

"How came it about, you ask? She fled from her father — from *Lord Henry* — because she heard him say that he wasn't going to dower her and was going to wed her to William de Bridgport, a man of sour nature and repellent character."

Burnell waved an impatient hand. "Of course Lord Henry wouldn't dower her, 'twas not his responsibility to do so. The king would. The king, who is in fact her father."

"She ran away, hiding in a wagon of wool bound for St. Ives Fair. She came here —

quite by accident. We were wedded, as I told you, two days ago."

"God's ways are miraculous to behold," Burnell said in a marveling voice. "I cannot wait to tell Accursi of this. He will not believe it." Burnell then shook his head and gazed at St. Erth's smoke-darkened beams high above, just as Lord Henry had done. Dienwald looked up too, hopeful of inspiration, but there was none, only Burnell saying complacently, "Well, now there need to be no agreements from you, sir. You have taken unto yourself the right wife. All is well. All has transpired according to God's plan."

"Don't you mean the king's plan?"

Burnell simply smiled as if the king and God were close enough so that it didn't matter.

Dienwald opened his mouth and bellowed, "Philippa! Come here. Now!"

She heard him yelling and lowered her brows at Gorkel. She walked past him, head high, into the great hall, and came to a halt, staring from her husband to the man seated in her husband's chair. "Aye?"

"Philippa," Dienwald bellowed, higher and louder, even though she stood not four feet away from him, "this man claims you are the king's bastard daughter, not the daughter of that damned fool Lord Henry.

He convinces me, though I fought it. No wonder Lord Henry wouldn't dower you. 'Twas not his duty to do so. He lied about de Bridgport just to keep Ivo de Vescy away from you. Don't you see, you're the king's daughter and thus his responsibility. Damn you for a lying, deceitful wench!"

She continued to stare at him a moment, then transferred her gaze to the other man, who was nodding at her like a wooden puppet. "But this makes no sense. I don't understand. Lord Henry isn't my father?"

Burnell had no chance to reply, for Dienwald howled, "I do have a father-in-law, curse you, wench, but it isn't that fat whining creature in my bedchamber. Nay, him I could have tolerated. Him I could have threatened and intimidated until he did as I wished him to do.

"Nay, my father-in-law has to be the cursed King of England! Did you hear me, Philippa? He is the *King of England*. I, a scoundrel and a rogue, a man happily lacking in wealth and duty and responsibility, have the wretched king for a father-in-law! You have ruined me, wench! You have destroyed me! You are a thorn to be plucked from my flesh. Foul mischance brought you to me, and the devil wove you into my mind and body until I was forced to seduce you!"

Burnell gaped at him. A tirade such as this was unthinkable and completely astonishing. He said in his most reasoned churchman's voice, "But, sir, you will be made an earl, the king has commanded it. You will be a peer of the realm. You will be the Earl of St. Erth, the first of a mighty line to hold power and land and influence in Cornwall. The king will dower your wife handsomely. She is an heiress. You will be able to make repairs to your castle, swell your herds, grow more crops. You will know no want, no lacks. Your lands will prosper and extend themselves. Life will be better. Your people will live longer. Your priest will save more souls, all of St. Erth will show bounty and plenty and —"

Dienwald raised his voice to the beams above, yelling in misery, "I repudiate this wretched woman! Before God, I won't have the king's daughter as my wife. I won't be bound to the damned king or to his damned bastard! I want to be left alone. I demand to be left to my humble castle and my crumbling walls! I demand to be left to my blessedly profligate life and sinful deeds! Give me ragged serfs and frayed tunics! Save me from this foul penance! Damnation, my people don't *want* to live longer. My priest doesn't *want* to save more souls!"

He turned on his speechless wife, snarled something beneath his breath — the only thing he'd snarled that no one hadn't clearly heard — and strode from the great hall.

"Your father, our gracious king, bids you good grace, my lady," said Burnell, for want of anything better. He rose and took her limp hand. Her face was white and she looked uncomprehending.

He sought words to comfort her, to bring her understanding, for he imagined it wasn't a daily occurrence to be told you were the offspring of the kine. "Lady Philippa, 'tis a surprise, I know it, this news has shaken you about, but all is known now and all is explained. The king . . . Naturally, he couldn't have acknowledged you before — he was wedded to his queen, even though at the time she was a very young girl. He wanted no hurt to come to her. But neither did he want to turn his back on you, for you were his dear daughter. He gave you for raising to Lord Henry. It was always his plan to come into your life when it was time for you to be married."

Philippa looked at him and said the most unlikely thing to him: "Why did the king wish me — a girl — to be taught to read and write?"

Burnell found his mouth open again. Had

the girl vague and token wits? "I . . . ah, really, my lady, I'm not at all certain."

"I suppose I had a mother?"

"Aye, my lady. Her name is Constance and she is wedded to a nobleman of her station. She was very young when she birthed you, the king told me. Perhaps someday you will wish to know her."

"I see," Philippa said. At least Lady Maude's dislike of her was now explained. The king's bastard had been foisted upon a woman who hadn't wanted her. It was more to take in than she could manage at the moment, for in truth it was her husband who now filled her thoughts. Her husband and his outrage at what had happened to him.

"My husband doesn't want me," she said, looking away from the chancellor. She saw Old Agnes, Margot, Gorkel, Crooky, and a host of other St. Erth people staring at her, marveling at what she'd suddenly become, chewing it over, and wondering what to do. Would they mock her for being a bastard? Despise her or curtsy to her until their knees locked?

"Your husband is merely confused, my lady. His behavior and his unmeasured words demonstrate that he has no real understanding of what has happened. He must be confusing his new status with that of someone else; he must not comprehend his good fortune."

"My husband," Philippa said patiently, shaking her head at him, "comprehends everything perfectly. Understand, sir, he is not like most men." *That is why I love him and no other.* "He doesn't appreciate the sort of power and wealth some men crave, nay, even covet unto death. He has never sought it, never desired it. He enjoys his freedom, and that means to him that he can do just as he pleases without others interfering in his life. Now all that has changed because of what I am. He would never have wedded the king's bastard daughter, sir. Offers of an earldom, offers of coin, offers of power and influence would have driven him away, not seduced him. You would never have convinced him otherwise. You could not have even threatened him otherwise. But fate arranged things differently for him, and for me. He wedded me and now he doesn't want what I've suddenly become. I don't know what to do."

Philippa turned away from the Chancellor of England and walked out of the hall.

In the inner bailey she came to an appalled halt. There was her father running toward Dienwald, Edmund on his heels, trying to catch the tail of his tunic. Her erstwhile father was shouting, "My precious boy! My honorable lord, my savior!"

He caught Dienwald and threw his arms around his neck and kissed him on each cheek.

Philippa shuddered at the sight.

Crooky came out of the Great Hall, observed the spectacle, and shouted to the blue sky,

> My poor master is now under
>   the king's thumb
> He wants to weep but his
>   brain's gone numb
> He's wed to a princess and
>   will never be free
> But he can't do a thing but
>   accept it and be
> — the king's proud son-in-law.

Philippa turned on the fool, cuffed him with all her strength, and watched him flail to keep his balance, then roll down the steps of the Great Hall, yelling loudly, "Kilt by a princess! The good king save me!"

# 21

Dienwald froze to the spot. Lord Henry had grabbed him firmly and was weeping copiously on his neck, kissing his ear, squeezing him so tightly Dienwald feared his ribs would crack, so great was Lord Henry's relief. "You're a fine, honorable lad, my lord. I knew it all the time, but I was just concerned and . . . well . . . Aye, 'tis God who has saved me and given me his blessing! I shall never again question the heavenly course of things, even though the course be a maze of blind turns."

Dienwald suffered Lord Henry for another moment, his mind still confused, when he looked up and saw Philippa cuff Crooky and send the fool flying. He grinned, then felt his face stiffen.

He pushed Lord Henry away. "Get thee gone, my lord! Take your *daughter* with you! I want her not. Just look at her — she even abuses my servants!"

"But, my precious boy, my dearest lord, wait! She's most desirable as a wife, Dienwald, she's quite comely —"

"Ha! Comely be damned! She's the king's daughter — that's her claim to comeliness!"

"Nay, not all of it. 'Twas I who raised her, I through my clerks and priests who taught her all she knows — and I saw to her lessons and to her prayers . . ."

"That certainly adds to her value." Dienwald didn't say another word. He just shook his head and broke into a run toward the St. Erth stables. Philippa walked slowly to where her father stood, looking in incredulous dismay after her retreating new husband.

"What ails him, Philippa? He's been given the earth and all its bounty. His father-in-law is the King of England! Oh, and you *are* comely, doubt it not, Philippa, truly. It matters not that you haven't the golden Plantagenet hair." Lord Henry looked upon his former daughter. "I don't understand him. He howls like a wounded hound and slinks off to hide. He acts as though he were to be hunted down and slain."

Philippa merely shook her head. She wasn't capable of more. Tears clogged her throat, and she swallowed.

Edmund tugged on her sleeve. "Are you truly the king's daughter?"

"It appears that I am."

Edmund fell silent, simply peering up at

her, as if to observe some magical change in her.

"What, Edmund, you hate me too?"

"Don't be stupid, Philippa." Edmund stared after his father. "Father's always boasted that his life was his own, you see. He's told me many times, since I was a very little boy, to be what I chose to be, not what someone else chose for me. He said that life was too rife with chance, too uncertain in measuring out its punishments and rewards, to be what someone else wished. He said he wanted no overlord, no authority to hold sway over him and to keep and hold what was his."

"Aye, I can hear him saying that. It's true, you know. It's what he believes, it's what he is." Philippa turned back to Lord Henry. "I wondered why I was so tall. The king is very tall, I hear. Is he not called Longshanks?"

Lord Henry nodded. "Listen to me, girl. I did my best by you."

"I know it well, and I thank you. It could not have been easy for Lady Maude. She always hated me, but she tried to hide it." At least in the beginning she'd tried.

Lord Henry tried his best to dissuade Philippa from this conclusion, but it was lame going, for Lady Maude had always resented the king's bastard being foisted upon her household. He stopped, unequal to the task.

Philippa looked thoughtful and said, "My hair — 'tis not Plantagenet gold, as you just said, but streaked and common."

"Nay, I simply spouted nonsense, that is all. Nothing about you is common. And your eyes, Philippa, they are the blue of the Plantagenets, a striking blue as vivid as an August sky." Philippa rolled her eyes at his effluence. "Aye," Lord Henry continued, rubbing his hands. "Aye, that is bound to please the king mightily when he finally meets you."

To meet the king. Her *father.* It held only mild interest for her now. All babes had to be born of someone. She was a royal indiscretion, nothing more, and that fact was going to ruin her life. "Please excuse me now, sir," she said. "I must decide what to do. If you wish to stay, you will use Edmund's chamber. If the chancellor wishes to stay, then he will sleep —" She broke off, shrugged, and walked away.

"Philippa's not happy," said Edmund to the old man who wasn't Philippa's father. Just imagine, Philippa was the king's get! It frayed the thoughts, such a happening. Did that make the King of England his step-grandfather?

"Your father, young Edmund, will make haste back to reason once he's had a chance to think things through. He's not acting like a man should act, given this heavenly gift."

"You don't know my father," said Edmund. "But Philippa does." Edmund left Lord Henry and walked to Crooky who was still sitting on the ground, rubbing his jaw.

"Aye, I was cuffed by a royal princess," said Crooky, his face alight with reverence and awe. "A real princess of the realm and she wanted to cuff me! Her fist touched me. *Me,* who's naught but a bungling ass and so common I am below common and thus uncommon."

"Nay, Crooky, she's the king's bastard and her fist did more than just touch you. I thought she was going to knock your head from your neck."

"Split you not facts into petty parts, little master. Your stepmother is of royal blood and that makes you . . . hmmmm, what does that make you?"

"Perchance almost as uncommon as you, Crooky." Edmund caught Gorkel's eyes and skipped away.

"The mistress is beset with confusion," Gorkel announced, "and so is the master."

"Aye."

Gorkel ground his teeth and stroked his

jaw. "You must speak to the master. You're his flesh. He must heed you."

Edmund agreed this was true, but he knew his father well enough to realize he could say nothing to change his thinking. In any case, there was no opportunity. Dienwald, astride Philbo, was riding out of the inner bailey, alone, a blind look in his eyes. Men called after him, but he didn't respond, just kept riding, looking straight ahead.

In her bedchamber, Philippa sat on the bed and folded her hands in her lap. The situation was too much to absorb, so she simply sat there and let all that had occurred flow over her. Words, only words out of men's mouths, yet they'd changed her life. She didn't particularly care that she was the king's bastard. She didn't particularly care that now the facts of her life had become quite clear to her. She didn't care that Lady Maude had made much of her life a misery. And finally, she didn't care that she now knew why Walter had wished so much to wed her. She could only begin to imagine what prizes he believed would become his upon marrying her.

What she cared about was her husband. She saw his pale face, heard his infuriated words ringing in her ears, blanched anew at his rage over his betrayal. Betrayal in which she had played no part, but he didn't believe that. Or perhaps he did, only his outrage was so great, it simply didn't matter to him who had done what.

If King Edward had been in the bedchamber at this very moment, Philippa would have cuffed him as hard as she'd cuffed Crooky. She would have yelled at him for his damned perfidy — but then she would have crushed him with embraces for selecting Dienwald to be her husband. What was one to do, then?

Life had become as treacherous as Tregollis Swamp. She rose and began to pace. What to do?

Would Dienwald return? Of course he would. He had to, for he had no place else to go and he also had a son he wouldn't desert.

She knew she should give the women instructions; she should speak to Northbert about the lord chancellor's men as well as her fa . . . nay, Lord Henry's men-at-arms. She knew she should find out what Robert Burnell wished to do, and Lord Henry as well, for that matter. Thus, she finally left the bedchamber, duty overcoming loss and fear.

Lord Henry and Robert Burnell were drinking Dienwald's fine ale and chatting amiably. They would stay until the morning, they told her, both of them so ecstatic in drink that she doubted whether Burnell, that devout churchman who never flagged in his labors for his king, could stay upright for much longer. She sought out Margot.

The woman curtsied to her until Philippa thought she would fall on her face.

"You will cease such things, Margot. I am nothing more than I was before. Please, you mustn't . . ." Philippa broke off, stared blindly into space, and burst into tears.

She felt a small hand clasp hers and looked down to see Edmund through her tears.

"Father will come back, Philippa. He must come back. He'll soften, mayhap."

She could only nod. She retired to her bedchamber, rudely, she knew, but she couldn't bear to be with either Lord Henry or Robert Burnell, her *father's* chancellor.

Dienwald didn't return. Not that night or the following day.

Late the next day following, another man arrived at St. Erth, a man alone, astride a magnificent black barb, and he was searching for Robert Burnell. The chancellor had planned to depart that morning, but another long evening spent swilling ale with Lord Henry had kept him in bed — rather, the former steward's bed — until late that morning. Even now he was pale and of greenish hue.

For an instant Philippa thought it was Dienwald, finally come home, but it wasn't, and she wanted to kill the stranger for her disappointment.

His name was Roland de Tournay. She greeted him, not seeing him, not caring who he was, saying nothing, and merely led him to where Burnell and Lord Henry were sitting before a sluggish fire, trying to ignore their pounding heads.

Burnell leapt to his feet, his aching head forgotten. "De Tournay! What do you here? Is the king all right? Does he need to —"

"I am here on the king's orders," Roland said, waving his hand for Burnell to take his seat again. "I promised him to come speak to you about the heiress — the king's bastard daughter. He wants me to look her over."

Lord Henry bounded to his feet. "De Fortenberry is already the king's son-in-law, sirrah!"

Roland merely lifted a black brow. "The heiress is already dispatched, you say?"

"Aye, to the man the king intended her to have!"

Roland laughed. "A journey crowned

with a neat escape for me. So that knave won her, eh?"

Philippa, who'd been listening to this talk, now stepped forward and said, "The king sent you?"

Roland stilled all humor as he looked at the king's daughter. He hadn't known who she was before. But as he looked at her closely now, he realized she had the look of Edward, with her clear blue eyes and her well-sculptured features. She was lovely and she was tall and well-formed, and her hair — ah, it was thick and curling down her back, framing her face. Then, for a brief instant Roland knew a sharp flicker of disappointment that he was too late. But only for an instant. He assumed a bland expression and said, "The king — your esteemed father — simply asked me to see you."

"I am already wedded," Philippa said in a remote voice. "However, it is uncertain whether or not my husband still will claim me for his wife. He left me, you see, when he learned my father is the King of England."

Roland's black brow shot up a good inch.

Lord Henry inserted himself. "You needn't tell this stranger all these things, Philippa. 'Tis none of his affair."

"Why not? The king sent him. Perhaps next he will send William de Bridgport when this man says he doesn't want me. Who knows?" Philippa turned to Robert Burnell and added, her voice hard, "Even if my husband dissolves our union, I don't want this man. Do you hear me? I don't want any other man, ever. Do you understand me, sir?"

"Aye, madam, I understand you well, for you speak clearly and to the point."

By God, Roland thought, staring at the young woman, she was in love with de Fortenberry. How had this come about, and so quickly? There was a mystery here, and he liked unraveling mysteries above all things.

Lord Henry snorted. "It matters not what he understands or doesn't understand. Look you, Roland de Tournay, my daughter was wedded to de Fortenberry before either of them knew who her real sire was. All is over and done with. You can leave with good conscience."

And Lord Henry stared at him as though he'd like to shoot an arrow through his neck. Well, it mattered not. Nor was it such a mystery after all.

"Don't be rude, Fa . . . my lord," Philippa said. "I care not if he remains at St. Erth. There is room, and there is more ale. Why not? Indeed, if he plans to return to

London, he can tell the king what has transpired and . . .”

She stopped suddenly and just stared at Roland — not really at him, Roland thought, but through him and beyond him. There was a pain in her fine eyes, a very deep pain that made him flinch. Suddenly she turned and left the hall, simply walked away, saying nothing more.

“Damnable churl,” Lord Henry said. “I’d slit his throat if he weren’t already her husband.”

Roland shook his head. “You mean that her husband left when he discovered she was the king’s daughter?”

“Aye, that’s the meat of it,” Lord Henry said. “I’d like to smash the pea-brained young cockscomb into a dung heap.”

Roland smiled at blessed fate. His luck had held him through this brief foray into possible disaster. He could not understand de Fortenberry’s actions. Was the man mad? His own motives for not wishing to marry — even the king’s bastard daughter — were different; they meant something. Roland decided to stay the night at St. Erth and on the morrow pay his visit to Graelam de Moreton at Wolffeton. The king’s bastard daughter was no longer any of his concern. He’d done his duty by his king, and all, for him at least, had resolved itself right and tight. The heiress was already wedded and he had no more part to play.

He remarked upon the political situation with the Scots, the intractability of King Alexander and his minions, and forgot the purpose of his visit. The three men, without the presence of either the master or the mistress of St. Erth, ate their fill and consumed more of the castle's fine ale and kept watch and company until late into the night, talking, arguing, and yelling at each other, all in high good humor.

The master of St. Erth, the soon-to-be Earl of St. Erth, didn't appear. Nor did his discarded wife.

*Wolffeton Castle*

"Hold him down, Rolfe! Hellfire, grab his other leg, quickly, he nearly sent his foot into my manhood! You, Osbert, keep his arms behind him! Nay, don't break his elbow! Just keep him quiet."

Lord Graelam de Moreton rubbed his hand over his throbbing jaw and watched as two of his men held Dienwald down, another sitting on his legs and a fourth on his chest. Dienwald was panting and yelling and now he was gasping for breath, for

Osbert was not a lightweight. His blow had been strong and knocked Graelam off his feet and flat on his back onto the sharp cobblestones of the inner bailey.

Of course, Dienwald had caught him offguard. Aye, he'd taken Graelam by complete surprise. His so-called friend had ridden through Wolffeton's gates, welcomed by the men because he was a known ally. No one could have guessed that the instant Dienwald dismounted his destrier, he would attack him. Graelam looked down at his red-faced enraged friend. "What ails you, Dienwald? Kassia, don't fret, I'm all right. It's our neighbor here who's gone quite mad. He attacked me like a fevered fiend from hell."

"Let me up, you stinking whoreson, and you'll see how I split you with my sword!"

"Nay, sir," Rolfe said kindly. "Move you not, or I will have to twist your arm."

Kassia stared from Dienwald to her husband. "Ah," she said, "Dienwald has discovered what you did, my lord. He's come to express his disapproval of your interference."

"Aye, loose me, you coward, and I'll debone you, you lame-assed cur!"

Graelam hunkered down beside his friend, his face only inches from Dienwald's. "Listen to me, fool, and listen well. You needn't marry the king's daughter, and you know it well. Both Kassia and I saw Morgan or Mary or whatever her name is and knew it was she you wanted. We decided if you wanted to wed her, you would have her, and the king be damned. There was no reason for us to say anything. We knew you wouldn't bend to any man, be he king or sultan or God. Isn't that the truth?"

Dienwald howled. "I had already wedded her when Burnell came! She was already my wife!"

"So what is the matter? You're acting half-crazed. Speak sense and I will let you free."

"Her name isn't Morgan or Mary, damn you! Her name is Philippa de Beauchamp and she is our blessed king's cursed daughter!"

Graelam looked up at his wife. They simply stared at each other, then back at Dienwald. "Well," Graelam said finally, "this is a most curious turn of events."

Kassia knelt beside Dienwald and gently laid her hand on his cheek. "You're obstinate beyond all reason, my friend. You wedded the girl who was intended for you. And she was the girl you wished to wed. All worked out as it was intended to. Everyone is content, or should be. So you're now the king's son-in-law. Does it really matter all that much? You will perhaps have to become more, er, respectable, Dienwald, in your dealings, less eager to strip fat merchants of their goods, possibly a bit more deferential, particularly when you are in the king's presence, but surely it isn't too much to ask. We did it for your own good, you know —"

"Good be damned!" Dienwald howled, his eyes red. "Your mangy husband did it because he thought I'd stolen the wine your father sent you! Admit it, you hulking whoreson! You did it to revenge yourself upon me — I know it as I know you and your shifty ways!"

"You won't insult my lord," Kassia said in a tone of voice Dienwald had never heard from her before. It was low and it was mean. It drew him up short, and he said, his voice now sulky and defensive, "Well, 'tis true. He did me in, he did it to spite me."

Kassia smiled down at him. "You reason with your spleen and your bile, not with your wits. Hush now and behave yourself. Release him, Rolfe, he won't act the stupid lout again. At least," she added, giving a meaningful look to Dienwald, "he had better not. Yes, Dienwald, you will now rise and you won't attempt to strike Graelam again. If you even try it, you will have to deal with me."

Dienwald looked at the very delicate, very pregnant lady and grinned reluctantly. "I don't want to have to deal with you, Kassia. Cannot you turn your back for just a moment? I just want to smash your husband into the ground. Just one more blow, just a small one."

"No, you may not even spit at him, so be quiet. Now, come in and I will give you some ale. Where is Philippa? Where is your lovely bride?"

"Doubtless she is singing and dancing and playing a fine tune for the damned Chancellor of England and her fa . . . nay, that idiot Lord Henry de Beauchamp."

"You believe her wallowing in pleasure that you left St. Erth? That is what you did, isn't it, Dienwald? You shouted and bellowed at her and then ran away to sulk?"

Dienwald looked at the gentle, sweet, pure lady at his side, and growled at her husband, "Put your hand over her mouth, Graelam. She grows impertinent. She vexes me as much as the wench does."

Graelam laughed. "She speaks the truth. You've a wife, and truly, Dienwald, it matters not who her family is. You didn't wed her for a family or lack of one, did you? You wedded her because you love her."

"Nay! Cut off your rattling tongue! I wedded her because I took her and she was a damned virgin and I had no choice but to wed her since my son — my demented nine-year-old son — demanded that I do so!"

"You would have wedded her anyway," Kassia said, "Edmund or no Edmund."

"Aye," Dienwald agreed, shaking his head mournfully. "I will beget no bastard off a lady."

"Then why do you act the persecuted victim?" Graelam said. "The heedless brute who cares for no one?"

"Oh, I care for her, but I believed her father to be naught but a fool, and so it bothered me not. But no, her father must needs be the King of England. The *King of England*, Graelam! It is too much. I will not abide it. I will set her aside. She took me in and made a mockery of me. Aye, I will send her to a convent and annul her and she will forget all her besotted feelings for me. She smothered me with her sweet yielding, her soft smiles and her passion. She will hate me and it will be what we both deserve."

Kassia swept a cat off the seat of a chair and motioned Dienwald to it. "You will do nothing of the sort. Sit you down, my friend, and eat. You've eaten naught, have you? . . . I thought not. Here are some fresh bread and honey."

Dienwald ate.

Graelam and Kassia allowed him to vent his rage and sulk and carp and curse luridly, until, upon the third morning after his unexpected arrival at Wolffeton, Roland de Toumay rode into the inner bailey.

When Roland saw Dienwald, he simply stared at him silently for a very long time. The man looked to Roland's sharp eye to be at the very edge. His eyes were hollow and dark-circled for want of sleep, and he had not the look of a man remotely content with himself or with his lot. "Well," Roland said, "I wondered where you'd fled. Your wife is not a happy lady, my soon-to-be lord Earl of St. Erth."

"I don't want to be a damned earl! What did you say? Philippa isn't happy? Is she ill? What's wrong?"

"You yourself said she was besotted with you, Dienwald," Kassia said. "Would you not expect her to be unhappy in your absence?"

Roland marveled aloud at de Fortenberry's outpouring of stupidity. He said patiently, "Your lovely wife happens to care about you, something none understand, but there it is. As you say, she is besotted with you. Thus, in your unexpected absence, she is miserable; all your servants are miserable because she is; your son hangs to her skirts trying to raise her spirits, but it does little good. The chancellor and Lord Henry finally left because life at St. Erth had become so grim and bleak. No one had any spirit for jests, even your fool, Crooky. He simply lay about in the rushes mumbling something about the lapses of God's grace. I could be in the wrong of it, but it would seem to me that you are very stupid, my lord earl."

"I am not a damned earl! I don't recall having required your opinion, de Tournay!"

"Nay, you did not, but I choose to give it to you, freely offered. Your wife is a lovely lady. She doesn't deserve to be treated so meanly."

Dienwald appeared ready to attack Roland, and Graelam quickly intervened. "I expected you sooner, Roland. Dienwald, go lick your wounds elsewhere and look not to bash Roland. He isn't your enemy. And if you spit on him, Kassia won't like it."

Dienwald, still muttering, strode to Wolffeton's training field, there to besport himself with Rolfe and the other men.

As for Roland, he turned to Graelam and

smiled. "It has been a very long time, my friend, but I am here at last. This is your wife, Graelam? This beautiful creature who looks like a fairy princess? She calls you, a scarred hairy warrior, husband? Willingly?"

"Aye," Kassia said, and gave her hand to Roland. He touched his fingers to her palm and smiled down at her. "You carry a babe, my lady."

"Your vision is sharper than a falcon's, Roland! Aye, she will give me a beautiful daughter very soon now."

"A son, my lord. 'Tis a son I carry."

Roland looked at the two of them. He had known Graelam de Moreton for many years and called him friend. But he'd known him as a hard man, unyielding and implacable, a valued man to fight at your side, strong and valiant, but no show of tenderness or gentleness in his character to please such a fragile lady as this. But he did please her — that was evident. Roland marveled at it and thought it excellent, but didn't choose to see such changes in himself. No, never. He didn't understand such feelings and had no desire to, none.

Graelam said, "Come, Roland, I assume you have something of import to tell me. Kassia, I wish you to rest now, sweetling. Nay, argue not with me, for rest you will, even if I have to tie you to our bed." He leaned down, his palm gentle against his wifes cheek, and lightly kissed her mouth. "Go, love."

And Roland marveled anew. The two men sat in Wolffeton's great hall, flagons of wine between them.

Roland said without preamble, "I must go to Wales and I mustn't be Roland de Tournay there. You have friends amongst the Marcher Barons. I need you to give me an introduction to one of them. Mayhap I will need to pay a surprise visit."

Graelam said, "You play spy again, Roland? I have no doubt, my friend, that you could dupe God into accepting you as one of his angels. Aye, I have friends there. If you must, you can go to Lord Richard de Avenell. He is the father of Lady Chandra de Vernon. You know her husband, Jerval, do you not?"

Roland nodded. "Aye, I met both of them in Acre."

"It's done, then, Roland. I will have my steward, Blount, write a letter for you to Lord Richard. He will welcome you to his keep. Will you leave for Wales immediately?"

Roland sat back in his chair and crossed his arms over his chest, his eyes sparkling with mischief. "If I may, Graelam, I should like to remain just for a while longer to see what transpires between Dienwald and his wife and his father-in-law."

Graelam laughed. "Aye, I too would like to see Edward's face were he to be told that Dienwald cursed and fled when he discovered the king was now related to him! He would surely be speechless for once in his life."

*Near St. Erth*

Walter de Grasse wanted to spit, and he did, often. It relieved his bile. He'd argued fiercely with Britta, who'd clung to him and wept bitter tears and begged him to stay with her and not go after Philippa. But he'd dragged himself and his aching head away.

He would have Philippa, no matter the cost. He would have her and he would kill Dienwald de Fortenberry at last. Damned scoundrel! And he would keep Britta, no matter what either female wanted.

He'd cursed his men roundly, railing at them for allowing one lone women with a little boy to escape Crandall. But it had happened and they had escaped and now he had to devise another way of catching her again.

He and six of his most skilled and ruthless

men camped in a scraggly wood not a mile from the castle of St. Erth. One man kept watch at all times. It was reported to Walter that the master of St. Erth himself had ridden off, no one with him, and as yet he hadn't returned. Walter knew of the chancellor's visit and of Lord Henry's visit as well. The fat was now in the fire, and Philippa as well as Dienwald had been told who she really was.

Why, then, had Dienwald ridden away from his keep alone? It made no sense to Walter.

He saw the chancellor and all his men leave, which was a relief, for Walter had no wish to tangle with the king's soldiers. Then Lord Henry and his men left St. Erth. Walter sat back, chewed on a blackened piece of rabbit, and waited.

*Wolffeton Castle*

"The wench is what she is, and nothing can change that."

"That is true," Graelam, agreed.

"Do you love her, Dienwald?" Kassia asked now, setting her embroidery on her knee, for the babe was big in her belly.

"You women and your silly talk of love! Love is naught but a fabrication that dissolves when you but look closely at it."

"You begin to sound more the fool than your Crooky." Kassia sighed. "You must face up to things, Dienwald. You must go home to your wife and your son. Perhaps, if you are very careful, you could still raid on your western borders. Aye, I think my lord would wish to accompany you. He chafes for adventure now that there is naught but boring peace."

"She's right, Dienwald. There would be no reason for the king to find out. You could be most discreet in your looting and raiding. You would simply have to select your quarry wisely. Aye, Kassia speaks true. I should like a bit of sport myself, on occasion."

Dienwald brightened. "Philippa likes adventure as well," he said slowly. "I think she would much enjoy raiding."

"It is certainly something for the two of you to speak together about," Kassia said, lowering her head so Dienwald wouldn't see the smile on her lips.

Roland de Tournay, much to both Graelam's and his wife's appalled surprise, said suddenly, "Nay, I don't agree with Graelam. I agree with you, Dienwald. I think you should travel to Canterbury and explain to the archbishop what happened to you. I think he would annul his marriage.

After all, the wench wasn't honest about her heritage. She's a bastard when all's said and done. What man would wish to be wedded to a bastard? Aye, rid yourself of her, Dienwald. It matters not if she carries your babe in her belly. Let the king, her father, see to it. You will be happy again and your keep will resume its normal workings. You can return to your mistresses with a free heart and without guilt."

To Graelam's and Kassia's further surprise, Dienwald bounded to his feet and stared at Roland as though he'd suddenly become a toad that had just hopped onto the trestle table and into the pigeon pie.

"Shut your foul mouth, Roland! Philippa knew not that she was a bastard! None of it was her fault, none of it her doing. She is honest and pure and sweet and . . ." He broke off, saw that he'd been trapped in a cage of his own creation, and turned red all the way to his hairline.

"You damnable whoreson, I hope you rot!" he bellowed as he strode with churning step from Wolffeton's great hall, leaving its three remaining occupants to explode with laughter.

# 22

*St. Erth Castle*

Philippa stood in the inner bailey, her hands on her hips, facing Dienwald's master-of-arms. "I care not what you say, Eldwin. I won't remain here for another day, nay, not even another hour! Don't you understand? Your master is at Wolffeton — he must be there — licking his imagined wounds and whining to Graelam and his *perfect* little Kassia about what his treacherous wife has done to him."

"And you wish to go to Wolffeton, mistress? If the master is there, you want to berate him in front of Lord Graelam? Rebuke him in front of the men? Mistress, he is your lord and master and your husband. You mustn't do anything that would reflect badly on him. Above all, surely you wouldn't wish to leave St. Erth! Why, 'tis your duty to remain here until the master decides what he will do and —"

Philippa was at the end of her tether. Crooky, who stood beside her, looked knowingly at Eldwin and said, "You are naught but a stringy bit of offal, sirrah! Don't pretend to rise above what you are to tell *her* what she must and mustn't do. She is a princess, Eldwin, so bite your churl's tongue! A princess does what she wishes to do, and if she wishes to fetch the master, well then, all of us will go with her and fetch the master. And the master will be well-fetched, and that's an end to it!"

"Aye, I will go as well," said Edmund, "for he is my father."

"And I!"

"And I!"

Eldwin, routed, looked about at the two score of St. Erth people, who had obviously sided with the mistress. Old Agnes was grinning her toothless grin and flapping her skinny arms at him as if he were a fox in her henhouse. He gave over, but not completely. "But, mistress, all of us can't leave the castle! Old Agnes, you must stay and see to the weaving and sewing! Gorkel, you must keep the villeins at their tasks and see to the keep's safety."

"Aye, and what will ye do, Eldwin of the mighty arm?" Old Agnes said.

"I go with the mistress," Eldwin said, rose to his full height, and stared down at Old Agnes, who promptly moved back a few steps.

Philippa grinned, and Eldwin, pleased that he'd made her smile, and equally pleased that Old Agnes had retreated a bit, felt his chest expand. Perhaps they *should* fetch the master. Perhaps it was the best thing to do. Wasn't there more to his duty than to remain at St. Erth and command and protect the keep?

"Aye, mistress, it will be as our brave Eldwin says," Old Agnes shouted. "I'll keep all these rattling tongues at their tasks! I just hope Prink — the faithless cretin — gives me some difficulties. If Mordrid doesn't smack him down, then I'll have Gorkel flail off his wormy hide."

"Aye," said Gorkel the Hideous, "I'll keep everything and everyone in his place. You aren't to fret yourself, mistress. No one will fall into lazy stupor."

It was too much. Philippa looked from one beloved face to another and felt her smile crack. The past three days had been beyond wretched, and all of them had tried so diligently to make her feel better about her husband's defection. She swallowed her tears, and found herself nodding at Crooky with approval even as he cleared his throat and looked fit to burst with song.

We go to fetch the master

We go to bring him home.
We'll not take a nay from him
Unless he's torn limb from limb.

Crooky stopped, clapping his hands over his mouth, aghast at the shocking words that had come pouring forth. Philippa stared at him. Everyone stared at him. Then Philippa giggled; several nervous giggles followed. Finally Philippa sobered and turned to Eldwin. "Pick fifteen men and arm them well. We ride to Wolffeton within the hour. As for the rest of you, prepare the keep for your master's return. We will feast as we did the day of our wedding!"

*Near St. Erth*

Walter was livid. He saw her there, at the head of the men, riding away from St. Erth. Fifteen men — he counted them. Well-armed they were. Too many for him to attempt to capture her, damn their hides.

Where was she going? Perhaps, he thought, smiling, she was leaving her husband. Aye, that was it. She was leaving the perfidious lout.

At last he'd have her. Walter roused his men, mounted his destrier, and waved all of them to follow him. He would follow her all the way to Ireland if need be. He would find her alone at some point along the way. She would have to relieve herself or bathe. Aye, he'd get her.

*Between Wolffeton and St. Erth*

Dienwald patted Philbo's neck. His destrier was lathering a bit, beginning to blow hard now, but he plowed forward, ever forward, as if guessing they were homeward-bound.

Dienwald would soon have his wench again and he would kiss her and hold her and tell her he forgave all her multitudinous sins, even if she chose not to remember them. He would love her until he was insensate and she as well.

"Ah, Philippa," he said, looking between Philbo's twitching ears. "Soon all will be well again. Even though I'll be an earl, I shan't carp overly. I will bend my knee to your cursed father when I must, and will show him that I am a man of honor and a man who cares more for his daughter than the world and all its bounty.

"I'll learn to write so that I can extol her beauty in love poems, and recite aloud what I have written to her." Dienwald paused at those outflowing words. Philbo snorted.

Dienwald's vow rang foolish, so he quickly shook his head. "Nay, not poetry," he added quickly, "but I will show her how much I desire her and adore her by my actions toward her. I will whisper in her ear of my desire for her and wring her sweet heart with my tender tongue. I will never, ever yell at her in anger again." He smiled at that. Aye, 'twas good, that vow. It was a vow with meat and meaning, and he could hold to it; he was a reasonable man, he was controlled. It wouldn't be difficult.

Aye, he would tease her and love her and bend her gently to his will. He worried not about his own peculiar will, for he was not a tyrant to demand subservience. Nay, his was a beneficient will, a mellow will, a will to which she would submit eagerly, her beautiful eyes filled with pleasure at pleasing him, for she adored him and wanted above all things to delight him.

His brow lowered suddenly, and he added loudly, "I won't promise to become a shorn lamb in the king's damned flock!" He moaned, seeing himself in a royal antechamber, clothed like a mincing buffoon, waiting for the king to grant him audience. It was a hideous vision. It curled his toes and made his heart lurch.

Philbo snorted, and Dienwald ceased his

flowing monologue and his dismal imaginings, which, after all, needn't necessarily come to pass. In the distance he saw a tight group of men riding toward him. He counted them, sixteen men in all. What could they want? Where were they going? And then he recognized Philippa's mare and Eldwin's huge black gelding and his son's pony.

What was happening here? Where was Philippa going with his men? There she was, riding right there in the fore, leading them, commanding them. Where was she taking his son? Then he froze in his saddle.

She was leaving him. She'd decided she didn't want him. She'd decided that she was too far above him to belittle herself with him further. She'd left St. Erth — her home — where she belonged. She was going to London, to her father's court, to wear precious jewels and fine clothes and never again worry about being naked and having only a blanket to wear.

His fury mounted and he cursed loudly, raising his voice to the heavens. Aye, and he couldn't begin to imagine all the men who would be at court, wanting her, damn her beautiful face and body, not just because of who her father was, but because of how she —

"Damnation!" he bellowed, and urged Philbo to a furious gallop. He saw Edmund riding close to Philippa, Eldwin on his other side. And there was Northbert, his loyal Northbert, riding just behind her. She was stealing his son from him, and his men were helping her. Rage poured through his body.

"By God," Eldwin said, coming closer to Philippa's side. "That's the master! See, 'tis Philbo he rides! He rides right for us, as if he comes from hell."

"Or he rides toward heaven," Philippa said, smiling.

"Aye," Edmund said from her other side, " 'tis Papa!"

"At last," Philippa said, drawing her mare to a halt. Her eyes sparkled for the first time in three days and her back straightened.

Philippa forgot her anger at her husband at the sight of him galloping toward her. He'd come to terms with matters and realized that he wanted her, only her, and she was his wife, no matter who her sire was. How fast he was riding! She felt warmth pouring through her, knowing that soon he would be kissing her and holding her, not caring that his men were watching, that his son would be tugging at his tunic for his own hug. He would probably pull her in front of him on Philbo so he could fondle her all the way back to St. Erth. Philippa closed her eyes a moment and let the sweet feelings flow through her. He would love her and there would be naught but smiles and laughter between them again. No more arguments, no more boiling tempers, no more shouting down the keep.

She opened her eyes, hearing his pounding destrier, and now she could see his face, and she urged her mare forward, wanting to reach him, wanting to lean into his arms when he drew close.

Dienwald jerked up on Philbo's reins, and the powerful destrier reared on his hind legs, snorting loudly.

"Philippa!"

"Aye, husband. I am here, as is your son, as you can see, and your men with us. We were coming to —"

He allowed Philbo to come only a few feet closer to his men and his wife. He needed some distance from her. He'd stoked the fire and now he was ready to blaze. "You damnable bitch! How dare you steal my son! How dare you steal yourself! Aye, I know where you're going, you malignant female — 'tis to your father's court you were traveling with my treacherous men, to bask in the king's favor and gleam riches from him.

Perfidious wench! Get thee out of my sight! I don't want you, I never wanted you, and I will whip you if you leave not this very instant, this second that follows the end of my words! Hear me, wench?"

"Papa . . ."

"You'll soon be safe from her, Edmund. We'll return to St. Erth and all will be restored to the way it was before she blighted us with her presence. You were right, Edmund: she was a witch, a curse from the devil, rising out of the wool wagon like a creature from Hades, criticizing you, scorching all of us with her tongue with the first words from her mouth. You won't have to suffer her further, none of us will. You, Eldwin, Galen, Northbert! all of you, leave her side. Ride away from her. She's naught but the most treacherous of beings!" He paused, breathing hard.

"Master," Galen said quickly in the moment of respite, though he was awed by his master's flawed fluency. He waved his hand to gain Dienwald's attention, for the master was staring straight at the mistress, blind with anger. The master was confused; he didn't understand. Galen looked toward the mistress, but she was simply staring back at the master, white-faced and still. "What you think isn't what is true, master. You mustn't believe those absurd words you spout —"

"We return to St. Erth at once!" Dienwald roared. "Get thee gone, wench. No more will you torment me with your lies and tempt me with your sweet body."

Philippa hadn't said a word. She'd stared at him, at his mouth, as if she could actually see the venomous words flowing out. He truly thought she was leaving him, taking his son with her to London, to her father's court? She felt a hollowness inside, an emptiness that at the same time overflowed with pain and fury. She stared at him as he yelled and bellowed and insulted her. It was all over now. So much for her silly dreams of his love.

He was exhorting his men now, calling them faithless hounds and churlish knaves. Then he stopped and stared at them, and his men were silent beneath his volley of fury. A spasm of pain crossed his face. They'd all betrayed him. They'd gone over to her side. He felt blinding grief and anger. Without a thought, he galloped through them. He would return to St. Erth. They could do as they pleased; if they chose to follow her, then they could, curse them. His men fell back from him, scattering, their destriers whinnying in surprise. He heard Galen shouting, Northbert bellowing something he didn't understand or care to. He wanted only to get away from her and the misery she'd brought him. He whipped Philbo into a mad gallop away from her, away from his men, straight through them, back to St. Erth. Away from his son, who'd also chosen the damnable wench.

" 'Tis over now," Philippa said. Her lips felt numb, her brain emptied of feeling and thought. She felt utter and complete defeat. Nothing mattered now. It was better so. Then suddenly she felt the blood pounding through her, felt the heat of fury roil and churn within her, felt such black rage at his stupidity that she couldn't bear it. How dare he, the disbelieving fool!

"No!" Philippa yelled after him. She whipped her mare about and raced after her husband. She yelled back over her shoulder, "Eldwin, remain here! None of you do anything! I'll be back soon! Edmund, don't worry. Your father but needs a sound thrashing!"

Dienwald's men, their ranks already split by the master's wild ride, let her go through as well. She rode straight after her husband, her eyes narrowed on his back, her hands fisted over the mare's reins. She saw Dienwald twist in his saddle at the sound of her mare closing on him, saw the surprise on his face, the brief uncertainty, the renewal of rage.

Philbo was tired and the mare was fresh. Just as her mare came beside Philbo, Philippa, not for the last time in her life, thought with her feet. Without hesitation, she jumped from the mare's back straight at her husband, her arms flying around his back. He stared at her in that wild instant, then knew what was going to happen. He lurched around in the saddle, clutched her against his chest even as both of them hurtled from Philbo's back to the ground. Dienwald twisted and landed first, managing to spare Philippa the brunt of the fall. His arms tightened, and he grunted, the breath momentarily knocked out of him.

The road was narrow and curved, alongside it the terrain sloped sharply downward. They rolled over and over, locked together, down the grassy incline, coming finally to a stop in the middle of a patch of eglantine and violets.

Dienwald lay on his back, Philippa atop him. They were both breathing hard. Dienwald wondered if his body was intact or strewn in bits amongst the eglantine. Then Philippa reared back, looking down at him. She, he saw, was just fine. He felt her belly against him and his sex responded instantly, and he knew, at least, that this part of him had survived the fall, and further, would never be immune from her. Her thick glorious hair had come loose of its ribbon and was a riot of wild curls around her face. Her eyes sparkled with fierceness and he found himself waiting eagerly for her outpouring of rage.

"You stupid lout," she shouted three inches from his face. "I should break both your arms and your head! You ignorant clod! Aye, I'll break you into small pieces!"

"You already have," he said. "Ridiculous woman, I tried to protect you, take the brunt of the fall, but your weight flying at me was enough to crush my spleen and pulverize my liver. When we smashed to the ground, my breath died, as did all feeling in my chest."

" 'Tis the loss of your brains that should concern you," Philippa said, and began to pound him. "You had few to begin with, rattling around in that fat head of yours, and now you have none, my lord husband."

Dienwald grabbed her flailing fists — not an easy task — and finally managed to roll her beneath him. He jerked her arms over her head, clasped her wrists together, and came up to straddle her so she couldn't rear up and kick him.

"Now," he said, looking down at her, his chest heaving. "Now."

"Now what, you buffoon?"

He felt words stick in his throat. Something was decidedly wrong here. She seemed unaware of his mastery over her, whereas he was aware of nothing but the maddening effect she had on him.

"I suppose you've been licking your false wounds, with your perfect little Kassia giving you her sweet, tender succor. Is that it, you wretched ass? Have you spent the past three days bemoaning your hideous fate? Cursing me and all the saints for the misery that has befallen you? And did your perfect little Kassia agree with you and cry with you as you smote your feckless brow? Answer me!"

"Not really," he said, and frowned.

She jerked, trying to free her hands, but he only tightened his grip. He wanted to kiss her and thrust inside her and throttle her all at the same time. Instead, he said in his most commanding voice, "I am your master, wench. Only I, no one else. You came to me and seduced me and I wedded you and that is that. Now, hold still and keep your tongue quiet, for I must think."

"Think! Ha!"

"Where were you going with my men and

my son? You were escaping me, 'twas plain to see. You were going to London, weren't you? You were taking my son and going to your cursed father. Tell me the truth!"

She sneered at him and tried to kick him, but he held her securely and all she gained was the pressure of his sex, hard and demanding, against her. It drove her mad and enraged her at the same time. "Aye," she shouted so loudly she hurt his ears, "aye, we were all going to London! To my father — to cover myself with jewels and cavort and frolic and dance with all the fine courtiers."

"That's all you can think about? Gallants and jewels? And what would Edmund have done whilst you were cavorting and frolicking and flirting with these frivolous clothheads?"

That stumped her, for her brain had fallen into wayward paths. He was astride her, his legs tight against her sides, and he was panting, so close she could nearly feel the texture of his mouth on her. She wanted desperately to hit him and then kiss him until he was breathless and so hungry for her that he forget everything.

"Don't look at me like that, Philippa. It will do you no good. I won't give in to you. It won't spare you my wrath. Don't deny it — you're trying to seduce me again. No, you've been disloyal to me, you've —"

She suddenly heaved upward with all her strength, taking him off-guard. He fell sideways, not releasing her wrists, and they were lying there with naught but thick clumps of purple violets between them, face-to-face, their noses nearly pressed together. He couldn't help himself. He kissed her, then lurched back as if stung by a hornet.

"Dienwald . . ." she whispered, and hurled herself toward him, trying to kiss him back.

"Nay, I shan't let you debauch me again, wench. Stay away from me." Blood pounded in her head and with a furious cry she pulled free of his hands and smashed down on him, rolling him again onto his back. She was lying atop him once more, and then she was kissing him, even as he tried to duck away. She gripped his hair and yanked hard, holding his head between her hands, and she kissed him again and again, licking his chin, nipping at his nose, rubbing her cheek against his ear. He felt her belly hard against his sex and knew it was nearly the finish. The finish for him. He didn't understand her. She was yielding and taking both at the same time, and it astonished him and pleased him. He stilled his body, letting her have her way with him.

"Wench," he said finally when she'd momentarily left his mouth. "Wench, listen to me."

Eyes vague, heart pounding, Philippa heard his soft voice and raised her head to look down at him.

"You're my husband, you peevish fool," she said, and kissed him again. "You're mine. I would never leave you, never, no matter how great my anger at you and your crazy thinking. Do you understand me?" And she pounded his head against the violets. "Do you? I was coming to fetch you, to bring you home to me, where you belong. Do you understand?"

"Stop it for but a moment! By the saints, my head! You're breaking my head! There, stop! Aye, I understand you. But now you heed me. You're my wife and you won't ever leave me again, do you understand me? You will remain at St. Erth or wherever it is I wish you to remain. You won't ever go haring off to London to see your father without me. I won't have it, do you hear me?"

"Me leave you?" That made her stop her kisses and clear her brain just a bit. "You left me! For three days I didn't know where you were or what you were doing. Then I realized you would go to your beloved perfect little Kassia, so I was coming after you, your men and your son with me!"

In her indignation, she tugged at his hair all the harder and pounded his head several more times against the ground. He groaned loudly, and she stopped. "Your head is crushing the violets. How dare you think those awful things about me? You are impossible and I can't imagine why I love you more than I love —" She broke off, staring down at him, knowing that she'd left herself open to him, open to his scorn, his baiting, his insults.

He suddenly smiled, a beautiful crooked smile that made her want to kiss him until he couldn't think. "Were you really coming after me, to fetch me home?"

"Of course! I wasn't going to London. You honestly believe I would steal your son, leave my home? Command your men to attend me? Ah, Dienwald, you deserve this!" She reared back, her arm raised, yet at the last moment her fist stilled in midair. She stared down at him and saw the gleam of challenge in his eyes, the twist of a smile on his mouth. She cursed him softly, then leaned down and kissed him thoroughly. He parted his lips and let her tongue enter his mouth. It was wonderful. She was wonderful and she was his.

"Aye," he said into her warm mouth, "I

deserve all of you, wench."

She felt his hands stroke down her back and pulled her flat against him. His fingers were parting her legs, pressing inward through her gown, to touch her. "Dienwald," she said against his mouth.

He jerked up her gown and his fingers were now caressing the bare skin of her inner thighs, working slowly upward, until they found her woman's flesh and then he paused, his fingers quiet now, not moving, merely feeling her warmth and softness. He sighed deeply. "I've missed you."

"Nay, 'tis my body you've missed," she whispered between urgent kisses. "Any female would suit you, 'tis just that you are a lusty cockscomb and a man who is randy all his waking hours. I have heard of all your other women, I even know all their cursed names for Edmund recited them."

"You would surely make me the most miserable of men were I to take another woman to my bed. Do you know that I dream of coming inside you, deep and deeper still, and all the while you're telling me how it makes you feel when I push into you —"

She kissed him again, wild for him now, unheeding of their surroundings. Dienwald was very nearly removed in spirit as well until he heard Eldwin's soft voice, "Master."

Dienwald wanted nothing more than to let Philippa debauch him right here, in the nest of violets and eglantine, the soft warm air swirling about them. He cocked open an eye even as he pulled down her gown.

"What want you, Eldwin? There is an army bearing down on you and you must know where to flee?"

"No, master, 'tis worse."

"What in the name of St. Andrew could possible be worse?"

"It will rain soon, master — a heavy rain, Northbert says, a deluge that could fill this ditch in which you lie. Northbert reads well the clouds and the other signs, you know that."

Dienwald looked up. It was true, the soft warm air swirling about them was also dark and heavy and gray. But it didn't matter, not one whit. "Excellent, my thanks. You and the men take Edmund back to St. Erth. The wench — my wife and I will return shortly. Go now. Wait not another minute. Hurry. Be gone."

Eldwin wasn't blind to what he'd interrupted. He turned on his heel and hurried back to the waiting men. Soon Dienwald heard pounding hooves going away from them.

"Now, wench."

"Now what?"

"Now I shall have my way with you in the midst of the violets and the eglantine."

When the first rain drop landed on Philippa's forehead, she was glad for it for she felt fevered and so urgent she felt ready to burst. Dienwald brought her closer to his mouth and caressed her until she screamed, arching her back, wild with wanting and with the mounting feelings that filled her. Overflowing now. And when he left her, she lurched upward and pressed him back and he fell, laughing and moaning, for she was kissing his throat, his chest, her hands splayed over him, and soon she was crouched between his legs and her mouth was on his belly, her hair flowing over him, and she was caressing him with her mouth and her hands. When she took him into her mouth, tentatively, wonderingly, he thought he would spill his seed then so urgent did he feel, but it was as if she guessed, and left him, easing him gently with her fingers, before caressing him again until he cried out with it and pulled her off him. Then he was covering her, and his manhood was thrusting into her, deep and hard, and so sweet that she cried with the wonder of it. And when he spilled his seed within her, he tasted her tears on her lips.

Dienwald said as he kissed the raindrops

away, "I love you, Philippa, and I will never cease loving you and wanting you. We are joined, you and I, and it is for always. Never, ever, will I speak to you in anger again. You are mine forever."

And she said only, "Yes."

He was heavy on her, but she didn't care. She wrapped her arms about his back and hugged him all the more tightly. The rain thickened and it was only then they realized that they were lying in the open, sheets of rain pouring down on them, in the gray light. And then Dienwald saw there was something else beside the rain.

There was Walter de Grasse standing at the top of the incline, staring down at them, his face twisted with rage.

# 23

Dienwald slowly eased away from Philippa and pulled her gown down her legs, pretending not to see Walter.

"Love . . ." she said, her voice soft and drowsy despite the rain battering down on her. "Love, don't leave me."

"Philippa," he said as he straightened his clothes, "come, you must awaken now."

Sir Walter's voice cracked through the silence. "Are you certain you are through plowing her belly, you whoreson? If the little slut wants more, I shall take her and give her pleasure she's never known with you."

Walter! Philippa sat up quickly, staring at her cousin, who still stood at the top of the incline, his hands on his hips, rain long since soaked through his clothes. He'd *watched* them. She felt at once sick to her stomach and blindly furious. She scrambled to her feet.

Dienwald took one of her hands in his and squeezed it. When he spoke, his tone was almost impersonal. "What do you want, de Grasse?"

"I want what is mine. I want her, despite what you've done to her."

Dienwald squeezed her hand tightly now, and said in the same detached way, "You can't have her, de Grasse. She was never yours to have, save in your fantasies. She's mine. As you have observed, she is completely mine."

"Nay, you bastard! She'll wed me! She"ll have no choice, for I'll hold you to ensure her compliance!"

Dienwald stared at him. "Too late, de Grasse, you are far too late. Philippa is already wedded to me with her father's — the king's — blessing."

"You lie!"

"Why should I!"

That drew Walter up for a moment. He eyed his enemy of so many years that he'd lost count. De Fortenberry had been an enemy before Walter had even seen his face, his very name a litany of vengeance. So long ago Dienwald's father had beaten Walter's, but it hadn't been fair, it hadn't been unprejudiced. No, his father had been cheated, cheated of everything, his only son disinherited. "I should have killed you when I had you at Wolffeton. I broke your ribs, but it wasn't enough, though I enjoyed it. I should have tortured you until I tired of hearing your screams, and then I should have sent my sword into your belly. Ah, but no, I waited, like a fool I waited for Graelam to return, certain that he would mete out justice, that he would right the wrongs done unto my father and unto me. I was a fool then, I admit it. I didn't think that Lord Graelam's wife, that little bitch, Kassia — your lover — would dare rescue you. But she did, curse her. Hellfire, I should have killed her for saving you!"

"But you didn't," Dienwald said, bringing Philippa against his side. "And Graelam, not knowing the depths of your twisted hatred, made you castellan of Crandall. But you couldn't be satisfied with your overlord's trust. No, you couldn't dismiss your hatred and forget your imagined ills. You had to kill my people and burn their huts and their crops and put the sword to their animals. You went too far, de Grasse. Graelam knows what you did. He will not allow it to continue. He himself will kill you. I won't have to bother."

"Kill me? You? As for Graelam, you have no proof, de Fortenberry, of any burning or killing. Not a shred of proof do you have. Graelam would never act without proof. I know him well. He thinks he judges character like a god, when he is but a fool. And when he finds you dead, there will still be no proof, and he won't act against me."

"Then you stole Philippa and my son. You will die, Walter, and your enmity will die with you."

"Stole! Ha! I rescued my cousin! Your miserable brat just happened to be with her. I didn't harm him, the little vermin. Skewer not the truth for your own ends."

"Since there is no longer a rescue to be made, since Philippa is my wife with the king's blessing, then you intend now to take your leave of us? You intend to forget your plaints and return to Crandall?"

Even as he spoke, Dienwald saw Walter's men, in view now, yet blurred in the downpour. The shower was lessening a bit but they were still vague and gray. They looked miserable; they looked uncertain.

Philippa said, "Walter, I am wedded to Dienwald. I am his wife. Both Lord Henry and Robert Burnell, the king's chancellor, will attest to it. It is true. Leave us be."

Walter ground his teeth. He felt maddened with failure, his loss surrounding him, gashing into him, twisting him and taunting him. He'd not gained what was his by birthright. He'd gained nothing, less than nothing. Life hadn't meted out justice to him. There would be no retribution unless he gained it for himself. And now he'd stood watching his enemy enjoy the girl intended for him. He raised his face to the skies and howled his fury.

It was a grim sound, terrifying and haunting. Philippa clutched Dienwald against her side, turning her face inward to his chest. It was a howl of pain and defeat and ruin; a cry of loss of faith, loss of self.

Then Walter was silent; all his men were silent, though several were crossing themselves. The silence dragged on. It was frightening and eerie. The rain pounded down and the curving piece of ground upon which Dienwald and Philippa stood began to fill with water. The violets sagged beneath the weight of the rain.

Then Walter, without warning, drew his sword and leapt down the incline, his full weight landing against Dienwald's chest, battering him backward. Philippa was thrown to the side, splashing onto her knees into the water. She scrambled to her feet, flailing about to gain purchase in the swirling torrent.

Walter's sword was drawn, and in a smooth arc aimed toward Dienwald's chest. Dienwald had naught but a knife and he held it in his right hand, then tossed it to his left, back and forth, taunting Walter.

He said softly, "Well, you sodden fool? Come, let's see if you understand the uses for your sword! Or will you just stand there?"

Walter gave a roar of sheer rage and rushed toward Dienwald, his sword straight out in front of him. Dienwald sidestepped him easily, but his foot slipped on the slick grass and he twisted about, falling on his back.

Philippa picked up a rock and threw it with all her strength at Walter. It hit him square in the chest. He looked at her, surprise writ on his face. "Philippa? Why do you that? I am come to save you. You mustn't pretend you don't want to come with me, wed with me, there is no more need. I will kill him and then you will come with me."

Walter turned, but Dienwald was on his feet again, feinting to the right, away from Walter's sword thrust.

On and on it went, and Philippa knew Dienwald must fail eventually. His knife was no contest against Walter's sword. Suddenly there came shouts from the road above.

The men paid no heed.

Philippa paid no heed either. She had grasped another stone and was waiting for the chance to strike Walter with it, but the men were close, too close, and she feared hitting Dienwald instead.

"Philippa! Stand clear!"

She whirled about and looked upward. It was Graelam de Moreton and he was standing on the road above them. Beside him stood the man Roland de Tournay. She watched through the now gentle fall of rain. Roland drew a narrow dagger from his belt, its shaft silver and bright even in the gray light, aimed it, and released it. It slit through the air so quickly, Philippa didn't see it. She heard a suddenly gurgling sound, then turned to see the dagger embedded deep in Walter's chest. He dropped the sword and clutched at the dagger's ivory handle. He pulled it out and stared at the crimson blade. Then he looked upward at Roland de Tournay.

He looked confused and said, "Do I know you? Why do you kill me?"

He said nothing more, merely looked once again at Philippa, gave a tiny shake of his head, and collapsed onto his face in the water.

Dienwald stood panting over him. He frowned down at Walter's lifeless body. " 'Twas a good throw." Then he looked up at Roland. "I was very nearly the victor. You acted too quickly."

"Next time I'll let your wife hit your adversary with rocks," Roland shouted.

"By all the saints above," Graelam shouted, "enough! Come up now and let us ride to St. Erth. Dienwald, thank Roland for saving your hide. But hurry, for I am so sodden my tongue molds in my mouth!"

Within minutes Philippa was huddled in the circle of her husband's arms atop Philbo. One of Graelam's men was leading her mare. Walter's men hadn't fought, for Lord Graelam de Moreton was, after all, Sir Walter's overlord, and thus they, his men-at-arms, also owed allegiance to Lord Graelam.

Dienwald looked at Graelam. "How came you by so unexpectedly? I was praying, but 'twas not for your company in particular."

"We came by design," Graelam said. "Roland wanted to see the final act of the play he'd helped to write."

"What does he mean?" Philippa asked, twisting about to face her husband.

"Hush, wench. 'Tis not important. Roland is loose-tongued, but he does throw a dagger well."

"But —"

"Hush," he repeated, then said, "Will you continue to welcome me as sweetly as did gentle, perfect Kassia?"

She stiffened, as he'd expected, her thoughts turned, and he grinned over her head.

They were shivering, their teeth chattering, when they finally rode into St. Erth's inner bailey. Once in the great hall, they were overwhelmed with cheers and shouts and blessed warmth and trestle tables covered with mounds of food. All of St. Erth's people were gathered in the huge chamber, and it was noisy and hot and the smells of food mingled with the smells of sweat and wet wool and it was wonderful.

"Welcome," Philippa said, her wet face radiant as she turned to her guests. "We're home!"

She sneezed suddenly, and Dienwald swooped down upon her and picked her up in his arms. He pretended to stagger under her weight, saying, "My poor back, wench! I'm nearly beyond my abilities, with you so weighty with wet wool."

Graelam and Roland watched Dienwald carry her from the great hall, grinning at the wild cheering from all St. Erth's people. "The king's son-in-law is a fine man," Graelam said.

"Aye, and no longer a fool," Roland said. He fell silent, frowning. "I do find it passing odd, though."

"What do you find odd?"

"That Philippa, a girl of remarkable taste and refinement, preferred him to me. I am incredulous. 'Tis not normal in my experience. Why, the harem I kept in Acre, Graelam — you wouldn't believe the appetites of my women! And it was my duty, naturally, to satisfy appetites each night. And they never complained that I shirked my duty to them. But Philippa gives me not a look."

Graelam merely laughed, grabbed a hunk of well-roasted rabbit, and waved it in Roland's face. "You braying ass! Lying dog! Harem? I believe you not, not for an instant. What harem? How came you by a harem? How many women? You satisfied more than one woman each night?"

Crooky chortled and waved his hands toward all the food. "A feast, my lords. A feast worthy of a king or a king's daughter and her friends!" And he jumped upon Dienwald's chair and burst into song.

A wedding feast lies here untasted
The lord and lady care not it's wasted.
They're frolic and gambol without a yawn
They'll play through the night 'til the dawn.

In their bedchamber, warm and dry beneath three blankets, the master and mistress of St. Erth lay together listening to the rain and enjoying each other's kisses. They heard a sudden shout of loud laughter and guffawing from below in the great hall, and wondered at it, but not for long, for Philippa nuzzled Dienwald's throat, saying, "Have you restocked your seed?"

"What?" Dienwald said, and pulled back to look at his wife's laughing mouth.

" 'Tis what Old Agnes said, that I would fetch you home and keep you in my bed until you begged me to let you sleep and restock your seed."

"Aye, all is in readiness for you, greedy wench. I ask for nothing more in this sweet life than to be debauched by you each night."

"A promise easily made and more than easily kept."

# Epilogue

*Windsor Castle*
*October 1275*

Dienwald quickly closed the door to the opulent chamber, locked it, drew a deep breath, then let it out slowly as he sagged against the door, his eyes closed.

"My lord husband, you did well. My father thinks you nearly as wonderful as do I."

Dienwald opened his eyes at that. "He does, does he? Ha! I'll wager you he still thinks Roland de Tournay would have made the better husband and the better son-in-law. And I have to call Roland, that damned brute, friend! It passes all bounds, Philippa."

She wanted to laugh, but managed to keep her mouth from quivering, her eyes slightly lowered. "Roland is just a common fellow, husband, of little account to my life and of no account at all to my heart. And since my father no longer has any say in the matter, it's not important. What did you think of Queen Eleanor?"

"A beautiful lady," Dienwald said somewhat absently, then frowned, moaned, and closed his eyes again. "The king looked at me and knew, Philippa — he knew I'd raided that merchant's goods near Penrith."

Philippa laughed. "Aye, he knew. He was amused, he told me so, but he also hinted to me that I should scold you just a bit — 'never be a testy nag, my daughter,' he said — and somehow keep you from plundering about the countryside. I truly believe he said nothing to you because he doesn't want to break your spirit."

"He doesn't want to break my spirit! I don't suppose you told him that you were with me, riding at my side, dressed like a lad, laughing at how easily we sidetracked that merchant who'd cheated us?"

Philippa straightened her shoulders and looked down her nose at him. "Naturally not. I am part Plantagenet, thus part of the very highest nobility. Besides, do you think me an utter fool?"

"Next time we will take greater care," Dienwald said. He pushed away from the door and walked to the middle of their chamber and stopped. The room was dazzling in the elegance of its furnishings, and the overwhelming luxury of it stifled him. The bed was hung with rich velvet draperies, their thick crimson folds held with golden rope and ties. The velvet was so thick, so voluminous, one could suffocate if the hangings were drawn at night.

"The ceremony was moving, Dienwald, and you looked as royal as my father and his family."

Dienwald grunted. He looked down at his flamboyant crimson tunic, belted with a wide leather affair studded with gems. A ceremonial sword was strapped to his waist. He looked well enough, he supposed, but one couldn't scratch in such clothing, one couldn't really stretch. One couldn't grab one's wife and caress her and fondle her and fling her onto the bed and wrestle with her, tearing off clothing and laughing together and tumbling about.

" 'Dienwald de Fortenberry, Earl of St. Erth.' Or perhaps I prefer 'Lord St. Erth.' Ah, that has a sound of proud consequence and arrogant privilege. It fits you well, my lord earl. And Edmund will grow nicely into that appellation, for already he scowls like you do when displeased, and orders me about as if I were his wench."

Dienwald was silent. He sat down in an ornately carved high-backed chair, stretched out his legs, and looked morosely into the fireplace.

Philippa, her humor fled, knelt in front of him and gazed up at his distracted face. "What troubles you, husband? Do you wish now that you weren't tied to me?"

He stretched out his hand and lightly touched his fingers to her hair. It was arranged artfully, with many pins and ribbons and fastenings, and he feared to dislodge such perfection. He dropped his hand.

Philippa snorted and flung away the pins and ribbons, shaking her head until her hair hung free, framing her smiling face.

"There, now do what you will. As you always do when we are home."

Dienwald sat back, his fingers absently sliding through strands of her hair, his eyes still melancholy, as he gazed at the orange flames in the fireplace.

"I'm no longer just me," he said at last.

"True," Philippa agreed, leaning her cheek against his knee. "I'm part of you now, as is the child I carry."

His fingers stilled abruptly and his dulled expression vanished in a flash. "The *what?*"

"The child I now carry. Our babe."

"You didn't tell me." She heard the beginnings of outrage in his voice and smiled.

"Why didn't you tell me? I am the father, after all!" He was ready for an argument, a banging loud fight, but she didn't plan to give him what he wished just yet.

In a voice as calm as a moonless night she said, "I wanted to wait until after you'd met my father and dealt with your honors and position. Now that you've survived all your new privileges and awards and tributes, all the banquets and fawning courtiers, we can return to Cornwall, to our real life. Tomorrow we leave London, and we'll look back on this and know it was but a fragment of something not really part of us, Dienwald, something like a dream that scarce touches us."

"Save that I'm now a peer of the realm and have my coffers filled with royal coin. Royal coin I never sought."

"Aye, I know," she said, gently rubbing her palm on his thigh. And, she thought, grinning, you're spoiling for a fight. You can't bear that I'm being so quiet, so reasonable. Not just yet, my husband.

His fingers tightened in her hair. "Aye, none of this I wanted. I have been made to feel guilt over a bit of honest thievery, and that from a man who'd cheated me! I won't have it, wench! And now you deign to tell me you are with child! *You* decide it is time that *I* know of *my* babe. You have deceived me, and I shall make you very sorry that you did."

"Just what will you do?"

She was teasing him! He stared down at her laughing face, saw the dimples deepening in her cheeks, and wanted to throttle her. "I will think of something, and don't you doubt it."

Her voice was as demure as a virgin's. "Something worthy of an earl? Worthy of Lord St. Erth, that scoundrel and knave?"

He sought for words but couldn't find a single one, so instead he leaned down, grasped her face between his palms, and kissed her hard.

He pulled away and saw the darkening of her eyes, the sheen of passion building, the soft yielding to him. It was always so, and it always made him feel boundless satisfaction and immense male pleasure. He smiled and kissed her again. His hands left her face and stroked downward until they held her breasts. When she moaned softly, coming up on her knees to get closer to him, to come between his legs, he pulled back and grinned evilly down at her. "There, I have my revenge and it's worthy of any man in the realm who's worth his salt. I started to debauch you, and when you were reach to beg me for it, I stopped."

Philippa stared at him silently for a very long time. He fidgeted, but she didn't move, didn't speak. Then, as he looked at her, two tears seeped from her eyes and trailed down her cheeks. She didn't make a sound. Tears continued to gather and fall.

"Philippa, don't cry. I . . ."

He gathered her against him, wanting to pet her and fondle her and make her forget her tears. When he leaned forward to draw her up, she suddenly jerked back and smashed her fists against his chest. He lurched sideways, and the chair tipped and fell, sending them both flailing to the floor. But he didn't release his wife. They lay in front of the fire, facing each other, and she was grinning at him.

"You give over, husband?"

"I'll give you anything you want, wench."

"Will you love me here, on this soft Flanders carpet, in front of the fire?"

"Aye, I'll make you moan with pleasure before I'm done with you."

"Proceed, husband. I await your pleasure."

He laughed and drew her to him. She was his wife, this king's daughter, and he would wear his earl's laurels as would his sons and his sons' sons after them. And he would repair St. Erth and it would become a renowned and mighty castle, a bastion to defend the king's honor, a protector of those in his domain, in all Cornwall. And his wife would birth him a daughter who would likely marry the small son delivered earlier that summer at Wolffeton.

He knew himself unworthy. He prayed he would become more worthy as time passed.

He prayed also that worthiness had nothing to do with an occasional raid, an occasional theft, an occasional assault on some knave, who would, after all, deserve the fate that would befall him.

Philippa's hands stroked his face, and he kissed her neck. "I love you," he said, nipping at her earlobe. "As do my son and all the people at St. Erth."

"You don't mind that Edmund chooses to call me Mama?"

"Nay, why should I? 'Witch' and 'Cursed Maypole' don't go well with your new dignities. Now, enough of this nonsense that has nothing to do with what I want to do to your body."

"And what is that?"

"If you will close your lips against your silly female words, I will show you."

The employees of Thorndike Press hope you have enjoyed this Large Print book. All our Large Print titles are designed for easy reading, and all our books are made to last. Other Thorndike Press Large Print books are available at your library, through selected bookstores, or directly from us.

For information about titles, please call:

(800) 223-2336

To share your comments, please write:

Publisher
Thorndike Press
P.O. Box 159
Thorndike, Maine 04986